"I know your secret."

Alex Caine is a martial artist fighting in illegal cage matches. His powerful secret weapon is an unnatural vision that allows him to see his opponents' moves before they know their intentions themselves. When enigmatic Englishman, Patrick Welby, shows Alex how to unleash a breathtaking realm of magic and power, Alex is drawn into a mind-bending adventure beyond his control.

A cursed grimoire binds Alex to Uthentia, a chaotic Fey godling, who leads him towards chaos and murder, an urge Alex finds harder and harder to resist. Befriended by Silhouette, a monstrous Kin beauty, Alex sets out to recover the only things that will free him-the shards of the Darak. But that powerful stone also has the potential to unleash a catastrophe which could mean the end of the world as we know it.

Bound is dark urban fantasy at its best!

PRAISE FOR ALAN BAXTER AND THE ALEX CAINE SERIES

"If Stephen King and Jim Butcher ever had a love child then it would be Alan Baxter." —Smash Dragons

"I was completely blown away when I read this. The world he's built rivals anything by Jim Butcher…. I'm reminded of Benedict Jacka and Kevin Hearne…" —Kylie Chan, author of *The Dark Heavens*, *Journey to Wudang*, and *Celestial Battle* trilogies

"Kick ASS!" —Sean Williams, *New York Times* #1 bestselling author

"I had a lot of fun reading Alan Baxter's Bound…It's a teeth-gnashing, shadow-chasing, magesign-riddled sexy beast of a thing!" —Margo Lanagan, award-winning author of *Sea Hearts* and *Tender Morsels*

BOUND

ALEX CAINE BOOK ONE
ALAN BAXTER

Bound: Alex Caine #1
Gryphonwood Press | www.gryphonwoodpress.com

ISBN-13: 978-1-940095-74-5

Created in the United States of America

Cover & Graphic Design Coordinator:
Shawn T. King, STK Kreations

Books by Alan Baxter

The Alex Caine Series
Bound
Obsidian
Abduction
Omnibus Edition

The Balance
RealmShift
MageSign
Omnibus Edition

The Jake Crowley Adventures
Blood Codex
Anubis Key

Other Works
Hidden City
Primordial
Crow Shine
The Book Club
Dark Rite
Ghost of the Black
The Darkest Shade of Grey
Write the Fight Right

For Halinka and Arlo
And for Haines

ONE

A distant roar rose and fell, rose again. Dark gray concrete underfoot, bloodstained, hard. Alex circled to the left. He peripherally registered each panel of chain-link, each steel upright, never taking his eyes from the figure in front of him. The man known as Bull Finley.

Below a heavy brow Bull stared back, cautious. But not scared. He exuded feral, predatory strength, a calm resolve. His hands, raised before his face, were calloused and rough, like Alex's. Bull's energy pulsed. Alex watched the man's *shades*, the aura of his intentions, shifting around him, saw purpose swell, muscles bunch. One of Bull's meaty hands swept within an inch of Alex's nose, breath grunting out between clenched teeth, forward momentum carrying him through. Alex let him go by, twisted, gathered and whipped out a leg in a turning kick to the ribs.

Bull's exhalation finished its escape in a rush, his face registering shock more than pain. Alex pressed the advantage, following in, hands a blur of strikes and counterstrikes. Bull blocked well, but not well enough, his upper lip and nose flowered scarlet.

His intent changed, a slight desperation entering his mind. Alex saw the shades move, felt the man's desire to grapple, take the fight down to the hard stone floor. He disengaged, slipped out of reach even as his opponent made the conscious decision to grab. That surprised expression again. Confidence to surprise, surprise to concern, concern to fear, fear to defeat. A journey Alex had seen play out time and again. His opponent's eyes widened slightly, the corners of his mouth twitching downwards. Surprise to concern. Alex smiled inside. *So it begins.*

For several seconds they circled, the roar rising, falling, rising, falling. Bull's bulky frame heaved with his breath. Alex, leaner, more athletic, waited. He was calm. Bull looked for an opening, a gap that wasn't there. Alex feinted in and out, his opponent flinching, lips tight. Concern to fear.

The tension grew. Alex drew his breath in deep, sank his

energy low, gathered himself. A deliberate drawing away, taunting his opponent to follow him in, to attack. Fear brought with it a lack of focus, lack of patience, a desperate desire to take back control. That desire pulsed off Bull like a wave. Alex moved in and to one side exactly as Bull made his assault. A clumsy move, all physical strength, no breath, no finesse. The man closed the gap to where Alex had been, launching fast punches. Alex exhaled, struck back across Bull's arms, drove a knee up hard and sharp. The big man's nose and ribs cracked almost simultaneously, pain escaping in red and black waves. As his opponent stumbled, Alex whipped in one last punch and a kick to finish him. Broken and unconscious, Bull collapsed against the chain-link fencing as though his skeleton had been removed.

Alex turned away as the dull roar boomed into his ears. He honored his opponent by not relishing the defeat as he let the rest of the world back in. The stench of steel and concrete, blood, sweat and popcorn. The glare of overhead halogens, the stamping of hundreds of feet on wooden stands, hundreds of throats screaming approval, baying for blood. A loud, brash voice burst over loudspeakers and Alex walked past the man with the microphone, as he always did. A gate swung open and he let the darkness of the tunnel to the change rooms swallow him away from the spectacle.

Alex pulled a T-shirt over his sweat-slick chest, ran a hand over his close-cropped dark hair. He stretched as event officials jostled around him in the tiny room. A clipboard was thrust under his nose, accompanied by a chewed biro. He signed without reading, knowing the agreement by heart.

"Way to go, Alex. Man, how are you so fast?" He ignored the question, kept his head down, resumed his stretching. "Ha! You're a legend, man, a fucking legend!"

The man with the clipboard scurried away. A doctor tipped his head back, shone a tiny light in each eye. "Anything?" Alex shook his head. The doctor nodded once and left, scribbling on a clipboard of his own.

Alex rubbed his face and hair with a towel and concentrated on his breathing and stretching as the activity around him faded. He heard movement in the hallway, a voice raised in concern. Another voice, angry, and a man walked into the dressing room. The man was big and ugly, a product of mean streets and bad attitudes. An obsequious little rat scurried in behind. Alex sighed. "Go away, Eugene," he said. "You too, Karl."

Eugene sneered. "You gotta fight for us, Alex Caine. The boss won't have it any other way."

"*Your* boss can kiss my arse."

"You can't talk like that about King Scarlet," Karl said, his voice piping.

Alex laughed. "Really? Still calling himself King Scarlet? It's like a bad Saturday morning cartoon. Fuck off, the pair of you."

Eugene took a step forward, meant to be threatening. Alex watched his shades, saw the nerves and concern drifting off him like a bad smell. He stood quickly, took one fast step forward. Eugene staggered back, sudden concern clear on his face. He bumped into his insubstantial friend, sent Karl bouncing off the doorframe.

"Fuck off," Alex said again.

Eugene waved one finger. "You do what King Scarlet wants, Caine. Or else."

Alex raised his chin. "You threatening me, Eugene?" He made the man's name sound like a disease.

Eugene shoved Karl ahead of him out the door. "This isn't over."

Alex ignored them, let them leave. Finally everything was silent and still.

A moment later, a quiet presence moved just outside the door. Alex sighed. *No peace at all tonight.* "Can I help you?" he asked, not looking up.

"I know your secret." The voice was soft and friendly, with an impeccable upper-class English accent.

The man in the doorway was elderly, though vibrant looking, well dressed in an old-fashioned suit and waistcoat, impeccably polished shoes. "My secret?" Alex asked.

The old man gestured back over one shoulder. "Problems?"

"Nothing I can't handle."

"You know, you really are very good."

"I've done it for a long time."

The man considered Alex for several seconds. Alex let him, wondering what this man could want. People always wanted something. He read the man's shades and saw nothing but calm curiosity.

"Why here?" the Englishman asked eventually. "Aren't there more organised events held all over the world? Big promotion, massive prize money, fame and glory? Better rules and protective equipment? Legal?"

"You've just listed all the reasons I'm not interested."

The old man's eyebrows raised. "Even the money?"

There was a cough and movement in the corridor. "'Scuse me." A small, gruff-looking man with a shiny bald head pushed into the room. "Shit, Alex, one of these days you're gonna at least get hit, aren't ya?"

Alex smiled. "I get hit pretty often, Gary. Just not tonight."

Gary let out a strangely high laugh. "Thanks for stepping in at such short notice."

"No problem. Your other fighter going to be okay?"

"Yeah, just a training injury. He'll be fine."

"Glad I could help. Thanks for the chance."

"Any time. Dunno what I'd do without ya." He handed over an envelope and slapped Alex heavily on the shoulder.

"You still want me in next week?" Alex asked.

"Ah, give it two weeks."

"Sure. But I'm going to fight in London next month. Might stop in LA on the way back."

"Don't be out of Sydney too long." Gary turned, nodded at the old man before slipping back out the door, yelling to someone down the hallway. Alex held up the envelope with a half-smile.

"Is it as good as the mainstream prizes?" the old man asked.

"I get by."

"Which brings us back to my original point."

Alex leaned back against the wall, annoyed. "Which is?"

"I know your secret."

"Right. So what secret is that?"

"I see what you see. Not nearly so well, I think, but I see it."

"What do you mean?"

"Patrick Welby, by the way." The Englishman extended a hand.

"Alex Caine." He shook the man's hand, noticed manicured nails and very soft skin. He did his best to be polite, but wondered why he was bothering.

"I know. It took me a while to find you. These dos are bit hard to track down."

Alex ran out of patience. "That's kinda the idea. Listen, I don't have time for chitchat." He gestured at the door.

Welby's shades became urgent. "You fight for money, away from the limelight, you live quietly in the country and have very little interaction with anyone."

"So?" Alex said, hiding his concern at the extent of the stranger's knowledge.

"Am I right?"

"I trained to fight and never really had much interest in anything else. I don't play well with others." He gestured at the door again. "Now, out."

The old man held up both hands. "Please. I've been seeking someone like you for a long time."

Alex pushed down his anger, but let it burn gently below the surface. This old man bothered him. "Someone like me?"

Welby took a long breath. "I know that when you fight you see what people intend to do before they do it."

Alex raised one eyebrow, spooked. "Is that right?"

He had never really been able to explain his abilities, even to himself. He sensed a change in the shade of the air around a person, a sensation most similar to vision, but not something he actually saw. Sometimes that sense would blossom into waves of color at particularly powerful moments. He could read it and know what people intended to do. In the scenario of a fight it became particularly clear, less so in other aspects of life. "I've been told I was born for fighting," Alex said. The old pang of grief cut through as he remembered his Sifu's words.

Welby's face was sympathetic. "Is that why you don't play well with others?"

Alex shrugged. "The more you get to know someone the easier they are to read. Sometimes it's better not to know." He cleared his throat. "You need to leave, now. I've got nothing for you."

Welby's shades became agitated again. "You can't go on making a living like this forever."

Alex moved to the door. "My house is paid for and I don't get hit often. You have no idea what I can or can't do."

"But I can show you so much more, help you understand yourself."

"What's in it for you?" Alex asked.

Welby smiled broadly. "Good lad! Always the most important question. Well, I think that you'll be able to read a book that I can't, and I really want to know what this book says."

"That's it?"

"This particular book requires something special. I can pay you with knowledge you wouldn't find anywhere else, or money if you'd prefer. Or both."

Alex stared long and hard at Patrick Welby. Something was certainly being held back, but it was unclear. "No, man, sorry."

Welby frowned. "I can show you wonders. There are things you should know."

"I don't need any complications." He held the door open.

The old man reluctantly stepped out. "You like to stay in control, don't you?"

"Who doesn't? I just make sure of it."

"You'll lose that control."

Alex hardened his expression. "That a threat?"

"No. Just knowledge." Welby's shades fluctuated between defeat and hope. And something else fluttered like a dark moth, unreadable. "If you change your mind…"

"I won't." Alex closed the door, alone at last.

TWO

Alex walked along a dim alley, heading for the main street and a taxi to his hotel. He always treated himself to a fancy suite after a fight, a good room service feed and a big bed. The two-hour drive home in the morning was easier that way. Two silhouettes stepped into his path, one large, one small. They held long heavy weapons, bats or bars of some kind. Alex sighed. *This is getting old.*

"Piss off, you monkeys," he shouted. "I don't work for anyone."

"The King thinks differently," Eugene called back. "You cost him a lot of money tonight."

They faced each other, thirty meters apart. Alex read their shades, recognised the shifts and colors as nervous, especially the little one, Karl. But they both intended to do their boss's bidding. There would be a fight here. Alex shrugged his sports bag off his shoulder, put it down out of the way. "Come on then," he said. "Bring it!"

The shades throbbed and swam around the men as they raised their weapons and rushed him. Baseball bats, he noted. These guys were gorillas, street thugs using intimidation and numbers to win fights. They were no threat at all, even with bats. As the gap closed Alex danced between them, striking out as the bats whistled past. Two strikes each and it was over, the men squirming on the bitumen, groaning in pain.

A third man, not ten meters away, pointed a revolver. Alex cursed. *Stupid, stupid, stupid!*

"You're costing the King money, Caine. We can't have that."

Alex frowned. "Your king should start betting on me instead."

"Doesn't work like that. He controls. You'll work for him. Or you'll die."

Alex vaguely registered a car slowing at the mouth of the alley. "I don't work for anyone."

The man gestured with his gun. "You are in no position to negotiate. Come with us now or I kill you right here."

Alex tried to figure the best angle to move. The man knew what he was doing, positioned close enough that he would be unlikely to miss, far enough away that he would be hard to reach without getting a shot off. Alex centered his breath, about to launch forward, and a bright orange glow erupted over the man's shoulder. He yelped as flames licked the side of his face. He frantically tried to beat at his back, Alex and the gun forgotten. Alex rushed, wondering if more guns were trained on him from the car parked at the end of the alley. *How the hell did he catch alight?*

The man dropped and rolled, trying to smother the flames, and Alex leapt over him. He skidded to a halt when he saw Patrick Welby's face smiling through the window of the car. "Need a ride?" the old man called out as he pushed the passenger door open.

Alex jumped in and Welby peeled away as the man with the gun staggered, smoking, to his feet. A concussive crack followed them as he squeezed off a shot.

"What was that?" Alex said angrily.

"Looked like you were about to be shot." Welby's hands were steady on the wheel, a slight smile played about his lips.

Alex scowled. "I don't fucking need your help."

Welby said nothing and they drove in silence. Alex thought over the events. Why was nothing ever simple? Always someone trying to get a bite of your pie. The image of the flames bursting across the gunman's back returned. Welby slowed for a red light. "How did you do it?" Alex asked.

"Do what?"

"You know fucking well what." He caught his breath, catching his anger with it. "Did you throw a petrol bomb at him or something?"

"Never so ham-fisted."

"So how?"

"I simply threw fire at him."

"Threw fire?"

"Can I buy you a drink?" Welby asked. "I'd really like to talk with you some more."

Alex felt his world spinning, his control slipping away. He

refused to let other people dictate his life. "No, you can't. Just take me to my hotel. I'm at the Four Seasons."

Welby lifted a hand from the wheel, wagging one index finger at Alex. "How many people have you told about your... ability? The things you can see?"

"My life has nothing to do with you, Welby." Alex's anger burned. "Stop the fucking car, I'm done here."

"I can help you!" Welby said, desperation in his tone. "You don't owe me anything, but at least talk to me until I get you to your hotel. Please? How many people have you told?"

Alex ground his teeth. There was no point in denying the obvious. "None really."

"Why?"

He saw where the old man was heading with this. "Because in the first instance it's very hard to explain and in the second, it's unlikely anyone would believe me."

"And why wouldn't they believe you?"

"Because it's a hard thing to prove."

Welby grinned. "Exactly. But who has the better understanding of reality? You? Or them?"

Alex chose not to answer. Rhetorical question. Let him blather on, he didn't really care. He wanted to be in his hotel room, alone.

Patrick Welby said nothing for a few blocks. Then, "Your talent could be far better. If you can see as you do that means you have the ability to do all kinds of other things most people would consider supernatural. Magical. You just need to know how."

Alex smirked. "Magical? I'm an open-minded guy, I know most people wouldn't believe me about what I can see, but it's not magic."

"Isn't it?"

"Mine is just a well-developed natural aptitude," he said. 'empathy."

"Why do you resist the truth?"

"Resist?"

Welby pulled the car over to the kerb. They were nowhere near the hotel. "What are you doing?" Alex asked.

Welby took a bottle of water from the back seat. "I want to show you something."

He unscrewed the cap and raised his right hand before his chest, palm out, holding the bottle in his left. Alex watched the old man's hand curiously. Welby gestured subtly with his chin, drawing Alex's eye to the bottle. A sensation of static rose, coppery, tickling across the skin. The air seemed to swell slightly and he saw subtle shades shifting through the space between himself and Welby. The water shivered. Then it rose in the center, a finger of clear liquid standing up through the bottleneck against gravity.

Alex jumped like he'd been stung. Welby curled his fingers slightly and the column of standing water twisted in a graceful spiral, glittering in the light from the dashboard. Welby gestured again and the spiral of water unwound, stood taller, and fell back with a soft splash. Alex stared, his eyes hard.

"You *felt* it too, didn't you," Patrick Welby said quietly. "You didn't just see it, you felt the magic."

Welby was patient as Alex pondered. Some kind of trickery? He had been less than two feet away and watched everything in crystal clarity. He had felt the swell of something in the air between them, the charge of something preternatural occurring. And he knew he had felt it before. *Fucking magic? Really?*

Welby screwed the cap onto the bottle. "I realize all this is a lot to take in, but you really deserve to know the potential you have. It deserves to be nurtured."

Alex pursed his lips. "And you want me to look at this book," he said.

"You use your vision in a very practical way. I'm aware of my limitations. I think you'll be able to see what I can't."

"What's so special about this book?"

"There are many in the world that are powerful. The contained knowledge makes any book a magical item. Do you like to read?"

"Yes."

"Some books are designed to be specifically magical. Grimoires that impart arcane knowledge, ancient secrets, dangerous truths that men have killed and died for." Welby reached into his jacket and pulled out a small, leatherbound tome. It looked like an extra thick address book, but for the weathered age of its cover and the edges of its pages. As soon as Alex saw it he knew it was something infused with more than the leather and paper and twine of its construction. "You can feel it, can't you?" Welby said. "Already you're learning. Just by knowing there is more to know, you are improving."

Alex said nothing. He saw slight shifts in the shades around the small book. If he concentrated he could see them gently moving up over Welby's hand, up his arm and sleeve, like questing tendrils of translucent smoke. As if the book not only had some kind of power, but the power itself had a presence. A simple sentience that sought its own experience.

"This is a potent little item," Welby said. "It contains secrets of the elements, of air, water, earth, fire. It teaches methods of drawing on those elements. There's some commanding knowledge in here, more than the trickery I just demonstrated." He reached out, offering it.

Alex didn't move. "I'll take your word for it."

"You don't want to see? You don't want the understanding?"

He was certainly curious. So much so that he physically ached to open it up and read. But the way the book's magic slipped and slid around Welby's hand gave him pause. "Can't you see it?" he asked tightly.

"The magesign? Does it bother you?"

"Is that what you call it?"

"It has many names. Everything magical gives off 'sign. That's the name the ancient magi and wise men used. You could call it an aura or energy field or whatever you like."

"It's like the way I see people, only so much clearer, more intense."

"Yes. Arcanes, magical folk, have an aura like a lighthouse on a dark night. The more powerful they become the brighter they shine, so they learn to mask themselves. That's something you'll need to do. You shine quite brightly. It's something I can teach you."

Now Alex knew why Welby's shades seemed obscured. The

old man masked himself. "It's creeping around your hand. As if it's trying to escape and climb up your arm."

Welby cocked an eyebrow. "Is it?" He looked down curiously. "You truly have a clarity of vision." He held out the book again. "Really, it's harmless. Some 'sign can carry dangerous energies, but that would be very obvious, especially to you."

Alex took the book. It buzzed between his fingers, the magesign even clearer now he held it, swirling around lazily. But the sensation of sentience had passed. It seemed no more malevolent than the steam from a kettle, a simple by-product of the thing itself. His head ached as he tried to take everything in.

He flicked open the cover. The page was dense with tiny characters and diagrams, the writing unlike anything he had seen before. "This looks like a tough language to learn," he said, trying to discern the swirls and ellipses of the text, like a strange kind of Arabic or Sanskrit, complicated and beautiful. He read a line that poetically described the personality of water. With a start he looked up sharply.

The old man was pleased. "It's an eldritch language. A magical language. Those with talent can learn to read it. I must say I've never seen anyone decipher one quite so quickly." Welby's face was alight with an almost childlike joy. "You can hang on to that," he said through his mirth. "A token of my goodwill. It's worth a fortune and it might teach you some useful skills."

Alex closed the book, his heart racing. "This isn't what you wanted me to look at?"

"No, just an example. A way to show you the method of looking. I thought you might need a bit longer to get the idea but your skill is remarkable. What I need your help with is far older and more obscure. It's about the oldest and most powerful book I've ever seen, but I can't read it. No one I know can. The language is intricate and dense, something only someone with a rare clarity of vision could decipher. Which is why I've spent so long seeking someone like you." He sat back.

Alex's curiosity burned. "All right. So you want me to look, and then what? Translate it for you? Do you have it with you?"

Welby shook his head, becoming serious. "No, I don't. It's not actually in my possession. It's owned by an... acquaintance of mine. I'm hoping if I take you there to see it, and if you can read it, that he'll sell it to me. Perhaps I'll have to agree to share the information with him, I don't know. I wanted to find someone capable of reading it first. Will you come with me?"

"Where is it?"

"A small place in London."

"London?" Alex laughed. He held out Welby's gift. "Take me to my hotel."

Welby's face fell. He pushed the book back. "Please, Alex. Aren't you fighting soon in London anyway? I overheard you in your dressing room. You're facing a bit of trouble here right now too. Perhaps a sojourn might be a good idea, till the heat's off."

"The heat? This King Scarlet fool is going to continue hounding me. I can't just run away."

"That man was prepared to shoot you. To kill you."

"But he wouldn't have succeeded."

Welby's eyes narrowed. "Are you really so in control of everything around you?"

"Yes, I fucking am. Take me to my hotel."

Welby sighed. He pulled away from the kerb and they drove to the Four Seasons without speaking. Alex sensed the old man's frustration. He felt sorry for him, but not enough to upend his life. Too much had happened tonight, way too fast, and he had his own problems. He had contacts. He needed to get home, make some calls, sort out this King Scarlet thing.

They pulled into the driveway of the hotel and Alex recognised two of Scarlet's goons from previous encounters. They loitered just inside the lobby. "Shit!"

"What's the matter?"

"How did he know where I was staying?"

"This Scarlet fellow?" Welby asked.

Alex gestured to the hotel. "Two of his men are in there. Maybe more I can't see."

Welby slowed the car to a crawl. "He's not playing games, is he?"

"No."

"You can stay at my place," Welby said. "I have a flat here in Sydney."

Alex stared through the tall, plate glass windows, his brow furrowed. "My stuff is in my room, my car parked underneath."

"I daresay they've got that covered. He seems to have some influence."

"Drive into the car park. There's not much in my room, I was only going to be here overnight. Fuck it. I'll drive myself home now and sort things out tomorrow."

Welby nodded and headed for the garage doors. He used Alex's room key to access the basement car park and drove down the winding concrete path. As they reached the second level Alex cursed when he saw his car at the other end, the tyres slashed, lights and windows smashed, ugly scratches scarring every surface. Two men in suits stood nearby.

Alex slipped out of his seatbelt and dropped into the footwell, curling up out of sight. "Keep driving," he hissed.

Welby said nothing. He reached back and pulled a jacket off the back seat and dropped it over Alex. From under its edge Alex watched his face, impassive as he drove by. At the end he turned and the car began travelling up, spiralling back towards street level. "We're clear," the old man said.

Alex sat up into his seat. "My car! What the hell is wrong with these people?"

"You must be costing this Scarlet a lot of money. He's taking things very seriously."

"Maybe you setting his man on fire hasn't helped!"

Welby looked contrite. "I'm sorry. I was trying to save you."

Alex sighed. "I know, I'm sorry. It's not your fault."

"You want to go to my flat while you decide what to do?"

"Yes, I suppose so." Alex's fury boiled deep in his gut. "Thanks," he said through gritted teeth.

The flat was stylish. "Can't be cheap to keep a place in Double Bay," Alex said.

Welby closed the door, dropped his keys into a bowl on a mahogany bookshelf. "I'm very fortunate when it comes to money. Old family fortunes and all that."

"How long have you lived here?"

"Oh, I don't live here. I have a few places around the world. I tend to travel a lot. People pay good money to lease places like this for a few days or a week at a time and it gives me somewhere readily available when I need it. They pretty much pay for themselves."

Alex made a noise of derision. "If you have the money to get them in the first place."

"Well, yes. But let's not talk about money. It's an ugly subject."

"Fair enough."

Welby seemed uncomfortable. Alex let him wallow in it. Given how strange this evening had been already and how freaked out he was by it, he certainly wasn't about to make things easy for this weirdo. He realized on some level he wasn't being fair to Welby, but nothing seemed very fair right now.

Welby cleared his throat nervously. "Listen, Alex, I am sorry. I'm aware this whole turn of events must be incredibly unsettling."

"You could say that."

"What do you plan to do?"

"It's late and I'm tired. If you don't mind me crashing here I'll make some calls in the morning. I've had enough for now."

"Not a problem. And please, consider my offer to come to London. I mean it when I say you have much to gain from this. Knowledge is the most valuable thing in the world and I can give you a lot of it."

Alex made a wry expression. "Knowledge can be a dangerous thing."

"Of course. I'm going to go to bed now, leave you to think and have some space. That door leads to the guest bedroom. Make yourself at home."

"All right then."

Welby pointed to the pocket of Alex's olive green combat surplus jacket. "Have a look at that grimoire before you go to sleep. Read about the elements."

"Maybe I will."

"Good. Night then."

Welby turned and strode across the room, disappearing behind a dark oak door. Alex slumped down on the soft leather sofa. A remote sat on the coffee table and he reached for it, flicked on the oversize television. A few channel skips found a mindless late night American chat show. He watched vacuous Hollywood celebrities trying to convince an equally vacuous audience they really did have causes they believed in. Empty programming that gave him something to stare at while his mind ticked over.

This situation had become serious, but there was nothing to be done right now. Some calls would hopefully start to put things right. Perhaps he would have to avoid Sydney for a while. There were plenty of other venues. It pissed him off that Scarlet was making his life difficult.

His thoughts drifted back to Welby's water trick in the car, the uncanny, beautiful moving sculpture the old man had conjured. It was mind-blowing. Something seemingly simple that obviously wasn't stage trickery.

A new part of him had woken up. His ability seemed so much more than he had ever imagined. And the fact he knew, absolutely, positively knew, that he had felt people practising magic before, weighed heavily on his mind. He hadn't recognised it for what it was. What else did the world have to offer? What else had been concealed under this patina of normality? He remembered his father, sitting with him in a sunny garden. It had been mid-summer, hot and bright. He had been barely in school. *This world is an amazing place, son, full of fascinating things. Take a moment once in a while to look around and take it all in.* His father spoke a deeper truth than either of them could have realized at the time. The familiar old rock in his gut grew heavy, as it always did when he thought about his parents. It brought with it the usual melancholy and cold rage.

He pulled his leatherbound book from the pocket of his jacket.

Welby was certainly trying to buy his favour. For a long time he held it, watched the drift of magesign around it, gently swirling and twisting, mesmerising. He realized there had been times in the past when he'd seen magesign, only he'd had no idea what it was. And not knowing meant he hadn't really seen it properly, hadn't focused on it. The thought made him uncomfortable, made him feel like a fool. Perhaps the world was peppered with people laughing at folks like him, *Look at the blind idiots, stumbling through life.* But he wasn't blind any more. A veil had lifted. Now he planned to spend every minute with his eyes wide open.

He turned to the first page and began to read. It took a moment for the words to become clear, like adjusting a pair of binoculars until the image sharpened, but once through it stayed. He read it as easily as a newspaper. It described the nature of the elemental forces in the world, the physical and magical properties of water, air, fire and earth. It talked of their personalities and how they could be manipulated, conjured, controlled with the fifth element of will. Magic.

He read for a long time until his eyelids grew heavy and he began to blink long and slow. He was keen to read on, but his tiredness outgunned his resolve. The knowledge seemed to settle deep in his brain, more than words, mere information. He realized the book contained more than the script on the pages. It imparted magic directly to the reader. "Fuck me," he breathed.

THREE

A sharp, insistent rapping. For a moment, he stared at the fancy glass light fitting above and wondered where the hell he was. "Alex? Are you awake?"

Welby's accent brought everything back into focus. "C'm'in," he managed through dry lips.

The door cracked open and Patrick Welby's face slipped into the gap, his expression almost comical in its concern. "Ah, you're... er..."

Alex rubbed his eyes. "I'm still here. I must have slept like a log." He sat up, stretching muscles that hadn't moved since he lay down hours before.

Welby came into the room. "I was mildly concerned that you'd slipped away in the night. I can see you're still tired."

"Really?"

"Magesign. Remember I told you how the magus has to learn to mask himself? It doesn't do to wander around like a beacon."

"Right."

"Hungry?"

Alex raised an eyebrow. "Bloody starving."

"Come on, I have eggs boiled and bread in the toaster."

Alex sat sipping gratefully at a large espresso, his stomach full of eggs, toast and sweet, fresh tomatoes. "You're looking after me well," he said over the rim of his mug.

"I'm still hoping you'll help."

"How old are you?"

Welby looked up from his plate, toast halfway to his lips. He stared deep into Alex's eyes. Alex maintained his gaze, looked carefully at the play of shades around the Englishman. Something told him Welby was older than he seemed. A lot older. He thought about how much more he might be able to see if he put his mind to it. Welby's lips curled in a smile. "Trying out some new tricks?" he asked, and pulled his shades in dramatically, like an old school thespian whipping a voluminous cloak around himself.

Alex willed his sight to pry under that thick cloak of shades, to see past them all. To his surprise the shades burst open again, laying bare all the colors Welby had to show. Welby's eyes widened in shock and Alex realized he could see not only past the shades Welby had pulled about himself, but past shades even the poor man could not have known about or controlled. He felt as though he had mentally stripped Welby naked and flayed him as he sat before his breadcrumbs and eggshells. He saw Welby for the age he truly was, saw everything about the Englishman laid bare, wide open, raw. He could see the fibers of the man's being and he knew everything there was to know. He pulled away his vision, mentally and physically, turning his head. "Fucking hell, I'm sorry!"

Welby's hands flopped to the table, his shoulders slumping. "Good gods."

Alex couldn't bring himself to look at the old man, turned in his seat to further avert his gaze. "Really, Patrick, I'm so sorry. I didn't know I could…"

"It's all right." Welby's voice was weak. "By all the gods, you have some power."

Silence, heavy and uncomfortable, for several moments. Eventually Welby said, "So you see me a little more clearly now?" There was humor, sarcasm in his tone.

Alex kept his back turned. "You're, what, a hundred and fifty years old?"

"Almost. One hundred and thirty-eight. I was born at the height of Victoria's reign, a truly marvellous time of innovation and expansion. For those of us who could afford it, of course. I began studying the arcane arts as a young man. When we develop our skill we also develop an unusual longevity. The magic tends to preserve us."

Alex sat stunned, still reeling from what he had been able to do to Welby as well as the revelations that kept coming. He knew now what he hadn't been able to see before. Welby's everyday shades were a construction, a mask of normality placed over the real colors the man bore, concealing all the truths about him. Alex had torn everything away and seen deep inside.

"It really is all right," Welby said. "You'll have to face me again eventually. I've never been laid quite so naked before in my life, but at least you know beyond a doubt now that my intentions are as I stated them."

Alex swallowed hard. "Your intentions are also a bit crude."

"Well, forgive an old man his desires. But I would never have let on about those feelings, much less acted on them. More's the pity."

Alex could hear a measure of mirth in Welby's voice and couldn't help smiling himself. Some of the tension, the shock, lifted from the room. "I guess I should be careful what I search for."

"Just be careful how hard you look. You said yourself not long ago that it was easier not to learn too much about people."

"I had no idea how much I could know."

"Now you do."

Alex was unable still to turn around. He knew Welby's mind, his intentions, desires, fears and elations, almost as well as he knew his own. He had looked into the very soul of the man and absorbed nearly one hundred and forty years of life experience and emotion in an instant. He felt as though he had run full speed into a solid wall, his mind and body battered by the experience. But more than that, he bore an incredible sense of guilt, of sorrow. He had committed an unforgivable invasion of privacy. He didn't know what to say.

Welby moved around the table to stand in front of him, forcing him to look. "Let it go, Alex. It's all right, really. This will be harder for you to reconcile than for me to forgive."

He looked into Welby's eyes and knew him in minute detail. He refused to focus on the shades, but he could see peripherally that Welby meant it when he said it was all right. "I'm sorry," he said again, quietly.

"I probably shouldn't have been quite so theatrical. I rather tempted you to pull against me. Of course, I had no idea how easily and deeply you would be able to go."

Alex realized he had learned something else. "I know how to do that now, how to mask." He willed his own shades, his presence, his personality, to draw within the confines of his skin and wrapped it down with the intention that no one would be able to see his true aura. He created a sheen of normality—a shield—so that no one would know he was anything but a normal man.

Welby looked him up and down, eyebrows rising as he did so. "Very good. I honestly can't see a thing." He felt Welby's mind probe over him, like the stroke of a ghostly hand. The old man barked a short laugh. "Not a thing. Good lords, boy, your talents are manifold! You appear as mundane as a post box."

"I can stay like this too. It doesn't feel like it would take any effort to remain like this as a… well, as a sort of default position."

Welby nodded. "And so you should. You'll attract much less attention that way. So what now?"

Alex pulled his phone from his pocket. "I need to make a call."

"I'll give you some privacy."

Welby left the kitchen and Alex dialled a number. After a few rings a voice said, "Alex, you dog! Long time, my brother."

Alex felt immediately reassured at the sound of something normal, familiar. "Hey, Amir. How's things?"

"Oh, you know, fucken."

As if Amir would ever tell him what was really going on. "I need some help," he said.

"Anything, brother."

"You know this King Scarlet dickhead?"

Amir made a noise of disgust down the line. "He's a pain in my arse. Starting to get heavy all over town."

"He's insisting that I fight for him. Really insisting."

"We fight for no one but ourselves, brother. Since Sifu died anyway."

"I know. But he's starting to get upset. Last night I had a gun pointed in my face and he trashed my fucking car, man."

Amir cursed violently in Lebanese. "There's a bit of a war going on, my friend. I've heard rumors of the moves he's making and your name has come up a few times."

"You didn't think to warn me?"

"Ha! You can look after yourself, fucken! But you shouldn't

even be here this week."

"Gary called me to step in for an injured fighter. Now I'm thinking that guy was Scarlet's plant, supposed to take a fall."

"I can see things have escalated," Amir said, his voice resigned. "I hoped he would leave you be, but you're too good, my brother."

"Can you help me out?"

"Sure. But not quickly. There's a lot of balls in the air here. I can put you in my stable, but Scarlet won't take that lying down."

Alex pursed his lips. "No offense, but I don't want to work for anyone, even you."

"Of course, of course, but Scarlet doesn't need to know that. I tell him you're mine and it's just one more thing we're fighting about."

"I'd really appreciate it."

"But he won't be happy. He'll come for you. I can try to sort this out, but maybe you should take a holiday for a little while. These guys are getting serious."

Alex stared at the tabletop, seeing his control spinning away again. He hated relying on anyone for anything. Right now it seemed he had little choice. "There is something I could do for a week or two, overseas."

"Anywhere is good to be safe. I'll keep you up to speed."

Alex sat back, morning light through the window bathing his face. "Take this fucker out, Amir. And get me his car."

"For certain, fucken! I'd like nothing more. Leave this with me."

"Thanks, brother." Alex hung up and wandered into the lounge.

Welby sat reading a newspaper. "Any luck?" he asked.

"Sort of. For us both really."

"Is that so?"

"I have friends who can hopefully sort this out, but I've been advised to leave town for a while."

Welby folded the newspaper onto his lap. "So maybe a trip to London is just the ticket?"

Alex shook his head, frustrated these decisions didn't seem to be his own. "Just the ticket," he said. "Sure."

"We can go right away. All expenses paid, of course," Welby added.

"I need to pack some stuff, Patrick. And get my passport."

Welby stood, dropped the newspaper onto the coffee table. "Money is no object. I can buy you anything you would have packed and fly you first class."

Alex paused, taken aback. "My passport is at home," he said eventually.

"I can teach you how you don't need one. I can show you how you really don't need any of the things most people consider essential, even compulsory."

Alex let out an exasperated breath. "Fair enough then, Patrick Welby. Show me."

"Excellent! I'll get us on a flight this afternoon."

"Really?"

"Certainly. We can buy a bag and some clothes and things for you at the airport shops after we check in."

Alex sighed. *What the hell is happening to my life?*

At Sydney airport's international terminal Alex stood nervously in line. He had listened to everything Welby had explained, marvelled at the mind tricks he pulled on their taxi driver, making the poor man take wrong turns and do weird things with the radio and indicators. All with nothing but insubstantial will. He had listened, seen and understood, but remained anxious. He wasn't sure how Welby would use those trickster skills to get them through airport security.

The airport employee smiled. "Tickets and passports please," she said with practised jollity. Welby handed her two tickets and Alex focused in on his magesign, watched the shades as Welby's mind worked. He saw and felt the 'sign swell, ebb and flow. "Any luggage to check in?" she asked with another broad smile.

"No, thank you. Just carry-on."

"Thank you, sir. Departing at gate 36. Have a nice day." She handed over two boarding passes, waved them through. The old man glanced back and winked before walking away. Dumbfounded, Alex followed, the only thought in his mind being, *These aren't the droids you're looking for.*

He followed Welby through to the departures area, dropping his phone and wallet into a plastic tray as he went through a metal detector. On the other side numerous shops enticed with bright neon and shiny displays, coaxing weary travellers to empty their wallets while they killed interminable hours before take-off. Shopkeepers smiled and opened their palms, offering succour from the boredom of international travel. Inside an hour Welby had bought Alex a stylish leather travel bag and stocked it with new jeans, a few T-shirts, a collared shirt, a warm jumper and underwear. He bought a washbag and filled it with toothbrush, toothpaste, shaver and more. Alex pulled his phone from a jacket pocket. "I'll need a charger for this," he said. Within minutes he had one.

It was something of a revelation that if one had the money, nothing else seemed necessary. Welby's wealth had taken care of everything. Combined with his magical skill in negotiating the red tape of modern living, there seemed very little that couldn't be accomplished. *Magic and money. All you need.*

"Something amusing?" Welby asked.

"Just trying to get my head around the last few hours. It was only last night that I was doing what I do best. I fought, I won, I collected my pay and I planned to go home. Since then the world has flipped on its axis."

Welby gestured to a seat at the departure gate. "And I must say you're taking it all extremely well. It's not often, even in my long life, that I've opened up this world to people. On the few occasions I have it's been difficult and slow. Not with you. You soak it up like a dry sponge drinks water."

Alex sat, rested his new bag between his feet. "I hope my mind can continue to keep a grip on it all. Why do you need money when you can mind-fuck people into believing they've seen our passports?"

"Good question. When someone expects to see a passport it's

quite easy to convince them they have. They hold onto nothing but the knowledge. When they're expecting to take money and keep it, well that's very hard when they clearly have no bills to put in the till."

That made a kind of sense. "So much to take in."

"We have twenty-four hours on a plane," Welby said. "First class really does pamper a person. You can actually lie down. Let's call this next twenty-four hours a new experience-free zone. Give you time to catch up a bit, eh?"

The thought appealed. "Sounds good. Though I want to read more of that element book."

"Grimoire."

Alex smiled. "Right. Grimoire. It's amazing, not like learning. The words seem to become a part of my mind."

"That's right. Reading eldritch texts is itself a kind of magic, if you can decipher them. Therein lies their power."

The lamplit streets of London were a blessed relief from the cramped and artificial confines of airports and aeroplanes. Even in the comfort of ridiculously expensive seats the fluorescent lights, air conditioning and pressurisation all got under the skin after a while. Alex breathed deeply of the cold, polluted air. Only after flying for twenty-four hours would taking deep breaths in central London feel refreshing. However filthy it might be, it was real, with genuine smells and sounds carrying through it. He had insisted they get out of the taxi a few blocks early in order to stretch their legs and take in something tangible. Welby had looked as though he would never have considered such a thing, especially at night, but clearly appreciated it as he walked alongside, looking around as though seeing things for the first time.

Alex felt swollen from reading the grimoire. He'd been fascinated, unable to put it down. For hour upon hour he had consumed the knowledge in its pages, absorbed the fantastic things it had to say until he'd read everything. Then he read it again. Now he understood the elements in a way he could never explain. He knew them like close friends, understood their personalities and intricacies. He knew intrinsically their make-up, and more, the energies that bound them to each other. It frightened him when he considered how much understanding that tiny book had forced into him. How much stuff like that could a mind take? At the same time he felt invigorated by it, desperate for more.

After a walk not nearly long enough to really appreciate the freshness of an English autumn evening they arrived at Welby's place—a tall three-storey Victorian house in a row of similar stately two-storey homes. The street was quiet and tree-lined, with flagstone pavements and high, rough-hewn kerb stones dropping into deep gutters. Crackling brown leaves like fragments of old parchment skittered across the ground in a chill breeze, the leafless fingers of the trees scrabbling silhouettes against the night darkened sky. Dark but with a gentle orange sheen, cityglow from the bustle beneath.

"Let's get inside, shower and change," Welby said jovially. "The best way to recover from travelling is to wash off the experience."

Alex had to agree. "Sounds good to me."

"And then we'll go and have a look at this book."

"Tonight?"

"Certainly. We don't need to worry about the opening hours of this particular shop."

"For a man who's been around as long as you, you don't seem to have much patience."

Welby stopped, his key in the lock unturned. "I suppose it would seem that way," he said. "It's just that I've looked for so long for someone like you." He twisted the key and pushed open the door, stepped back to let Alex through.

Inside the house was immaculate and elegant. Fine art and antiques throughout, leather sofas and armchairs. Extensive bookshelves, all bowing under the weight of books, seemed ubiquitous. It appeared to be a cross between a museum and a library, but it had the general feel of a home, lived in and cared for. "I spend as much time as I can here," Welby said. "This house has been the only constant thing in my life."

They passed through a lounge into a dining room and on into the kitchen. Turning, Welby led the way back through a hallway to the foot of the stairs by the front door. An informal tour of the ground floor. Welby took the stairs. At the landing he pointed to doors in sequence. "Bedroom, bathroom, bedroom. That one's yours." Without waiting he headed up to the top floor, casting a strange smile back over his shoulder as he went. As they climbed Alex shivered, static lifting the hairs on his arms and neck.

At the next landing Welby pushed open a door and stepped back. "This is my favorite place." The room was large and lined floor to ceiling with books. A desk with a computer stood under the only window, a large leadlight bay recess. In the middle of the space were more leather armchairs and sofas. "This is the actual library, my personal study. All the most important volumes are here."

Alex opened his vision to see the magesign. Every shelf swam with it, the whole room seemed soaked in magical energy. He whistled softly.

Welby grinned. "This is a priceless collection, which is why it's also protected. You felt the wards as we climbed the stairs?"

"Is that what that was?"

"Yes. Without a considerable ability to break the spells you wouldn't even see those stairs leading up here. From the outside this appears as a two-storey house like the others. You'd never suspect anything more than the roof would be where we're standing now."

Alex didn't feel like letting on that he had seen three storeys from the outside without even trying. "So much to learn," he said instead.

Welby nodded. "Indeed. That's my bedroom over there. Go on back down, shower, change, whatever. I'll meet you back in the front room in half an hour or so."

"Fair enough."

FOUR

The taxi ride to the bookshop was entertaining, Welby almost buzzing with excitement. Alex used the time to center himself, take back some kind of control. He lived life according to his own plans, but this whole bizarre adventure had become a game for which he had no rule book. If everything this evening turned out to be too complicated, if he felt as though his grip slipped on what little authority he had left, he would walk away. If Welby was so desperate for help, then Alex could dictate his own terms. And after that unfortunate event when he had stripped Welby's defenses away he felt as though the old man acted slightly less confidently anyway. There had been a distinct power in what he had done. He regretted it. Valuing his own privacy so highly left him under no illusions about what a violation his act had been, unintentional or otherwise. But he remained glad of the control it gave him, the small sense of power over Welby in an environment where he would have been otherwise powerless. He might be a stranger in a strange land, but he would not be lost.

The shop itself looked like something from a storybook. Down an old cobbled lane, ancient buildings of worn stone with lattice windows and heavy wooden doors. They walked past a coin collector's emporium, a boutique clothing store and stopped by a black door with BOOKS painted on it in peeling gold, the word repeated above the multifaceted window. Nothing else. No names, no open or closed sign. Shelf upon shelf stood visible in the dim interior, watery light leaking through from a curtained-off area at the back. Welby rapped on the door.

After a few moments he tried again. "He'll take a while to respond. Stubborn bugger, he is."

"Looks like he relies on reputation for business, rather than passing trade," Alex said.

"Yes. He's been around a while. He has an established clientele."

"Been around a while like you have?"

Welby gave him a wry look. "Yes. But he's something of an

adept rather than a magus. His skills are very limited though he thinks he's something special. He's actually incredibly irritating."

"I've met people like that in my game."

Welby rapped the door again.

"What's the name of this guy anyway?"

"Mr Peacock," Welby replied, deadpan.

Alex laughed. "Really?"

"Yes. That's what he insists on being called by everyone. Refuses even to admit to having a first name. Like I said—irritating. Here we go."

The curtain whipped aside and a tiny, wrinkled man peered towards the window. Welby tapped on the glass. "Open up, Peacock, it's Patrick Welby."

Peacock waved a hand petulantly. "Come back tomorrow, you old fruit. I'm closed up, can't you tell?" His voice was high, harsh.

Welby gave Alex an apologetic look. "Don't be a fool," he called out. "Open the bloody door."

Peacock stomped heavily through his shop, theatrical exasperation. He made a meal of sliding bolts, turning keys. When the door swung in he opened his mouth to bark at Welby then stopped dead when he saw Alex. His eyes roved down and back, his mind probing instantly, rudely. Alex let a pulse of anger wash through his tightly held shields for a fraction of a second, magical bitch slap. Peacock staggered a pace backwards as Welby snorted with mirth.

Peacock was suddenly politeness personified, curiosity drifting off him like cheap cologne. "Welcome, gentlemen, welcome. What brings you here at this strange hour?"

"This is Alex, a friend of mine. He's going to read the book."

Peacock's eyebrows leapt skywards. "Is he now?"

"He is."

"He's going to try, you mean?"

"No, he's going to read it."

"Hmm. Well, you'd better come in."

The inside of the shop was soaked in magesign. The books on the shelves swam in a mist of it, most of them simply old, beautiful things. Some, hidden here and there, were clearly something more. Not as powerful as Alex's elemental grimoire, though similar. But the sensation from the back of the shop, leaking past the curtain like blood swirling in clear water, was far more compelling. It exuded a pull, a mental magnetism, the desire to stride in almost overwhelming.

"He going to be all right?"

Peacock's high voice pushed a cold knife through Alex's thoughts.

Welby patted Alex on the shoulder. "Yes, he's fine. Just very sensitive. Lead on."

When Peacock pulled back the curtain it felt as if a furnace door had opened, blasting arcane winds. "Deep breaths, Alex. Relax and let it drift by you." Welby kept his voice low, whispered close.

Alex rubbed one hand over his face. "So much magic here!"

"I know. Trust me, you'll get used to this."

Peacock turned. "What are you two whispering about?"

"Nothing, old chap. Lead on."

They entered a room lined with more shelves, enclosed behind glass. The books were all grimoires of some description, every one heavy with magic. Alex felt the wards and shields as Peacock dropped them to allow entry. He got impressions of not only intruder shields, but fire, water, all manner of protection. He knew some of the methods used from his recent reading. The collected works here must be priceless. So much knowledge, so much power. He became dizzy. Peacock sat behind a huge mahogany desk, waving one hand impatiently at them.

An empty chair sat before the desk. Welby dragged another over from a corner. Seated at the dark wood, the three men observed each other. Peacock's desire to look into Alex was obvious, though he wisely resisted the temptation. Alex scanned the bookseller's shades and saw a variety of conceits, arrogance and superiority. Welby was right that Peacock thought himself something special. But his colors were dull. Alex knew better than to trust that now, having learned that a skilled magus would use such shades as a shield to their true self. He kept an eye on the small man anyway, watching for any slip. Several uncomfortable moments passed.

"Well?" Welby said eventually.

Peacock sank his chin into one gnarled hand, fingers seeming too long for his diminutive frame. He stared, brows knitting in a frown.

Welby made a sound of exasperation. "What?"

"I'm not sure I should show you the book."

"I've seen it a hundred times."

"What's in it for me?"

"Ah, you fear Alex here may actually be able to read it?"

Peacock harrumphed. "Fear, no. But *if* he can, what's in it for me?"

"Well, you'll get an idea of what the book is about. Anything Alex reads he'll read aloud. Right?"

"If you say so," Alex said. "You're both a lot more convinced I'll be able to read this thing than I am."

Welby opened his palms on the desk. "Come on, show us the book."

Peacock, still frowning, fumbled in a drawer then leaned down out of sight. A sound of metal on metal and he sat up again soaked in swirling 'sign, wrapping itself around him like a hundred tiny smoke dragons. Alex was unsure what he had expected, but visions of some giant leatherbound tome were in his mind. A magnificent book with heavy parchment pages. What he saw seemed ridiculous. No more than four by three inches, maybe half an inch thick, like a pocket notebook, the cover stiff leather, tooled around the edges in an intricate design. It looked like something you'd buy in a shop that sold incense and 'Protected By Angels' stickers, though the power swelling off it was undeniable, almost pulsing with a sense of desperation to be out. The book begged to be opened, consumed.

Peacock turned it and placed it on the desk in front of Alex, leaving his hand on it a moment before sitting back, eyes suspicious. The old men sat with a sense of urgent expectation. The book was dark crimson red, almost black. Strange symbols were faint on the cover, pressed into leather worn shiny smooth with years. Leaning forward, staring at the alien shapes, realization dawned. Simply by wanting to decipher any meaning in the design Alex read it as easily as reading his name. "Darak Uthentia."

Peacock sat up in his chair like he'd been shocked. "What?"

Welby smiled.

"It says "Darak Uthentia". Those are the words, but I don't know what it means. The symbols kinda impart the sound of the words, but the words are... I don't know, they don't make sense."

Peacock turned on Welby. "Who the fuck is this whelp, Patrick?"

Welby held up one hand. "No need for anger."

"He can read it and not know what it means?"

"Apparently."

Realisation dawned on Alex. "Oh, they're names. Proper names, that's why."

Peacock fumed. Patrick sat smugly confident, clearly waiting. Alex felt trapped between them. For want of anything else to do he picked up the book, opened it. Peacock and Welby's attention became avid, intense.

The pages were dry and slick to the touch, some kind of ancient vellum. The age of this thing was hard to imagine. The script appeared similar to that in his grimoire, though more complicated, somehow denser. Alex focused on the first line, let his eyes slide around the writing, trying to peer past the indecipherable lettering and seek the meaning within. ""Darak was broken before history began, nature of the universe changed,"' he read quietly. ""The Eld split the rock, the King betrayed and trapped. Nothing ever the same again." Sounds like a bad epic fantasy novel," he said with a smirk. He looked up when there was no reply. Welby and Peacock sat open-mouthed, Welby entranced, though the old bookseller seemed furious. "I can read on..." Alex said.

"Could it really be a history of the Darak?" Welby asked quietly.

Peacock shook his head, suddenly agitated. "I don't know what to think. It's all just legend and bollocks anyway. Isn't it?"

Welby stood, paced back and forth. "Well, who knows anything for certain? Let him read more."

Peacock snatched the book from Alex's hand, diving under the desk with it, a clang as his safe door closed heavily.

"What are you doing?" Welby cried.

Peacock still wore a livid expression. "I don't like any of this. I don't like that you've just brought this boy here. Who the fuck does he think he is? Who the fuck do you think you are?"

"Peacock, you're being irrational, man! Let him read it. The things we could learn!"

"No. I need time to think about this."

Welby pulled a cheque book from his pocket, slapped it on the desk. "Name your price."

"What?"

"Name your price. Absolutely any price you can imagine. Name it. I'll pay it. That book is useless to you without someone to read it. If you won't let him read, then sell it to me and you'll be richer than you could possibly imagine."

Peacock's mouth worked like a beached fish. "Are you mad?" he managed eventually. "I'm not selling it, especially now. It's worth more than even you have squirrelled away. Maybe I'll get the boy to read it to me and then I'll decide on a price to tell *you* what it says."

Welby sat down, steepling his fingers. "That's a ridiculous suggestion. I found the boy; I'm hardly going to let him work for you."

Alex had heard enough. "Who the fuck do you two think you are? I'm not some servant to be bartered over. Some "boy" for your uses. You can both fuck off." He stood and turned to leave. The pull of the book, even locked away under the desk, was strong. He was desperate to read more, to simply hold the thing, feel its power. But he refused to sit there and be argued over like a commodity. He strode off through the shop. He heard Welby curse the old bookseller and jump up to follow.

Alex didn't look back. He headed down the cold cobbled street, hands thrust deep in his jacket pockets. He could hear Welby puffing as he caught up. "Alex, please, I'm so sorry."

"Whatever."

"No, really, please forgive me. That vile man never fails to bring out the worst in me."

Alex looked over his shoulder, pinning Welby with his gaze. "I'm not your property."

Welby shook his head, wringing his hands. "No, please, it's this bloody book. I've tried for so long to fathom something about it. When you started to read it like that, well, it was overwhelming. Alex, we really need to read it. Surely you can feel how magnificent it is. Don't you ache to know?"

Alex stopped dead, turned to face the old magus. "I'm learning more and more by the minute since I met you and I'm not sure how far I want to take that. All this is pretty fucked up."

Welby put a hand on Alex's forearm. "But you do want to know about the book, don't you?"

Alex ground his teeth. Of course he did. He had never wanted anything more in his life. There was something primordial, commanding, seductive about that tome and he was desperate to hold it, read it, absorb it. He had no doubt the thing contained incredible power. And he could read it when it appeared no one else could. Welby smiled. Alex wanted to punch him.

"Let me buy you a drink and tell you a little bit about what you read," Welby said. "At least understand better what you've revealed already."

Alex sighed. He could certainly use a drink.

A pub was never far away in London. As Welby led him into the warm, wood-panelled comfort of a traditional ale house Alex paused. He felt something. Turning slowly his eye fell on a beautiful blonde across the road. She seemed to be in her mid or late twenties, fit and lithe, eyes smouldering as she watched him. She wore tight jeans and T-shirt, short leather jacket, practical boots. He let his vision expand, wondering if he sensed more than simply the stunning good looks. Something lurked beneath her passive exterior. The everyday presence she maintained appeared almost flawless; he couldn't see through it without forcing the issue, but he knew there was something else there. The blonde tipped her head to one side.

Alex blinked, confused. Too much happening too fast. He had no idea how to respond to anything anymore. Was this girl hitting on him? She smiled crookedly. It was one of the loveliest things he had ever seen.

"What are you doing?"

Welby's voice broke his concentration. Looking at the old man, he smiled ruefully. "Just distracted by..." He stopped, mouth slightly open, leaning to look down the road.

"What?"

"That blonde over there," Alex said quietly.

"What blonde?"

"Exactly. She was right there. I've never seen anyone so dazzling."

He walked across the pavement, looked up and down the road. Shaking his head he pushed past Welby into the pub. "Why should that be any more normal than anything else today?"

Welby followed him to the bar.

Sitting in a quiet corner with pints of London Pride, Welby's mood was somber. "I really am sorry for how I behaved."

Alex grunted.

Welby sipped his beer thoughtfully. "I can't expect forgiveness right now," he said. "But I did promise you an explanation. Darak Uthentia refers to a stone of power. Darak is a stone that used to be wielded by a commanding group of magi known as the Eld. They used the stone to destroy a Fey King, known as Uthentia. Well, Uthentia is an honorific. Of course, to know his real name would give you enormous power over him. But I digress into irrelevancy." Welby paused.

Alex shook his head, amusement twisting his lips. "You sound like Tolkien or something."

Welby ignored the comment. "Uthentia was an evil creature and he was trapped somewhere outside the known realms by the Eld. Some even considered the Eld to be ancient gods. They exiled

Uthentia millennia ago. But doing it cracked their stone, so the legend goes."

Welby paused again. Alex felt a wave of discomfort. The old man challenged his mockery, dared him to scoff. After all that had happened recently, was a story of Fey kings and magic rocks really so preposterous? "Peacock called it all legend and bollocks," he said, trying to hang on to some kind of normality.

Welby sipped again, clearly pleased Alex was listening. "Of course it is. Or maybe it is. Or maybe it's all true."

Alex rolled his eyes. "Fuck me. What is it you want from me?"

"If that book really is some kind of history of the Darak and Uthentia then it's possible it might lead us to the stone itself. At least, to the missing pieces of it."

The sounds of the pub wrapped around them, the hubbub of voices, clinking glasses, electronic beeps from fruit machines. Over it all an old rock song played that Alex couldn't place. "Or it might just be a load of old bollocks," he said.

Welby raised both hands. "In which case it's still priceless. That book is an ancient grimoire, written in an eldritch text I've never seen before. You can read it when no one else I know can. Even if it's only a story, don't you want to read it? There's enormous power in stories. Look at the Bible or the Koran."

Alex's beer tasted good, dark and hoppy. He sipped at it rather than engage in more conversation. Why should he care about the strength or value of this book? He had enough to think about without more complications. But it was fascinating.

Welby grinned. "You do. You've got the bug. You want to know."

Alex, though loath to admit it, was hooked. He could still feel the smooth, aged leather of the book on his fingertips. He could smell the vellum of the pages, feel the magic that soaked through the tiny tome. Surely it contained more than a story. The magic seemed to even soak through time and space to where he sat, stroking something at the base of his hindbrain, too seductive to be safe. There had to be something dangerous about all this. But the seduction remained nonetheless and it was strong. Welby's eyes were serious again. "What?" Alex asked.

"What if I told you it's not all legend?"

"You know more about it than you're letting on, I suppose. More than Peacock?"

Welby laughed disdainfully. "That old fool has no idea. He thinks he knows a lot but he's like a child with an encyclopaedia. The pictures intrigue him but he has no idea of the deeper understanding he's missing."

"And you do?"

"The Fey King was the most powerful creature Faerie had ever known."

Alex smirked. "Faerie? Really?"

Welby scowled. "Don't be distracted by cartoon fairy tales. The Folk, Fey, Faeries, they have many names. And they are very dangerous. I'd advise you to do some research at my house. To continue, the Fey King wrought havoc in the mortal plane and started to break down the few rules that kept any kind of balance. Only these rules stopped the Fey Folk from over-running the mortal world and enslaving humanity thousands of years ago. Certain humans, and, some say, gods, constantly waged a war against Faerie.

"Eventually it was postulated that if the Fey King's power could be weakened even briefly, there existed the opportunity to control him long enough to exile him. With him exiled, Faerie would have a far weaker grip on the mortal realm. That's what the Eld managed to do, shattering their stone of power in the process. The Fey King has been lost between realms ever since.

"Rather than risk anyone else having that kind of magic, the Eld scattered the pieces of the Darak, across the world. Anyone potent with that stone? Too much to contemplate."

"So it makes a person stronger?" Alex asked. "Like an amplifier?"

Welby wagged one finger. "Exactly! Like an amplifier. There are a number of things that a person can use to amplify their ability. This was the greatest of them all."

"So what?"

"So what? Well, if this book really is some kind of history of the stone and that struggle then it might give us clues to find the remaining pieces."

Alex sensed something in Welby's tone, a smugness. "The remaining pieces?"

Welby reached inside his shirt, pulled out a leather cord that hung around his neck. On the end of the cord was a silver locket, the leather woven through it and back several times so it nestled in a criss-cross pattern of laces. "This is how I know it's more than just myth and legend."

The locket, though warded heavily, still leaked 'sign. Welby looked around the room then popped the locket open. Alex rocked back in his chair as magesign flooded out, hitting him full in the face and chest with a physical force. Welby sat almost lost in the twist and swirl of arcane energy flooding from the tiny silver box. Sitting inside, strapped into place with fine silver banding, was a shard of gray stone. It looked like nothing more interesting than a chip of slate, but the magic burned deep. It glowed as if a volcano were trapped inside, desperate to blow. Alex gasped as Welby snapped the locket shut again and dropped it back inside his shirt.

"That's one piece of the Darak," Welby said. "I'm sure of it. Legend says it was split into three pieces. The Eld scattered those pieces around the world. But of course, the world is a far busier place these days. What might have been a wasteland miles from anywhere then could be a bustling town now. When I came into possession of this shard my very meager powers were increased exponentially. And this stone led me to Peacock and the book. It wants to be found."

That sounded like something very dangerous. "Wants to be found?"

"It has a certain presence, a personality almost. I can't explain how, exactly, but it drew me to Peacock and his strange store. Peacock knew he had something special in that book, but he had no idea how special. I became convinced the stone and the book were connected. When you read the title of the book today I knew I was right. I'm sure the book can lead us to the remaining two pieces."

Alex didn't like the sound of any of this. A stone with a personality and a book that wants to be found? These were things he definitely couldn't control.Eventually he shook his head. "No, this is all too fucked up. I can still feel that book, like it left a stain on me. This stuff is dangerous. Way too dangerous to screw around with. I'm out." He drained his pint and stood.

Welby remained in his seat, his eyes wide, pleading. "Alex. I can't read it."

Alex stared down at the old man. He had promised himself he'd come along for the ride and retain whatever control of the situation he could. But that control had quickly slipped away. However much of this stuff was true, one thing remained certain: everything about it was drenched in danger. Like the fool who goes to investigate the noise in the basement in a B-grade horror movie, this whole situation was a road to trouble. "I'm sorry, Patrick. You'll have to find someone else." He felt a wave of guilt as Welby's shades swelled in abject disappointment.

Welby twisted in his seat, hands supplicating. "Alex, please!"

He left the pub without looking back. As he walked he started to wonder how he might get home. Getting into the UK with Welby's assistance had been one thing. It hadn't occurred to him that he might need to get back on his own and he had no passport. Perhaps he could go to the Australian consulate and claim he'd lost it and needed to get a replacement. It might take a while, but he had ID in his wallet and that struck him as a better idea than trying to replicate Welby's mind tricks.

He saw the blonde girl standing at the end of the street. She looked right at him, that crooked smile still in place. Something about her eyes grated, as if he amused her. He raised a hand in half a wave. "Hey there," he called out. "How you doing?"

The smile spread and she turned down an alleyway out of sight. Alex quickened his pace, knowing she'd be long gone when he got there.

He needed space and time to think. Across the road a park stood shrouded in darkness, black iron fencing around a small square of grass and stunted trees. A gate stood open in the center of each side, paths forming a cross. Alex walked in and sank onto a cold bench, elbows on his knees, and put his face in his hands.

He also realized now that, for some reason, he had been living his whole life in denial. Of course, his vision was more than some overdeveloped empathy. Somewhere deep inside he had known it was beyond natural, but had refused to admit as much to himself. Why? Perhaps because it allowed him the lifestyle he wanted. Allowed him to dominate as a fighter and fighting had been all he wanted to do, ever since his parents died. He'd found somewhere to focus his rage and he'd used it. He trained, he fought and he lived in peace. House in the country, space, solitude, friends here and there when he felt like company. A good life and, on some subconscious level, he had known if he looked too deeply into why, that life would get complicated.

He cursed Welby and the moment the old man darkened his changing room door. Right then something had shifted. Was it often a person could recall with crystal clarity the exact moment their life had jumped the tracks? He had trusted his deeper instinct and told Welby to leave him alone, but events conspired differently. And the carefully, intuitively constructed shield around his life had shattered.

He sighed, leaning back on the bench. Crossing his arms he stared up into the inky city glow. If he were at home the sky would be awash with stars, a glittering shroud laying over eternity. Here, nothing but pollution and electric light, trapping him.

He could feel the elemental grimoire in the inside pocket of his jacket, pressing into his chest. His heart pulsed one extra heavy beat as the image of his new leather travel bag passed through his mind. The bag with his new clothes inside, the button- down side pocket. He had taken his wallet and phone from the pocket when he'd left Welby's house, leaving the grimoire in there. He could see it in his mind's eye, 'sign gently swimming out over the top of the bag and across the bed. So what sat in his jacket pocket now?

Trembling, he reluctantly pulled the Darak Uthentia grimoire out into the air. The power it emanated burst around him, coiling over his hands and arms, almost wrapping around him, as if it tried to gather him into its pages. The smooth leather of the cover felt warm under his fingertips, alive. He had watched Peacock snatch it away and lock it in the safe under his desk. How had it come to be in his pocket now? No wonder he felt the stain of it stay with him. It *was* with him.

Ramming the book back into his pocket he sat breathing hard, trying to think. He wanted no further part of this. He shouldn't have let himself be dragged into it in the first place, but what was done was done. He remembered a lesson with his Sifu, so many years ago. *Don't concentrate on the fact that you have just been hit. The fight is fluid, time doesn't wait for you. When you get hit, let it slide by you, instantly in the past, and concentrate on the now. Always the now. Act and react in the present moment.*

Alex stood and strode back towards the pub. Anger burned alongside fear in his chest. He didn't like to fear anything. He planned to take control back.

Welby sat where Alex had left him, staring disconsolately into his pint glass. He looked up, surprised, when Alex stood over him, eyes dark and furious.

"Alex! I... I'm sorry. I can't imagine how confusing all this..."

Alex leaned forward, both hands palm down on the table, his nose an inch from Welby's. "Shut the fuck up. Here's how it's going to go. You're coming with me back to Peacock's shop and I'm returning this book." Welby's eyebrows shot up, but Alex continued before he had a chance to speak. "Then we're going to your house and I'm getting my fancy new bag and clothes, which I plan to keep. Then we're going to the airport and you're getting me on the first plane to Sydney. And you're coming with me to get me through customs and passport control at the other end. Then you're going to pay a taxi driver to take me all the way home, regardless of how much that driver decides to charge for a two-hour ride. Then I'm going to get into that taxi and you're going to fuck off to wherever you like. And if I ever see you again, I will rip you into hundreds of pieces. Got all that?"

Welby's face softened. "Return the book?"

Alex ground his teeth. He wanted out of this whole situation, yet his rage was impotent and he knew it. "Yes." He pulled the book from his jacket pocket and slammed it down on the table. Welby stared at it for several moments then nodded softly. Alex felt his anger begin to dilute, fear washing away his fury. "Why do I have that?" he asked.

"I think perhaps it's chosen you."

Alex shook his head. "Fuck that."

Welby's face was resigned, even disappointed. "After all that."

"All what?"

"All my trying to convince Peacock to sell it to me, trying to bargain with him. I even tried to break into his shop once but his wards are too strong for me to breach. Obviously put in place by someone far more powerful than Peacock himself. He just opens and closes them. Whoever his ally is, they probably charged him a small fortune for that job."

Alex sat heavily into the chair opposite. "Job?"

Welby looked up from the book for the first time. "There are plenty of freelancers around, willing to do work for those less capable. If they can pay."

Alex hung his head, unsure what to say. It had chosen him?

"I really am sorry," Welby said.

"Fuck sorry!" Alex's raised voice caused several heads in the pub to turn, though they all quickly turned away again. "I'm over this. I want out. I don't want to be *chosen* by a fucking book! I'm returning it to Peacock, I'm going to apologize for any inconvenience and I'm going to tell him he'll have to find someone else to read it for him. And so will you."

"I don't think you'll be able to give it back."

"I don't want this thing, Patrick. It feels alive."

"All knowledge lives."

Alex picked up the book, waved it accusingly in Welby's face. "No. This itself feels like an evil, dangerous, living thing. I don't want it." He pushed the book across the table. "Here. Take it."

Welby took the small, dark book. He ran his fingertips across the leather, opened it and slowly thumbed through the pages. The dense script flickered past. All the time Alex watched the 'sign swirling, twisting over Welby's hands and wrists before curling back and reaching across the table. Reaching for him.

Welby closed the book with a soft snap, held it out for Alex to take. "It's yours, I'm afraid."

"I don't want it."

"I *do* want it, Alex, but I don't think I'll be able to keep it."

Alex pushed back his chair and stood. "I'm not touching it. I'm going to your house to get my stuff and then I'm going to the airport. Do what you like with it and come, without it, to the airport and you're taking me home." He turned and left the pub again. Glancing back from the door he saw Welby slip the book into his jacket and pick up his pint. He didn't look like he planned to go anywhere.

Knowing what would happen, yet refusing to accept it, Alex walked down the road towards Welby's house. Within a hundred yards he felt the weight in his jacket. Stopping, feeling weak, he took the book out. The 'sign leapt and danced around his hands, reaching up towards his face. It was something incredible, something so desirable he felt his heart crack, yet so clearly dangerous. Malevolent, wicked in indescribable ways. And he couldn't get rid of it. He turned and walked back to the pub.

Welby stood outside the door, leaning on the Victorian glazed tiles of the wall. "I'm so sorry, Alex."

"Did you know this would happen?"

"No, really I didn't."

Alex rubbed his eyes with the heels of his hands. "I don't want it, Patrick. I don't want any of this."

"I know."

"So what do I do?"

Welby pursed his lips. "If you want to try one last time to be rid of it, then perhaps you should try to return it to Peacock."

Alex could see how much it pained Welby to say that. "Yeah?"

Welby shrugged. "I really didn't mean for this to happen. I just wanted you to be able to read the book. The quest for knowledge has ever been a double-edged sword. Perhaps Peacock's wards can hold the book. Return it, explain what's happened. Ask him to raise as many wards as he can before you leave. Perhaps you can slip out and the book will remain with him."

Alex sighed, leaning heavily on the tiles beside the old man. "You don't think that'll work, do you?"

"Not really. But you can try."

"Come on then."

Welby held up one hand. "If I go with you it'll only infuriate Peacock. Go alone, blame me, whatever. Try to give it back. I'll see you at my house and then I'll take you home."

"And if I can't give it back? If I'm stuck with it?"

"It's up to you, Alex. I won't force you to do anything. If you want to go home with it and tell me to never darken your door again, I will."

"Bullshit."

Welby made a rueful face. "I'll try. I'm so sorry, Alex. This hasn't gone how I'd planned at all."

FIVE

A lex knew someone followed him as he made his way to Peacock's shop. His senses vibrated, yet everywhere he looked remained stubbornly empty. He slowed his pace, tried to look all around. He was beyond caution. He stopped dead. "Who are you?" he yelled at the dark street.

Nothing. Yet he was sure someone lurked in the velvet shadows. He could feel them, almost certainly the strange, attractive blonde. Since he had admitted his vision was more than he had previously allowed, it seemed to be growing, his sensitivity increased. So why not use it? He closed his eyes. The ancient *chi gung* breathing techniques taught to him by his Sifu always proved useful in his training, his fighting. And in everyday life. Perhaps they could be useful in the less mundane skill set he was being forced to develop. Centring himself, drawing his energy, his *chi*, down into his lower belly, he let his consciousness slip out. His magesign swelled from beneath his shields, seeking out any similar energy. With a gasp he looked up at the roof of a building beside him and caught a glimpse of a surprised face, a whip of pale hair and she was gone. He felt her run and leap over the roofs at a preternatural pace before disappearing from his senses. Who was this girl, so desirable and clearly some kind of magus? Her physical skills were impressive. Why was she following him? Something else beyond his control.

If she meant him harm she'd had plenty of opportunity to ambush. She obviously watched with another agenda and perhaps he would have to ignore that for now. If this mysterious woman chose to spy on him, so be it.

When he arrived at Peacock's shop he could see the glow from behind the curtain at the back. He banged on the door. When he got no response, he rapped on the glass of the window and banged on the door again. He crouched and pushed open the letterbox flap. "Open up, Peacock," he called through. "I know you're in there. You want this book back or what?"

The curtain whipped aside and Peacock hurried between the

shelves. He threw bolts aside and swung the door open, his face angry. He swept his eyes and mind up and down, rudely trying to pry through Alex's shields. Alex sent out a wave of magesign, making Peacock stagger backwards. Slamming the door behind him Alex grabbed Peacock by the shoulder and turned him. Shoving the old man in front he marched them into the office at the back.

"I didn't want any of this," he barked. "I'm pissed off with Welby for getting me into it and you for... for being you and having this fucking book."

Peacock struggled but Alex's grip held like an iron vice. "How did you take it?" His voice was high, scared.

"I didn't. It came with me. I didn't even know I had it." He took the grimoire from his pocket and threw it onto Peacock's desk.

The old man gasped. "Be careful! That's ancient!"

"I don't give a fuck. I want out. Lock it up, put up your wards, lock this place down. Then let me out and the book can stay."

Peacock's animation stilled. "Will that work? Can you get past my wards?"

"Fuck knows. Welby thinks it's worth a try."

Peacock looked guilty, shifting uncomfortably. "Ah, Welby suggested you give it back to me?"

"I told him I was going to and he argued against it. But when I insisted he suggested this." A cold feeling crept into Alex's groin. "Why?"

Peacock looked down at his threadbare carpet.

"What have you done?"

Peacock shuffled his feet. "I thought you two had managed some elaborate theft. I sent... friends to Welby's to get the book back."

"What kind of *friends*?"

"My gargoyles."

Alex was stunned. "Gargoyles?"

Peacock looked remorseful, though unrepentant. "You came here and then my property went missing. I'm not sorry for sending them."

"Gargoyles?"

Peacock became angry again. "Yes, yes, gargoyles. You are a child in all this, aren't you? They've gone to Welby's and they will look for the book."

Alex pointed to the desk. "It's there."

Peacock shrugged. "That won't stop them looking. They're rather dumb and single-minded."

"Call them back!"

"I can't. They'll come when the job is done."

Alex's mind spun. He simply could not get any control however hard he tried. He imagined Welby fighting against ugly stone, winged creatures. "Can Welby cope with gargoyles?" he asked, the words sounding ridiculous to ears.

Peacock walked around his desk, sat heavily into his oversize chair. He stared at the book on his desk with trepidation. "I doubt it. That's why I sent them."

Alex bit down his fury and grabbed Peacock by the front of his shirt. "Lock this place down. Hold onto that and let me out. It should stay with you."

Peacock looked up into Alex's eyes, trembling, his mouth working silently. Alex grabbed the book and thrust it into the man's hands. "Start putting up your wards or whatever you do to protect this place."

Magesign wafted lightly off Peacock and Alex felt the protective shields overlapping each other all around him. He opened his vision, looked through the normal range of sight and watched for magic. He saw the wards, shimmering in a plethora of impossible shades. He could see the impenetrable bubbles of magic yet at the same time he could see where they pressed together. Using his own 'sign to cleave a path he slipped in and among Peacock's wards, letting them close tightly behind. He heard Peacock's gasp of surprise but ignored it and left the shop. He turned towards Welby's house and ran as fast as he could.

He managed to flag a taxi and gave the driver an extra ten pounds to jump every red light back to Welby's. Standing in the street outside, looking up through the witch's fingers of the leafless trees, he could see movement in the supposedly invisible third floor room. A lead ball of dread sat in his gut.

The front door stood damaged and ajar. As he tentatively stepped into the hallway he could see the remaining impression of massive bursts of magic, visual echoes of an arcane struggle. He felt a coppery charge in the air. As he stalked through the house, evidence of fighting lay everywhere. Broken and turned over furniture, scorch marks on walls and ceiling, torn, smouldering carpets. He tried to sense ahead of himself.

As he climbed the stairs he felt Welby moments before he saw him. Sprawled on the first floor landing, twisted unnaturally, the old man's eyes were wide and quite blank. Blood pooled darkly around his head, soaking into the luxurious carpet. Alex could feel the creatures up above. He crouched, double-checking what he already knew to be a fact. Welby was dead. Swallowing his fear and anguish, Alex closed Welby's eyelids and looked up the stairs to the secret floor.

As carefully as possible he reached into Welby's shirt. The locket on its leather cord still hung there, burning with magic under Alex's palm. It was like the book, had the same urgent desire to be held, owned, used. Alex recognised another tipping point in his life. Upstairs or down? Take the locket or leave it? A fundamental moment of choice and probably his last opportunity to get away. Or was it?

He lifted his hand slowly to his chest and pressed. The small hard rectangle of the Darak Uthentia sat hot and desperate in his pocket. Alex's head dropped. One hand on the book in his jacket, the other on the locket inside Welby's shirt, the power of those unfathomable objects coursed through him. Muffled as they were, they made the magic in him expand, swell.

And the creatures that had killed Welby had been sent to get what he held. Alex's eyes crept up to the top of the stairs. In the shadows he saw two pairs of deep, red eyes staring back.

His heart raced, adrenaline dumping into his system. His stomach felt liquid, his mind suddenly wrapped in cotton wool. And his training kicked in. Centring, gathering his energy and his focus, he slipped the locket from around Welby's neck without taking his eyes from the malevolent silhouettes above. When he dropped the leather cord over his head the stone sang out to him, a crystalline song of belonging and joy. The book in his pocket cried out, sending desire across subconscious airwaves he couldn't begin to explain. A flood of power washed through him like an orgasm. He gathered that power, along with his adrenaline, breathed it through his flesh. He let his shields down, let his 'sign wash forth, and stood. "Come on then, you fuckers!" he yelled.

They burst from the shadows with a rush of leathery flapping and snapping of grotesque, tooth-filled snouts. They reached for him with black-clawed hands, sinewy muscles beneath dark, warty, thick hide flexing, twisting, fast and strong. He'd expected them to be made of stone.

Alex stepped between them as they swept down. His vision enhanced, he saw their intentions with ease, read their shades effortlessly. He grabbed one by its reaching arm and used its momentum to send it past, tumbling and squealing down to the ground floor, cracking stairs and tearing the wall as it went. As the first fell he drove his elbow into the snot-riddled snout of the other. A satisfying crunch and wail made up somewhat for the impact-blossom of pain that lanced through his arm. They didn't look like stone, but they felt like it, tough leather stretched over moving boulders. Pushing the creature across the landing, Alex made space and powered out a front kick, driving his heel up under the gargoyle's chin. Its head whipped back and dirty ivory fangs snapped and spiralled into the air. The creature howled.

Alex heard the other scrambling to its feet, clawing at the walls and stairs as it rushed back up to him. The voice of his Sifu rang in his memory. *When the fight isn't fair, be sure you fight dirtier than them. When there is more than one enemy, use them against each other.*

Alex grabbed the gargoyle he had kicked and swung around behind, slipping one forearm under the creature's chin. He cranked up, bracing with his other arm against its back. It stood up taller, trying to shake him free. As its fellow appeared Alex shifted the gargoyle in his grip and used it as a shield, his muscles straining with the effort. The rushing horror slammed into the chest and belly of its mate, snapping and clawing around it, reaching for Alex's face.

Driving forward, thighs burning as they worked, Alex forced the creatures to the top of the stairs. His chokehold had no effect, the gargoyle thrashing in his grasp. With a roar of rage he used all his strength and pushed the creature away. He pumped out a leg and kicked hard in the center of its spine. It arched in pain as something cracked and the momentum carried both abominations down again.

Grabbing a leg from a broken table on the landing, Alex leapt down behind them, gathering all his own energy and wrapping it up with the power from the stone at his neck. He could see with such clarity, feel every mote of dust in the air around him, every sensation of the monsters below. He could smell the leather of the furniture, musty books, his own sweat. He could hear every sound. He was alive with the instant, knew everything. The gargoyles fell into a tangle of pustulent flesh and Alex landed on them, stamping down with both feet, desperate to break whatever bones these things might have. As they struggled to part he lifted the table leg high and drove it down, broken end first, flooding it with energy from the shard of the Darak, directly through the eye socket of the gargoyle on its back beneath him. It screamed an ear-shattering wail, scrabbling at the wooden table leg, before spasming and dropping still. Alex felt the stone against his chest singing out in joy as he utilised its power. He knew the book's insane elation at the murder, not revelling in the magic, but in the death, and it was dark. He concentrated on the Darak, as though it were a part of him, its energy flooding through his veins, invigorating and terrifying.

The second gargoyle twisted and pushed away, knocking Alex over. He landed with a grunt of rushing breath and the thing dropped onto him, grasping for his throat. He grabbed both its rough, hard wrists and tried to force it up. It snapped and spat at him, turning and pressing. Alex had the strength of years of training, but nothing compared to this. He knew he had seconds before its might overwhelmed him.

Bucking up, using his hip to escape the weight of the creature, he slipped free, keeping a grip on one of the gargoyle's wrists. He stood and turned the wrist, wrenched the creature's arm up and back, forcing it to move sideways. His muscles screamed in protest at the effort. Without letting go of the wrist he stamped hard into the hideous face. Twisting the wrist further, using the creature's own shoulder joint against it, he kicked again. Hanging on against its thrashing desperation Alex twisted, kicked, punched, again and again. Teeth and claws swiped this way and that, but Alex refused to release his grip, doggedly hanging on to the one small advantage he had. His abilities gave him extra milliseconds to move, yet even then he couldn't avoid every blow. Bruises thundered into his body, burning welts from flailing claws danced across his chest, stomach, legs. A leathery wing cracked into his head, made his vision cross. His hands and feet felt battered and broken as he repeatedly struck the stone-hard creature's head and body.

The strength began to wane in the gargoyle's thrashing defense. Its head lolled dizzily and Alex let go of the wrist, leaping into the air, drawing up both knees and landing with a double stamp on the creature's skull. He drove down as much power as he could muster, letting the force from the stone rush through him, and the gargoyle's head cracked with a sound like a gunshot.

Alex stood panting, shaking, bruised and bleeding. He looked from one gargoyle corpse to the other as they both lost color. Pale gray seeped across their skins and in moments they were broken granite grotesques. They shivered and shattered into dust and gravel.

"Defeating two gargoyles barehanded? Impressive."

With a gasp Alex looked up into the blue eyes of the blonde. His vision swam. She stepped forward, reached out for him. "Easy there," he heard. "Looks like you…"

Strange sounds washed in Alex's ears, a soft *whump, whump, whump.* Keeping his eyes closed, breathing deeply, he realized it was his heartbeat. Every inch of his body burned with pain, as though he had been flayed. The image of the blonde swam into his mind and his heart rate increased. As his senses came online he knew he lay on something soft and she was still there, right beside him. She felt strong.

"I know you're awake," she said softly. Her voice had a Scottish lilt, almost lost but defiant.

Without opening his eyes Alex assessed his energy levels and the extent of his injuries.

"You're safe for now," the girl said.

He had just had a fight to the death, almost his own, with two living, moving, deadly creatures that should be nothing more than adornment on gothic buildings. What the hell was happening to him? A flash of realization branded another image on his mind: Welby's corpse, broken on the landing above. That fucker Peacock had gone medieval with all the wrong assumptions and left Patrick Welby dead and Alex lost and broken. All because of this fucking book. He should never have left Sydney.

The stone against his chest, like a second heart, pulsed in its locket. What would it be like to open the locket, wear it right against his skin? Power throbbed through the tiny shard. Only a third of the whole? If only it was a wishing stone and he could wish himself back to his peaceful house surrounded by paddocks and cows, with no knowledge of it or the grimoire or Welby. Or magic and gargoyles and idiot booksellers. Or beautiful, mysterious blondes.

"You going to open your eyes and talk to me?" Her voice had an amused edge. He could imagine her crooked smile and it fired his desire.

His eyes flickered open. Even his eyelids hurt. He lay on a sofa in the front room, the blonde kneeling beside him. She watched him with humor. "Hello there."

"Hey." He sounded like a wino after thirty years on the streets with meths and old cigarette butts.

"I've patched you up a bit. Luckily there was a pretty good first aid kit in the kitchen. I'm sure you hurt all over, but it's all pretty superficial, nothing broken. Which is a surprise, given what you were hitting."

"Lots of practice."

She raised an eyebrow. "Really?"

Alex laughed softly and winced at the pain it put through his chest. "Well, not against... those things. It's always been people before now. But the conditioning still counts, it seems. Who are you?"

"You can call me Silhouette."

"Which isn't your real name, I'm guessing."

"It's what everyone calls me."

"Fair enough. I'm Alex. Alex Caine."

They watched each other for several moments. Alex had to assume he had an ally in this girl, though he was still suspicious. She hadn't helped with the fight, but she had fixed him up afterwards. At the very least she was no immediate enemy. He felt lost and keen to hang onto anyone friendly, but remained wary. More than anything he wanted to be back home, on his own. He was fairly sure he would never again enjoy the simplicity of the life he had known.

Without a word Silhouette stood and left the room. He heard her in the kitchen. She returned with a glass of water. "Hold this."

He struggled up into a sitting position, grimacing at the needles of pain in his body. He gritted his teeth, took the glass.

Silhouette dug around in a small leather pouch on her belt and pulled out what looked like a screwed up green leaf. She carefully unwrapped it and took out a pinch of dark brown sand between index finger, middle finger and thumb. She dropped the sand into the water, brushing every last grain off her fingers. It sank lazily, spiralling slightly. With a burst of tiny bubbles the water effervesced and turned dark purple. "Drink it."

Alex looked at her with concern.

"Alex, if I meant you harm I've had plenty of opportunity. Quickly, drink it all down before it's wasted."

With a shrug, he took a deep breath and gulped the glassful down. It was strong, like over-stewed tea, and so sweet it tasted thick like treacle. He winced as he forced himself to swallow the last of it.

Silhouette smiled. "You like that? That's the definition of bittersweet, huh? It's good for you."

"What is it?"

"Not of this earth." She flicked him a wink.

Alex felt the liquid spread through him. His muscles relaxed, the burning in his skin and the ache in bones softened. A lopsided smile twisted one side of his face. He felt inexplicably happy, almost silly. "Is nice," he slurred.

Silhouette rolled her eyes. "I gave you a bit too much perhaps."

Alex giggled. "Not at all. In fact, I'd like a bit more..." He was getting sleepy. As his eyes closed he saw Silhouette shake her head. He was sure he heard her say "Humans' in a derisive tone as darkness folded in from the edges of his vision.

SIX

When Alex woke, he saw light outside. Silhouette lay on the floor on her stomach, chin propped in her hands, reading a large leatherbound book that lay open before her. "Morning," she said, not taking her eyes from the pages.

"Morning." He tentatively swung his legs off the couch, sitting up, assessing the level of hurt. Surprisingly little. His hands ached, his knuckles still throbbed, but the majority of his pain had eased. The cuts and bruises that weren't covered by dressings looked several days healed. "How long have I been out?"

Silhouette flipped a page. "All night. "Bout six or seven hours."

"Are you sure?"

She looked up at him. "That drink I gave you speeds healing. Feeling better?"

"Immeasurably."

"Good." She turned back to the book.

Alex watched the 'sign swirl around the pages, snaking lazily across the patterned rug. He let his eyes move from the book to the girl, looking over her colors. She was physically gorgeous, moreso than anyone he could remember, but she had an inner beauty too. A power and grace that stupefied him. He was desperate to look beneath her almost flawless facade and see what kind of person she was. What kind of power she had.

"Careful there, big fella. You haven't even bought me a drink yet."

With a gasp Alex sat back, pulling his vision with him. "I'm sorry. I was just..."

"I know. It's cool."

"Who are you?"

Silhouette swept up into a sitting position, cross-legged on the rug, the grimoire forgotten beside her. She moved with a dancer's grace, though Alex could see the fighter beneath. He found that unbelievably sexy. "You're very new to all this, aren't you?" she asked.

"All this?" He knew what she meant, but was unsure how

much to discuss.

She smiled. Gods, he liked it when she smiled. "You're very wary, and that's good. But you can trust me," she said.

"Really?"

"Sure. You can't trust many people these days, but I promise I don't mean you harm."

"You've been watching me."

She nodded. "Yeah. You intrigued me."

"Why?"

"Well, firstly because you were with Welby. We always keep a casual eye on him."

"We?"

Silhouette pursed her lips. That was even better than her smile. "It's complicated," she said eventually.

Alex flexed his shoulders, stretched. His back popped softly. "So why are you interested in Welby?"

"He's an interesting guy. Well, he was."

"That fucker Peacock," Alex said with a wince. "I should go and settle that score."

Silhouette smiled again. "Nice. Yeah, maybe you should. Exercise out the kinks from last night. No one would miss that desperate wannabe. Anyway, Patrick Welby is an old magus, by human standards. He's been around a while, largely self-contained, furthering his studies, developing his skills. Nothing out of the ordinary. There are hundreds like him."

Alex laughed, shook his head. When Silhouette raised an eyebrow he said, "Nothing. Just trying to get my head around… well, everything."

"The reason we watched Welby is because he suddenly seemed to increase his power a couple of years ago. We were wary, but he still seemed interested in his own thing, so we let him be. Just watched. He spent the last year or more travelling all over the place, clearly looking for something."

"I think that might have been me."

"But when he found you, all kinds of shit hit the fan. What happened?"

Alex decided to tell her everything. If she could help him get home, that would be great. If she could help him get rid of this book, even better. "I can see things," he said. "I can see magesign very clearly, apparently, and I read people. I see the shades around them."

Silhouette paid close attention. "I know what you mean."

"Well, according to Welby, my vision is far greater than most, even his."

Silhouette laughed heartily, her blonde hair swaying with her mirth. "Even his? He was little more than a conjuror." At Alex's confused expression she waved a hand. "Never mind, go on."

"Welby knew about this book and he couldn't read it. The whole thing is written in an eldritch text that no one could decipher. Welby thought I would be able to read it."

"And?"

"He was right."

"Really? Well, well. Aren't you the prodigy."

"I wish I wasn't."

Silhouette leaned back on her hands, legs still crossed. Alex couldn't help his gaze roving over her flat stomach, the generous swell of her breasts, her lithely muscled shoulders. He flicked his eyes away, catching sight of her half-smile as he did so. "So what happened between you reading this book and the mayhem here last night?" she asked.

"I read the book and it sort of attached itself to me. I didn't take it, but when I left I had it in my pocket. I tried to give it to Welby and leave and it reappeared. I can't get rid of it. I tried to take it back to Peacock, but he'd already sent those fucking monsters here thinking Welby had stolen it."

Silhouette offered no comment. She sat stock still, eyes narrowed. "And," she said quietly.

"Welby seemed to think the book and this stone he had were connected. That's all I know."

"The locket you took from him right before the fight?"

Alex nodded. "Wait a minute! You saw that and you didn't help me?"

"I wanted to see how you did. I might have stepped in if you were in danger of losing."

"Might have?"

She gave him a condescending look. "I don't owe you anything, Alex Caine."

That cut a little. "So why are you here now?"

"I'm here because you fascinate me," she said. "You're so young and green and completely unaware of what's going on around you, yet you have an unusual power. Now you have that stone too, which only makes you stronger. The combination of strength, youth and ignorance can be a dangerous thing."

Alex felt mildly offended. He was well aware of his ignorance in this world rapidly unfolding around him, but Silhouette did him a disservice. "You call me young. What are you? You look about twenty-four, twenty-five, but I'm guessing you're not."

Her face softened, her crooked smile returning. Alex reddened. "Have a look," she said.

His heartrate increased. He let his vision slip over her, gently seeking past the shields she held so naturally. She let him look a certain distance while keeping the majority of herself concealed. He felt like a schoolboy, allowed to put his hand under the blouse of his girlfriend behind the bike sheds. With a sharp intake of breath he sat back, pulling his vision away. "You're…"

"Older than Welby? Yes. You see what I mean about youth and ignorance?"

"Sorry."

"It's okay."

Alex was confused again, unsure now how to interact with this girl. She was young and beautiful, yet also ancient. "Sorry," he said again, for want of anything else to say.

"Just carry on as before," she said. "You were doing fine." Her face became serious again. "But we need to get back to the point. You said Welby felt the book and his stone were connected. You could read the book. What was it called?"

"The Darak Uthentia…"

Silhouette's hardening expression gave Alex pause. It appeared he didn't need to explain any more. "And this is the book that's bound to you?" she asked.

"Yeah. And the stone…"

She waved a hand at him. "I can imagine. Well, you're certainly in the shit."

"Am I?"

"You know you are. Don't you?"

Alex looked down at his feet. "Yeah. I don't know what to do."

"Did Welby set you up for this? I didn't think the old poof had it in him."

Alex sighed expansively. "No. At least, he claimed not. He got the stone, I don't know how, and the stone led him to the book, but he couldn't read it. He had his suspicions but he seemed genuinely sorry when he realized what had happened."

Silhouette made a wry face. "Hmm. Little more than a conjuror, see? For all his studies, he wasn't very smart."

"So what do I do?"

Silhouette stared hard at Alex. After a while he became uncomfortable, his cheeks flushing, but he refused to look away. "You're a hardass, huh?"

He didn't know if she was mocking him or not. "What do you mean?"

"You're a fighter—that much is obvious from what I saw last night. Is that all you do?"

"Pretty much. I'm good at it, it makes me a solid living. I like to fight and I like the peace and quiet I earn between bouts."

"Your life has just flipped arse upwards, young Alex." She seemed genuinely sorry for him.

"I know." He was desperate for this strange girl to help him. He needed someone to tell him what to do.

"I don't think I can help you," she said softly.

"What?"

"There's so much you don't understand and I think you're too deep too soon. I can't help you."

Alex could feel himself trembling. He cursed his weakness. "Please," he said. "I don't want any of this."

Silhouette sat forward, taking his hand in hers. Her touch felt warm and electric, her fingers strong and soft at the same time. "Something tempted you."

"Tempted me?"

"There's always choice."

He thought back to the dressing room in Sydney. The goons in the alley, Welby's magic trick with the water, the element grimoire, his car at the hotel, the airport. His hand had been forced by Scarlet but he had been seduced all the way by Welby and what he might learn. He could have gone anywhere while Amir did his thing, but he'd followed Welby to London, intrigued. In his gut he'd mistrusted the man, but had let himself be dragged along. "I knew better," he said, his voice weak.

"Then it was too late."

He looked into the ice blue eyes under her blonde fringe. "Please help me!"

She looked down at their hands. "Alex, I really don't think I can. But maybe my Clan Lord can."

"Clan Lord?"

She looked up again, that crooked smile making his stomach flutter. "You think you've seen a lot already? You better brace yourself. And I need to warn you, you'll have to earn the right to talk to my Lord."

Alex was happy for any thread of hope. "Sure, sure. If there's someone that can help…"

"It might kill you," she interrupted.

"Kill me?"

"I'm being honest with you. My Clan Lord *might* be able to help, but to find out might kill you."

Did he really need to go through with any of this? He couldn't give the book back to Peacock, so would that old fucker keep sending creatures like gargoyles after him? If the buck stopped with Peacock then a path seemed clear. And he owed some kind of vengeance to Welby, surely. If he couldn't get rid of the book, and the only real issue was Peacock, then take Peacock out of the picture and put the book on a shelf somewhere and forget about it.

The thing hung heavy in his pocket. He got a sensation of warmth, almost as if it approved of his train of thought. He sensed it cajoling him, urging him on.

He looked up into Silhouette's eyes. "Can you try to help me first?"

"You got an idea? Call me crazy, but I kinda like you. I should warn you that you might not like me so much, the more you learn."

"Really?"

"Yeah. My history might not sit well with you."

That wasn't something he wanted to consider just yet. "Well, you've done the right thing by me so far. I'm happy to leave it at that for the time being. Especially if you help me."

She laughed. "Cute. What are you thinking?"

"Well, I can't get rid of this thing. Peacock is the only one who knows about it now Welby's dead. Before Peacock sends any more fucking monsters after me, I'm going to kill him." He said it so easily the words shocked him. "Peacock murdered Patrick and nearly killed me, so fuck him, right? Kill Peacock and end it there. Forget about the book and get on with my life."

Silhouette grinned at him. "I really don't think it's going to be anything like that simple, but it's certainly a bloody good place to start. And it takes care of at least one loose end."

"So you'll help me?"

"I don't think you'll need any help, but sure. I'll come along. Be a shame to miss a good revenge slaying."

Alex frowned. "You're pretty dark, you know that?"

Silhouette flicked him a wink and stood. "Alex Caine, you have no idea."

The street outside Peacock's shop was quiet in the wan autumn sunshine. Alex and Silhouette stood on cold cobbles, staring at the black painted door.

"So what's the plan?" Silhouette peered up at Alex under her fringe. She was only a couple of inches shorter than his six feet, yet she deliberately taunted him.

Her icy eyes teased him, had him imagining the parts of her he couldn't see. "Not sure," he said. She did that half-smile thing again and Alex looked away. He needed to focus and she was playing with him. "I suppose," he said, "that I'll just walk in there and smash the fucker." He felt heat swell out from the book in his pocket. The pendant around his neck remained warm constantly, like a tiny hand lying against his skin.

"You ever done anything like this before?"

He laughed. "Stroll into someone's place and kill them in cold blood? Funnily enough, no. This'll be a first for me."

"You seem quite collected, all things considered."

He did feel calm. "It's the right thing to do. I'm protecting myself and avenging Welby. The rules of my life have changed."

"You really need to avenge Welby?"

"I thought you were all for a good revenge slaying?"

"Oh, I am. I love a good killing. But it seems like you're making some major changes here."

Alex pursed his lips, thinking. "Yeah," he said eventually. "I'm taking control back."

Silhouette seemed to accept that. "Fair enough. Can I offer some advice?"

"Definitely."

"This place is wrapped in all kinds of magic which I'm guessing includes alarms and security. I suggest you don't make a meal of this. Get in there, use your familiarity to get close and take him out quickly."

"Cold."

"But effective."

"Fair enough."

"Hesitation will kill you, Alex."

He watched her for a moment. "Why are you helping me?"

"Call it a weakness of character." She looked away. "That's what my Clan would tell you."

Alex turned back to the door, took a deep breath. "You coming in?"

"No, I'll make him suspicious. I'll be right here. If things turn ugly I'll help if I can."

Alex nodded and rapped on the door. After a moment, he knocked on one glass panel of the window and called out, "Peacock, open up. It's me." He felt reluctant to yell out his name. He wondered briefly about cameras and quickly put it out of his mind. He hadn't seen any before in the shop and it seemed unlikely Peacock would have technology along with all the magical countermeasures he had in place. It wouldn't hurt to check once inside, but the truth was he didn't care. Something nagged at the back of his mind. *Why don't I care?*

The curtain at the back shifted and Peacock shuffled nervously into the shop. "What do you want?" he called out, voice betraying his fear.

"We need to talk, Peacock."

"Welby?"

Alex decided honesty was the best policy. "Dead. Thanks to you. Me too, nearly."

"Nearly? You faced my gargoyles?"

"Yeah."

"I wondered why they weren't back yet."

Alex laughed without humor. "They aren't coming."

Peacock shook his head, eyes downcast. "Bloody hell." He looked up sharply. "You have any idea what it costs to bind gargoyles?"

Alex was stunned. With everything else happening this old fuck was complaining about cost? "You have any idea how little I care about that? Call it a fee for killing Welby."

Peacock waved his hands. "Stop yelling that stuff in the street, boy! What's wrong with you?"

Alex pounded the window. "Open the fucking door then. We need to talk."

Peacock retreated, shaking his head. "No. Not a chance. You're not here to talk. You still have my book and I can't get it back, can I? And you destroyed my gargoyles. I'm calling it quits right here. I fold. Go away."

A red rage swelled up in Alex's chest. The stone and book vibrated in harmony with each other, crying out for Peacock's death. With a roar of fury Alex lifted his knee and hammered out a kick at the shop door, letting the power of the Darak flow through him. The door exploded in a shower of wood shards and splinters. He heard Silhouette gasp, out of sight somewhere beside him.

Peacock squealed like a child and hurried towards the curtain. Alex felt the wards popping up as the despicable little man ran, shadowy films of magic swelling into existence. He dropped his own shields completely, let his presence, his own magic, flood out. He opened his vision and saw every ward and drove his 'sign, his very will, into all the gaps between them. As he strode into the shop Peacock's shields flexed and burst, colors and shades popping and spinning away. Peacock cried out, diving through the curtain.

Alex ripped the curtain away in time to see Peacock stand up behind his desk, the malevolent anodised steel of a revolver rising with him.

Alex watched the colors, calm, collected. He focused his rage and let it merge with the stone against his chest. He could see everything, every intent. Peacock began pumping the trigger of the pistol, the gunshots deafening in the enclosed space. Alex ducked and turned, moving more quickly than Peacock could adjust his aim. The little man managed to squeeze off four shots as Alex covered the space between the ruined curtain and the desk. He felt the heat of each shot passing, but knew none would touch him.

He slapped the gun aside. As Peacock whimpered, his mouth flapping almost silently, Alex put one palm behind the old man's head. He raised his other hand and drove iron-hard fingers through Peacock's eyes. The hot warmth of gray matter and blood burst over his hand and he stepped aside to avoid the gout of gore as he pulled his fingers free. Peacock slumped, his head bounced once off the corner of his desk with a sick crack, and he rolled to the floor on his back. Dark, thick blood and brains oozed from the black orifices where his eyes used to be.

Alex stood panting, rushing from the flood of power coursing through him. The exhilaration was orgasmic, firing neurons all over his body. He took long, strong breaths in through his nose, forcing himself to settle, drawing his shields back tight. He felt the book in his pocket, throbbing with thick waves of exultation, revelling in the death.

"Well, fuck me."

He turned and saw Silhouette standing in the doorway, hands on her hips. He'd done what he had said he would, removed the threat of Peacock from his life. And avenged Welby, for whatever that was worth.

Silhouette walked around him to look down at the corpse of Peacock. "That was quite impressive," she said, crouching. "The way you dodged and everything. I'm genuinely impressed here."

"I'm glad."

"No, seriously. Do you have any idea how hard it is to impress me?"

Alex concentrated on his breathing. The energy began to calm with him, settling back to a more normal level. He heard a slurping sound.

Silhouette crouched low over Peacock's body, lapping at one ruined eye socket. Alex staggered back, horrified. "What the fuck are you doing?"

The blue of her eyes had given way to a swirling black, shining and infinite. Blood stained her lips. Even through his horror Alex was aroused by the sheer primal beauty of her. "I told you I had a history, Alex."

"As a fucking vampire?"

"I'm not a vampire. Though some of us choose to live that way. I figured it was only fair to make sure you knew exactly who I was. Besides, I couldn't resist this, still thick with the adrenaline of fear."

Alex came up sharp against a wall behind him. He stared at Silhouette, his bile rising as she bent back over the corpse, drinking again. "What are you?"

She licked her lips. Alex wasn't sure whether what she did or the fact that it turned him on disgusted him more. "I'm Kin, sweetheart."

Alex staggered from the bookshop and turned down the road. He had no idea where he was going. Away, simple as that. *She drank Peacock's blood, right out of the empty socket!* He was shocked, but it perturbed him more that he wasn't as horrified as he would have expected. And part of him remained strongly attracted to this creature, whatever she was. When would he get a chance to catch up? When would his world stop spinning over and over and let him take stock?

He turned out into a busy street, people bustling back and forth, consumed with the normality of their daily lives. Unaware of magi and blood-drinking women. Blissfully unaware of books that wanted to be owned and stones that made people powerful enough to explode a solid oak door with a single kick.

He struggled for breath as he grappled with everything flooding his mind. He'd killed a man. An arsehole, to be sure, but he had walked into that man's space and murdered him, in cold blood. Worse, he'd enjoyed it. His hands shook, his knees were weak. The stone burned against his chest, its power coursing through him, almost as if it tried to console him. The book felt different, like it approved of the killing and tried to make Alex proud of it. It radiated dark glee. How could a book and a stone make him feel anything?

He bumped into a group of young punks gathered on a street corner, hair spiked and attitudes keenly tuned to disapproval.

One staggered as Alex barged through. "Fucking watch it, ya cunt!" the punk said, punctuating the sentence with a half-smoked cigarette.

Alex stopped dead, spun on one heel to stare the young man in the eye. "What did you say?" His entire body trembled, engorged with power. "Come on, you fucking parrot. Give me one reason to rip that ridiculous hairstyle clean off your fucking scalp!"

The punk's eyes widened and he took a step back. "All right, mate. No need to be aggressive."

Alex laughed. "Aggressive? You haven't seen aggressive yet, fucker." He wanted to kill this young man. He wanted to tear the guy's face off and feed it to his friends. He wanted to be in the middle of the group as they tried to attack him and he would shred each and every one of them limb from limb. And he knew he could do it. With a cry of despair he shoved the man out of his way and strode across the road. Car horns blared and tyres screeched. The hollow pop of impact and a tinkling shower of headlight glass receded in the distance as he jumped over a pedestrian fence on the opposite pavement and turned down a side street. He ignored the raised voices behind him and turned into the welcoming warmth of a pub doorway.

Quiet this early in the day, it seemed safe. He walked to the empty bar and sat on a stool. "Give me a double whisky," he said to the barman's raised eyebrow. "In fact," he put his wallet on the counter between them, "give me two and keep an eye open for empty glasses." He had never been a drinker, but needed something to calm this rage.

The man shrugged and poured the drinks, putting them on the draining tray without a word. Alex handed him a twenty-pound note and sank the first in a single gulp. As the barman put his change beside his wallet on the scored old oak Alex sipped at the second drink.

He sensed her come in, his mind still wired. As she walked casually through the pub to sit next to him he concentrated on locking down his shields. The booze helped. He waved, holding up the empty glass, staring at nothing but the oak bar.

"Give me the same," Silhouette said, though it sounded a thousand miles away.

The barman delivered the drinks, helped himself to Alex's money. Alex sipped again, breathing, sipping, breathing, sipping, letting thoughts drift across his mind's eye like a movie screen. He ignored Silhouette, ignored the pub, ignored everything. He was a warrior, this is what he did. He remained calm in desperate situations. The voice of his Sifu drifted across his mind. *You must be aware of your emotions, but not a slave to them. You must be aware of the emotions of others and use them to your advantage. Throughout it all you must remain calm. Anger, fear, doubt, these things will ruin you. They will stiffen you and you'll snap in the winds of adversity. Control them, control yourself, bend in the wind like a willow.*

He began to settle, his mind his own again. Since he had raised his knee to take down Peacock's door, he realized, he had been barely in control. At any moment he could have gone berserk. He was thankful he'd managed to hold onto himself as much as he had. The warm, soft glow of inebriation played along with his breathing exercises. The crowing of the book had dulled. The irony wasn't lost on him. Alcohol, the great control destroyer he'd always avoided, working in his favour now.

Silhouette laid a hand on his shoulder, her palm hot. "You back with us?"

Alex nodded, saying nothing. He still had very mixed feelings about her, but at least she knew exactly what had been happening. He took great comfort in knowing he wasn't completely alone in all this.

"You're a remarkable young man, Alex," she said, her voice low, seductive.

"I wish I wasn't."

"You said that before. But you are. Nothing you can do about it."

"Fuck." He sipped.

She squeezed his shoulder. "So. What now?"

"What now? I'm going to have a couple more drinks and then I'm going to destroy this fucking book and stone, that's what now."

EIGHT

Silhouette left her hand on his shoulder, warm and reassuring, as they drank. Alex knew getting drunk was a bad idea in the long run, but it seemed to be dulling the insistent presence of the book in his pocket and the Darak against his chest.

Welby lay dead in his own house. Peacock lay dead in his shop, murdered by Alex's hand. Silhouette drank the blood from a dead man's eye socket. These things in his possession had turned his life upside down. What next?

He knew Peacock's death was his own desire, yet there was more to it than that. Would he really have acted so defiantly, so violently, without feeling as though the book and the stone were urging him on? He wondered how much control he had. How much he knew his own mind. He had skills others couldn't imagine. He had learned more about that in the last couple of days than he would ever have dreamed possible. And those powers were exponentially increased with this shard around his neck. But at what cost? And how connected were these items? He truly intended to destroy them both, but deep down felt certain he wouldn't be able to. It wouldn't stop him trying, but if he couldn't destroy them, then what?

He needed help and the only people he knew that might have a clue were dead. *My thoughts are going 'round in circles.* He looked disdainfully at the glass in his hand. Help and hindrance in one tiny package.

But there was someone else that could help. Silhouette. Devastating and terrifying, young and old, sensual and animal. His only ally. A monster. Alex turned to her, taking his eyes off the bar for the first time since he'd sat down.

"So what are you really?" Alex asked.

She smiled, a predatory baring of teeth at once alluring and frightening. "I told you. I'm Kin."

Alex nodded. "Then I suppose the question is, what are Kin?"

"What do you think?"

"I think you're some freak animal that lapped up the blood from a dead man's eye. Beyond that I daren't consider."

"Really?"

Alex sighed. "I'm starting to think I've lived my whole life blind. I've seen magic, I think I've used magic. I fought two fucking gargoyles! So, I'm not sure I can really get my head around what you might be."

Silhouette stroked his cheek. "You're doing pretty well."

"You drank his blood, Silhouette! Your eyes turned black." She nodded, letting her hand slip away. He frowned. "But you say you're not a vampire."

"I'm not. I would have eaten his flesh too, but that would have been too confusing for the police who might find him. A bit of smeared blood is less... incriminating. But being a vampire is a lifestyle choice."

"What?"

She gestured over her shoulder, out the door of the pub. "Those punks you nearly tore to pieces out there. They dress and act a certain way. They choose a particular style of being, right?"

"I suppose."

"Same thing with my people and vampirism."

Alex shook his head. "No, no. Just because someone chooses to act like a vampire, that doesn't make them one. You're more than playing some twisted role."

"I told you, I'm not a vampire. Just like you're not a punk."

"Yeah, but I could be a punk if I chose to be."

Silhouette finished the last of her drink. "And I could be a vampire. Some of my people dig the whole gothic thing. I'm not a fan."

Alex sipped, buying time to think. He couldn't really think of anything. "But you drank his blood."

"Like I said, it was too good to miss. Such adrenaline and fear. Delicious! It was so hard not taking a bite too."

"How is that not being a vampire?"

Silhouette turned on her stool to face him, took his hand in hers. "I told you I had a history that might not sit well with you. I figured the easiest thing would be to show you outright. Plus, I couldn't resist. I'm not a vampire, but I do feed on people. My *kind* feed on people, and not just on their blood, but flesh, bones, the whole thing."

Alex swallowed hard, a rocky lump of bile rising in his throat. She sat there admitting a hideous truth and he still found her so enthralling. He was drawn to her, desperate to explore every centimeter of her. She looked at him with soft eyes, her usual casual cheeriness giving way to a seriousness she didn't seem comfortable displaying. "What the fuck?" was all he could manage.

"Humans always have to categorise and pigeonhole, Alex. Vampires and werewolves, demons and angels. We're all of those things and none of them. We are Kin. We're the monsters under the bed, the bogeyman in the closet, the fear in the dark."

"Humans?"

She reached out for his cheek again. "You're human, Alex. I'm not. At least, not entirely. That's what makes me Kin. My people don't generally mix with yours. If you see us, you don't live long enough to talk about it. That's where the vampire and werewolf legends come from. And all the others. Some of my people got into the idea and started to live out the human perception. They like that, get a thrill out of it. Sometimes they settle into that way of being for decades, even centuries. Sometimes they bore quickly. But we're all Kin. You're human. But I'm a bit different. I've always had a soft spot for people."

Alex shook his head, trying to keep up. "So you like to butter the cow up before you eat it?"

She grabbed his chin, tipped his face up, planted a kiss on his lips. It was hot and passionate, arousing him instantly. "I don't tend to eat the people I befriend." She sat back with a wink.

"So why have you befriended me?"

"I'm weird like that."

He laughed in spite of his confusion. If he ignored the fact that she was not entirely human, and that she fed on humans, she was actually pretty cool. He laughed harder at the ridiculous chain of thought.

She grinned at him. "You're a bit weird too, aren't you? Maybe that's why we're getting along."

Alex's laughter faded as reality swung back in front of him. "I need help," he said, casting his eyes down at the floor.

"I know. And I don't think I can really give you the help you need, but I can be there while you try."

And there it was again. The only reason he wasn't completely alone in all this. He knew he looked past the mind-bending revelations of what she actually might be primarily because of that. And because she was smoking hot. More than anything he needed someone to cling onto while the world fell apart around him. "I need to try to destroy this stone and this book," he said quietly.

"I think the stone is fairly safe. It's a tool. And a powerful one at that. I don't think you should give it up so easily. The book is another matter."

His eyes searched hers. "You think I should destroy the book?"

"I think you should try. But I don't think you'll be able to."

"And then what?"

She shrugged. "The offer still stands to talk to my Clan Lord. If you earn the right to speak to him, if you survive, he might be able to help you."

Alex swallowed the last of his whisky. He picked up his wallet, leaving the few remaining coins on the bar, and stood. "Let's go."

"Where?"

"First we'll get a cab to Welby's for my stuff. And maybe some of his."

A man and a woman, sharp corporate dress and expensive shoes, stood looking down at the corpse of Peacock. Blood dried in a sticky patch around his head, congealed on his cheeks like a frozen flood of dark scarlet tears, smeared by something.

The man clasped his hands together, steepled index fingers gently tapping his lips. The fluorescent light from above reflected off his pale, completely bald head. "Well, Ms Sparks," he said eventually. "It would appear that our friend Mr Peacock really upset someone this time."

The woman smiled, long blonde hair half covering a coldly attractive, severe face. "Indeed, Mr Hood. You have to admire the handiwork."

Hood nodded, looking up at the doorway to the shopfront, the wooden frame splintered with bullet holes. "Whoever did this avoided extremely close range gunfire and didn't waste any time completing their objective." Peacock's gun lay in his slack palm. Hood tapped it with his toe. "Either our miserable little bookseller was truly useless with this, or his assailant was very fast."

"Maybe a bit of both," Sparks said thoughtfully. "Not to mention avoiding the various protective wards." She crouched, looking closely at Peacock's ruined eyes. After a moment's silent contemplation, she stood, smoothing her tight, dark skirt. "So, looks like we won't need to continue trying to negotiate with Peacock for all this." Her hand swept the room, taking in the bowed shelves of grimoires and scrolls. "Instead of trying to convince him to give us a price we can turn a profit on we can take it all and clear a very healthy margin."

Hood nodded absently, still staring at Peacock's corpse. His index fingers tapped away at his lips, eyes narrowed.

"What are you thinking?" Sparks asked. "I'm sure Peacock pissed off plenty of people. This was inevitable really, given enough time."

Hood lowered his hands. "Certainly. But think about it. This kind of targeted, ruthless violence doesn't come from a simple dispute." He pointed to the bullet-riddled doorway. "Someone destroyed the front door, came in while Peacock squeezed off several shots. They covered this distance and killed him without any unnecessary activity. And then they left." He pointed at a book on Peacock's desk. "Look at that. Very valuable that is. And the stuff on the shelves is untouched. Why didn't they take anything? Why not ransack the place?"

Sparks looked around, shrugged. "You think this was about something else?" Hood nodded. "Something specific?" Sparks asked.

"I built Black Diamond Incorporated by sourcing the kind of

things that most people don't even believe in," Hood said. "I've made an obscene amount of money by learning to spot those items and find buyers for them. I notice details." He gestured at Peacock. "This situation bears the hallmarks of something very intriguing. I want to know who killed this despicable little man and why. Have the boys get around here and gather up anything of value before the police or some other busybodies stumble across it all. We can't let an opportunity like this slip by. Any authorities will think it a simple robbery. There's nothing to trace back to us if we're clean."

Sparks nodded. "Yes, sir. And the killer?"

Hood smiled. "I think we need to call in the Subcontractor."

Sparks's face split in a wide grin. "Excellent!"

"But first." Hood ran a long, thin hand through Sparks's hair. "This whole situation rather thrills me. Bend over that desk, Ms Sparks. I have some excitement that needs releasing."

Sparks dipped her head coyly, her grin staying put. "Why, Mr Hood!"

Alex and Silhouette stood outside Welby's house, looking up through watery light at the stuccoed Victorian facade. "What do you see?" Alex asked.

"What do you mean?"

"Describe to me what you see."

Silhouette looked the house up and down, at the others either side. "I see a mostly white, two-storey house. It's kinda dirty, but looks in good condition. Tile roof, new windows. Pretty much the same as every other house along this street. What am I supposed to see?"

"Look at the roof again."

"Yeah? Tiles, chimney. What?"

Alex frowned at the plainly obvious third storey, windows with the curtains drawn. The house stood head and shoulders over every other home in the street. He laughed, shook his head. "Come on then."

Silhouette planted her hands on her hips. "What the hell? What am I supposed to see?"

"It'll be easier to show you. Come inside."

Alex paused as he shut the broken front door behind them, wedging it closed with its broken catch. He studied the devastation from his fight with the gargoyles. He fought for a living, but he'd never had a battle like that in his life. Hoped he never would again. Drawing a deep breath, he started up the stairs, bracing himself for Welby's corpse. "Don't like, lick him or anything," he said.

"Okay then. Just for you."

He led her to the second floor and stood with his back to the stairs leading to the third, secret storey. "You see anything you don't expect."

"What are you going on about? What am I supposed to see?"

Alex turned and walked up the stairs, feeling a shiver of magesign as he passed through Welby's wards. Silhouette gasped behind him. He turned, looked down at her. "See now?"

She laughed, wide-eyed. "Well, of course I can see now you've shattered the wards for me."

"They're still here, I think. Can you follow me up?"

Silhouette made a strange gesture with her hand then shrugged. She mounted the stairs and followed him. "Bloody clever," she muttered. "Certainly not Welby's own work. He must have paid a lot for this."

"I don't think money was much of an issue for him."

"Clearly."

In Welby's study Alex started looking more closely at the books that lined every wall. Nothing made a lot of sense to him. There was a wealth of information here, not to mention massive monetary value, but it wasn't worth the paper it was written on at this stage. What could he use? Silhouette walked slowly around the room, running one finger along the spines of the books.

"This is amazing," she said. "Do you realize how amazing this is?"

"Sure. But I need something to help me with my situation."

For hours, they pored over Welby's library, looking for anything that might shed some light on Alex's dilemma. A small pile of books grew crookedly in the middle of the floor, all incredible, all containing unbelievable degrees of knowledge and magic. Tomes that mentioned anything about Fey history or curses or stones of power. Eventually, tired, despondent, Alex stared at the works they had gathered.

"None of this is really helpful, is it?"

Silhouette smiled ruefully. "I'm not sure there's anything that *can* help you with your current predicament."

Alex spun on his heel. "Fuck this! I'm going to burn this book."

Silhouette trotted to catch up. "I'm not sure burning's a good idea."

Alex glared over his shoulder, his eyes alive with fury.

Silhouette held up both palms. "All right, easy there." She giggled. "Give it a go."

Alex went into the front room. He pulled aside a decorative grate from an open fireplace and stuffed newspaper and kindling into the hearth from a large basket. Bigger logs of firewood were stacked neatly in a box beside it. Within a few minutes he had a fire raging, bright orange flames licking at the blackened bricks of the chimney. He felt Silhouette moving behind him. He looked around to see her standing in the hallway, one hand on the front door. "What are you doing?"

She seemed fairly amused by his actions. "Just being cautious."

Alex deflated. "It's not going to work, is it?"

Silhouette shrugged.

"Fuck it!" He pulled the book from his pocket. Magesign swam urgently around his hand and arm. Holding the book towards the flames he felt a flood of desperation and entertainment combined. The book had a presence, a personality almost, and it mocked him. Dared him. With a growl of anger he threw the small book into the dancing flames.

Nothing happened. The fire seemed to slide around the book without touching it. Then the flames bit and gathered across the smooth leather cover. The page edges began to blacken. Then spark.

Silhouette's voice was concerned. "Er, Alex?"

Alex stood, backing away. "What's it doing?"

"Not exactly burning." The front door clicked open.

The book expanded, as though the fire filled it rather than burned it. The sparks became blue arcs of lightning, snapping and popping around it and the charcoaled wood it sat on. A feeling of pressure filled the room, like the air before a massive storm.

"Alex, you might want to move further away."

As a sharp, ear-drilling howl joined the lightning in the fireplace he turned and ran, diving out the door as heat and light burst all around. Silhouette caught him as he flew through the air, pushed along by an explosive force that shattered the windows and blew the door from its hinges. Roaring flames bulged from the shattered frames and grasped the entire house in white hot fury.

Silhouette dragged him with her, forcing him to find his feet and run. "Move!"

Heads low they charged away from the house as it exploded. Car alarms wailed and trees cracked as the masonry of the walls and roof rained down. Several houses either side of Welby's split and collapsed. Windows on both sides of the street burst with orchestral rains of glass.

Alex and Silhouette ran for their lives, ducking around a corner as debris fell around them. Casting a glance back Alex saw Welby's street devastated as if an air strike had targeted it. They ran on for several more blocks before slowing to a walk, panting.

"So much for any of Welby's books being useful," Silhouette said.

Alex didn't care. "I don't think there's a book anywhere that can help me." He reached into his jacket, pulled out the Darak Uthentia, completely unscathed.

Silhouette nodded. "I'm not surprised. I think that was a lesson in the futility of trying to destroy it."

Alex winced, remembering his bag in Welby's spare room. "All my stuff was in there, what little I had."

Silhouette squeezed his shoulder. "It's just stuff."

He remembered the element book. That hurt most of all, as that had been a fine gift. But he'd read it all, twice, mesmerised by it, and the knowledge lived on in his mind. He could feel it there, nestled in his brain. It would take time to think on it, practise it, get to know it, but the book itself had become irrelevant. He felt some comfort in that. He had his wallet and phone in his pocket and the clothes on his back. Maybe, with his newfound powers, he didn't need anything else after all. Of course, he had the Darak Uthentia too.

He felt desolate. "I can't throw it away, I can't give it away, and I can't destroy it."

Silhouette made an apologetic face. "So keep it."

"No. This thing is evil. It approved of me killing Peacock. It urged me on. Fuck, Silhouette, it made me not care about killing a man until after I'd done it! What else can it do?"

Silhouette put a hand on his forearm. "Let's go and see my Clan Lord. It might kill you, but that's one answer, right?"

A white transit van slid to a stop at the corner. Two men sitting in the front seats watched Alex and Silhouette walking down the road.

"Who are they then?" asked the driver.

The man in the passenger seat drew on a cigarette. "Fuck knows. Doesn't matter really. Sparks said to follow up on Peacock's known associates. These two would appear to be connected."

"Why did they blow up Welby's 'ouse?"

"Dunno. Don't really care. We came to ask Welby questions, but her ladyship will want to talk to this couple, I shouldn't doubt."

"Shall we take 'em now?"

The man flicked his cigarette out the window, pulled a phone from his pocket. "I'll call some boys. Follow them to somewhere more quiet. This road's a bit busy."

NINE

The Subcontractor stood in the doorway of the King's Arms, his nose twitching. The aroma of beer inside and cigarette butts on the street muffled the trail. The general miasma of odors from the street added to the confusion—petrol, diesel, dust, piss. City grime coated everything, a skin of humanity lying over the land like a shadow. The Subcontractor closed his eyes, tipped his head back, sniffing. He let the scents that didn't interest him slip away, searching out the unique fragrance of his quarry. Those two single strands of pheromone and psychic identity, one human, one Kin. He'd identified them around the corpse of Peacock, though that hadn't been easy in a place of such intense activity.

It didn't help when the whole scene was soaked in the stench of that idiot's cum and his whore's juices. What kind of freaks were they? He charged them extra because of the bizarre shit they always carried like baggage. They could pay it. What kind of professional would he be if he didn't charge as much as he could for his unique skills? He charged extra for city work too. He hated working in cities, yet found himself invariably called to them. People seemed to sink to their lowest, commit their basest acts, when they lived in the highest densities.

A human male and a female Kin. Their trails came through more clearly as he emptied his mind of petty concerns. The trail that led him here had been weak, but a stronger one snaked away again. With a quiet hiss of pleasure he snapped his eyes open.

Two young men stood before him, strange expressions on their faces. "You all right, mate?" one asked, all attitude and long hair.

The Subcontractor sneered. "Perfectly."

Long Hair gestured at the doorway. "Mind if we come in?"

"I don't care what you do."

The man laughed. "Right. Well, get the fuck out of the way then, eh?" He elbowed his friend, who guffawed obligingly.

The Subcontractor's eyes widened. If one thing really bothered him it was a lack of respect. He was a small, wiry, strange-looking character, and people invariably underestimated him. "How about I eat your face?"

Long Hair barked a laugh, reaching for the Subcontractor's shoulder, presumably to push him aside. That simply wouldn't do. Long Hair staggered forward as his wrist was grabbed and pulled sharply. The Subcontractor stretched up, opening his mouth impossibly wide. He sank his teeth into Long Hair's cheek and whipped his head away, spraying the man's friend with blood and saliva. Long Hair screamed, collapsing to his knees. His friend staggered back, eyes terrified, mouth working soundlessly. Blood poured onto the dirty concrete of the path. Long Hair's howls of agony and his friend's frantic gibbering for help faded as the Subcontractor strolled away from the pub, chewing happily on the foolish man's cheek. He kept the trail of the human and the Kin uppermost in his senses, following easily now he had a firm mental grasp on it.

Alex and Silhouette froze in their tracks as a white van parked across the street some ten meters ahead of them. The side door slid open and two men trained guns on them.

"What the fuck is this?" Alex hissed. He turned to look back down the street and saw two more men, pistols in hand.

"No side streets," Silhouette said, eyes scanning the quiet area. "They've got us pinned. Who are they?"

Alex ground his teeth, a dull rage swelling up from his belly. "I have no idea."

The driver of the white van emerged and another man walked around the front from the passenger side. "Hello there," the passenger said in a broad cockney accent. "I'm Dan Butler and you'll be coming with us."

"What is this?" Alex asked. "What do you want?"

Butler grinned broadly, positioning himself between the two gunmen still perched in the van. The driver, moving off to one side, had a gun of his own drawn. Butler didn't seem to consider the need for one himself. "We wanted to ask Patrick Welby some questions," Butler said. "But his "ouse was all blown up and there's you two running from the scene. So you'll do."

Alex frowned, wondering what the connection was. "You've got the wrong guy."

"Is that right?" Butler said with a grin.

Alex looked back at the gunmen approaching from behind. "We can take this lot," he said quietly to Silhouette. "You can move fast enough, right?" He felt empowered by his encounter with Peacock. He opened his vision, studying the shades around the men. Their colors were tense, nervous. He started mentally plotting a course of movement. "Can you deal with the ones behind us?" he asked.

Silhouette gave him a look that froze his stomach. "Sorry, Alex. I don't like guns." She stepped away from him, her hands up over her head. "If this boy's in trouble, I want nothing more to do with him."

Alex felt as though a knife had shredded his guts. "Silhouette, no."

"Really?" asked Butler, his eyes suspicious.

Silhouette smiled disarmingly. "I'm just a working girl who was going to suck his dick. I don't need this, so I'll just walk away."

Butler pointed one stubby finger at her. "We saw you run away with "im when Welby's "ouse exploded."

Silhouette kept moving away, heading towards the side of the street. "Yeah, that was all him," she said, pointing at Alex. "He takes me to this house, and I think that's where we're going to do the deed, but he sets it up to blow. Destroying evidence, he said. Thought it would turn me on to see how *bad* he was. You get all sorts. We only just made it out in one piece and I told him to fuck off, but he's so desperate for a blow job he offered double if we went to a hotel. I need the money."

Alex couldn't believe his ears. Was she playing out some bizarre act? She didn't seem to be placing herself anywhere advantageous. And her eyes had been so serious when she left his side, so final. *What did I expect? Why should she help me?* A part of him couldn't blame her.

"Shall I grab her?" one of the men behind them said.

"It's true," Alex said. "Let her go." He strode forward a couple of paces, drawing the attention of the gunmen. "She's nothing, just a hooker." He felt empty as he said it. From his periphery, he caught the flash of movement as Silhouette ran, inhumanly fast.

Several pairs of eyes turned back to where Silhouette had been, faces registering surprise. Except Butler, who never moved his gaze from Alex. "Get after her!" he barked.

The two men approaching behind ran past, the men at the van still pinning Alex at several gunpoints. Within moments, the men were back, panting for breath.

"Nowhere," said one. "Just bleedin' vanished."

Butler flapped one hand. "Fuck this, we've still got you, eh? Now you'll have more questions to answer. In the van, please."

He was alone with six men, five guns. He had no plan against those odds. He felt the book urging him to lay waste about himself, felt the stone throbbing against him. But these men were too well positioned. On his own there was no way to take them all, or to escape and avoid the shots. For now, he had no choice but to play along.

The Subcontractor stood at a taxi rank, frustrated. Modern transport constantly proved to be the bane of his life. But he wouldn't be beaten. He remained patient as cab after cab travelled through. Every one he leaned in, sniffing, ignoring the driver's protestations and outrage, before waving it away. It took a couple of hours before he finally found it, sweet and sour, the aroma of his prey. He got into the big black car. The driver half twisted in his seat. "Where to, mate?"

"I need to know all the fares you've taken in the last few hours."

"You what?"

"All the places you've been in the last few hours. Since, say, ten o'clock?"

The driver turned fully to stare at him. "Are you mental? I can't remember that and I couldn't tell you if I could."

"Why not?"

"Confidentiality."

The Subcontractor laughed. "You're not a doctor. Tell me where you've been."

The driver shook his head. "Just get out, mate. Find another bloke to be a nutter with. I've had it up to here already today."

There were so many ways to get information, but he could do with this man not only telling him where he'd been, but taking him there too. The tried and tested methods were often the best. After all, those Black Diamond freaks could afford it. "How much?" he asked.

The driver frowned. "For what?"

"How much to *remember* all the fares you've had today?"

"Oh, right. Well, that kind of memory ain't cheap."

"A hundred pounds?"

"Fuckin' "ell! Yeah, all right."

"How many couples have you had today? A man and a woman. The man is quite young and I imagine the woman would appear to be quite young too."

The driver lifted his chin, defiant. "Money first, eh?"

The Subcontractor sighed. He pulled a wad of notes from the pocket of his long, dark coat, counted off five twenties. "How many?"

The driver eyed the cash ruefully. He probably regretted agreeing so easily to a hundred. "Well," he said, "there's been a few couples today. Mostly people on their own though." He stared up at the grubby lining of the cab roof, face twisted in thought. "There was a couple arguing about renting a flat. I took them to Highgate. Then, towards lunchtime, there was a couple wanted to go out towards Kensington. They both reeked of booze. Bit early I thought."

The Subcontractor whipped up one finger. That rang true with the scent in his nose. "I'll give you another twenty pounds if you drive me now on the exact route you took them, to the same location."

The driver raised one eyebrow. "The fare'd be that on its own. What's in it for me?"

"The hundred I already gave you?"

The driver nodded towards the Subcontractor's pocket. "I reckon you can stretch to a bit more than that, eh?"

Why were people always so greedy? This man might have lived to spend one hundred and twenty pounds. Now he would die with nothing. "What about another fifty?"

The driver grinned. "Lovely jubbly. Off we go then."

He pulled away from the kerb and made a right turn. The Subcontractor cracked the window open a fraction, letting the odor drift in from the street, infinitesimal though it was. Like a shark homing in on a single drop of blood in a wide ocean, he hung onto the trail. Before long the cab pulled over.

"I dropped them right here," the driver said.

The Subcontractor opened the door, leaned out close to the pavement. "Yes," he said. "So you did."

A few minutes later he stared at the wreckage of the street. One house was nothing but a pile of scorched rubble, houses either side collapsed and ruined. Emergency services and police vehicles stood inside an area of over one hundred meters cordoned off at both ends, damage and debris everywhere. Television crews and newspaper reporters swarmed around the yellow tape, calling out questions like seagulls cawing for chips.

The Subcontractor dabbed at his hands with a brown and scarlet stained handkerchief. Stuffing it deep into a coat pocket he turned, nose twitching. The trail, clearer now, led away from the bombed street. He turned and strolled along with it.

TEN

Alex stumbled into a walk-in fridge, shoved from behind by two nervous gunmen. They slammed the door and his breath puffed in frosty clouds as he fought to control his anger. He'd sat in the van staring down the barrels of five guns while Butler drove and talked to someone on a cell phone, the words lost in the rattle of the road and the growl of the diesel engine. At no point had an opportunity presented itself for him to break free. He felt a certain pride that every man's shades had been tinged with trepidation. They were genuinely scared of him, but they had guns and numbers on their side. He couldn't blame Silhouette for deserting him. The odds had swung swiftly against them. He remembered her words in Welby's lounge. *I don't owe you anything, Alex Caine.*

The cold soaked into his bones, his body trembled with shivers. The whiskies from earlier had worn off, the chill and the fury sobering him up. "Keep him in the fridge," Butler had said. "Secure and cold, to slow him down a bit, eh?"

The rage in Alex broke suddenly free. He let the power of the Darak flood through his body and thrashed at everything around. He smashed shelves and hurled boxes of produce at the hard plastic walls. He pounded kicks into the thick, reinforced door, revelling as the plastic split and the hinges groaned. Insulating foam burst out in clouds of choking particles.

A voice hollered from the other side. "We will fucking shoot you!"

Alex paused, gasping for breath. His hands shook as vapour swam around his head.

"You gonna calm down?" the voice asked. "Seriously, we will hurt you. At the very least you'll lose your knees."

Alex tried to calm the rage that soaked his rational thoughts in a red veil. This wasn't the time. He believed them when they talked about killing him. In the van their shades had clearly betrayed their willingness to pull the trigger. He'd considered setting them off, hoping he could avoid the bullets while they shredded each other, but hadn't fancied his chances in the confined space.

A distant sound caught his attention. It sounded like a scream, cut quickly short. He heard a frantic, muffled conversation outside the door, too disrupted by the walls of his prison to understand.

Shoes slapped the concrete floor as one man ran away. Alex clenched his fists in anticipation. Only one man stood guard now. Only one gun. He could happily play those odds.

"Don't you make a fucking move," the man outside the door called, as if reading his mind.

"What's going on?" Alex shouted. "Who the fuck are you people?"

"None of your business." The man sounded distracted.

Alex decided it was his best chance. He remembered Peacock's heavy oak door. Could this fridge be much stronger? He concentrated, let the stone swell into his body. He pictured his leg lifting, the kick flying out. Another distant cry floated to him, cut off like the last, then two gunshots punctured the pause. He hammered out a kick and the fridge door burst off its hinges. The man outside half turned before the heavy metal and plastic struck him, knocking him to the ground. Alex leapt out into the strangely warm air and swung a kick at the man's head. His shin connected with a sickening crack and the gangster slid across the floor, flaccid as a rag doll.

A shape moved across the dimly lit space ahead, like a huge animal of some kind moving swiftly on all fours. Alex dropped into a corner, blinking. *Did I really see that?*

He crept along the hallway, trying to force back the darkness with his eyes. Another shadow moved, this one definitely shaped like a human. A very familiar human. "Alex? Is that you?" Silhouette sounded nervous.

Relief coursed through him. "Yes, it's me." He stood, hurried along the hallway.

Silhouette stepped into view, her smile mocking him. "Tell me you didn't really think I'd deserted you? I can't believe that worked, to be honest."

Alex felt a tinge of guilt, but remembered it was justified. "You once said you owed me nothing."

She patted his cheek. "True. But you're not like other humans I've known. Come on, there might be back-up coming any minute."

She led him along the corridor and through a room with a table and chairs, tatty sofas and a TV playing *Judge Judy*. Bodies were scattered among the furniture with blood spilling copiously across the floor from rents and gashes in their flesh. In some, large chunks of that flesh were missing entirely. He saw a skylight in the high ceiling had been smashed through, shards of frosted plastic scattered throughout the room.

Alex swallowed hard. "What the fuck, Silhouette? Did you do all this?"

She ignored the question and pulled at his jacket, dragging him through the door. They emerged into a warehouse, the white van parked in one corner. A side exit led out into an industrial estate, warehouses all around, trucks and cars moving slowly between them, fork lifts carrying precarious loads. Silhouette took Alex's hand and they walked casually but swiftly, heading for the main road. "Looks like you got away with that unscathed," she said.

"I guess so," Alex agreed. "Listen, thanks for coming back for me. It's good to know I'm not alone in this."

"I think you were managing pretty well. What was that, a fridge they had you in?"

Alex could see a certain humor in the situation. "Yeah, it was," he said with a laugh. "They thought if they kept me cold it might slow me down."

"Well, more fool them. We need to get to my Den. On the way we can try to figure out just who the hell they were."

The Subcontractor fronted up to a huge metal roller door, sniffing casually. The trail had become less clear along the way, like they were travelling in a vehicle again, but it definitely led here. The closer he got, the fresher the trail, the easier it was to follow, even wrapped in the metal and oil of a car. He knocked and waited. Nothing.

Pursing his lips, he walked around the building, looking for another way in. A side door stood open. As he approached the door the scent became very clear, leading away. Intrigued, he carefully entered the warehouse. The stench of fresh blood swamped all other aromas.

In a lounge room, he found the bodies and evidence of quite a struggle. He smelled gunpowder and panic. Down a long hallway he saw more damage and destruction. These two were certainly leaving a pretty obvious path but it was messy and confusing. What had led them here? Why had these unfortunate men become victims? Peacock murdered, Welby's house destroyed, now this. He tipped one man's face up with his foot and sighed, recognising one of Sparks's hired goons. Such redundancy, always hedging her bets, trying to win the boss's favor. And with useless thugs like this? It was an insult to professionalism. These men must have got lucky and it killed them. But it did prove the danger presented by this pair he tracked. That gave him a small rush, the thought that perhaps they might prove to be at least a bit of a challenge. Life could be so boring. Anyway, with these hired guns out of the way, perhaps he would be able to get on with his job now, as contracted.

Back outside the trail hung in the air, unmistakable. He sniffed appreciatively and headed for the main road.

Alex and Silhouette stood outside huge wrought-iron gates in a quiet street in Wandsworth. Conifers shivered in the cold breeze, tall behind a red brick wall to either side, shielding the house beyond. Alex's phone beeped. He cast an apologetic look at Silhouette and checked it. One new message from Amir.

situation heating up, brother. stay quiet, will call when everything fixed. won't be long.

He smiled ruefully. With everything else happening he'd forgotten all about that. It seemed a lifetime ago. With a slight shake of the head he tapped out, *thanks brother*, and pocketed the phone.

Silhouette gave him a quizzical look.

"Nothing important."

"Okay," she said. "Remember what I told you. Let me do the

talking."

She pushed open the gates and dropped into a crouch. Alex waited. Two Doberman Pinschers came bounding over, growling deep in their throats. Silhouette held out both hands. She spoke in a strange, lilting tongue, her voice soothing. The dogs sniffed and cocked their heads to one side, looked up at Alex. He stiffened while doing his best to hide his trepidation. Silhouette spoke more soft words and the dogs turned and loped away into the gardens.

A Victorian mansion stood among manicured lawns at the end of a gravel driveway, the lower storey of worn russet bricks, rough white stucco above. Weathered, lichen-covered tiles marched up the steep roof to several tall, intricate chimneys. The grounds appeared to spread far and wide beyond the house.

"This place must be worth a fortune," Alex said.

Silhouette laughed. "Most probably. We've been here a long time. Joseph had this house built for us, back when this was a distant suburb of London and land was cheap. The building is just the facade though."

"Facade?"

"You'll see."

The front door stood in a shadowed porch, clay tiles on the floor. The door itself a heavy, dark oak, studded with iron bolts. A green tinged copper gargoyle head gripped a massive iron ring in a distended jaw. Silhouette ignored it, using a key from her pocket. "Follow me," she said. "And don't say a word."

Alex followed her into a long, wood-panelled hallway. Oil paintings lined the walls, Victorian furniture laid out neatly in every room. The whole place stood cold and still, unlived in. An odor hung in the air, a musky scent that tickled the back of the senses. Otherwise nothing but dust and silence.

Silhouette led him into a giant kitchen, a freeze-frame from a previous century. Copper pots hung in rows above marble benchtops. A black iron stove, big enough to cook up a feast for an army, took up a large portion of one wall. Huge ceramic sinks lined another. They looked as though they hadn't been used in decades. A dark wooden door, arched to a steep point at the top, dominated the center of another wall. Silhouette walked straight to it and tapped a foot impatiently.

The door opened. A tall, imposing man, ebony skin taut over bulging muscles, stood in the shadows beyond. He smirked, showing inhumanly sharp teeth. "Playing with your food again, Sil?"

"Shut up, Ataro. Come on, Alex." Silhouette pushed past the big man, not sparing him another glance.

Alex, trembling slightly with nervous tension, followed her. He nodded at Ataro as he passed. Ataro leaned down to take a long, deep sniff of Alex's head. Alex flinched away, casting a frown back at the man. Ataro laughed and licked his lips, a quick, lascivious action.

"Ignore him," Silhouette called out. "He's a big idiot."

The small room had a black and white tiled floor, no more than three meters square. Presumably a walk-in larder at one point it now housed a couple of old leather armchairs and a television on a small table. A bookshelf stood against one wall. Shadowed stone steps led down into darkness from the far side. Ataro slumped heavily into one of the chairs, picked up a book left on the arm of it, an airport thriller.

Silhouette started down the steps. "Come on, Alex."

The steps wound down into a wide chamber. Large gray flagstones spread across the floor, similar stone carved into smooth blocks made the walls. Red bricks vaulted to a high ceiling, curving up into a dome with intricate patterning. Columns stood throughout, carved with patterns and topped with grotesques, dragons, imps, angels. A large archway at the far side led through into a much bigger room, warm, flickering light from flaming brands around the walls danced over everything. Alex sensed enormous power. People milled around, sat on comfortable chairs or at tables, read and played games. Every one of them paused to watch Silhouette and Alex enter. They all wore an expression of amused interest.

A pale woman with long, raven hair stepped over. She might have been attractive if not for the feral twist to her face. She laughed softly and two sharp canine teeth shot down to press against her thin, scarlet lower lip. Alex jumped, his fists clenching. "You brought us a plaything?" she asked.

Silhouette gave her a disdainful look. "He's with me, Caitlin. Put your fangs away. Joseph in?"

Caitlin looked Alex up and down. "Shame. I'd like to play with him."

Silhouette sighed. "Joseph in?"

"What am I, his secretary? Go and see for yourself, bitch."

Silhouette smirked, flipped Caitlin the bird. "Come on, Alex."

She led him to a corridor on the far side. Alex kept his attention on the back of her head as they walked, determined not to catch any of the eyes that followed them. "She doesn't seem to like you," he whispered.

Silhouette's shoulders hitched slightly. "None of them like me much. I'm something of a pariah."

"Among your own people? Was she a vampire?"

"It's a lifestyle choice, remember. Fucking try-hard is what she is."

"Try-hard?"

Silhouette paused, half turning to him. She opened her mouth and her own canine teeth quickly grew to long, sharp points. Alex took a step backwards. Silhouette shifted her jaw and all her teeth lengthened and sharpened. She moved again, her nose and jaw extending into a lupine snout before snapping quickly back to her recognisable face. "We are Kin, Alex," Silhouette said. "We can be whatever we want to be. She's nothing special. I also told you not to say anything."

She turned away. Alex followed her along the corridor, desperately trying to process everything. As soon as he got used to one incredible revelation, another knocked it for six.

Several other doors led off on both sides, most closed. Through the few open ones Alex could see lounge rooms or bed chambers. What had he got himself into? Every step he took led him deeper into danger. Or simply changed one menace for another, equally life threatening. Amir's text seemed ludicrous in the face of his new experience.

At the end of the corridor a massive door dominated the wall. Silhouette stood before it, silent, patient. She didn't knock. After several seconds she reached for the handle. She turned to Alex, drawing one index finger across her lips. He nodded.

A luxurious apartment spread before them, deep red silks and velvets, rich, intricate Persian rugs, old, cracked leather furniture. Doors led from the room to other chambers. A man lounged on a deep, soft sofa in the middle of the room. Two more people sat across from him in armchairs, a tall man and a woman, both dark-haired with icy eyes. All three examined Alex and Silhouette. Alex returned their inquisitive gazes.

The lounging man radiated an authority that left Alex in no doubt that he must be the Clan Lord. With long, blond hair, a thin, sharp nose and narrow, dark eyes he was both handsome and frightening. His shades were completely unguarded and powerful beyond anything Alex had ever seen. It was like trying to look at the sun.

His guests were equally enthralling. The woman had a stunning beauty and power about her, but a softness too. She looked at Alex with a curious kindness. The man next to her had a similar look of concern, though his presence seemed colder. He emanated strength, his entire being seemingly carved from granite. He wore a tattered leather jacket and jeans, tousled dark hair hung down to his shoulders. If not for the arrangement of the seating Alex could easily have mistaken this man for the Clan Lord. He had an age about him, an undeniable aura that humbled Alex, made him feel small, insignificant. Both their shades were guarded, closed, but Alex had no doubt they concealed considerable power. Neither guest was Kin, but both seemed far more than mortal human.

Silhouette touched gently against his chest, staying him. She stepped forward, bowed low to the man lounging on the sofa. He languorously held out one hand. Silhouette knelt, taking his hand in both of hers. "My Lord Joseph," she whispered, kissing his knuckles. "It pleases me to see you again. I apologize for disturbing you."

Joseph stroked her cheek then looked over at Alex. His eyes penetrated Alex's own, his mind sliding up and down with no concern for propriety. Alex stiffened again, but held himself immobile. He left his shields as they were, didn't tighten or relax them. Silhouette had warned him that Joseph would look at him closely and he had anticipated that would mean looking inside and out. "Who's he?" Joseph asked. He sounded tired.

"My Lord, his name is Alex and he's a friend of mine. He needs our help."

Joseph looked disgusted. "A friend? Really, Silhouette, I loved your mother dearly and I love you like a daughter, but why must you constantly act so... human?"

Silhouette sat back on her heels. "My Lord, I can't change my nature."

Joseph laughed. "No, you can't, can you. He needs our help, you say? You may do whatever you wish, dear Silhouette. But why should we help? You'll be lucky to leave here with him alive." He seemed about to dismiss them both.

"Joseph, please. He can earn the right to your counsel."

Joseph laughed, his head rocking back in genuine mirth. "Earn the right? Silhouette, please, you'll get him killed quicker than ever that way."

She smiled sweetly, like a toddler charming her father. "I'm serious. He can do it. And he doesn't care if he fails."

"If he fails he dies."

"I know."

"He knows?"

"Yes. He has a considerable problem and he'll either earn your help or die trying."

Joseph looked over to the man and woman opposite him. "Please, excuse me for a moment." The granite man gestured politely with one hand, a small smile curling his lips. He scanned Alex up and down, nodded almost imperceptibly. Alex was too tense to return the acknowledgment.

"Alex, is it?" Joseph said.

He jumped slightly, realizing he had become the focus of the Clan Lord's attention. "Yes, sir." He inwardly cursed the tremor in his voice. He took a deep breath, the words of his Sifu in his mind. *Trust always in your own skills. Never think another man above you, beyond you. You'll have lost before the fight begins. Should you lose, acknowledge your opponent's abilities and congratulate him, learn from him and beat him next time. Half of every fight is in the mind.* He cleared his throat. "Yes," he said more forcefully. "Alex Caine."

Joseph smiled, one eyebrow creeping up. "Well, Alex Caine, don't you have balls of iron."

"Yes I do."

Joseph laughed, swinging his legs to the floor. He sat forward, elbows on knees. "You must have, tiny human. You really understand what you're offering to engage in here?"

Alex concentrated, determined to maintain his center. "Not exactly, no. But I know that I'll either succeed or die."

"You have to fight, Alex Caine. Can you fight?"

Silhouette winked and nodded encouragingly. Fight? Well, that was one thing he certainly could do with absolute confidence. *Maybe something's finally going my way.* "Oh yes, I can fight. I love to fight. That's pretty much all I do."

"Really? I wonder if you've ever *really* fought, Alex Caine."

"My Lord." Silhouette put one hand on Joseph's forearm. "I saw him defeat two gargoyles, single-handed. He really can fight."

Joseph appeared impressed. "Well, Alex Caine, you might survive to talk further with me. Our disputes are settled in combat. We are great believers in the trial of the warrior. If you fight here and win, you may ask me whatever you wish. If you lose, well, you'll lose. Are you ready?"

Alex drew himself up. "I'm always ready."

Joseph seemed pleased by the turn of events. He turned to the man and woman opposite him. "Shall we?"

"Certainly," the man said. "I'd quite like to see this."

"Really?" Joseph asked. "I thought you'd try to save your fellow human."

The man shook his head. "I think he can save himself."

Joseph turned back to Alex. "Well, well. If Isiah here thinks you can prevail then maybe you really can."

The huge arena Alex was led to had a ceiling rounded in the same vaulted brickwork as the rest of the Den, only much higher. The sprawling rooms, corridors and halls under the Wandsworth house were like a small town underground, and this space was the largest he had seen. Torch-topped stone columns ringed a circular center, open and flat, and an eldritch light emanated from the dome high above, bathing everything. Silhouette crouched before Alex, strapping his hands tightly in boxer's wraps. He had been given a pair of loose cotton trousers. His bare feet were cold against the stone floor, his naked torso cool. The people gathering around, all standing or sitting beyond the columns, were otherworldy creatures, despite their human-like appearance, but he thought of them as just another crowd. This was just another cage. This whole bizarre situation just another bout.

This was his territory, his area of expertise. He did this all the time and today would be no different. The faces around him, smirking and derisive, were irrelevant. He let them fade away, focused on nothing but the space inside the columns. Silhouette finished the wraps and stood. She planted a quick kiss on his cheek and slipped away. He sat alone on the edge of the combat arena. *Every battle has rules,*he remembered. *Some are competition and have many rules, some are to the death and have none but the rules of physics. Always know the rules, know the field of battle, know everything that can be used against you or that you can use against your foe. When the fight begins, nothing exists but you and your opponent, and the space you occupy. Own yourself, own the space and own your opponent. Then own victory.*

There was nothing here but a wide circle of flagstone floor. Silhouette had told him the crowd would push them back into the circle if they got near the edge, a problem he'd try to avoid. No weapons were allowed. Joseph might stop the bout, but only Joseph could. His opponent would certainly be trying to kill him. A simple set of rules. He had tucked the locket holding the shard of the

Darak into the waist of his trousers, winding its cord together with the one that held the waistband tight. He could feel its power swelling through him and he drew on it. Not a weapon, Silhouette had assured him, perfectly permissible. He was as ready as he could be.

Joseph walked into the center, the raised hubbub of voices quickly hushed. Alex became vaguely aware of the granite man, Isiah, and his companion, off to one side. Silhouette sat not far from them and a large chair stood empty next to them, presumably for Joseph. He let the image go. Nothing but the circle of stone floor existed. He stared calmly at his wrapped hands as Joseph spoke.

"A human has come among us this day. Alex Caine. Remember that name, Clan, as it may go down in history. Or it may go down on the menu for dinner tonight." A ripple of laughter, with an undertone of growls, swept through. "There is some speculation," Joseph continued, "that Alex Caine may prevail this day. I, for one, am quite excited to see that. But I will not let him win easily. His opponent, Ataro!" Another murmur spread through the crowd as the giant doorman stepped into the light. He wore nothing but a pair of knee-length shorts, his hands wrapped like Alex's. His dark skin shone. He gripped his fists in front of his chest and flexed, massive muscles bulging as he roared, an animal sound. The crowd cheered.

Alex walked into the middle of the arena, feeling the familiar surge of adrenaline course through his stomach, fire through his skin. He breathed it into his muscles, welcomed it like a favorite drug. *Every man has strengths and weaknesses. Every man can be beaten. And every man can lose. Step up knowing you can win. Find your opponent's weakness and use it to defeat him.*

Ataro stood head and shoulders taller than him, towering with muscles and malice. The insipid disrespect had been replaced with a bloodlust. A primeval urge to kill. He leaned down towards Alex and roared again, his face flexing through a parody of wolf before returning to Ataro's human visage. Alex was calm, prepared. These games were his strength. The big man's shades were all anger and rage. He exuded a desperation to destroy as quickly as possible.

Alex could use that.

He looked into Ataro's snarling features, pinned the man's eyes with his own. "Did you finish your book?" he asked. "Or shall I tell you the end before I kill you?"

Joseph laughed and Ataro roared again. "Oh, I like you," Joseph said. "It's a shame you'll die here."

"Die here!" Ataro snarled.

Alex gave the ghost of a smile. "What are you now, an echo?" he mocked.

Joseph laughed again, shaking his head, bemused. "I think we'd better get this fight started. Step apart."

Alex and Ataro shifted a few paces from each other. Ataro's face twisted in fury, his hands curled into claws, the muscles of his forearms and chest bulged. He opened his mouth wide, his teeth a forest of sharp, black fangs. His shades had colors and shifts Alex couldn't recognise—Kin aspects he supposed. But there were others he knew all too well. Alex stood calm and relaxed, breathing deeply. This was combat, the essence of life. He would fight and prevail. If he lost, nothing would matter, so all that remained was to engage the battle. Ataro was massive, had unknown abilities, magic and shapechanging, at his disposal, but it all boiled down to the same thing. Seek out the weakness, exploit it and win.

Joseph retreated to his chair at the edge of the arena. He raised one hand high then let it drop. "Fight!"

Ataro barrelled forward, charging Alex like a bull. Alex had seen the shades, knew he would do exactly that, and sidestepped, lifting his knee to deliver a heavy turning kick to Ataro's thigh as the man passed. It was the kind of kick that would usually cause a significant amount of damage when landed well. Alex landed it well, but felt a shock arc up his shin. Ataro's leg was like stone. The big man spun, grinning.

When a technique doesn't work, don't concentrate on injury or despair. You've learned something about your opponent. Use that knowledge.

Alex danced back, ignoring the pain, breathing it away. He watched the shades shift around Ataro, read the man's intent. Ataro charged again, swinging one colossal arm to collect Alex. Alex dropped, planted one hand firmly against the stone floor, and swept his leg around at ground level. He connected with the back of Ataro's ankle and swiped the man's feet out from under him. With a grunt, Ataro fell. The crowd howled as Ataro hit the ground, rolled and regained his stance with preternatural speed. Alex barely shifted his weight in time as Ataro swung again, huge dark knuckles cracking into the side of Alex's head just above his left eye.

Pain lanced white hot through Alex's skull as he ducked and turned. He made a space between them, determined not to press his palm to the throbbing hurt. A warm trickle passed under his left ear and he knew Ataro's iron hard knuckles had split the skin just behind his eyebrow. Ataro grinned. "First blood to me, little human."

Alex feinted forward, reading Ataro's shades for timing. Even as the man decided to move, Alex ducked through, driving the heel of his hand up, letting the stone at his waist flood his arm with power. Ataro grabbed air and Alex's palm crunched into the big man's nose. Dark red gouted, spraying Alex. Alex leapt to one side, twisting away as the huge man roared in pain and frustration, his own strike missing. The crowd roared with him.

The combatants kept their distance, circling each other. Ataro wiped scarlet and snot from his mouth with the back of one hand.

"Second blood to me," Alex said. "You breathing okay?"

Ataro's eyes were wide, incredulous, as he flicked the blood away. Confidence to surprise, surprise to concern, concern to fear, fear to defeat. *This* was a rhythm Alex recognised.

Alex circled, reading the shades. He would wait, let Ataro make the next move. Let the man's frustration and anger make him clumsy. The shades shifted and Alex saw something he had never seen before. He read the movement, but didn't know what it meant. It became clear as Ataro crouched, his legs bunched, his muscles stretched and warped. His arms and face lengthened, his hands became claws, his teeth extended to long ivory razors, all in a fraction of a second. A monstrous creature, part wolf, part man, part hideous denizen of nightmares, flew at Alex. So much for surprise to concern.

Alex jumped to the side, twisting in the air to avoid one great, swiping hand. Talons raked four deep lines across his ribs. Hot, searing pain folded through him, forcing him to clamp his elbow and upper arm against his body as he hissed with agony. Ataro landed and sprang instantly, changing direction, moving quicker than Alex could read. A desperate duck and roll saved him meeting Ataro head on, but four more scorching tracks ripped across his back. For a fraction of a second his vision swam, panic threatening.

The fight is not over until you are no longer standing. If you have time to think, "I'm beaten', then you have wasted an opportunity to win. Only the instant exists.

Alex spun as he landed, no longer trying to get away from the marauding creature. He gathered his energy as he turned, whipping one foot up and out in a blur. He let all the power of the Darak shard flow through his body, let it harden his leg like steel.

Ataro ran directly onto Alex's spinning kick, Alex's heel connecting with the side of Ataro's head with a sickening crack. The crowd howled as Ataro staggered sideways, his form morphing insanely between wolf and human.

Alex drove off from his grounded leg, sticking with Ataro as if glued there. He drew the magic up through his arms and hammered a flurry of punches into Ataro's face.

The monumental man whipped one elbow across even as Alex's blows knocked his head stupidly to one side. The elbow caught Alex across the cheekbone; a numb whine of injury sang through his mind, sent him stumbling to the side.

Ataro fell to one knee, hands waving drunkenly. Alex sucked breath in as deep as he could, staying conscious by force of will alone. His vision crossed as he tried to focus on his opponent. He had to move first, had to finish this. The shades around Ataro altered again as the man drew energy from somewhere. Alex drove himself forward with one pumping leg, gathering every last bit of strength he had, and drove his other knee up and out.

As Ataro shifted his feet, trying to stand, Alex slammed his knee up under the man's chin. Ataro's head flipped up, his teeth snapping shut like a bear trap, and he keeled over backwards. Alex went with him, blackness circling in at the edges of his mind like hungry vultures. As Ataro collapsed onto his back Alex landed over him, drawing his elbow back, fist clenched, visualising his knuckles like iron bolts crashing through Ataro's head. The bloodlust overwhelmed him, the urge to kill surged like an orgasm. He felt the book, wrapped up with his clothes, calling out for murder.

"Stop!" Joseph's voice lashed into the room like a whip crack, clear over the roaring crowd and the surging through Alex's head.

Alex ignored him, drove his fist down. His knuckles pounded into Ataro's face and clear through, crushing the big man's head to mince. A shock ran up to Alex's shoulder as his hand cracked into the stone beneath. The behemoth bucked once beneath him and lay still. The crowd fell silent.

The Clan Lord strode in as Alex struggled for breath, shadows chasing each other at the peripheries of his vision. "It's over!" Joseph yelled. He looked at the corpse running red across the flagstones. "You should have stopped when I called it," he said, quietly so only Alex could hear.

"You said to the death," Alex whispered. He felt exhilaration from the kill, but shame overwhelmed it. The influence of the book had driven him on when he had heard Joseph call a stop to it. No true warrior acted that way.

Joseph made a strange sound, part amusement, part annoyance. He turned slowly, addressing the room. "Alex Caine, the human with balls of iron, has won," he said. A susurration of muttering and chatter swelled in the high chamber.

Alex staggered up, backing away from Ataro's supine form. Joseph had one eyebrow raised. Isiah nodded softly, though his face appeared troubled. Silhouette clapped excitedly, grinning. He let blackness take him.

ELEVEN

Sounds stretched and folded over each in thick darkness. One resolved into a female voice. It sang to him, a song of triumph. Noise melted and folded again and the voice became clearer. "Drink this, you fuckwit."

Alex's eyelids flickered. He felt pressure at the back of his head and something cold pressed against his lips. He gave in to the reflex to swallow and tasted a familiar tingling sweet bitterness. Silhouette's healing potion. He tried to open his eyes again.

"Give it a minute, Iron Balls."

He collapsed back, taking deep breaths, and let the bittersweet tingle travel into his chest. Almost immediately some strength and sensation returned. His heart hammered a couple of extra beats and settled.

"I only gave you a tiny amount this time, considering you're such a lightweight for the stuff."

Alex opened his eyes. Silhouette's face floated over him, her hair hanging down, almost touching him. A wash of relief and ecstasy poured through him. He'd won the fight. He reached a hand up and pulled Silhouette's head down, pushing her lips against his, taking a long, passionate kiss. She kissed him back for a couple of seconds before moving back angrily. "I've killed men for *far* less than that!"

Alex grinned, closed his eyes again. A dark shadow of shame flitted through his mind with the image of Ataro's mangled head. What had he become? Never before would he have let a bloodlust overwhelm him like that. He had been fighting for his life, Ataro had been trying to kill him, but he had the big Kin beaten and Joseph called a stop. Alex considered himself a true warrior, an exponent not only of fighting, but of the essence of the martial arts. That included honor. There had been no honor in what he'd done.

He let his body soak up its renewed energy and slowly raised himself to a sitting position. He was on a sofa in Joseph's quarters. Silhouette stood beside him, arms folded tightly across her chest, face set in a furious scowl. Joseph, Isiah and his companion sat across the room in armchairs, all looking quite amused.

Joseph leaned forward. "So. You really are quite the fighter."

Alex gave Silhouette an apologetic smile. She huffed and turned away. "Thanks," he said to Joseph. "I'm very sorry, I should have stopped."

"I told you to fight to the death. I understand the nature of bloodlust and the heat of battle." Joseph nodded to his side. "Isiah and Petra here are both very accomplished fighters. They're also rather impressed with you."

Petra smiled, nodding. Isiah's expression was unreadable. "You're pretty undisciplined," he said softly. "But you have remarkable potential."

Alex frowned. "Undisciplined?"

"Yes."

It seemed Isiah's opinion was not open for discussion. Something about the man made Alex's teeth itch. He had a presence, a barely contained authority. There was no doubt the man was every inch the warrior, every atom of his being attuned to battle. The shades around both him and Petra were excellently constructed masks, impenetrable. "Perhaps you can teach me some discipline sometime?" Alex said.

Isiah smiled. "Good. Perhaps I can."

"If we've finished the love-in," Joseph said, "perhaps we can conclude any outstanding business."

Silhouette sat on the arm of Alex's sofa, clearly still annoyed, though her eyes had softened. "You feeling okay?" she asked.

Alex felt as if he'd been hit by a train. Twice. But he was alive and fundamentally unbroken. That made him pretty okay. "I'm fine, thanks." He turned to Joseph. "So you think you can give me some answers?"

Joseph shrugged. "You've earned respect here, which means a civil tongue and none of this Clan will hunt you. I agreed to talk some more, but that's all."

Alex's clothes were piled by his feet. He retrieved the Darak Uthentia from his jacket, held it up. "I'm stuck with this. I can't get rid of it or destroy it and it... affects me in ways I don't like. I want to be rid of it." The book's presence swelled out. Alex was shocked, realizing it had been concealing itself from the others all along.

Joseph's eyebrows shot up as he scooted back in his seat. "Kid, you're fucked. If I'd have known you had that I wouldn't have let you fight here."

Alex sat dismayed, shocked by the fear he saw in Joseph's eyes. "What?"

"Where did you get that?"

"A man had it and another man asked me to read it. When I did it seemed to lock onto me. What is it?"

"What were you told?"

"Some kind of history of a Fey king and a stone of power. It's called the Darak Uthentia. Apparently Uthent—"

"I know who Uthentia is, child." Joseph seemed both angered and amused. "Put it away. You have no idea what you're into."

Alex slumped back on the sofa, dropped the book into his lap. "I know. That's why I need your help."

"Put it away," Joseph said again. "I can't help you. I don't think anyone can."

Silhouette put a hand on Alex's shoulder. "Can you at least tell us what all this is, maybe help him find a way out?"

"Why do you insist on getting wrapped up in the mundane affairs of humans, Silhouette?" Joseph asked with a pained expression. He looked quickly at Isiah and Petra. "No offense!"

Isiah inclined his head. "None taken."

"It's my weakness," Silhouette said icily. "Indulge us?"

Joseph sighed. "Silhouette, you know exactly what Uthentia is."

"I know, but I can't explain this. My Kin history is a little patchy. I don't really know what Alex is caught up in."

Joseph rubbed his palms together. "All right. I'll tell you, and then you'll leave. Both of you. I don't want that kind of chaos in this Den."

"That's fine. Thank you," Alex said, grateful for anything he could learn. Knowledge was power. Whatever Joseph could tell him must help in some way.

Joseph pursed his lips, gathering his thoughts for several moments. Eventually, "Firstly, Uthentia is not a Fey king. That's a poor translation. It's more like a Fey god, but even that isn't a very accurate description."

"It's no god I've ever heard of," Isiah said. "And gods are my business."

Joseph nodded. "Exactly. Uthentia is *like* a god, but it doesn't need any faithful or any worship. It just is. It's an eternal creature of pure chaos, utter anarchy. It's older than the *idea* of gods. Millennia ago it strode the realms and the Fey Folk rejoiced in its mayhem and played along with it. Between them, Uthentia and the Fey were destroying this realm. For sport.

"Every thin day, the Fey can cross from The Other Lands into this world. Every time they do, they bring a little chaos and death with them. Forget your fairy stories, Alex, the Fey are evil in the purest sense. We're Kin, we have Fey blood in our veins. That's what makes us what we are, but we have human blood too. The tiniest drop of humanity in our bodies ties us to this realm. We're stuck here, we have power, we feed on people, we're the monsters, but we're nothing compared to true Fey. And the Fey are disgusted by us as much as they are by humans, even though they made us. So we're every bit as vulnerable to their whims as you are, even if we are more able to defend ourselves."

Joseph sat back. "The point is, the Fey and Uthentia were taking too much of a liking to the idea of shattering this world and we were as threatened as the humans and everything else here. So a long time ago, before anything you'd call history, a group of powerful Kin, known as the Eld, came up with a plan, and found a way to weaken Uthentia enough to banish him from here, trap him *between* realms where his power was irrelevant.

"The trap worked *almost* perfectly, but it destroyed the Eld and a tiny thread of Uthentia's consciousness slipped back through. The whole episode was considered a success and that tiny piece of chaos was thought a small price to pay. To anchor itself in this world it bound itself to things and those things became indestructible and dangerous. For a long time now, hundreds of years, it's been a book." He pointed at Alex's jacket. "That book. It occasionally ensnares a human or a Kin, plays with them until they die and moves on. This time, young Alex Caine, that's you."

Alex sat and stared. "So this book...? It's a piece of this god?"

"Not a god," Joseph said. "*Like* a god, powerful like a god, but pure chaos. Pure evil. Only so diluted now it's no real threat to the world any more. Of course, that doesn't make it any less deadly to you. And perhaps you could become a threat to the world. Many dangerous and destructive people through history have actually been driven by that book or a previous incarnation of it."

"So how do I get rid of it?"

"You can't. Eventually it'll kill you, after it's caused as much damage as it can, and then move on to someone else. The Eld did an amazing job really, reducing the power of Uthentia to that."

"Oh, well that's good then!" Alex rubbed his eyes with the heels of his hands. "I thought the book was special, that it could only be read by someone with a powerful vision. Welby told me..."

"Welby?" Joseph laughed. "Is that where this all leads back to? That whelp?"

"Welby is the one who roped Alex in," Silhouette said. "He was aware of the grimoire, but couldn't read it. He discovered that Alex could, but by then I think it was already too late."

Joseph gestured dismissively, his face resigned. "Of course it was. The book always tacks itself onto someone with power, someone who can wreak as much havoc as possible before they're overwhelmed. Welby, for all his studies, certainly isn't powerful enough. But there are plenty of people who are. Welby really has no idea of the world he dabbles in."

Silhouette made a noise of understanding. "Welby's dead," she said. "So's the man who originally had the book, although it was Alex who killed him."

Joseph laughed. "You see! This is what it does. It led you here indirectly and if you'd died in the arena one of us would have got stuck with it. Look on the bright side, Alex. You're one in a long, long line of poor suckers paying the debt incurred by the Eld to save the world."

Alex dragged a hand over his short, dark hair. "What about the stone? The Darak?"

"There are many items of power." Joseph pulled a leather cord from around his neck, exposing a smoky gem that writhed in magesign. "This is one. There are many others. Most Clan Lords have something like this."

"A dragon's tooth, for example," Petra said quietly.

Joseph grunted. "Absolutely, but good luck finding one of those." Petra smiled. Joseph narrowed his eyes for a moment before turning back to Alex. "The Darak amplifies a person's natural abilities. Items like that tend to bind with people, become a part of them. No one could take this without killing me." He dropped his gem back into his shirt. "When the Eld were trying to find a way to banish Uthentia they fashioned the Darak, reputedly the most powerful arcane item ever made. The story goes that when the Eld sprang their trap the magic that caught Uthentia and killed the Eld also shattered the Darak."

The stone burned in its locket against Alex's waist. "So what happened to it?"

Joseph shrugged. "The Kin leaders were left to clean up the mess and decided the Darak, even broken, was too dangerous a thing to be ignored. The item which had given the Eld power to banish Uthentia could potentially free him too. Three guardians were selected, one for each shard. They hid their piece then committed suicide, so the hiding places would never be known."

Alex felt a thread of hope and dread. If he could find the other parts of the Darak, he could have incredible power. Maybe enough to rid himself of the book. But if it could free Uthentia... Was destroying the world the only way to be free? And what kind of freedom was that?

The book cajoled him. It had fuelled his violent and remorseless slaying of Peacock, his bloodlust against Ataro. What could it make him do if he had the strength of the full Darak?

He pulled the locket from his waistband, held it up. "This is one shard."

Joseph's eyes widened as he, Isiah and Petra all sat forward in their seats, entranced. "What?"

Alex popped open the locket. Magesign burst into the room, snaked through the air, feeling its way around the people gathered. Joseph, Isiah and Petra released magesign of their own as they looked, feeling around it, inside it with their magic. Alex pulled his protections down and closed the locket, threatened and overwhelmed by the energy of these three. "Hey! Back the fuck off!"

They pulled their power away. Isiah and Petra both made apologetic eyes at him. Joseph whistled through his teeth. "No wonder you smashed Ataro like you did. That thing makes my gem look like a sideshow trinket. Where did you get it?"

"Welby. I took it from his corpse."

"Well, that explains Welby's strangely unbalanced abilities and knowledge. And even with that the book didn't want him. It obviously waited for someone with more potential."

Alex shook his head. "How can that be me?"

"You're more than you think," Joseph said. "No one has ever beaten Ataro before. No Clan member here would even dream of trying. That a human slew him is causing quite a stir. Now I understand how you did it. Your natural ability and that stone? A serious combination."

Alex hung the locket back around his neck. "So this is part of the Darak?"

Joseph raised his hands. "I don't know. But it's about the most powerful single thing I've ever seen. So yeah, I reckon it might be. You're going to be dangerous until that book kills you."

"I'm not going to let it. I'm going to beat it."

"What an admirable position to take. You should commune more closely with that little rock, meditate with it, let it in to become a true part of you. You've barely tapped into it yet. But regardless, the book will kill you."

"If I find the other two parts," Alex said, "will the stone be whole again? Or just three powerful pieces?"

"The legends suggest that if the three were physically put back together they would rebind into one. If you did somehow manage to find and repair it you would have remarkable power. But you would still be a slave to the shred of Uthentia bound into that volume. And Uthentia might cause untold damage with you before you're dead."

Alex drew a deep breath. "Or perhaps I would have enough strength to be rid of it."

Joseph's laugh was derisive. "The Eld were the most prevailing Kin of their age, working together to banish Uthentia, and the act destroyed them and the Darak and still didn't quite finish the job. Even with the whole stone, you're more than arrogant to think you could finish what they couldn't."

Alex refused to be intimidated. "Even so, I plan to try."

"Your prerogative. Your balls truly are pure cast iron, I'll give you that."

Isiah leaned forward again, his face serious. "Alex, if you become too powerful, and are controlled by this Uthentia as Joseph suggests, you could be a liability to the world."

"So?" Alex wanted control back.

"So? So there are people and agencies that would stop you. Forcefully."

"Like you?"

Isiah smiled. "No. This whole thing is a little outside my jurisdiction. But someone would."

Alex frowned. "Shame there aren't any *agencies* out there that would think to help me."

"Perhaps there are," Petra said.

Isiah looked sharply at her. "Petra?"

She returned his look icily. He laughed and shrugged. "I'm busy right now." She indicated Isiah. "*We're* busy. But I'll ask my people to assist you. We have unrivalled resources for research. Perhaps we can help you track down the pieces of the stone."

Joseph sat up. "Wait a minute! You can't help him."

Petra gave the Clan Lord a withering look. "We have to give him every chance to escape this."

"It can't be done!"

Petra shook her head. "If we thought that way, we'd never help anyone. People would never have achieved anything. He deserves the chance to save himself. If we stand for anything, it's compassion and learning. By helping him we could learn a lot about this thing that has tainted the world for so long. Perhaps finding the pieces will give him what he needs."

Isiah looked exasperated. "To do what?"

"That's up to him. It might kill him, it might cause chaos, it might mean he needs to be stopped or even killed. But right now he's a young man, scared and in trouble. We should help him. He might find a way out, and we stand to learn a lot."

Isiah shook his head and squeezed Petra's hand. "Your biggest flaw is also your greatest strength. Your compassion will be the end of us all one day!"

She laughed. "Screw you."

Joseph slumped back in his chair. "I'm amazed that shard has shown up," he said. "If it actually is part of the Darak. The chances of him ever uncovering the other pieces are less than slim."

"There you go then," Petra said. "No harm in offering him a bit of hope."

Alex felt like a tiny child in a room full of adults, discussing things he had no hope of understanding. These people seemed to think it some kind of game. A potentially dangerous game, but one they considered entertaining more than threatening. "I want to try," he said, the sentiment sounding lame even to his own ears.

"Of course," Petra said with a smile. "Free will is the single most important thing we are bound to protect. It may create a mess that we or others might have to clean up later, but right now it's your decision. All I ask is that you share everything you can with us."

Joseph stood decisively. "Right. Enough. Alex, get dressed. Take your book and your stone and leave my home. You've been given ample courtesy and I want those things gone before they cause any more havoc. Silhouette, you are always welcome here, this is your Den. But not with him."

Silhouette nodded. "Thank you, Joseph."

Alex stood, discarded the light cotton trousers and pulled his own clothes on. "Yes, thank you. Really, I appreciate it more than you could imagine."

Joseph laughed, though there was no humor in it. "Whatever. You're a remarkable human, but you're doomed. It's very sad, but there you go." He leaned close to Silhouette and whispered in her ear. She looked at the floor, nodded once. Joseph turned to Isiah and Petra. "Shall we?"

Isiah and Petra stood, following Joseph across the room as Alex and Silhouette headed for the door. "I'll send someone to talk to you," Petra called out. "They'll find you shortly."

"How will they find me? Even I don't know where I'm going."

"They'll find you, if you let them. Be open."

Alex frowned, confused. "Thank you." As he opened the door Isiah called his name. He looked back. "Yes?"

"Have you read it?"

"What?"

"The book you have. Or that has you, more accurately. Have you read it?"

In all the mayhem, that hadn't occurred to him, which suddenly seemed very strange. "Actually, no. I've just been trying to get rid of it."

Isiah smiled. "Know your enemy, Alex."

They left the room. As Alex and Silhouette walked through the Den, the eyes of the Kin burning into them with mixed fascination and hatred, Alex asked, "What did Joseph say to you then, right before we left?"

Silhouette looked sour. "He was just reminding me that I'm Kin."

The Subcontractor lurked outside the big house in Wandsworth for several hours, hidden. He watched a few Kin come and go and wondered what his quarry were up to. And why Hood had such an interest in them. But he knew better than to try to infiltrate a Den. Even he had limits. It was a long time before they finally emerged and he saw them for the first time. The man was young, tall, well-built without being bulky. He moved like a well-trained athlete. He had short hair, jeans, a dark green army surplus jacket with big pockets and black cross-trainers on his feet. All very practical. The female was lovely and lithe, oozing sexuality. She dressed for action too, short lace-up boots and jeans, a small leather jacket over a tight T-shirt that accentuated her curves. What was she doing with a human?

The Subcontractor stayed hidden, taking deep draughts of their physical and psychic scents, locking them in for future tracking. The day had waned and the pair looked tired. He followed them to a hotel not far from the Den. They checked in and disappeared up into the building.

The Subcontractor slipped away to report back to Hood.

TWELVE

Alex sat on the edge of the bed and stared at the root of all his woes. The title, which he now understood, meant nothing. Just the names of two problems that had hooked themselves into him and wouldn't let go. As Alex stared the words slipped and slid on the old leather cover. He could feel the personality of the book in his hands, its mirth. He let his vision open, deciphered the new configuration of arcane symbols.

Uthentia's Legacy.

He made a noise of annoyance. Silhouette hopped onto the bed, slipped her legs around him from behind and looked over his shoulder. "What is it?"

"This thing is playing with me."

"Really?"

"The title just changed. Uthentia's Legacy." He felt a surge of excitement at Silhouette's sudden closeness.

She rested her chin. "It's evil."

Alex dropped the book on the bed beside him. "I know that now. And I'm trapped with it. Aren't you scared?"

"No, not really. No offense, but it's stuck to *you*. I don't think it can or will be any threat to me while you're still alive."

"So you're enjoying watching me suffer then?" His tone was angry.

"Hey, fuck you! I'm the one who's been kind to you. Been *helping* you." She stiffened, hurt.

He reached up one hand to her cheek, desperate not to scare away the only thing left in his life he could consider good. He wouldn't help himself by letting his anger out at her. "I'm sorry." She relaxed, resting her chin again. "I'm sorry, Sil. I'm just scared."

"I know."

"Why *are* you helping me?"

"I like you."

"Why?"

Silhouette sighed. "My people don't understand me, but I like humans. I find you all so fascinating and clever and funny and intriguing. The Kin have grown to see you lot as nothing but sport and food. They resent your numbers, always forcing them to live in the shadows. But I've never understood that. Humans are amazing."

Alex laughed. "You're very charitable."

"And people like you, the ones with power, are a lot more like Kin than most of my kind would admit."

"But you still feed on us." Alex stared at his hands, trying to figure out how he felt about Silhouette. She was alluring, incredible, but a monster.

"We do, but we don't have to all the time. Not like you need food. I try to only feed on bad people. And only when I really have to. We can go a long time without feeding. And we can subsist on other things in the meantime."

"Like what?"

"A nice rare steak. Nothing compares to human flesh and blood, but we don't have to gorge like you lot three times a day."

Alex shook his head. Could he really accept her eating habits?

"Is it really so different to eating any other animal?" she asked, as if reading his mind. "Humans are animal. Flesh is flesh. I can't help what I am."

There was a simple, undeniable logic to her statement. "I suppose so," Alex said quietly. "Besides, right now I really need a friend and, like you said, you're the only one being nice to me. But I still don't really understand why."

She sighed. "My mother was human."

"Really?"

"Like Joseph said, Kin have Fey blood. But we've all got human blood too, and that ties us to this realm. Over centuries, millennia, the Kin have grown into themselves. Most Kin are Kin born; two Kin fuck and a little Kin comes along. But once in a while a Fey son of a bitch rapes a human and makes a brand new Kin. That's how come I'm here."

Alex frowned. "So you're a first generation Kin?"

"Exactly. Rare among my own kind. And I grew up with a human mother. I didn't even know I was Kin until I hit puberty and all this weird shit started happening. Weirder than regular puberty anyway."

"How did you cope?"

"Joseph. He found me one night, figured me out. He liked me and took me under his wing. For all his talk of hating humans, he's been close to a few in his time, including my mother. But, you know, he has a reputation to protect." She smiled, lost in reverie. "He showed us into his Den and took care of us. Of course, my mother grew old and died a long time ago, but I guess I've always been closer to humans than most Kin because of her. And for that, the majority of Kin hate me."

"You lot are some fucked up individuals."

She laughed. "You think?"

Alex tried to imagine the implications. Sil's history made fairy tales sound dull. But she was right—she couldn't help what she was.

"What about you?" she asked.

"What?"

"Well, while we're getting all deep and meaningful, what's your story? What made you?"

Alex felt the old hurt turn its knife in his guts. "I don't like to talk about it."

Sil wrapped him in her arms. "Wow, you really have some pain inside." She kissed his neck. "You can tell me."

Alex sighed. "My parents were killed by a drug-fucked psycho who ploughed them down in the street in a stolen car. He was running from the police and they were just leaving the cinema." Alex took a shuddering breath, emotion flooding up. "Wiped out in an instant. I was home with a babysitter when the police came to the house."

Sil squeezed him tighter. "Shit."

Now he was talking, the floodgates were open. He wanted to tell her everything, though didn't know why. "I was only six. The police had no idea I was awake, listening from my room, so I got all the gory details I wasn't supposed to hear. That fucking junkie took everything from me. I went from one foster home to another and I fought everyone. I was angry, belligerent, mean. I was an arsehole. Then I found my Sifu and something I could direct my anger into. He taught me ways to control and channel my hurt. It helps."

Silhouette rested her head against his. "And you've been fighting ever since, huh?"

"I guess so."

She kissed him again. "I'm sorry."

"Me too." The pain burned deep in his gut.

They sat in silence for some time. Eventually Silhouette relaxed her hold on him. "So, you gonna read that book?"

Alex sucked in a breath, picked up the grimoire. He thumbed through, letting the dense arcane script flitter by in a blur. *Know your enemy*, Isiah had said. There was wisdom in that. *Never pass up an opportunity to learn about your opponent. No information, however seemingly insignificant, is ever useless.*

He turned to the front and looked at the first page. The characters swam in magesign, blurring and shifting. He concentrated, letting his eyes and mind penetrate beyond the physical text, looked deep. Like reading the intent in a person's shades, he gleaned the meaning from the eldritch letters. It seemed different to the passage he had read in Peacock's shop. The words swelled in his consciousness, *The mind of a power beyond this universe swims and sings above and outside you, within and beneath this. Your life is wrapped in the fronds of a creation palm, older than life and bigger than intellect, playing, dancing, singing, ecstasy.*

Alex looked up with a sound of discomfort. "Fuck me."

Silhouette slipped her arms around his waist. "What is it?"

"It's like reading madness."

"What does it say?"

He shook his head. "I'm not entirely sure." He looked again, picking his way through the shifting lettering, *Power is universe alive and allowed, power is always outside the grasp and underneath the mind. Power is yours when power is taken. Your desire will lead you to power, and power in the universe is yours.*

Silhouette ran the back of one finger across his brow, smoothing out the frown. "You okay?"

Alex closed the book. "I can feel some meaning. I *think* it's talking to me. It's not like a normal book, that's written and can be read. I think it's communicating directly with me, in a kind of bookish way." He made a wry face, apologetic that he couldn't explain it better.

"And what's it saying?"

"I think it's telling me to pursue this stone. That I should try to get it."

Silhouette stroked his brow again. "I hear a but in there somewhere."

Alex barked a humorless laugh. "But. But it seems to think that the power of the stone will be for me. I can't help but think that means just for it. How can I trust anything this thing tells me?"

"You can't. It'll play with you and tease you, it'll try to get you to do awful things and try to engineer some kind of destructive and spectacular death for you when it's ready to move on. That's what I got from what Joseph told us. But you have to try to resist the urges it puts on you and take the reins for yourself. I think you have a chance with this."

"What kind of a chance do I have? I'm a fucking ant in the cosmos! In the last few days I've discovered there are vampires that aren't really vampires, gargoyles attacked me and I had to fight a shapeshifter. I'm a fighter. I fight for money. I fight *humans* for money and that's that. How can I fight this?"

Silhouette slipped around him, sitting on his lap, her legs locked behind. She took his face in her hands. "I was damned impressed with the way you fought Ataro." Her eyes smouldered. "The others are right when they talk about your potential. You're a very impressive human. Your vision is just the start of your abilities. I think you have it in you to face this."

"What if I don't?"

She pulled one hand away and slapped him across the cheek, hard enough to shock him. "Then you die, Iron Balls. But so what? You don't fight, this thing will drive you mad and kill you. If you do, you might die, but at least you'll die fighting. Those are your options."

He stared into her icy blue eyes. She was right. He had very few choices. It really did boil down to give up or brawl. And he didn't have it in his nature to give up on anything. If he had to fight he needed all the weapons at his disposal, every advantage he could find. The tiny shard of stone around his neck drenched him with a kind of power he wouldn't have believed a week ago. If he could find the rest surely there was nothing he couldn't do. The battle didn't end until you were out cold on the floor.

"So I guess we just have to wait until Petra's people contact me," he said. "See what clues they can give me and start trying to find a way out of this."

She smiled at him. "I guess so."

He threw the book across the room, far away from the bed. "So, what shall we do while we wait?"

She leaned back, that half-smile pulling at her lips, starting a fire in his groin. "Well, I don't know. What shall we do?"

Alex put a hand behind her head and pulled her to him. She came willingly and they kissed, hard and urgent.

Ms Sparks did nothing to hide her anger, knuckles white around the cell phone. "What do you mean, Butler's dead? How?"

The voice on the other end trembled. "Well, pretty much ripped to pieces, ma'am. Him and his whole crew."

"By whom?" Sparks demanded. "And why?"

"They must have found something too big for them to handle, ma'am. Beyond that, I have no idea."

Sparks revelled in the man's fear, as much terrified by reporting to *her* as he was by what he had seen. But it was small consolation. Her initiative in sending crews to all of Peacock's known associates had almost paid off, obviously, but she'd ended up with less than nothing, a crew dead. Whoever killed the bookseller seemed more dangerous than she had suspected. She would have to think carefully about whether or not she told Hood. While he appreciated her proactive approach most of the time, it's what made her such a valued PA, when things went badly he was... less than appreciative, and enthusiastic about laying blame.

"Search the place for any clues, however small," she snapped down the phone. "Then get back here without delay!"

"Yes, ma'am."

She hung up and took a moment to compose herself, then pushed open one side of a garishly carved dark wood double door.

Mr Hood, behind an enormous mahogany desk in an ostentatiously decorated office, acknowledged her. Glass cabinets stood around the room containing all manner of arcana, crystal balls and ancient scrolls, leatherbound books and shrunken heads, strange coins and yellowing bones. A larger than lifesize painting of the man himself hung behind the desk, dominating the room with a condescending smile. Hood, wearing the same expression, reclined in a huge wing-backed chair. The Subcontractor occupied one of two leather chairs opposite. Ms Sparks perched on one end of the desk, legs crossed, and began filing her nails, her long, straight hair half hiding her face.

"You found them?" Hood asked.

The Subcontractor smiled, a baring of teeth with nothing friendly about it. "Of course. They're quite an interesting pair."

Sparks breathed a soft sigh of relief. No need to report her failure.

"A pair?" Hood said.

"Yes. A human male and a female Kin."

Hood raised his eyebrows, stroking one finger along his livery lips. "Really? And which of them killed Peacock?"

"The human."

"Ah."

They sat in silence for a while. Hood liked to make himself seem as important as possible, but the Subcontractor seemed to have no interest in such games. He waited for Hood to ask more.

Eventually Hood spoke. "So, why do you think they killed Peacock?"

The Subcontractor shrugged. "Impossible to say. I didn't know the man and have no idea what they might have argued about. Maybe for sport. The human is colluding with Kin, after all, and they don't need an excuse to kill."

"You don't sympathise with that kind?" Hood asked, a smile tugging at his lips.

The Subcontractor sighed. "I'm not one of them, so don't try to lump me with those freaks. Stop fishing. We have an understanding and I'd hate to have to stop working for you. You pay well."

"No one walks away from me."

The Subcontractor stood, turned to leave. "You're far from my only source of income." He started towards the door.

"Sit down, sit down. No need to be so touchy."

He turned back to Hood, eyes narrowed. "What do you want?"

Hood smiled. "Postulate, if you will. Any ideas why this strange pair might have killed Peacock?"

The Subcontractor sat back down, his hatred of Hood barely concealed. "Peacock specialised in arcane texts. Perhaps a disagreement over one of those. The human shields himself, but he's not practiced at it. He can't cover the fact that he's carrying a couple of pretty powerful items. No idea what they are, but he's sweating 'sign from every pore."

Hood leaned back, a lascivious expression sliding across his face. "Ah! Well then. Perhaps you're onto something."

"And?"

"And? My dear Subcontractor, as if you need to ask. I want whatever it is this human has."

"You're want me to *retrieve* things now?" His tone dripped with distaste.

"Yes. Kill them both and bring me whatever they're carrying."

"Right. Pay me for the tracking first."

Hood opened a drawer and pulled out a thick wad of notes. He slid them across the desk with one thin, pasty hand. "Here you are, my good man. Worth every penny, as always. Usual rates for this next part of the job."

Shaking his head, the Subcontractor took the money and slipped it into a deep pocket in his long, dark coat. "One of them is Kin remember."

Hood wearily inclined his head. "Naturally. But remember, I do not pay for failure."

The Subcontractor nodded and left.

Hood sucked a long, deep breath in through his nose. "Ms Sparks, get Jackson to put a bird on him. Just to keep an eye on things."

Sparks hopped off the desk and walked around next to Hood. She bent over, reaching for the phone on the far side of the enormous desktop, smiling over her shoulder at him. "Of course, Mr Hood." She pressed a button and listened at the receiver for a moment as Hood stared at her arse through the tight fabric of her skirt. "Jackson?" she said after a moment. "A bird on the Subcontractor, if you will. Have it report back to us every hour."

She hung up and turned back to Hood. He sat, leaning his chair back, his cock hard in his hand. "Excellent work, Ms Sparks."

With a smile, Sparks dropped to her knees.

On the roof of the Black Diamond tower, Jackson limped towards a wood and chicken-wire coop. His beauties chittered and squawked, became animated as he approached. He pulled open the door and stepped inside, instantly mobbed by his leathery charges, like ravens without feathers. Their drawn heads, shining eyes and clacking beaks shivered all around him as he stroked them, cajoled them, cooed to them like they were children. Their black, bat-like wings flapped and scuffed. "Ah, pretties," Jackson said, his voice like gravel in a tin can. "Who's it gonna be then, eh? Who wants to fly for daddy?"

The activity redoubled, a frantic cloud of skin, beaks and claws. Jackson held up a fist and several of the nightmare creatures battled to alight. Finally one caught a grip, black claws digging through the skin of the old man's knuckles. He hissed in pleasured pain.

Outside the coop Jackson whispered to the bird, gave it names and descriptions, pressed an old, wrinkled forehead to the bird's tiny skull stretched with taut dark skin, and thought images into its frantic brain. He threw his hand up into the air and the bird swooped and dipped once and disappeared over the edge of the roof, barrelling towards the busy streets.

Far below, the Subcontractor paused, sniffing the air as he

stood on the pavement outside Hood's building. He caught the dusty, parchment scent of one of Jackson's planesbirds and rolled his eyes. Hood and his paranoia. No matter. Let the thing follow and report, it bothered him not a jot. He flagged a passing cab and climbed in. The planesbird would earn its meat tonight. He gave the driver the address of the hotel. "Drive fast," he said, smirking up at the cab roof, smelling the bird circling high above.

THIRTEEN

Alex rolled over, pinning the sweating Silhouette beneath him, gasping as he moved with her. Her eyes darkened as she slammed two hands against his chest, nails digging deep into his skin. His blood roared in his ears, his pulse pounding against his forebrain like a punch against a jaw. Silhouette arched up on the bed, breathless, heading for climax. Alex went with her, driving down against her, stroke after stroke, the shudder of orgasm rippling through every nerve in his body. He let out a primal cry as he came and felt sharp heat across his cheek as claws raked his face. Snarling, he looked down at his hands wrapped around Silhouette's throat, her face half animal, a canine snout, bared teeth, her eyes furious yellow slits. He felt his pulse surge and squeezed tighter and she bucked up, growling deep in her chest. She sent one leg out from under them, using the mattress to bounce them both off center.

As they rolled she hit him again, her face morphing back into the beauty he recognised. "That's enough, Alex!" She twisted, struck out against his chest, sent him flying into the wall six feet away. He hit the ground, rolling instantly into a low crouch, thinking only of finishing the act, killing what he'd fucked.

"Alex, snap out of it!" She rolled onto all fours, her whole body shifting into something feline, half lovely, half terrifying. She roared in his face.

Alex staggered back from her beast ferocity and sat down hard against the wall, sucking in breath. He put his hands against her broad, deeply furred chest as she slipped back into human form. "What the fuck?" he gasped. "Silhouette, I'm sorry."

She sat back, naked and gorgeous, and laughed. "Well, I like it rough sometimes, Alex, but that's mental."

He shook his head, staring at the carpet. "What the hell?"

"The book, you idiot. You have to learn to resist the influence. It wants you to kill and maim and desecrate. You have to resist it."

Alex felt his control spiralling away again. Cold-blooded murder, slaying in a controlled bout, violent sex. These things were not in his nature. "I don't think I can."

"Of course you can. You just did. With my help." She leaned forward, that half-smile again. "Come on, be honest. That was pretty hot!"

He was ready to shout and rant, but her eyes mesmerised him. Against his better judgement he laughed. "Just as well you're as strong as you are," he said.

"Exactly. I can handle you, Iron Balls. In fact, I think I'm going to enjoy handling you. You're more like Kin than you realize."

"I don't know if that's a compliment or an insult."

"Take it any way you like. I reckon we should do a lot more of that," she nodded towards the bed, "to see if we can't help you learn to command those urges."

"You are one messed up chick."

"I know."

A knock at the door made them both jump. Alex raised an eyebrow at Silhouette, who shrugged. "Who is it?" he called out.

"Petra sent me." A female voice, heavy accent of some kind.

"Oh, right. Just a minute."

They dressed quickly and straightened the bed, doing their best to conceal the shredded linen. Silhouette wet a towel and dabbed the thin lines of blood her claws had left on his cheek. Alex went to the door. Through the peephole he saw a small, completely bald woman, young and vibrant looking, her skin so black it shone with an almost blue sheen. She smiled, wriggling her fingers at the peephole in a friendly wave. He opened the door. "How did you find me?"

"Your mind-print. Petra passed it to me. You're surprisingly easy to track down, especially when you…" She stopped, smiling slightly.

"When I what?"

She seemed embarrassed. "When you let your guard down, you know. When you're lost in… something else."

Alex felt his cheeks burning. "Oh, shit. Right. Er… sorry about that."

"No need to apologize. I'm Meera."

Alex shook the offered hand. "Alex. This is Silhouette."

Meera and Sil nodded to each other.

"Please, come in." Alex stepped away from the door.

Meera came into the room, shut the door behind her. She handed Alex a piece of folded paper. "I'm afraid our records don't have much information readily available, but there are a couple of snippets. I've jotted down the key points. I'll keep looking and our archive keepers are still searching. There is one location you should investigate. It's off the coast of Canada, a very remote island, supposedly uninhabited. We don't know any more at this stage."

"How did you get this information?" Silhouette asked.

"We're specialists," Meera replied, with no small amount of pride. "If it's written, we'll find it. There's a fragment of a tale, an enduring piece of folklore, about a dark Kin tracking another, trying to prevent him from completing an important task. The dark Kin was killed and the other, if he's who we think he was, killed himself after completing his mission. How did the story survive? We don't really know, but it did. It's written, it's recorded, it's ours."

Alex unfolded the paper. Co-ordinates, sketched maps, some place names. And a dense account of the story Meera had told, with a few extra names and details. He looked up from the page. "Who are you people?"

"We are the Umbra Magi, the Shadow Mages."

"And why are you helping me?"

"We seek knowledge. By helping others, we learn more. The more we learn, the more knowledge is preserved."

Alex held up the paper. "I can't tell you how grateful I am."

"Just promise you'll share with us anything you find. We'll keep digging." She stepped forward, placed her palm on his forehead. He felt a surge of energy, something sank into place in his mind and gut. "Can you feel me now?" Meera asked.

"Yes."

"Then you can call on me when you need me. And I can find you more easily." She looked past him to Silhouette. "He has much to learn."

Silhouette smirked. "You're not wrong. But he's doing okay so far."

"Perhaps, but you must teach him how to conceal himself more thoroughly. You will draw attention. Unwanted attention."

"Fair enough."

Meera and Silhouette both stiffened, Meera dropping to a crouch as she turned to face the door, Silhouette hissing through her teeth. A moment later Alex sensed a presence nearby and the door exploded in a shower of splinters. "Go!" Meera shouted. "I'll hold it, whatever it is. Get away!"

Silhouette shot to Alex, dragged him to one side of the door. As a wiry, dark figure burst through the shattered wood Meera ran and clashed with it head on. Silhouette pushed Alex through before the assailant had a chance to realize they were behind him. Alex turned, his bloodlust rising, and drove a kick into the attacker's back. It stumbled, directly into Meera's savage and skilful assault. He had a moment to marvel at her prowess before Silhouette dragged at him again, pulling him across the corridor, into the fire escape stairwell. He wanted to stay and fight, but Silhouette wouldn't let him, towing him along. They ran, barrelling down the stairs and out into the street.

"Run!" Silhouette barked, and sprinted off.

Tearing himself away from re-entering the hotel, getting back into the action, Alex pounded after her. They bolted for block after block, putting as much distance as they could between themselves and the mysterious assailant. Silhouette skidded to a halt at a junction, a line of vehicles standing idle, their drivers staring disconsolately at the traffic light, waiting for green permission to move on. She pulled open the door of the front car and yanked a startled woman from the seat. The woman screamed, tumbling into the road. Other drivers began opening doors, people on the pavement stopped to look, point phone cameras at the sudden excitement.

"Get in!" Silhouette yelled, dropping in behind the wheel. Alex jumped into the passenger side and Silhouette tore away, swerving between screeching cars coming from either side.

Now he had stopped running Alex could feel Meera, her desperation and her spirit to stay alive. She defended, doing nothing to end the fight, just trying to hold up whatever it was and not get killed in the process. But whatever the thing attacking her was, she couldn't hold it for long. Alex got the impression of something that looked human, almost insignificantly human, but felt stronger and more predatory than anything he'd ever imagined. A thought from Meera flashed in his mind. *I'm sorry, I can't hold on any longer.* A surge of magesign through their connection and she flashed out, simply disappeared. He heard the roar of rage of whatever she fought as she vanished.

"What the fuck!" Alex shouted. "What are we running from?"

Silhouette stared hard at the road, swerving between cars that skidded and blasted brash horns. "I have no fucking idea, but I am not waiting to find out."

"Where are we going?"

"Heathrow."

"The airport? To go to Canada?"

"Yep. That's what Meera there said and it's a good distance from here, so I'm all for it."

FOURTEEN

Alex and Silhouette stood at the Air Canada counter. "That was a piece of luck," Silhouette said with a smile.

Alex stared at the wallet in his hand and felt the weight of his phone in his hip pocket and the book in his jacket. The sum total of his possessions, along with the clothes he stood in and the shard of the Darak. So little, yet the one thing he desperately wanted to be rid of he was stuck with. The rep returned with his credit card and printed tickets. "There you go," she said cheerily. "You'd better hurry and check in before it's too late."

Silhouette led him away. "Let me do the talking at check-in."

"You know I have no passport, right?" His voice sounded slurred to his ears. Tiredness dragged on him like a wet blanket and he didn't know if he could pull off Welby's mind tricks.

"Only mundanes use passports."

They lined up in the human cattle farm of fabric tape and chrome stands, shuffled forward a few paces at a time. When they reached check-in Silhouette handed the smiling attendant their tickets. Alex felt a surge of magesign and knew she was pulling the same trick Welby had a few days before. Then he had been fascinated, now he was resigned. Sydney airport seemed like a lifetime ago, certainly part of a life he'd never know again. Silhouette took their boarding passes, shaking her head politely when the attendant asked if they had any baggage to check in. They moved on, Alex plodding disconsolately, his mind a blank slate. He was spent, used up. He'd never experienced an exhaustion like it. Used to training his body and focusing to the point of collapse in pursuit of martial excellence he might be, but this was different. Total emotional, psychological fatigue. He could only follow like an old dog.

He walked through the metal detector without sparing the officials a glance and trudged behind Silhouette. The plane would be boarding in less than thirty minutes. Sil led them into a couple of shops, bought a backpack and a few clothing items. She didn't bother to talk to him, just occasionally held a T-shirt against his chest or looked appraisingly at his legs and waist. If he did catch her eye she offered a soft smile and nothing more. She bought toothbrushes and other bits and pieces in a pharmacy store that reeked of artificial pheromones and expensive perfume. Everything they did had an uncomfortable déjà vu about it.

Before he knew it Alex found himself shuffling along the aisle of a plane. Silhouette guided him gently into a seat and clipped his seatbelt for him. "You can rest now."

Blackness wrapped him up in soft, dark eternity.

A pressure on his shoulder and Silhouette whispering in his ear. "Wake up. You need to eat."

He opened his eyes, eyelids popping apart like clam shells. An airline meal sat on the tray table in front of him. "How long have I been out?"

"Quite a few hours. I let you sleep through most of the flight, but they're feeding us again now and we'll be landing before long."

He felt immeasurably better, though still battered, his exertions hung like an anchor around his neck. "I was so tired."

"I know. I think everything's catching up with you."

"No shit." He started eating and found himself almost inhaling the food, suddenly ravenous. When had he last had a feed?

Silhouette smiled at him ruefully. "You're going to have to remember to eat. It's not the sort of thing I'm going to think about. And you won't want to eat with me."

He nodded, mouth stuffed with reconstituted mashed potato and suspiciously sweet bread. Within a couple of minutes the plastic dish was clean. "I need to eat more."

Silhouette slid her meal onto his tray, taking his empty containers. He attacked it. "We'll get you something else when we land if you still need it," she said. "You got that paper Meera gave you?"

He handed it to her. "What attacked us back there?" he asked.

"I hope Meera's okay," Silhouette said as she unfolded the note.

"She's fine. She kinda zapped out of there. Why do you think it's after us? Not your people, is it?"

Silhouette shook her head, her face serious. "No. Joseph promised you'd be safe with our Kin. None in our Den would hunt you or bother you. Besides, there's no reason to. I've been thinking about it and the only thing I can come up with is maybe some friend of Peacock."

"Really? How the fuck did they find us?"

"I don't know. But maybe we left some kind of trail. I can't think of anything else. You hadn't been in the country long enough."

She had a point. Unless Scarlet was a more serious threat than he'd ever imagined, though he trusted Amir to take care of that. "You think we've shaken them off?"

Silhouette made a disgusted face. "I doubt it. That thing seemed pretty tenacious. We should stay on our guard. With any luck it'll take a while to catch up again."

She read Meera's note. "Well," she said eventually, "we're heading into Halifax now. This says Meera's legend came from Beothuk natives who heard it from Icelandic Norsemen. The important part is that there's a magically protected island off the coast of Newfoundland that we need to find." She paused, thinking. "So we'll need to charter a flight to Bonavista then convince someone with a boat to take us out to sea."

Alex stole a long look at Silhouette's profile, part of him drinking in her lines, another part wondering what was going on. "Magically protected?" he asked in a tired voice.

"What?"

"The island?"

"Oh, right. Yeah. Probably means it's warded, cloaked. People could sail and fish all around there for decades and never see it. Occasionally someone might accidentally crash into it and wreck and they'd be considered lost at sea."

Alex laughed sharply. "That sort of thing happen a lot, does it?"

Silhouette turned to him, put one hand against his cheek. "Not a lot, but it's not unheard of. You're living a new paradigm, Iron

Balls. You have to adjust."

He sighed. "So how are we going to find this island?"

"It's protected, but we can probably find it, if we take our time. Especially with your talents. In fact, we should probably charter someone to fly us around out there until we do find it, then log the co-ordinates."

Alex rubbed his eyes, nodding into his palms. "How are we going to afford all this?"

"You don't have money?"

"I have some savings, but flights like this, chartering aircraft and whatever the fuck else. I'm not a millionaire. My money will run out. Then what?"

"Then we get some more. Don't worry, we'll manage."

Alex stood back while Silhouette negotiated with a private charter pilot. So much for the control he had intended to regain. Silhouette's willingness to help him still made him nervous. If he took her at face value, believed her when she said she found him fascinating, that led to problems of its own. It meant she was capricious. She could just as easily decide he had become boring and disappear. She was part Fey. It bothered him how easily he accepted that, but it was an undeniable truth. That's what made her Kin. Beauty and the beast. And he knew leaning on her carried dangers, but he had paddled way out of his depth and needed time to re-center.

In the meantime, he would let her ease his burden, and brace himself for the possibility of that help suddenly vanishing. Or worse. Deep down he knew he also braced himself for losing more than her assistance. Whatever else she might be, he grew increasingly attached to her and that scared him most of all. He wondered if she had anything like a similar attachment. Or was he just the current plaything, a momentary whim in her deviant longevity?

She turned back to him with a smile, winking as she strolled across the tiled floor. "He'll fly us out over the area in question and then land us at an airstrip about twenty miles from Bonavista township. He took some convincing because I wouldn't tell him why I was asking for such a strange charter, but enough money usually answers the difficult questions." She tapped her temple with one finger. "And a little gentle coercing, of course."

Alex nodded. "Cool. Let's go then."

"You've perked up a bit."

"I feel better for the rest and the feed. Besides, I can't let you take all the weight." He paused, looking deep into her eyes, ready to gauge a reaction. "I really appreciate all you're doing."

She smiled, all the way up to her eyes. "It's no problem. I know you're suffering, but I'm having fun. It's difficult to find new things to do when you've been around as long as I have."

"Happy to give you something to do."

She laughed. "Happy to do you."

The pilot emerged from his office. "Come on then, we'd better get going. It's getting dark early now, we should use what day we have left." He reached for Alex's hand. "Jim Daley."

Alex shook. "Alex." That was as much information as this guy needed.

Daley led them onto the tarmac. Alex went last, enjoying the movement of Silhouette's butt in her jeans as she walked ahead of him. She did seem to be taking this situation seriously. Maybe it *was* so hard to be entertained at her age that she would take his misfortune as an opportunity. Maybe there was even the chance that she was growing to like him as much as he liked her. But that thought needed to be tempered with the knowledge that he must seem like a child to her. They approached a small twin prop plane.

"This here is a Piper PA-44-180 Seminole," said Daley proudly. "It's old as hell, but in better condition than most things a fraction of its age."

Alex smiled. That sounded like a good description of Silhouette. On board was all cramped leather seats and a sloping roof that barely cleared his head. They strapped in, put on the offered headphones and waited while Daley cleared them with the tower. The headphones were cold and heavy, crackling with static. Alex leaned over to Silhouette, shouting as Daley fired up the props. "Does this seem as surreal to you as it does to me?"

Silhouette shook her head, smiled. "Actually, for me this is incredibly mundane."

Before long the old plane labored up into an overcast sky. Daley's voice came distorted over the intercom, tinny. "It'll take us a while to get where you want. I'll tell you when we clear the far coast near Bonavista, then you're gonna have to direct me around." He sounded like he was humoring children.

"No problem," Silhouette said.

Alex sunk down into his seat, let the incessant white noise of the engines lull his senses. He closed his eyes. At some point he slept. He dreamed of insectile creatures stalking him through darkened rooms. Every time one got near it tried to touch him. He cried out, yelling at it to leave him alone as he ran away, mystified that he didn't stand his ground. *I always fight!* He would duck around a corner and run, watching for the inevitable return of those clawing, scrabbling, chitinous hands. Every time something reached for him, he changed direction, his mind soaked in fear, some primal, certain knowledge that if those hands touched him they would kill him. His frustration grew; no exits to be found, no light to guide him. He wanted to battle, to stand tall and meet these things head on, whatever they were, but fear kept him sprinting. He whimpered as he went, his terror irrational. *Why don't I just stop and smash them?* He forced his feet to stop pounding, spun around, sweat pouring down his face, eyes searching the darkness. Long, clawed fingers shot out of the shadows all around.

Something pulled at his mind, sucking on his thoughts like a drain drawing water into a spiral. A sharp slap stung his cheek and he jerked upright in his seat.

Silhouette stared hard into his eyes, her magesign washed over him, her expression furious. Her magic probed and prodded at his shields.

"What's going on?" he asked, scared by her intensity.

"Were you just dreaming?"

"Yeah."

"What about?"

"I don't remember exactly. I was being chased, hunted. Something tried to... I dunno, kinda yank the thoughts out of my head."

Silhouette growled, deep in her chest. "Pay attention to me. Do exactly as I do. Use your vision."

Shaking off the gossamer veils of sleep, trying to hear clearly over the loud drone of the twin props, Alex sat up straighter. "What's going on?"

"Something is hunting. I can feel it."

"Hunting? Me?"

"It was incredibly weak, but there. Shut up and watch me."

He watched the shades around her. She opened herself up, let more of herself be revealed to him. He watched, mesmerised, hypnotised by every aspect of her. Everything snapped shut, like a color television suddenly switching to black and white. He started.

"Did you see what I did?" she asked, her voice as intense as her expression.

"I'm not sure. I dunno..."

"Damn it, Alex, concentrate!" She opened her shields again.

Alex watched nothing but the mechanics of her magic, studied the way she manipulated her own 'sign and controlled it. He resisted the urge to enjoy the show, remained clinical in his observation. She slammed everything shut once more, like the way he had learned to conceal his true self, the trick he'd learned from Welby. Only Welby's method was a cardboard box to Silhouette's cast-iron safe.

"Can you see it?" she asked.

He nodded, trying to apply her methods. He used his mind as a cloak, wrapping himself up in the security of ordinary nothingness.

"That's it," Silhouette's voice hissed, muffled by the tinny headphones. "Tighter. Lock everything up."

He did as she asked, closing off from outside of himself. Every time he learned something he had barely got used to it before he discovered it could be deeper, stronger, better. It felt good. Safe.

Silhouette nodded, her face finally relaxing. "That's it," she said.

"That needs to be your natural state."

The pilot looked over his shoulder, his expression confused and a little concerned. Silhouette raised one eyebrow, challenging. He shrugged, flicked them a quick apologetic smile and turned back to face the horizon.

Alex let the feeling settle into his bones, set it to default. He shifted the headset, leaning close to talk directly to Silhouette. "What just happened?" he asked, not sure he really wanted to know.

Silhouette frowned. "I think whatever attacked us back in London is trying to track you down again. Remember how Meera found us? She talked about your mind-print?"

"But I was there when Petra looked inside me. In Joseph's quarters, I felt her. I've felt nothing else like that."

"Well, it would appear whatever attacked us was able to do the same without you noticing. It must have watched us somewhere before it attacked. Now it has your print, a psychic signature that drifts in the ether. Either he's a dreamweaver or he's got one on the case."

"A dreamweaver?"

"I can't think of anything else it would be. Fuck me, but it's strong, whatever it is. Tracking you down over half the planet? That's incredible. It obviously has quite a gift."

"So he's going to come for us again."

Silhouette didn't answer, but her expression confirmed his fear.

The dreamweaver opened her eyes in the smoky gloom, a sharp tongue flicking across dry lips. She rubbed withered hands across her deeply wrinkled face. "He's gone again."

The Subcontractor cursed in an old, foul tongue. "Did you get anything?"

The old crone shifted in her seat, settling back. "Not much. They were off the ground again. Seems he only sleeps while he's flying."

"What did you get?"

The woman turned to an ancient, yellowing globe. "When I

found him before, he was around here somewhere." She stabbed at the globe with one blackened nail. "This time, somewhere around here."

The Subcontractor tried to breathe as shallowly as possible, disgusted by the rank closeness of the dreamweaver's home. "They must have used commercial airlines first, to get that far so quickly. You think he was sleeping again on the same flight?"

The dreamweaver shook her head, lank, greasy hair, gray like lead pipe, dancing over her sunken eyes. "No. The environment around him felt different."

They'd changed flights, so they must have landed somewhere. Given what this crone told him there weren't many options for where they had landed. He stared at the globe, his eyes coming to rest on Halifax. It felt right. He couldn't keep wasting time waiting for his quarry to sleep. Go to Halifax and sniff out the trail again from there. If he couldn't pick up the trail… well, he'd have to think of something else.

Hood's scrawny bird kept coming and going, reporting back. He could smell it outside again. Perhaps he should report himself, let Hood know the price was rising rapidly.

"Thank you." He stood, handed a roll of bills to the old dreamweaver and left. The fresh air outside felt like a cold shower on a hot day. He pulled a phone from his pocket and dialled.

"Black Diamond Incorporated, how may I help you?"

"I need to talk with Hood."

"I'm afraid Mr Hood…"

"Tell Hood it's the Subcontractor and I need to talk to him right now."

The line clicked and muzak piped through. Within moments the line clicked again. "What are you doing sitting around?"

The Subcontractor abhorred such rudeness. One day the contract would come in from someone requiring his services to take out this pompous fool. That job couldn't happen soon enough. "Hello to you too, Mr Hood. Suffice to say this job is more complicated than first thought. They're a slippery pair. The cost is going up."

Hood barked down the line. "Because of your incompetence you're going to charge me more?"

"You want them dead or not? You want what they're carrying or not?" He knew his employer. Once he'd decided on having something, he simply could not let it go. Like a dog with its jaws locked on a rabbit, the man would not leave off till the twitching stopped.

"Yes, I want it! Get on with the job, damn the expense. But don't drag this out!"

The Subcontractor clenched his teeth. "You insult me." He hung up before Hood could shout back at him.

Gathering his energy he let space bend and fold around him. This trail would be hot again in no time. As the realms shifted, making a space for him to slip through, the featherless raven-like creature swept down, eyeing him closely. Not of this world itself, the macabre thing read the realmshift. As the Subcontractor dematerialised and vanished, the planesbird cawed and followed.

FIFTEEN

Their pilot's annoyance grew with his impatience. "We're running out of light and fuel equally fast," Daley said, his voice gruff. "We're gonna pitch into the drink or crash land in the dark if we don't turn back soon."

Silhouette squeezed his shoulder. "Bear with us just a bit longer, please?" She turned to Alex. "Anything."

"No, I can only see water everywhere I… wait a minute." He twisted in the seat, trying to see back behind the plane.

"Turn about," Silhouette said to Daley. "One-eighty, please."

The pilot grunted and cranked the stick over. The plane lurched and wing-tipped. Alex ignored the unpleasant lift in his gut and scrambled across Silhouette's lap to look out the other side as they came around. "There!" He pointed. "Can you see it? Like a craggy, kinda teardrop shape?"

Silhouette leaned in close to the window, straining to see. "I can't see anything. You're sure you can see it?"

"Definitely."

"Jim, can you please log these co-ordinates?"

"Can we go home then?"

Silhouette smiled at him, disarmingly sweet. "Yes, Jim. Thank you so much."

Daley rolled his eyes. He scribbled something into a notebook on his console and cranked the stick again, powering up and away.

Silhouette squeezed Alex's hand. "Nice going."

He didn't share her enthusiasm. "You really think that's it?"

"It's an island in about the right location that I can't see. That makes it well warded. It also makes it a pretty solid candidate for what we're looking for."

"But I didn't try anything particular to see it. It was just there."

"To you, maybe. Don't worry, love. I think we're onto something here."

Love? Maybe she was genuinely into him. If he could get this stone together and become as powerful as the others thought he would then maybe he would actually be worthy of someone like her. And if he mastered the magic and learned to use it, maybe he would live long enough to enjoy her company. Welby had looked pretty good for nearly one and half centuries, seemingly a very healthy man in his sixties. *The magic tends to preserve us.* But he had been fairly insignificant according to the Kin. Silhouette appeared no more than twenty-five and she was far older than Welby. His train of thought disturbed him. Mastering magic and living for centuries to enjoy the love of a monster? Paradigm shift didn't begin to cover it.

Silhouette stroked his cheek. "What are you thinking?" There was a softness in her eyes.

"Just trying to get my head around it all."

"You'll be all right, Alex. You're doing pretty well."

"I wish I had your confidence."

She planted a kiss on his lips, hot and firm. "Trust me."

Standing on the apron at the tiny airstrip outside Bonavista, Jim Daley frowned. A technician chewed lazily while he refuelled the aircraft. "I hate flying at night," Daley said.

Alex scanned the darkening sky, deep inky blue behind dark gray clouds. "Do you have to be back anywhere in particular?"

"Nah. My wife left me years ago. All I got to go back to is shitty TV and a can of beans."

Alex sighed. He felt as though he owed something to this guy. He was earning from it, but he had been gracious about their weird requests and asked very few questions. "How about you ride with us into Bonavista and I'll cover the cost of a meal and a room for you. You can get back out here early and fly home in the light."

Daley grinned broadly. "Very kind of you, pal. Thanks."

Alex felt like he'd just been played.

The airstrip technician called them a cab from Bonavista and the cab driver directed them to a shabby hotel. It was cold, close to freezing, as they piled into the hotel lobby and organised rooms. Alex's concern that they might have trouble finding a place to stay was quickly allayed.

"You've got to be kidding!" The hotel clerk laughed, her

enormous bosom shaking over an even bigger stomach. "People are leaving this island like rats on the proverbial ship. There's less than four thousand people left here now and we're hardly a prime holiday destination, especially this close to winter."

Alex smiled, feeling foolish. He also wanted to punch the woman out and had no idea why. He bit down on the urge. "Sorry, I didn't realize."

"You here on holiday, then?"

"No, er, not holiday. Sort of a business trip."

"Right. What's your business?"

Silhouette interrupted them. "Does the double room have a bathroom? Like with an actual bath?"

The clerk stared at Alex for a second longer then turned to Silhouette. "It can have, if that's what you want."

Sil smiled her disarming smile. "That would be awesome. I'd love a nice hot bath."

The clerk handed over two sets of keys. "Single for you. Double, with a bath, for you guys."

"Thanks! Come on, Alex." Silhouette dragged him away. "Before she asks any more questions," she hissed in his ear as they went. From the foot of the stairs she turned back. "That place over the road, does it serve good food?"

The clerk raised her hands slightly. "It serves food."

"Cool. Jimbo, we'll see you over there in an hour?"

The pilot nodded. "Sure."

In the room upstairs Silhouette locked the door and turned Alex, forcing him to sit on the bed. "You okay?"

"Why?" He could hear the impatience in his voice, felt a sense of frustration knotting his gut.

"You're... buzzing."

Alex ground his teeth. "You noticed that, huh?"

"Yeah. Kinda hard to miss. And the last couple of minutes it's got a lot more noticeable."

"It's been building up in me for a while. Since I spotted the island, maybe. Certainly since we got here. I feel like I need to smash something, or someone. I want to break things, or fight or..."

or…" His heart started pounding, the adrenaline in his system hard to control.

"Or fuck someone?" Silhouette's eyes gleamed.

With a visceral growl Alex lifted her and spun her onto the bed, tearing at her belt. She worked with him, doing her best to save her clothing as they both got naked as quickly as possible. "Come on, then, Iron Balls." Her eyes flashed with golden slits, her teeth lengthening slightly then retracting again. "What have you got?"

Alex almost howled, smothering the need by kissing her hard.

The mattress hung half off the bed, the sheet torn in two. Alex and Silhouette sat on opposite sides of the room, soaked in sweat, gasping for air. Alex shook all over. Silhouette smiled darkly. "Man, you fuck like a Kin."

Alex grunted. "That a good thing?"

"Depends. In this case, yes it is."

"I nearly killed you again."

"Don't flatter yourself."

"I really wanted to." He hated himself for it.

"I know. We'll manage this. If this is how we help to control the bloodlust the book gives you, then that's no bad thing."

Alex's heart slowly returned to something like a normal pace. The primitive frustration that had been building in him eased with it. "What if I get the better of you though? What if you can't stop me one time?"

Silhouette laughed. "Oh, Alex, you're sweet. But I'm perfectly safe."

"Are you? Really? I killed Ataro and Joseph said he had never been bested. Ataro couldn't beat me when I really meant it. Do you have better stopping power?"

Silhouette became serious. "Maybe not. And there's no way I'm as strong as Ataro. But there's a big old human part of you that doesn't really want to kill me, right?"

"Well, yeah, but…"

"But nothing. You hang onto that part however much the

bloodlust is on you and I'll take my chances."

"I hope we can control this." He wanted her to be right, that he could keep hold of the part that had deserted him when he'd fought in her Den.

Silhouette headed for the bathroom. "Come on. Jim'll be waiting for us."

They managed to eat a half decent meal and enjoy a few beers with the pilot without talking about anything in particular. Having company prevented them from talking about what was really happening and turned out to be a good distraction. By the time they returned to the hotel Alex felt a lot less tense. He told Silhouette as much.

"You went straight to a pub and drank after killing Peacock too."

Alex sat heavily on the bed. "I know. But I'm not going to start drinking every time I feel the rage building in me. That's no answer. Drinking takes my edge and I can't allow that."

"True."

"Besides, having a couple of beers is a lot different to getting drunk."

The book dragged at his pocket, its presence insistent and angry. It pushed at his mind, tried to goad him. It was trying to make him start an argument with Silhouette, but spending his energy against her earlier and a couple of beers with dinner had certainly dulled its influence. Though the potential of its antagonism frightened him. It seemed to be getting stronger all the time and he wondered if his resistance would decline accordingly. What if he killed Sil next time?

She sat down next to him. "You say you're less tense, but you look worried."

Alex's eyes were heavy with fatigue. "I don't know how long I can hold off against this urge. It's relentless."

"But sated a bit now?"

"Yeah."

"Even before you had a beer?" Silhouette's eyes glittered, her expression seductive.

"Yes, before the beer." He wanted to tell her they could manage it, but he didn't believe it. "I don't like this violent sex, Sil. I mean, I love the sex part, but the violence, the killing rage, it's not me. And I'm frightened it will eventually take over."

She stood, ran one hand over his hair. "For now we've got a method. Don't give up on it. You're stronger than you think."

He kicked off his shoes. "I hope you're right. You coming to bed?"

She kissed him. "I'll come to bed soon. That steak wasn't enough for me, I need to feed. I spotted something on the way back."

A sudden chill swept in as she opened the bedroom window. She stepped out onto the fire escape and her shadow twisted and morphed as she slipped away into the night.

Alex stared into the blackness, letting the night cool his skin. Could he really accept what she was? Could he trust her? He needed to see.

With a grunt of annoyance he pulled his shoes back on. Outside the window the fire escape led up to the roof and down to the street. Which way? He hurried to the roof and crouched low, scanning all around. Movement in an alleyway opposite caught his eye, a dark shape slipping swiftly through the shadows. He climbed down the fire escape, ran across the road. Holding his breath, ensuring his shields were as tight as they could be, he slunk along the alley, close to the wall. Muffled voices drifted to his ears. He crept closer.

"Don't be afraid." That was Silhouette.

"What the hell, lady? I ain't got nothing." A man's voice, old and worn, gravelly with years of alcohol and cigarettes.

"Oh, but you do," Silhouette said.

The man cried out briefly, his shout cut short with a wet tear. Alex flinched, horrified and fascinated. He knew this was Silhouette's life, but could he handle it? He peered around the end of an overfilled dumpster and saw Silhouette in the shadows, holding the limp form of a man in raggedy clothes as easily as if he were a small child. She tore and worried at his throat, steam rising around her feline face in the cold night air.

Alex clenched his teeth together, forced himself to watch. That poor man, suddenly stripped of what little dignity and humanity remained to him, reduced to nothing more than an unlucky gazelle on the savannah. Silhouette tipped her head up to the sky, her face contorted into a long snout with sharp, gleaming teeth. She took an ecstatic breath and sunk her face again, tearing a wad of flesh from the wino's neck and chest. She seemed to swallow it whole before burying her nose in the huge wound and sucking down the blood.

Alex was frozen, mesmerised. Was she a beautiful woman who would sometimes have to do this, or was she this all along and only sometimes pretended to be a beautiful woman? Did that even matter? And if this was Silhouette's true nature and she was the only friend he had, what did that make him? A shrill tone disturbed her feeding. With a curse she dropped the corpse and wiped her hands on his clothes before digging into a pocket.

She pulled out a cell phone as her face resumed its human shape, flipped it open. "My Lord."

Alex frowned. *Joseph?*

Sil listened for a moment, then, "Yes, sort of. It's hard to tell."

She listened again.

"Well, we think we've found the second piece. Yes, I know, but I think we really have."

A tremor rippled up Alex's spine. *Why is she telling him this?*

Silhouette sighed, clearly exasperated. "Joseph, I'm fine. I can take care of myself." A pause. "Yes, I know, but all the time he's alive, he's stuck with it. It can't hurt me." Pause. "I know he can but I can look after myself."

Alex's mind spun in neutral. He'd been a fool to think that she wouldn't have told her Clan Lord everything. But did Joseph's interest really lie in Silhouette's welfare?

Silhouette crouched, hooking one long fingernail into the wino's rent chest. She plucked out a string of meat and chewed it lazily. "I know," she said. "But we can't separate the stone and the book, so the danger remains the same as ever." She paused again, looking up at the night sky. "Yes, of course. First chance I get.

Okay, talk to you soon." She flipped the phone closed and fell on the wino again as if she were starving, ripping open the filthy shirt and tearing off a hunk of meat with feline teeth.

Alex looked away, swallowing against her animal feeding. He took painfully slow steps backwards, trembling in shock. First chance for what? He went back to the hotel, his mind filled with fears and suspicions.

SIXTEEN

Morning dawned bright but overcast, the sky a gleaming white lid on the world. Sil snuggled against him and pressed her face into his neck. Alex kept his eyes on the world outside the window and tried to relax. His suspicions had kept him awake half the night but he couldn't address his concerns without admitting he'd followed her, spied on her. Would she forgive that? Would she care? He didn't even know if his apprehensions were fair. That she talked to her Clan Lord was no crime. If she conspired with him, that would be different. But right now Alex had no way of knowing. He wanted to trust her, *needed* to trust her.

He slipped out from under her, pulled his clothes on. "We should get going."

She looked disappointed, frowning at him. "You okay?"

"Yeah, yeah. Just anxious to get on."

"Okay then." She got up and walked naked to the bathroom.

She was breathtaking, firing his passion instantly. But was that a mask? If it were a mask, it was a bloody good one and real enough. Alex rubbed at his eyes, confused and lost. *My life has gone truly bizarre.*

An hour later, full of coffee, toast and bacon, they stood on the docks of Bonavista. Several jetties protruded into the choppy harbor, tiny wavelets forced through the narrow concrete mouth of the harbor causing the boats to bob randomly against their moorings. A sharp, chill wind cut across from the open ocean under a sky turned slate gray. The breeze and the salt smell helped clear Alex's head. Silhouette was in conversation with a rough-looking fisherman. The man wore oilskins, a heavy jacket and an expression of deep suspicion.

Silhouette tipped her head and a hip, eyes batting under her fringe. The man's misgivings melted away. After another minute she walked back to Alex, obviously pleased with herself. "He'll lend us his boat."

"Lend? I thought you were going to convince him to take us!"

"Where's he going to take us? He can't see the island."

"I can't believe he's just going to give you his boat!"

"I have a way with human men."

Alex narrowed his eyes at her.

"Don't worry. With you I mean it."

The exchange did nothing to allay his fears. "I don't know the first thing about boats, Sil."

"You don't need to. I can manage that. I've been around a while, collected a few skills. I can get us to the co-ordinates. You have to make sure we don't hit the island when we get there."

Jim Daley landed at Halifax, still bemused by the last couple of days. The strange couple had seemed nice enough but there was something wrong about them. And about their requests. Flying for hours over open ocean, treating him to dinner and drinks afterwards. It made no sense. Still, it was good money and he'd had nothing better to do.

Walking across the tarmac, heading for the office to check his schedules, he caught sight of a small man in a long, dark coat. Something about the guy gave him pause. The way he moved, like he was searching for something. Was he sniffing the ground?

The man looked straight at him, his stare unnervingly intense. Jim drew himself up tall as the thin man strode purposefully over. "Help you?" he asked.

The man leaned uncomfortably close, staring into his eyes. He sniffed sharply, across Jim's face and down one shoulder.

"What the hell is wrong with you, man?" Jim pushed a hand into the guy's chest, forcing him back.

The man stepped away willingly, a broad smile spreading across his face. He seemed to have too many teeth. "My apologies," he said. "You and I need to talk."

Jim didn't like anything about this strange guy. "I don't think so, buddy." He turned away.

The man grabbed hold of Jim's shoulder, his fingers biting deep into the flesh. "I said, you and I need to talk."

The journey was cold and rough. After a little over two hours Silhouette told Alex to start looking out for their destination. Within another few minutes he'd seen it. Tall, dark gray rocks made a ragged cliff of one side. The island sloped from east to west, seemingly nothing but desolate, deserted stone.

"Aim a bit to the left," Alex called out over the wind and the diesel engine.

Silhouette cast him an amused glance. "Aim?"

He pointed. "Go a bit that way. I don't speak nautical!"

As they rounded the western side, the shape he'd seen from the air became more apparent. Tall, broken cliffs made up the rounded belly of the teardrop. The west coast of the island, leading towards the point, lay lowest in the water, with natural bays between the rocks where waves bit at shingly beaches, with no sign of any kind of vegetation. Cold, wet rock led up from the sea to slick plateaus. Basalt columns stood strangely geometric in natural sculptures. The isle extended about two kilometers on the longest side by his best guess. Alex strained his eyes, looking for any signs of life. Signs of anything other than naked rock.

Silhouette slowed the boat to a drift. "Well?" she asked.

"Can't you see it?"

"It's all just open ocean. What do *you* see?"

"A massive rocky island. It looks dead. Deserted."

"Is there anywhere we can land?"

Alex scanned the rocky shore, numerous tiny bays and miserable beaches. "I can't really tell where would be safe to head in, but there are beaches."

"How close are we?"

"About fifty meters away."

Silhouette turned the boat. "Are we facing the island? Near a beach?"

"A bit more to the right."

She gunned the engine again.

"That's it," Alex called. "We're pointing right at a beach."

Silhouette revved again, propelling the fishing boat forward.

"Tell me when we're about twenty meters out."

"You're turning away again!" Alex shouted.

Silhouette scowled at him. "I am not. We're going in a straight line."

"Turn right some more."

Sil turned the boat back towards the beach then almost immediately began veering away.

"You're doing it again. Turn right some more."

Silhouette made a sound of annoyance. "Are you sure?"

"Definitely!"

"There's some powerful magic at work here." She closed her eyes. "Guide me if I go off course again."

"Right again. That's it. Nearly there."

As they chugged towards the island, a sense of trepidation welled up from deep inside Alex. A thick malevolence wept off this rocky lump, washing over him, a chill far colder than the ocean wind. "That's it," he called out.

Silhouette killed the engine, went to the stern. She cranked a lever and a heavy anchor dropped into the choppy waves. Chain slid with a metallic rattle over the gunwales. They both watched it and jumped when it stopped within seconds. "Well, that only went a few meters. We should be in open ocean," Silhouette said.

"Told you."

She moved to a wooden locker and pulled it open, dragged out a heavy canvas parcel. The weight didn't seem to bother her, but Alex helped anyway. Holding onto a yellow plastic tag in one hand and a piece of attached rope in the other, she threw the thing overboard, yanking on the tag as it went. The parcel burst and hissed into a rubber dinghy, bobbing at the end of the rope. "Get the oars."

Alex retrieved two plastic and aluminium oars from the chest and they clambered into the rocking dinghy. Alex set the oars and rowed the short distance to the beach. He watched Sil's face as they went. As they scraped into the shale of the beach her eyes widened and she looked frantically left and right. "It's fucking huge!"

"You can see it now?" Alex asked as he jumped out onto slick gravel and dragged the small craft and Sil up out of the water.

She stepped out. "Yeah, of course. The illusion only works against the eyes and mind. No illusion of this size can work against a physical contradiction. But seriously, Alex, your vision is strong to see through this. Now that I'm inside the magic I can see it at work. It's powerful, intricate stuff."

"I wonder who put it here."

Silhouette pursed her lips. "It feels like Kin magic. I wonder if whoever hid the shard here hid the island too."

"If the shard is here."

"I'm pretty sure it will be. Come on." She dragged the dinghy further up the beach, rolled a rock over the lead rope to stop it washing away, and headed between basalt columns.

As they gained higher ground, Alex's trepidation grew. The book almost buzzed. It urged him on, anxious excitement drifting through his mind from his jacket. The stone in its locket was hot against his chest. "Can you feel that?" he asked.

Silhouette stopped, turned around. "What?"

"Something is going on here. The book and stone are alive with it. I feel... I don't know exactly. Scared. I feel like killing."

"The book is driving you on. Resist it, as best you can. Try to channel the sensations and use them how you want. Don't *let* them drive you."

Alex drew a long, deep breath in, centring himself. His *chi kung* training proved useful, helped him to calm the frantic throbs of the book. "There's going to be a fight," he said, with absolute certainty.

Sil raised her eyebrows. "Is there?"

"Yep. I can't tell you how I know, but I do."

"Okay. Come on then. Neither of us have a problem facing up to a fight."

They moved on through the rocks. Eventually the dips and peaks gave way to an open view and they both stopped, catching their breath. Across a rough scree, only a hundred meters or so from where they stood, a ramshackle town of stone houses spread haphazardly up to the point of the island. The homes were simple, built of stacked slate and shale, closely packed, low roofs with a shallow slant, small doors, no windows. At the head of the town, standing on the point of the island, a larger structure, squat and wide, loomed over the others. People wrapped in heavy sealskins, pasty faces peering out from dark hoods, moved slowly between the buildings. They were bent and weak-looking, shuffling as they moved.

Alex and Silhouette dropped out of sight behind a low outcrop of dark rock. "What the fuck?" Alex asked in a low voice.

"Those people look… wrong," Silhouette said, spooked.

"I know. What the hell are they doing here? How can anyone survive here?"

"Do you have any idea where the stone might be?"

Alex let his mind be guided by his shard. He could feel it drawing him on. "I'm guessing we need to be in that big building at the end."

Silhouette peeked out from their hiding place. "I wonder how friendly the locals are?"

"There's gonna be a fight, remember?"

"Come on then. Let's try to sneak around. If we have to fight, so be it."

She crept along under cover of the rock, heading back towards the ocean. Alex kept low, following. They used rocky outcrops to hide, moving down towards the water when they had to. It was painstaking work but they slowly made their way along the island. The cold wind and ocean spray froze their fingers and faces as they went, but neither complained. A sense of urgency and concern for the strange denizens of this rock made a welcome distraction of the cold. Eventually they found themselves on a steep slope of shale and basalt, the side of the large building looming over them.

Hundreds of thousands of slate pieces stacked tightly together made the walls. Like the smaller structures, there were no windows, no gaps. Alex knew from their first glimpse of the place that a low, wide door stood in the middle of the front wall. How would they get in there without being noticed?

Silhouette climbed, heading for the back of the building. Alex followed. Climbing proved difficult with his numb fingers, but

Silhouette made the ascent look easy. He wasn't about to admit that it was any harder for him. She quickly scaled the rocks and immediately found fingerholds among the slates of the wall and climbed towards the roof. Waves crashed and hissed against rocks a hundred feet below. Not chancing vertigo by looking down, Alex focused on Sil's butt and used his breathing to calm his fear and the buzzing desperation of the book. She reached the roof and pulled herself flat on her belly onto it.

Alex slithered up beside her and they both lay still, catching their breath. Across the wide roof they could see the strange town again. The bent, shuffling people moved around seemingly without purpose. Smoke rose from some homes, sickly orange glows dancing through the doorways.

"What do they burn for fire?" Alex asked.

"Seal shit? I wonder if they have any contact with the mainland."

Alex stared across the desolate settlement. "What now?"

"Well, maybe we can slide across here and drop down in front of the door without being noticed. We can slip in without alerting any of that lot, maybe."

"And if there's anyone inside?"

Silhouette said nothing.

"Well, I guess I don't have a better plan."

They moved as carefully as they could across the wet surface. When they reached the edge, looking down for the door, both gasped in shock. Ranged along in front, hanging from tall, squared-off rocks, were human skeletons, tied in place with braided ropes of dried seaweed. Weathered, bleached arm bones were crossed above hanging skulls. Rib cages and untied leg bones shifted in the ocean wind.

"I count nine of them," Silhouette said.

"Yeah. And that one looks fresher." The figure hanging on the furthest obelisk still bore blackened flesh in patches, bits of it freeze-dried, flapping in the blustery weather.

"So we're not the first visitors then."

"The stones do offer a bit of protection between the building and that lot," Alex said. Each obelisk stood about six feet high and two square.

Without a word Silhouette slipped off the roof, dropping easily the ten feet or so to the ground like a cat, and rolled up against one of the carved stones. Her eyes scanned left and right, checking the door of the building. She nodded up at him.

Drawing a deep breath, checking again that no one shuffling around the town looked his way, Alex swung off the roof and dropped. He ran in a low crouch to the stone next along from Sil's, put his back against it. The power of the book coursed through him. It goaded him to break cover, cry out a challenge to the pale denizens. He imagined his fists and feet flying as he brought harsh justice to these freaks who had people strung up against some sick mockery of Stonehenge.

Silhouette hissed at him. He started, a furious expression on his face.

"It's trying to get you killed," Sil said in a sharp whisper. "Focus, Alex!"

She was right. The rage and frustration of the book, the slice of entity within it, railed at him. "Fuck off," he whispered at it, almost silently. The shard burned at his throat and he concentrated on that.

Silhouette gestured towards the doorway. "I'll go first," she said. "Wait for my signal."

Magesign swam over her and she morphed into the feline form he was beginning to increasingly associate as a part of her. The colors of her skin shifted, her clothes merged into fur, mottled gray and indistinct. If he had skills like that all this scurrying about might be avoided. She slipped from cover and into the darkness.

Alex crouched nervously, the cold stone hard against his back. He tried not to think about the bones hanging on the other side, who they might have been, why they died. Did these freaks eat them or just hang them up to rot? All kinds of horrible scenarios flashed across his mind. Silhouette had been too long. What if she couldn't call out for help? Inaction was unbearable.

He pushed up from the rock and ran into the building, slipping to the side of the door, pressed his back against the wall inside. He paused, let his eyes adjust to the smoky gloom.

Guttering orange light flickered from sconces around the walls. What looked from the outside like inky blackness was a ruddy, hazy murk inside. He crouched, eyes and mind scanning. He caught sight of shades of magesign by the far wall and saw Silhouette, still shifted and camouflaged, glaring at him.

A raised dais against the center of the rear wall drew his attention. Waves of power emanated from it, washing across the big, open space. Several pale creatures like those outside knelt on the steps leading up to the dais, bowing and rocking in strange obeisance. A low, keening sound accompanied their movements.

Silhouette appeared to be trying to get around for a better look. With a slight shake of her head she crept along again, staying pressed to the wall. Alex could feel the Darak shard at his chest dragging at him, trying to burst free from the locket and fly up. He used his *chi kung* breathing again, controlled the almost overpowering urge to rush the dais. Waves of magesign rose from it, like steam from a boiling pan. Something resided up there and it filled Alex with dread.

A voice boomed out, sharp, staccato words in a tongue Alex had never heard. The worshippers leapt up as one, spinning about, their unnaturally large eyes panning left and right. Alex growled, low and angry. The time for stealth had passed.

He rushed forward, heading straight for the raised platform. As the shambling people staggered down to meet him, Silhouette shot across the room to join them.

The pale skin of the flock was damp, slick. Their mouths hung loose, the skin under their eyes sagged. They chattered with low coughs and barks, animal sounds that bore something more than simple noise, some semblance of language. Pasty hands stretched out from the depths of their patchy, stinking hide clothes, reaching for him. Some had too many fingers, some too few. Some ended in soft, rubbery stumps, wobbling with their movement. Most of the faces bore strange mutations, the mouths misshapen, some with teeth growing crookedly from cheekbones, skin distended around yellow bone. Here and there an eye socket held nothing but stretched white skin.

Alex didn't waste any time testing their skills. He drove a hard, straight kick into the stomach of the first one. It dropped with a primal howl, to squirm in pain on the floor. It had felt soft and vulnerable under his foot. Already he was striking left and right, raining blows on the lumbering, coughing horrors, pushing his way up the steps. The book in his pocket sang with joy.

Silhouette struck across from him, helping clear his path. She moved in her cat form with a grace and agility that astounded him, seeming to fly from one victim to the next, laying waste about her. The loud, harsh voice boomed out again, frustration and anger evident.

The twenty or so worshippers swung almost randomly, trying to overwhelm Alex with weight and numbers, shambolic, but he moved with a fighter's awareness. Wherever a gap appeared, he moved into it, striking and kicking, sweeping and throwing, creating new gaps in the swinging horde as he went. This was his place in the universe, his element. He laughed as he fought, the bloodlust empowering him, the stone lending new speed and strength, the book singing its endorsement. Silhouette's strategic attacks assisted his passage, the two of them operating in perfect harmony, an unspoken understanding of method, always aware of exactly where the other was. Within moments all the attackers lay still or writhing in pain. Dark blood leaked from many, howls and meeps of pain and low coughs of anguish filled the smoky air.

Silhouette moved in front of him, slipping back into her normal form, fur re-forming into clothes. "There will be more. Where's the stone?"

Alex looked to the top of the dais. "Up there. But there's something else too."

A sensation of raw anger and malevolence flooded from above them. Together they raced up the last few steps and gained the top. The surface sloped down, a shallow bowl of dark gray stone. In the center of the bowl sat something huge and once human. It wallowed in rolls of its own fat. White, slick skin stretched over fold upon fold of stinking, ashen flesh. A furious face stared out under a bald head, reflecting the dim glow of the torches. Two hands waved, thick, pudgy fingers writhing and clenching. The creature howled, its anger mingled with fear. Magesign washed from it.

Immense age emanated, centuries of existence drifting off it like a smell. Alex sensed its need for worship, its anger at anything but adoration. Its shades were all colors of self-absorption, self-importance, all-encompassing narcissism. It stuttered incomprehensible words, weaving them together with its magic, its 'sign spinning out in smoky tendrils. Alex was suddenly dizzy. He wanted to sleep. Nothing seemed more important than curling up where he stood and letting deep, dark oblivion take him. He staggered, looked at Silhouette beside him. Her eyes hung heavy, almost shut. She weaved in the air, as if asleep on her feet. Alex reached for her.

"So tired," she slurred. "It's… bad… magic." Her knees folded up beneath her and she collapsed, slid down across a few steps, and lay still.

Alex ground his teeth. The book howled through every fiber of his being, the stone at his chest pulled him forward, trying to drag him into the embrace of the wallowing, corpulent horror before him. The massive thing grinned and muttered, waving its fleshy hands. Its magesign pressed him down, tried to force him to sleep.

And he could feel this creature's magic came from the same source as his own power. The connection between his shard and the magic attacking him was undeniable. The stone at his neck sent shockwaves through him, shaking him into action. He forced his eyes open, searching with every facet of his vision. And there he saw it, embedded in this monster, buried deep within it, a part of it. He drew power from his own source and made his arms and hands as hard as steel.

With a snarl of rage he leapt into the air and came down amid the roiling, billowing flesh of the thing and drove his fists down onto its head. Its face arched in terror for a fraction of a second, stunned that its magic hadn't worked, before Alex's knuckles smashed through its white, plump skull. Dark red and gray ichor burst up and, in his fury, Alex kept going. He tore into the thing, ripping its flesh apart like uncooked dough, tearing it to pieces, seeking his prize deep within its fetid body.

Its magic died with it and sudden clarity and awareness hit Alex like a physical blow. With a cry of repulsion, he drove on, digging and tearing through the thing, pulling lumps of flesh and fat aside, grasping soft, weak bones and ripping them out. The stone pulsed inside, crying out to him, to his own piece. The two were desperate to be joined.

Alex stopped, mired in guts, and pulled his locket from inside his shirt. He opened it and magesign burst out like a sun exploding, hitting everything in a blinding flash of pure magic. The hidden stone rose up, drawn to its fellow. He was pulled forward as the two pieces attracted each other like powerful magnets. When they met he was thrown back by the burst of energy they created. He closed his hand around the locket as he landed on his back, winded by the impact, and slid painfully down the steps of the dais.

Released from her sleep, Silhouette ran to his side, dragged him to his feet. "Time to go!" she yelled, grimacing at the state of him.

He half ran, half fell across the hall. They stumbled from the confines of the building into a bright, cold, salty day and sucked in lungsful of air. Nothing had ever felt so good to Alex as the fresh ocean cold of the outside.

Dozens of white, wide-eyed islanders staggered towards them.

Gore covered his hands and arms, splattered all over his clothes, his feet and legs mired in it. Silhouette stood beside him, trembling. "They're between us and the boat," she said. "And there's a fucking lot of them."

The Darak pieces, still clenched in his hand, swelled with enormous magic. He had thought the shard he already had was powerful. Now it had doubled, the two merging together, exponentially increasing the strength they gave him. Pure magic coursed through him, dizzied him. He could do anything. And there was still another piece to find.

He remembered reading Welby's element grimoire. It had

seemed so incredible at the time, so outside anything in his experience. Now it seemed like child's play. The things he'd read about in there seemed obvious. He had power now to make those things a manifest reality.

"Hold onto something," he said.

"What?"

"Hold on to something really, really tight."

As he spoke he wound a hand through the ropes binding one of the unfortunate skeletons to an obelisk. Silhouette, eyes betraying her unease, did the same. She locked both hands into the ropes, twisting them around her wrists, and gripped tight.

Alex held the newly enlarged stone aloft, drawing on the lessons of Welby's gift. He spoke to the nature of water, understood and controlled its very essence. He sent his will out into the ocean around them and worked it like kneading clay. Letting the power of the Darak reach out he drew the ocean up towards them, enhancing the natural swell, instructing it with steadfast, undoubting command.

Silhouette gasped as a massive wave, tens of meters high, rose up behind the island. "Hold your breath," Alex warned.

The shuffling inhabitants raised their arms, their eyes and mouths wide, as the wall of water crashed over the island. The book in Alex's pocket throbbed in delight.

Alex locked his other hand into the ropes around the rock, praying they would hold. The water hit them with a breathtaking cold and dragged across the rocks with unstoppable force, covering everything with an icy, muffled silent rush. Time seemed to slow in an arctic green cathedral. As the wave slammed them and sucked back towards the sea, twisted bodies were carried with it, crashing and breaking against rocks and buildings. Some grabbed for handholds as they were carried along, some slammed against stone and were broken and held there. Swirling seaweed and churning white blurred past, all their cries lost in the roar of the water.

Alex's lungs burned, desperate to take a breath. His hands threatened to give up their grip on the ropes, fighting the inexorable pull of the wave. Then it passed and he and Silhouette were alone.

Alex unwound his hands. "Come on!"

Silhouette freed herself, sucking in frantic breaths, and followed, shaking her head in amazement. They forced frozen feet to take step after step. Their clothes, heavy and soaked, dragged on their bodies. Through a haze of exertion and desperation they made it back to the beach, grateful beyond words to find their dinghy wedged between high rocks. They dragged it free and rowed out to the borrowed fishing boat with numb hands, teeth chattering. Silhouette started the engine as Alex drew up the anchor and they powered away from the teardrop of rock, hidden in plain sight.

As the island shrank in the distance Silhouette locked the wheel and called Alex down below deck. "We need to get warm before we get hypothermia," she said, vibrating with shivers. "There should be some dry things down here, or at least blankets or towels or something."

Alex's body pulsated with the thrill of power even as the cold ate his bones. He trailed behind, trying to force rational thought through his frenzied mind.

They sat below deck wrapped in spare fisherman's clothes and ragged old blankets, huddled together for warmth. After a while Alex reached into his shirt, pulled out the locket. It was twice its previous size, misshapen like it had been melted.

He slid a thumbnail against the edge, prised the case open. It popped with a slight *tink* and magesign flooded out. The stone inside had grown. The fine silver banding holding it in place had stretched and warped, but still contained it. The locket and stone seemed combined into a single thing, one an integral part of the other, the leather binding melted in with them. The immense power of it coursed through him, firing every fiber. The exultation of the book was palpable. It seemed disappointed that he had survived the island, yet ecstatic at the chaos he'd caused, the deaths at his hands.

"What did you do there?" Silhouette asked. "With the sea."

He was utterly drained. "Welby's grimoire, a gift to me. I read a lot of it before I lost it in the explosion. I understand the elements. The book seemed so simple, but it gave me knowledge. It... imparted knowledge."

"Sounds potent."

"Must be. Water, earth, air, fire, I feel them all around, even more so now this has happened." He gestured with the newly altered Darak.

"You used an incredible amount of power back there, do you realize that?"

"Yeah. But it's the stone."

"It's you, Alex. The stone amplifies it. Most normal people would have been torn apart by what you channelled."

"How can something this small ...?"

Silhouette smirked. "Size isn't everything. It's not the physical attributes that make an item like that powerful. It's the magic that went into making it. Power stones like that, like Joseph's, they don't really occupy just the physical space you can see and touch. They direct energy through many realms. The stone itself, that's just an anchor point. Same as the book that holds a thread of the consciousness of Uthentia. It's just a physical fixture in this realm."

Alex rubbed his hand across his face. "It feels like it's tearing me apart. I feel like I could burst into atoms at any moment."

"Yet you handled it and survived."

"What were they?" Alex asked.

Silhouette's face twisted in disgust. "More to the point, what was that thing at the top?"

Alex closed his eyes. "It felt old. Centuries old. It used to be a man, I'm sure, but it had merged with that shard somehow. That was its downfall. It was so convinced its magic was unbeatable. I had the one thing that could resist it."

"A piece of the same," Silhouette said.

"Exactly. It was used to absolute control and adoration, constantly serviced by those weird fuckers. It must have found the stone and it turned into that thing over centuries. Could that happen to me?"

"No way," Silhouette said. "You choose how to use it. That...

thing was messed up. It had some freaky personality before, I expect. Those people it kept around were horrible, inbred things, all of them kept in a closed loop for fuck knows how long. Anyone who found them got put to sleep and hung up, I'm guessing. The skeletons, remember?"

Alex shivered, with more than the cold. "That could have been us."

"It would have been me. That thing's magic overwhelmed me in an instant."

Alex made a wry face, gesturing with the locket. "Thankfully this kept me going. It felt the other part of itself and pushed me on."

"And then there were two. One more piece to go."

"Then what?" Alex asked.

"That's for you to figure out, Iron Balls."

Silhouette shook Alex awake. He rose from sleep reluctantly, his mind swimming up through dreams like tar. She wore her own clothes again and handed him his. "They're still damp and reek of diesel, but I got them dried out a bit in the engine bay during the trip back."

He shook himself, throwing off blankets and dressing. "Sorry."

"What for?"

"I seem to keep falling asleep and leaving you to sort things out."

"You saved our lives," Sil said with a laugh, "so I don't mind driving the boat. You feel better?"

"I do actually."

The throb of the stone was stronger than ever. He laid a hand over it, through his jacket. The book in his pocket howled to be read.

"You okay?" Silhouette asked.

Alex pulled the book out, sat heavily on the bench. He hated the thing. It was like a cancerous tumour on the outside of his body. He didn't even understand it properly. Some thread of some entity that played with him while it tried to kill him. He didn't want to read it, to give it any more power over him than it already had. The fact that it was a book had become irrelevant. The thing inside was his enemy and he was reluctant to give it any voice. But its urgency caused a vortex in his mind. He opened it and read, *Universe layers and pools of unknown, the stone empowers. Great harmony, power of stars and oceans. More to extract, to uncover, reveal. Play on, with life, with death, with ecstasy.*

He slammed it shut. "It hurts my fucking brain to read this!"

"What does it say?"

"It's urging me on, that's all."

"Sure," Silhouette said. "It could wreak incredible havoc with you, if you let it. You're strong enough to resist. Get the power and use it to defeat whatever that really is."

Alex threw the book away over his shoulder, knowing it

wouldn't be gone for long. "Who am I fucking kidding? A group of your people, the strongest of their kind, were only partially successful. What chance do I have?"

"Don't doubt yourself. That's what it wants."

"Whatever. Are we back?"

"Yeah."

"Come on then."

They left the boat moored in the harbor and headed for the hotel. Silhouette assured Alex the fisherman would find it all in order. "I even tidied the dinghy away for him."

Alex snorted. "You're all heart."

"You should be ecstatic, you know."

"What do you mean?"

She stopped. "Can you feel your mood swings? You're acting sour when you've just survived the weirdest place I've ever seen and gained a massive increase in strength. You should be bouncing off the walls."

He stood still, unsure what to say. He felt bitter, absolutely miserable. He turned away, walking on. "I don't actually want all this. I never did."

"So why did you follow Welby back in Sydney?"

There was that moment of choice again. "I had to leave town for a while."

"But you didn't have to go with Welby."

"I was curious. I didn't think we'd even get out of the country."

"But when you did get out of Australia, you still followed him. You got to London and you still followed him."

Anger rose. "So what? I was fucking curious! I didn't expect to get caught up in anything like this."

"Of course not."

"Welby said he could teach me more about myself. More about my vision."

"You might be caught up in something you don't want, but you're here because of something you did want. You can't go around lamenting that things didn't work out like you hoped. Life rarely does."

"This is different."

Silhouette sneered. "It's no different at all. Play the cards you're dealt, Alex. That thing, whatever it is, is far from human. It's beyond any of our understanding and it's toying with you. You're a conduit for its frustration, can't you see that?"

"What do you mean?"

"You just had a major success. Uthentia wants you dead, it wants your demise to be as spectacular as possible. We should have been caught by those mutants, strung up and fucking eaten or something. I *was* caught by them, but the stone saved *you*. You beat them. The book is pissed about it, so you're feeling pissed."

The aggravated emotions ran through every part of him, convoluted and confused, she was right about that. And the book was angry. "Maybe," he conceded.

"Own your feelings, Alex. Don't feel what it feels. Differentiate yourself. You've just gained enormous power. The more power you have, the more chance you have of beating it. Rejoice in that. Defy the evil bastard!"

A fire rose in his mind and groin. "I want to fuck you so hard."

"Just as well we've still got a room."

They reached the hotel in minutes and almost ran up the stairs. Alex pulled at her jacket as they climbed, laughing as she batted at his hands. She was right. He should feel good about what he'd survived, and nothing celebrated success and survival like sex.

An image rose in his mind, the night before, blood in the alleyway, Silhouette's snout buried deep in the wino's body, her conversation with Joseph. Uthentia's laughter bubbled through his mind. *Fuck you, stop trying to turn me against her!* But perhaps he should consider that. Could he trust her? The fire in him, his rage and frustration, swelled. He growled his anger at the book, *I'll make those decisions, not you.* He pictured Silhouette naked, pictured her riding him, sweating and moaning, and his passion smothered his anger again.

"You okay?" she asked.

"Oh yeah, get inside!"

They fumbled at the door, finally getting the key straight, and fell into the room. They threw their jackets to the floor and stiffened instantly, lust freezing solid in their veins.

"Hello there," said a small, wiry man. He reclined in the old armchair, his dark trenchcoat lay around him like a cape. He had one foot resting on the opposite knee.

Silhouette dropped into a crouch, growling. Alex let the power of the stone flood through him, hardening his bones. Fucking or fighting, either or both were fine with him.

"Now, now," the small man said. "Let's not get all crazy."

"Who are you?" Alex asked, deliberately keeping his voice calm, level. "How do you keep finding us?" The shades around the strange, thin man were colors and shifts he didn't recognise, shades that seemed truly alien. But he read the man's calm confidence and iron resolve clearly. Whatever he was, he seemed to think his job was done and the rest would be easy.

"You smell unique," the man said. "You're not easy to track, but I'm something of an expert."

"Who are you?"

"People call me the Subcontractor."

Silhouette sidled around, putting a gap between herself and Alex. "And what exactly do you want?" she asked.

"Well, I've been given a task." He wriggled one hand at Alex. "You've got a couple of things there. Very interesting things." His eyes narrowed. "More powerful than they were before, even."

"That's no concern of yours."

"Ah, but it is. I am to take those things from you for my client. Technically, my job is also to kill you both, but it doesn't have to be that way. I know my client well. Give me what he requires and he won't care about you any more, so I can let you live if you comply."

Alex barked laughter. "You serious? You tiny little freak, I'm not giving you anything."

"Be careful, Alex," Silhouette said, not taking her eyes from the Subcontractor.

"Careful?"

"Whatever this is, it's very dangerous."

The Subcontractor grinned broadly, his mouth crammed with

teeth. "You see, Alex, she shows respect. You, on the other hand, are very rude. I cannot abide rudeness."

He moved so fast that Alex hit the wall on the far side of the room before he realized the fight was on. A wave of panic froze his limbs for a moment, adrenaline surging through his veins. He hadn't seen a thing. He had been watching the man's shades and they were alert, but there had been no indication of any movement. Silhouette slammed into the Subcontractor a millisecond before the thin creature's teeth snapped shut on Alex's throat.

Alex sucked air back into his lungs, aware of the book's joy. It wanted him to fight and lose. "Fuck you!" Alex yelled, to the book, the Subcontractor, the universe and everything in it.

He gathered the power of the Darak. The more he used the magic, the more expertly he could manipulate it. The Subcontractor rolled with Silhouette's attack and the two of them fell. As Silhouette rolled underneath, Alex closed the distance and collected the Subcontractor's head against one iron shin. The small man flipped up and over, crashing a tall lamp against the wall as he flew.

Silhouette gained her feet in an instant and they bore down on the Subcontractor. Magesign pulsed off the man and his human appearance dropped away like a discarded coat. Shining black chitinous armor covered him. Vaguely man-shaped, four limbed, but backward jointed, he crouched low. His face shone dark and featureless in the low light of the room, his mouth wide, row upon row of sharp, silica-like teeth. A long, forked tongue flickered out, tasting the air. His hands flexed, long, sharpened fingers writhing hungrily.

"What the fuck are you?" Alex breathed, moving cautiously.

Silhouette mirrored his movement, trying to take the other side. The Subcontractor shivered its head, several tiny eyes glistening under a ridge of chitin. Alex tried to read its shades, but they were all textures and colors he couldn't understand. The creature sprang towards Silhouette. As Alex moved to go with it, it changed direction, kicking out at Sil and slamming into Alex with bone-crunching speed.

Silhouette cried out, flying over the bed to land in a heap on the floor. She writhed in pain as Alex tried to keep his breath, hammering blows across the creature's slick, hard skull as its hands swiped, tearing the flesh of his arms and chest. Wherever it struck it drew blood and left stinging agony.

Alex's vision crossed, his lungs burned, his knuckles bled along with everywhere the thing struck. An unfamiliar terror rose in his mind. It was stronger than him, and faster. It had shades he couldn't decipher. He kicked out in desperation, forcing a space between them, and staggered away, trying to buy time. *Everyone has a weakness, Alex. Defend until you find it.*

It was on him again, moving in unnatural patterns, exercising techniques he couldn't predict. He blocked and dodged, diving across the room. He'd be damned if he'd die here and give the book any pleasure. The creature stayed with him, snatching and snapping. If it got a grip with those teeth he'd be done for. He dropped low, spinning on one hand and one foot, sending a kick around into the side of its head. He was rewarded with a dull *thwack* and the thing stumbled sideways. Alex sprang in the opposite direction, watching it closely as it moved.

It twisted on hard, spindly legs, the reversed knee compressing as it bunched up to spring again. Alex drew all the considerable power of the stone and used it for speed, diving away as the Subcontractor came at him. As it moved again he saw his opportunity.

He rolled aside, fiery agony from a long claw arcing across the back of his shoulder as he moved. As the Subcontractor turned to spring Alex reversed his own movement and leapt back underneath. The creature flew above him and Alex grabbed one thin leg and rolled. He twisted, using his bodyweight to slam the thing into the floor and locked one forearm against the knee joint. He cranked with all his might. The thing clashed its teeth as its knee disintegrated with a wet snap. It hissed a high scream of pain, its hands a blur of sharpened torture as Alex rolled clear.

It became harder to concentrate through the pain. Alex knew he was losing blood. This had to end. The Subcontractor staggered to its feet, balancing on one leg, the broken limb swinging useless beneath it. *When you gain any advantage, press the attack.*

Alex gathered everything he had left and dived straight for it. The body was armored, its weapons deadly, but its joints were thin. Alex drove one elbow up under its head, wrapped his legs around it and grabbed an arm. As the other arm raked fire down his back, he locked and twisted the arm he held, separating the elbow. The creature howled. Alex kept his weight going forward as it fell, rolling with it, slamming another elbow into the side of its head.

Pain whined through his arm from the impact with the hard chitin of the Subcontractor's skull. A stuttering hiss of laughter came from between those rows of sharp teeth as it twisted and turned over once more, rising to sit across Alex's hips. It was surprisingly heavy, pinning Alex to the threadbare carpet. Its legs and arms clamped across his own, even its broken limbs effective in holding him down, tiny barbs hooking into the carpet, locking it in. Panic swelled through Alex's mind, *I'm going to lose! I'm going to die.*

He saw Silhouette face-down on the carpet, blood leaking from her mouth. *We've both lost.* He bucked his hips, trying to escape the thing mounted above him. He drew power from the stone and used it to give him strength, harden his body, anything to get out from beneath certain death, but his panic blurred his thoughts. The Subcontractor seemed glued to the ground, trapping Alex like a barbed-wire blanket. Waves of exultation pulsed from its shades as it raised one hand high, long fingers like hard black knives pointing at Alex's eyes. "Hood will be pleased," it said, close to Alex's ear, its voice harsh and muffled by its unnatural mouth. "Black Diamond gets the goods again!"

Alex rained blows upwards, crying out in desperation, pinned, trapped. Beaten. The Subcontractor hissed laughter again and drew its elbow higher. Alex stared at the shining sharp tips of its fingers, refusing to look away from death. He sucked in a last breath and screamed, "Fuck you!" and the Subcontractor's head exploded.

Alex's ears rang with the sound of thunder as shudders went through him. The hard, plastic-like body of the creature collapsed limp over him, the remains of its head dripping bile-colored viscosity and yellow, liquid brains over his face and chest. He scrambled from under it, pain and exhaustion threatening his consciousness. The hotel clerk stood in the doorway, her huge stomach and bosom wobbling with her shocked trembling, a shotgun hanging loose in her hands. "What in the high holy fuck is that?" she said in a strained voice. Her eyes were wide and terrified, her face white as snow.

Alex tried to think through his pain and the desolation in his mind. He had lost a fight. He'd been saved by this fat woman and her gun. He didn't know how to feel. "I have no idea," he said, gasping, trying to regain some composure.

Silhouette lay across the smashed room, moaning softly. *Thank fuck she's still alive.* He dragged himself across the floor to her, fumbling in her pockets for the healing powder.

"I'm calling the cops," the hotel clerk said.

"No, please, no police."

"What? Are you kidding?"

She was right. What excuse could he have not to call the police? He couldn't tell her the truth. His eyes beseeched her. "Please, no police."

She backed out the door. "Fuck you and fuck that!" She turned and barrelled down the hallway.

Alex cursed and pulled Sil's pouch from her waistband.

Outside the hotel window the planesbird hovered, leathery wings beating the air. It watched the mayhem in the small room. As the fight ended with a flash and a boom, it swooped away, slipping through a fold in reality with a coppery flash of realmshift.

EIGHTEEN

Alex mixed the bittersweet medicine and sipped it, hoping he hadn't made it too strong. Or not strong enough. Trying to ignore the burning lacerations all over his body, he lifted Silhouette's head and tipped the glass against her lips. She drank, eyelids fluttering.

"I hurt inside, Alex." Her voice was weak.

"Drink this. It'll fix you, right?"

Her eyes flickered open. "I hope so."

They passed the glass back and forth till it was empty.

"I have never been beaten up so often," Alex muttered. "And I fight for a living. That thing fucking beat me." His clothes hung ragged and bloodstained.

Silhouette said nothing.

"If that woman hadn't had a gun," Alex said, his face haunted. He could already feel the potion infiltrating his wounds, reknitting his flesh.

"She did," Sil said. "There's a million what ifs in the world. This time you got lucky."

"I don't use luck," Alex said angrily. "I don't lose fights!"

"You lost this one. Get used to it. So did I. Move on."

Alex grimaced.

She dropped the empty glass to the carpet beside her. "My powder's nearly finished. I can make more, but not easily. I need rare ingredients."

"How rare?"

"Not from this realm. Things that grow in The Other Lands."

Alex frowned, trying to comprehend the statement. "You've been there?"

"Fuck no. I buy from dealers, but it's hard to find and damned expensive."

"Can you go there?"

"I guess so. I have Fey blood. If they can get here on thin days I don't see why I couldn't go there. Screw that, though."

Alex stared at the human-insect hybrid on the floor, yellow

ichor thickening on the carpet all around what used to be its head. "What the hell is that thing?"

"I have no idea. I've never seen anything like it. Of course, there's more in these realms than I could possibly know about."

"It said Hood will be pleased and Black Diamond gets the goods again. What does that mean?"

"Best guess is Black Diamond's some kind of organisation and this Hood character is in charge. I suppose Hood sent that thing after us."

The stone pulsed against Alex's chest, keeping time with his calming heart as the medicine worked. "This Hood seems to want my book and stone. I wish I could give them to him."

"Alex, you have to dissociate the two. The book needs to go. The Darak is your greatest ally. Don't let the book poison your mind against your greatest weapon."

"The power it gave me against that thing *was* intoxicating, even if it wasn't enough."

Silhouette struggled into a crouch. "Exactly. Uthentia wants you dead, but the stone is your friend. Let it in."

"I keep remembering that thing on the island. I don't want to be like that."

"You won't. That thing must have been utterly self-obsessed when it first found the shard. You're not like it."

Alex stood, every muscle protesting. "We have to go. That woman is calling the police. How are you feeling?"

"Fucked. But I can walk."

She went to the window, snatching up her jacket on the way. Alex grabbed his own from the floor, their backpack from the bed and followed. They clambered out onto the fire escape, darkness creeping in, bringing more wet and cold with it. They gained the roof, ran across to the edge. A gap of about twenty feet, dropping down into a dark, wet alley, greeted them.

"Look." Sil pointed at a police car pulling up to the kerb out front. "We have to go."

The next building was fifteen feet down and twenty feet away, with nothing in between. "I can't make a jump like that!" Alex protested.

"Yes. You can."

"No way."

"Alex, you're about the fittest, most capable human I've ever known. And you have a talisman that makes Joseph's gem look like something from a Christmas cracker. Use it, ignore the book. I bet you could have beat that thing back there if you'd really opened yourself to the Darak."

That gave him pause. There was some truth in it, which only made the loss harder to bear. He remembered the power surging through him as he fought the Subcontractor. The thing would have torn any number of normal humans apart, but the Darak had made him hard, fast, strong. Not strong and fast enough, but maybe that was his fault. Whatever the Subcontractor had been it was an enemy he hoped never to meet again. With only a single shard he'd fought against two gargoyles and won. He'd fought Ataro and won. Maybe it was time he listened to Silhouette and took true ownership of it. He wouldn't end up like that abomination on the island. His was a better destiny. The book whined in his mind, frustration and anger. He smiled. *Good. Am I annoying you?*

He took several long strides backwards, gathering energy from the Darak as Silhouette's powder healed him. He let its magic soak through him, pictured himself leaping easily over the wide gap. Letting out a deep breath he sprinted for the building's edge and sprang forward, his legs like pistons, driving him up. He cleared the alleyway and another dozen feet beyond, crashing and rolling onto the opposite roof in a spray of gravel.

Silhouette landed lithely behind him and strolled over. "You're lacking a certain finesse, but that's kinda the idea."

He laughed, buzzing with power. "That felt wicked!"

"Good. Let's do it again. Try to keep up."

She ran, sidestepped an air-conditioning unit, and bounded over the next gap. Alex whooped, his body feeling more alive than it ever had. He chased her, leaping easily over another alley, springing up to grab the edge of the next roof, twenty feet above. Silhouette was already airborne as he dragged himself up, on her way to the next building. He doubled his speed, the cold evening air whipping past his face. He ran, leapt, rolled and laughed, catching up to Silhouette in seconds. Together they cleared several more rooftops before heading down a fire escape, hand over hand, and flipping to the back street below. They slowed to a jog and strolled out into the main road, panting.

Alex couldn't wipe the grin off his face. "I feel like Batman!"

"Welcome to my world. You kept up well."

"I love this!"

"No shit." Her smile faded as she looked him up and down. "You look like you've been wrestling a tiger. Change clothes."

They slipped into the darkness of the back street and Alex shrugged off the backpack, changed quickly in the gloom. He stuffed his torn, bloody clothes into a dumpster behind a burger bar and they headed back out into the main street.

"I vote we get out of this one-horse town," Silhouette said. "The main airport is in St John. Let's get there and try to organise a flight back to the mainland."

"How do we get to St John? And what do we do when we get back to the mainland?"

Silhouette shrugged. "I'll get us to St John. You worry about finding Meera, because we're fresh out of direction right about now."

Mr Hood sat behind his giant desk, painstakingly cleaning a Nordic idol with alcohol solution and cotton buds. He frowned at the phone on his desk, a voice coming through tinny over the speaker. "I don't want anything illegal, Mr Hood." The voice had a strong Asian accent.

"Nothing illegal? Please, Mr Choy, what do you take me for?"

Crackling laughter burst out. "You don't want me to answer that. Your reputation is not unsullied."

Hood tutted. "My reputation is what led you to me. It's what enabled me to meet your needs in the past. If you don't like it, you can deal elsewhere."

"No need for hostility. I just don't want illegal goods."

Hood barked a laugh. "Who's to judge the legality of the things I supply you? You want to run anything you've bought from me by the police and see what they have to say?"

"No, no, no. Let me rephrase. I don't want anything that has a history attached. A history that might come looking for it, you understand?"

"Yes, Mr Choy, I understand. This latest selection comes from a deceased estate that I had been negotiating with for some time. Let's just say I got lucky with my timing on this one. The previous owner certainly won't be coming after these things." He looked up at Sparks, mimed stabbing himself in the eyes with two fingers, grinning.

Sparks grinned back. She sat in one corner, bathed in winter sunlight flooding in through the window, tapping away at a laptop perched on her knees.

"Very well," Choy said. "If you're sure these items come without repercussions then there are several grimoires in that collection which interest me."

"I thought there would be. Use the usual encrypted channel to list the items and I'll have secured example files sent over. If you're happy then we can arrange a visit for you."

"At the prices you're suggesting, I hope you'll meet the expense of my visit yourself, Mr Hood," Choy wheedled.

Hood rolled his eyes. "Tell me what you're interested in and I'll see what I can tee up."

"Very good, very good. I'll contact you again soon."

"You do that." Hood viciously stabbed a button on the phone, scowling. "That fucking Choy," he said, derisive. "Always has to haggle."

Sparks laughed. "It's his way. It's cultural."

"Fuck culture. He'll try to get a discount too, you wait and see."

"I know he will. But let's be honest, we have a pretty broad margin on this collection." She smiled at him, one eyebrow cocked.

"Well, yes, there is that. But I'll never reduce a profit margin, however wide. Real power is not in magic but in the commerce of magic, Sparks. It's a shame my poverty stricken mage of a father didn't realize that." An urgent rapping on the door interrupted him. He sighed, putting down the half-cleaned idol. "Come."

The door creaked open and Jackson looked in, his face nervous. One of his hideous birds perched on his shoulder. "Er, Mr Hood, sir?"

"Yes, yes, come in. What is it?"

"This little one just reported back, sir."

"Yes. And?"

"The Subcontractor, sir. He's dead." Jackson stared at the floor as he spoke.

Hood stilled, mute, for several moments. Ms Sparks stopped typing, watching with pursed lips. "What?" Hood said eventually.

"The Subcontractor's dead, sir."

Muscles twitched in Hood's cheeks. "How?"

"There was a fight, apparently. In a hotel room. The two he was tracking."

Hood's teeth creaked together, audible across the large office. "Those two defeated the Subcontractor?"

"Yes, sir. Quite a battle it was too. The Subcontractor dropped his disguise and everything."

Hood's eyebrows shot up. "How much of it can you actually see? How much detail does that creature give you?"

"Images and sensations, sir. Not really clear pictures."

"Do you have any idea what the Subcontractor was?"

"No, sir. Not like anything I've ever felt before."

Hood stood, his chair flying back to crash into the wall behind him. He stalked out from behind his desk, paced across the office.

Sparks closed the laptop, rested her hands on it. She watched thoughtfully, keeping silent. Jackson scuffed at the expensive Persian carpet with one scruffy boot toe.

"The human still has the items presumably?" Hood asked.

"Yes, sir. He was quite overwhelming for my little beauty here. He burns so brightly. She fears him."

"For those two to defeat the Subcontractor... Oh, I really want whatever it is he has now. I want it so badly. Can your bird still track them?"

"I should imagine so, sir. If they haven't gone too far yet."

Hood spun to face him. "What? Well, send it now, you imbecile! Don't lose them!"

Jackson shuddered, turning to face the thing on his shoulder. He muttered and whispered to it, stroking its head. The bird leapt up, beat its wings once, and vanished with a bright flash. A metallic scent hung in the air. "She'll find 'em, sir. And keep an eye on 'em."

"Good. You'd better pray she does. We need to send someone else after them. Someone stronger than the Subcontractor."

Jackson and Sparks held their tongues, both knowing Hood well enough not to risk his wrath by speaking. "But who is stronger than the Subcontractor? That freak, whatever he was, has never failed me before. Bah! All his secrets have died with him."

He turned and strode to the window, standing beside Sparks, paying her no attention at all. He stared out across London's Docklands, his hands gently massaging each other. "But he failed *this* time," he said, addressing no one in particular. "Whatever that boy has it must be incredible. I want it, whatever the cost."

"Are you sure?" Sparks asked, immediately regretting it.

"What?"

She plunged on. "Whatever the cost? If they beat the Subcontractor the price might be high indeed."

Hood slapped her hard across the cheek, knocking her to the floor, laptop spinning across the rug. He walked back to his desk, slumping into his chair as she struggled back to her feet, wiping blood-spattered lips with the back of one hand.

"I need powerful allies here," Hood said, his fingers drumming on the dark mahogany. "I need something stronger than the Subcontractor." *Tap-tap-tap-tap.* "But what *is* there?" *Tap-tap-tap-tap.* "Maybe not just one ally. Perhaps many." *Tap-tap-tap-tap.* A smile spread across his face. He turned to his computer, typing rapidly. "Perhaps I need the Dark Sisters." His eyes scanned. With a noise of satisfaction he stood and strode to a sealed bookcase, heavy glass locked before dark wood and leather spines. Pulling a key from inside his suit jacket he unlocked the doors, fingertip tracing the ancient grimoires.

Sparks watched in trepidation, standing still, hoping not to be noticed again. These were the ones he would never sell. Too dangerous, he said. The kind of thing that people might one day use against him. Her lip throbbed and a deep part of her wished someone *would* turn against him.

"Yes," Hood said, mostly to himself. "Here we are. Yes, perhaps that's the answer." He pulled a large volume from the shelf. "Their price is very high. But worth it!"

He rounded on Sparks as he passed her. She flinched. He grabbed her chin, tipping her face up to meet his violent kiss. She melted, kissing him back with passion. Jackson seemed interested only in the floor.

Hood broke away and Sparks staggered as he released her. A look of drunkenness cleared from her face as he moved on. "Yes. The Dark Sisters," he muttered. "But how to reach them?" He sat at his desk, started thumbing through the large book.

Sparks pulled herself together. "The Dark Sisters? I've never heard of them. Who are they?"

"Death, that's who. Evil. Relentless. Their fee is usually too high to ever consider, but in this case I'm prepared to compromise."

"Are they mercenaries? Humans?"

Hood grinned. "Mercenaries? Of a sort. Humans? Good God, Sparks, no. They're about as far from human as I imagine anything gets."

NINETEEN

Silhouette drove the car she'd hotwired carefully, staying under the speed limit, avoiding attention. The roads weren't particularly busy. A kind of dread lurked deep in Alex's soul, but it was a seductive feeling. Every moment that passed with this woman the more he wanted to stay with her. He was becoming addicted. And becoming more like her. Falling in love with a monster. Was he becoming a monster too?

He had a malevolent force dragging at his life, a force that would surely kill him eventually, causing untold mayhem along the way. He had to shake himself free of it. Did he have to free himself of Silhouette too, before it was too late? How many would he kill saving himself? Those freaks on the island were messed up, but did he really have any right to wipe them out? If he'd died there and Silhouette had died with him that would have been an end to it, the book stuck, never to darken the real world again. Perhaps that would have been the best outcome. The book pushed its presence into his mind, revelling in the deaths. It urged him to kill again, to cause chaos, never to abandon it on some remote island. Alex knew, beyond a doubt, that these thoughts came from Uthentia. Its evil tendrils sank deeper into his consciousness all the time. Anger roiled in his gut. The urge to slaughter rose up, filling his chest with a fire.

Silhouette looked at him sharply. "What's going on, Alex?"

He ground his teeth, trying to suppress the surge of fury.

"Alex, chill the fuck out. You need to control this."

The book pulsed like his heart, racing with him. He remembered the fight with the Subcontractor and the animal joy of it. Even the defeat gave him a rush, under no illusion that luck had saved him. Luck in the form of a shotgun-toting, obese clerk. He wanted more havoc, more adrenaline, more death. He tipped his head back, yelling frustration at the heavens.

Silhouette hit the brakes, pulled the car off the road into a long darkened driveway lined with trees. She stopped in the deepest shadows and killed the engine. Alex clenched his fists on his lap, resisting the urge to strike out at her. "I feel like an explosion!"

She grinned at him. "Good. I'll give you one."

In one quick movement she was on his lap, knees astride his legs, grinding into him. She leaned in, biting at his neck, kissing his lips.

His desire for her flamed. He wanted to take her and then rip the life from her while he came. The real Alex, disappearing in a sea of rage, hated himself. He gasped. "I don't know if I can control…"

She slapped him. "Shut the fuck up." She put his hands around to her butt, pressed down on him harder, kissed him more urgently. She sat back, pulling her shirt off, pressing his head into her breasts. He reached beside the seat, pulled a lever. The seat fell back with his weight. Silhouette fell with it then sat up again, hands on his chest. She looked magnificent in the darkness. She struggled to pull down his jeans and her own, her body twisting in the confined space. He helped her, occupying his hands, trying to focus on her body, blot out the fury. Her features morphed as she growled, her own passion feral and powerful. "Come on! Fuck me!"

The car rocked, their heat steaming the cold windows.

Hood sat back with the old tome from his private bookcase, the leather seat of his private jet creaking as he moved. Sparks watched him. "Where are we going?" she asked. Clouds built swollen sculptures far below the plane, golden with sunlight.

He spoke without looking up. "Scotland, Sparks. The middle of bloody nowhere."

"That's where these Sisters live?"

"It's one place to reach them."

Sparks couldn't hide her concern. "I understand how badly you want whatever this boy has, but I can't help wondering how high the cost might be."

Hood lowered the book, his expression bored. "Why don't you let me worry about that? I seek sport as much as money. This whole thing has me entertained. I haven't had something like this to get my teeth into for a while. You could always find… something else to do."

Sparks shook her head vigorously. "No, no. I'm with you all the way. You know that. So what are these Dark Sisters? How do we deal with them?"

Hood gestured with the grimoire. "If you shut up and let me read I'll figure it out."

Sparks's eyebrows raised in surprise. "You don't know? Have you ever dealt with them before?"

Hood sighed, closed the book on his lap. "No. I met a man many years ago. He and I did a lot of trade together. He unearthed this for me, and it tells the tale of the Dark Sisters, how they can be bargained with and so forth. I've never used them before, as their price is very high. This is a special case."

"Sounds dangerous."

"Of course it's dangerous, Sparks. Everything we do is touched with danger. That's where the sport lies. But I have the power and the ability to pay what they ask, so I'll employ them and task them with getting me what I want. I'm a businessman, and this is business."

"You made a lot of calls before we left."

"There was a lot to arrange."

Sparks wasn't really mollified. She didn't like it when Hood conducted activities without including her. She had proved time and again how valuable an asset to him she could be, yet so often he left her on the outer. He seemed to revel in it sometimes, often claiming it was for her own protection while a self-satisfied smirk played across his lips. "I hope the book tells you all you need to know," she said.

"It will. It cost me enough. Now shut up, and let me read."

Alex lay back, gasping for breath. Cold air came in where the passenger door used to be, chilling his sweat-soaked body. Silhouette crawled back into the car through the ruined doorway, pressing the back of one hand to her rapidly swelling lower lip. "Fucking hell," she said between pants, dropping heavily into the driver's seat.

"I'm sorry," Alex said. "Are you okay?" His shame threatened to drown him. The rage had been diluted again, the pressure valve of frustration and anger released once more with their union, but every time he came closer to killing her.

She pulled her clothes back on. "Yeah, I'm fine. That was a good one!"

"I'm glad you like it."

"I'm glad it works. You feeling better?"

He pulled the seat up, dragged his jeans back on. "Yeah, it certainly calms the anger." He wanted to tell her that he had no idea how long he could resist the desire to kill her, but how could he possibly approach that truth?

Silhouette pursed her lips, looking at the shattered windscreen, glass like a giant confused spiderweb. The dashboard sat cracked and crooked, the passenger door lying in the darkness a few feet away. "Well, this is all pretty fucked up."

Alex nodded, flexing knuckles that still throbbed with the impact of repeatedly punching a car. He managed to direct a lot of the fury away from Silhouette while she helped relieve it, but not all. He hated what he had become. "What now?"

"I guess we have to get another one." She opened her door, looked down the dark driveway. "They'll probably have a car down there somewhere. I'll go and check. Can you do anything with this one?"

"Like what?"

"Well, burning it is the best way to make sure we don't leave prints or anything. Maybe you can find something to siphon some petrol out and douse it?"

"I'll try."

Silhouette disappeared into the shadows. Alex stared after her for a moment then climbed out. He thought about Welby's element grimoire, the powerful stone. He remembered the giant wave standing up over the island. Water, air, earth and fire. Those were the things he'd read about. Things he understood now with such clarity. He pictured the car on fire, visualised a roaring incandescence consuming the carpets and vinyl seats, flaking the paint off in a furious inferno. The Darak spread its own warmth through his body. He drew on it, saw twisted and blackened metal in his mind's eye. He tried to draw raw heat from the air the same way he'd drawn up a giant wave from a choppy ocean. He let his guards down, let his magesign swell out. Within seconds his arcane energies flashed into manifest flames, the entire car an inferno of blistering heat. He threw one arm up in front of his face, staggering away from the furnace. The metal frame of the car glowed a piercing red, the bodywork and chassis twisting and curling, melting like wax on a bonfire.

Silhouette jogged along, one hand pressed to her aching ribs. Alex got more violent every time, his fury harder to control. Fun it might be, and she did enjoy herself every time, but it was starting to scare her. The passion and animal intensity thrilled her. Alex's humanity, deep inside him, made for so much more than callous Kin couplings. But when would the influence against Alex push that humanity away? She pulled her phone from her pocket as she went, the screen informing her of numerous missed calls and messages. She sighed and dialled Joseph's number.

It rang once then, "How dare you ignore me, Silhouette? Who do you think you are?"

"I'm with him all the time, my Lord," she said, careful to keep her voice level. "I can't talk with you unless I'm alone."

His breathing sounded calm over the line. That disturbed her more than if he'd been furious. "Well?" he asked. "What news?"

"Alex has the second piece."

"Really?" Joseph was clearly impressed. "This human is proving to be quite resourceful. How much of your help did he need to get it?"

"Well, he actually saved me," Silhouette said with a wince.

"Interesting. So now what?"

"We're off to see if we can track down the third part."

"Do you think he'll find it?"

Silhouette frowned, unsure what to say. "It's hard to tell, really. We've nothing to go on so far."

"I want that stone, Silhouette."

"I know you do."

"Have you seen anything that might help us separate the stone from the book?"

Silhouette stood in deep shadow under a large pine. Two cars, a sedan and a pick-up, were parked in front of a ramshackle house. "No," she said. "Only his death will release them. But how to get one and not the other is still beyond me."

"Think of a way, Silhouette. Only my protection saves you from the Kin. You're too much human *and* too much Fey. But if you do this for me, *prove* you are true Kin… Get me this stone, little one. I want to hear more news soon."

The line went dead. Silhouette stood in the darkness for several moments, phone gripped tightly, teeth worrying her lower lip. With a growl of annoyance she turned her attention to the vehicles.

Over the roar of the flames Alex heard another sound, an engine revving. Silhouette skidded a big black pick-up truck to a halt beside him. "Nice work," she said with a smile. "Get in."

Alex jumped into the passenger seat. He trembled, buzzing with the magic he'd channelled.

"You okay?" Silhouette asked as she gunned the engine and powered out onto the main road again.

"Yeah. Just a bit shaken."

She narrowed her eyes. "You didn't siphon petrol, did you?"

"No."

"Then how?"

"Fire's an element."

"Yeah. And you're pretty scary. You're developing skills at a furious rate, Iron Balls. You need to be careful."

"Do I?" he asked, confused.

"You're running before you can walk. Fuck, you're sprinting before you can crawl. A person can screw themselves up using magic like you're doing."

"You're the one that told me to embrace the stone's power. Own it."

"Sure. But go easy, a bit at a time. You immolated that car!"

"Well, I did the job."

"You did. But remember, power is nothing without control. You have to learn to protect yourself from… well, from yourself."

They drove in silence for a while. Silhouette had it right. The power that surged through him back there had felt like it might burst him open, shatter him into atoms. He thought about his fight training, his Sifu's lessons. *First and most important is technique, Alex. Excellent technique will always lead to maximum speed and power. If you're all speed and power with no technique you'll only ever be a brute, never reaching your full potential. You'll have lost to yourself before you ever face an opponent.*

The same thing applied here. Slow practice would lead to mastery. Massive bursts would inevitably lead to disaster. *Power is nothing without control.* His Sifu had said that more times than he could remember, and now Silhouette echoed his dead master's words. She embodied control for him, taking the hit every time the book tried to overcome him. Without her he'd have run rampant by now, slaughtering who knew how many. If a human tried to calm him down like Silhouette did, that human would be destroyed in an instant. As much as she seemed to genuinely enjoy it, Silhouette was saving his life every time, at enormous risk to herself. He owed it to her as much as himself to regain command over his situation. He wished he could trust her, but regardless, he needed control.

He pulled the book from his pocket, watching the 'sign swim around it like a smoky octopus, reaching for his face. He opened it and read, *A universal song of power glides above you, through you, with you. Together and immortal, energies to shatter worlds. Three parts, two stolen, one lost, beyond you. Become the universal power without, give in, let fly, worlds collide.*

He slammed the book shut with a gasp.

"What did it say?" Silhouette asked, not taking her eyes from the road.

"I think it's telling me to give up. That I won't be able to find the last piece."

"Sounds to me like it fears what might happen if you do."

"Yeah, maybe," Alex conceded. "It's so desperate for chaos. It desires nothing more than absolute bedlam."

"You think it's worried you might get the better of it with the complete stone?"

"I don't know. I think it's pissed off that every time it tries to drive me to violence you take the fury away."

She winked, blew him a kiss. "Glad to be of service."

Alex looked at the closed book in his hands. "But I'm scared, Sil. I'm getting more dangerous all the time. What if I get too powerful for you?"

"Don't get ahead of yourself, Iron Balls. I've got plenty of fight left in me yet."

"I'll try to learn to control it."

"Yeah, you do that. Will you contact Meera?"

He closed his eyes, picturing the Shadow Mage. Unsure how to actually make contact, he simply willed her to hear him. "Meera?" he said aloud while he concentrated. "Are you there?"

I'm here. He jumped, her voice in his mind, like she whispered from inside his ear.

"I need to see you."

You're moving. When you're next still I'll come to you.

"Okay."

Silhouette looked over, one eyebrow cocked.

"She'll come to us when we stop."

"Clever bitch, ain't she."

TWENTY

The hotel room in St John was simple, little more than a bed and side tables. On a rickety table under the window stood an old TV and a kettle and tea bags. Silhouette hung up the phone. "We're on a flight back to Halifax at 8 a.m. tomorrow."

"And then what?"

"I don't know. I guess we have to wait for Meera. She coming?"

"She's supposed to. If she doesn't show up soon I'll try to reach her again."

Silhouette turned on the kettle. "Cuppa while we wait then?"

Alex slumped onto the bed. "Sure. I've been thinking."

"Sounds dangerous. What about?"

"You lot."

"Yeah?"

Silhouette sounded suspicious, but he had to know more. He had to try to figure out where her motivations might lie. Perhaps by learning more about the Kin he could learn more about Silhouette. "You say those people back at your Den weren't actually vampires, right? They just choose to live that way?"

"Right."

"So are there really vampires too?"

Silhouette gave him a withering look. "No, Alex. There's just us. Vampires, werewolves, whatever—it's all us."

"So some Kin have decided to live that way and that gave birth to the legends among humans, or the other way around?"

"No idea. Chicken and egg."

Alex pursed his lips, thoughtful for a while. Then he said, "So if there are no actual vampires, just you lot choosing a lifestyle, then humans have got the whole vampire thing pretty wrong."

Silhouette poured boiling water over the tea bags. "What do you mean?"

"You walk around in the sunshine, for example."

"Yeah. And I don't even sparkle."

"So the whole thing about vampires being burned up by the

sun is bullshit?"

She handed him a cup of tea, sat on the bed beside him. "Yes. Vampires are Kin and sunlight doesn't bother us at all. Neither does holy water or crucifixes or anything else."

"What about silver bullets?"

"Well, bullets in general are pretty savage. We're a lot tougher and can take a fair pounding, but riddle us with enough bullets and we'll go down, silver or otherwise. But there's nothing special about the silver."

"So it's all wrong."

Silhouette cradled her teacup in both hands. "Of course. The Kin are shapechangers and predators. We fulfil the expectation of vampires or werewolves or whatever, but all the frailties put upon us are inventions. When something makes its way into legend, humans always put a weakness on it, a way to defeat it. It makes people feel better to think that way. But the world doesn't actually work like that."

"So all the monsters are actually Kin and none of the supposed secret weapons work?"

Silhouette stared into her teacup. "No, Alex. Not all the monsters are Kin. That thing we fought back in Bonavista was no Kin. The world is full of dangers, for all of us."

The thing in Bonavista had me beat, he thought. "And what about the Fey?" he asked, to take his mind off thoughts of defeat.

"That's another story again. They're an entirely different race from an entirely different realm. Evil fuckers. On the thin days they come through and cause havoc, maybe make more Kin like me."

"You've used that term before. What are thin days?"

"Days when the realms are closer. Midsummer, equinoxes, stuff like that. On those days the Fey can slip between briefly and cause a bit of chaos here. It's when the Wild Hunt rides, for example."

Alex watched steam rising from his tea. "All that stuff is real?"

"Depends what you mean by all of it. The Fey are. The Wild Hunt exists. There are lots of Wild Hunts actually."

"But all the vampire legends are wrong," he said, exasperated.

"It's hard to know what's real, what's dangerous, what's made up." The same could be said of Silhouette.

"You can say that about the most mundane aspects of life too," she said with a smile.

They looked up at a soft knocking. Alex put his cup down, crept to look out the peephole. Meera stood outside. He opened the door. "Hi there. Come in."

Meera stepped in and closed the door behind her. She looked Alex up and down. "You've had some success?"

"You could say that. We've had a hell of a time, but your tip was right. I got the second piece."

"Excellent. Well done. Tell me all about it."

Alex recounted the gory details while Silhouette made more tea.

Meera listened intently, asking searching questions here and there. At the end of the tale she said, "I'll pass it on. This knowledge is invaluable, thank you. We might go to visit this place and see what's left."

"You might have trouble finding it," Silhouette said. "I couldn't see it until Alex stood me right on it."

"So what now?" Alex asked. "We're a bit stuck for what to do next. Any more leads?"

"I'm sorry. You got lucky the first time, but we've searched extensively and turned up virtually nothing."

Alex grunted. "Fuck it."

"Virtually?" Silhouette said.

Meera took out another piece of paper, faintly lined, dense with neat handwriting. "There are various mentions of things that could be related, but it's very hard to tell. I can find no record of the third piece. However, the Norse legend of the second piece also tells of Kin from a Den in Rome. If that's true, then perhaps all the Kin tasked with hiding the shards were from the same Den."

Alex frowned. "All that time ago they *might* have come from Rome? How does that help us now?"

"Do the Kin keep good records?" Meera asked.

"Nothing like you Umbra Magi, I'm sure," Silhouette said.

"But every Den keeps an account of its history, members and genealogy. I don't see how that can help."

"It's the only lead you've got. If the Den in Rome has enough detailed records you might be able to track down any tasks its members were given. If you can find mention of three Kin given a very serious job to do, you might get a clue where they went."

Alex let out a sigh. "Tenuous fucking link, that is."

"I'm sorry," Meera said. "It's the best I can do. I'm afraid that's it from me." She stood to leave.

"What, no more help?"

Meera took Alex's hand. "I'm sorry. We were prepared to offer you any information we had and we've done that. We try to observe and not interfere as much as possible. We have no more information and can therefore offer you no more help. If you would like to share anything you learn with us, we'd be very grateful, but otherwise yes, that's it."

Alex looked crestfallen. "We're on our own then. I don't suppose you could teach us how you turn up all over the place? We could certainly use that skill, it's far cheaper than airfares. I'm close to broke."

"That takes an awfully long time to learn and I wouldn't know how to begin to teach you."

"Why do you always knock on the door when you can zap in and out so easily?" Silhouette asked.

Meera smiled. "Just to be polite. It's rude to turn up in someone's room when you can arrive outside the door. Good luck, Alex. Silhouette."

Silhouette nodded once, saying nothing. Meera let herself out.

Alex fell back onto the bed. "Well, shit. What now?"

"I guess we go to Rome," Silhouette said. "There's no other lead to follow and I'm fresh out of ideas."

"And what do we do there?"

"We try to work out what really happened back when the Eld cast out Uthentia. If we can figure out who was involved and where things were taken, we might be able to find the third piece."

"Is there much chance of that?"

"Rome is one of the oldest Dens there is. There are Kin there older than the Bible."

Alex's eyebrows shot up. "Seriously?"

"Yeah. Some Kin count their age in millennia. Let's go and see what we can learn."

"And then what? If I do find the third piece of the Darak, what do I do then?"

Silhouette kissed him. "That, Iron Balls, is something you need to think about. Power is one thing, but you badly need a plan too."

Hood and Sparks pulled the collars of their heavy coats tight against an icy wind and ran from the plane to a waiting Land Rover. Inside, the heater worked overtime to push back the Scottish autumn, already worse than the deepest winter of London. Two burly men in fatigues, ex-military, sat in the front. "Long time, Mr Hood," said the driver.

Hood slapped his shoulder from the back seat. "It is, Curly. Good to see you again."

"You too, sir. This is Higgs. New boy."

"Good to meet you, sir," said Higgs.

Hood acknowledged the other man then turned back to Curly. "So there might be a fair bit of work to be done, and done quickly."

"Fair enough, sir."

"You got what I asked?"

"Yes, sir."

"Good lad. It might get unpleasant."

"Righto, sir."

"Haven't grown a conscience or anything recently, have you, Curly?"

"Not one that can't be paid off, sir. And you pay so very well."

Hood sat back. "Excellent. You got the directions I sent through?"

"I did."

"Let's go then."

The engine revved, reverberating through the vehicle, and they headed out of the tiny airfield onto a single track road. The North

Western Highlands loomed all around them, mountainous folds of dark green and gray, whitecapped with early snow. A sleety rain pushed sideways across the landscape, turning everything sparse and inhospitable. The road they followed led deeper inland, passing-spaces cut into the roadside periodically to let oncoming traffic through. They saw very little on the journey, most of the land barren and lifeless as a moon. Occasionally, low, scrubby heather hung on in desperation, stunted trees fought the weather in gullies and glens. Striated gray rock drove up from the brown and dark green earth, moss-covered and heavy with geological age.

After more than an hour Curly pulled off the single track tarmac onto single track gravel, little more than a path. The Land Rover bounced and rocked, Hood and Sparks hanging on to straps riveted to the roof. The way became progressively less maintained as the miles passed, the vehicle eventually crossing open terrain, slipping and shifting on tussocks of yellowing grass and brittle heather. Curly checked regularly with a compass and military GPS unit on the dash, roughly following a line of glens deep into a huge valley. It took another hour before he braked to a stop. Sloping green and brown led to ancient gray up to their right. The gray rose undulating, its sharp edges rounded by aeons, to a top lost several thousand feet up in the clouds.

Curly consulted a map then pointed to a rough trail, vaguely visible up one shoulder of the mount. "That's the track that leads to the caves," he said.

Hood squinted past Curly's finger, studying the hills. "Come on, Sparks. Got your walking boots on?"

Sparks considered the hillside ahead of them through the driving sleet. "I'm glad I have. You told me to prepare for rough conditions, but I didn't anticipate this."

"Who could ever anticipate this?" Hood said.

He opened the door, the wind instantly sucking all the warmth from the car. Curly and Higgs climbed out with him. Sparks pulled thick socks up over the cuffs of her heavy combat trousers and zipped her jacket up. Tightening the hood around her face, she followed the men. The things she did for this man sometimes made her wonder at her life choices. But no one had ever been better to her than Hood and, despite his occasional moods, no one treated her so well or did the things she liked quite like he did. This situation had definitely got the better of him and she couldn't help thinking it would cost him dearly. But long ago she had decided to follow him wherever it led and nothing would change that decision. Wincing against the weather, she trotted to catch up.

The track was little more than a goat or sheep trail that meandered with the rock, always creeping slowly higher. Loose shale made a shallow wave downwards to their left as they climbed, cracked and tumbled rock building the mountain to their right. Deep puddles and saturated bog made the going slow, arduous. Curly and Higgs stayed in front, setting a gruelling pace, regularly checking back on Hood. Every time they looked he flapped one hand at them to carry on. Sparks dropped further and further behind. There was nowhere to go but along the rugged track, so she kept her head down. She'd catch up eventually.

They trudged for an hour to reach a massive overhang of granite, high on the side of the mountain. Their clothes were soaked through and heavy. Sparks caught up to the three men as they waited for her in the lee of a shoulder of rock, shivering.

"Bracing, no?" Hood shouted over the wind, a spark of glee in his eyes.

Sparks forced a smile through numb lips. "That's one way to describe it."

Hood pointed behind her. "It's beautiful up here."

The valley snaked away below them between green and gray undulations until it disappeared in rain and cloud. It was an awe-inspiring landscape, endless and ancient. But Sparks would rather be admiring it from somewhere warmer. "Incredible," she yelled, more to appease Hood than anything else.

"We go this way," he said, pointing.

As the rock folded back on itself she saw three dark holes in the face of the stone, blackness in the shadow of the overhang. The caves looked like mouths wide open, waiting to feed. No point in protesting now and anything had to be better than this wind and freezing rain.

Hood turned to Curly. "You lads bunker down here and wait for us. We shouldn't be too long."

Curly nodded, pushing himself against the rock to let Sparks past. He and Higgs crouched in as much shelter as they could find, seemingly unbothered by anything about their predicament. Sparks followed Hood to the caves.

He passed the first opening without looking and turned into the second. The darkness swallowed them. The ground inside was earthy and wet, smells of mould and damp pervaded. The wind howled past the cave mouth, but inside was mercifully still and quiet. Sparks loosened the drawstring on her hood, pushed it back with a sigh of relief. "You take me to the nicest places," she said, looking around.

Hood kissed her, his lips like ice. "I take you where no one else ever would."

"That much is certain."

His face became serious. "Now let me do the talking. These creatures are dangerous."

"Is there really something living here?"

"There better be!"

Hood led them deeper into the cave. The light from outside didn't reach far and he pulled a torch from his coat pocket. The powerful beam cut through the gloom, glistening wetly from slick rock all around. The way twisted into the mountain, the floor rising at first then angling rapidly down. The passageway narrowed disconcertingly for several yards, making them duck as they walked, then opened into a large chamber.

Hood stopped, playing the torch beam around the cavern. Strange shapes cast shadows against each other, indiscernible even in the artificial light. Hood took a deep breath. "I seek the Sisters," he called out in a strong voice. "I know the price and come willing to pay."

Nothing happened. Sparks drew breath to speak and Hood shot one hand up, silencing her before the first word passed her lips. A distant sound, like a quiet moan, drifted up. It seemed to come from very far away. Sparks wondered how deep the cave system went. The moan sounded again, this time like more than one voice, twisting around rocks as the voices twisted around each other. They carried a soft, cold breeze with them.

"Knows…"

"…the…"

"…price?"

The sudden speech made Sparks jump. She cringed close to Hood and felt his trembling as she clung to him. Was he cold or scared? Or both? The voices seemed to come from all around them at once.

"I do," Hood said. "I know the cost."

"Knows…"

"…the…"

"…cost!"

The voices were sibilant, laughter bubbling along with the strong Scottish accented words.

A low, blue-tinged light swelled up through the caves. Movement caught her eye and Sparks stiffened at the sight of three figures crawling over the rocks towards them. They moved like lizards on all fours, elbows and knees sharply out to each side, heads low, dark hair hanging lank and wet. Ancient women, wasted and rotten, wrinkled, gray skin stretched across thin bones. Their eyes glowed a deep yellow in the pale light. Their faces were too long, with sharp jaws open and black tongues flickering out, tasting the air across the gap between them. They stopped a few yards away, shifting slightly on their hands and feet, the way a preying mantis stalks its prey. Sparks felt Hood still trembling, even through her own shakes. She swallowed hard.

"So," said one.

"What is it," the next said.

"That you want from us?" said the third.

"I want you to find and kill a couple who've cost me dearly," Hood said. "And bring back to me the magical items they carry."

All three laughed heartily.

"What ridiculous…"

"… irrelevant trivialities…"

"… are these?"

Hood clasped his hands together. "Forgive me, I am just a man with very human desires. I'll pay your price."

"You will…"

"… pay our price…"

"… or die."

"Yes, yes. I have influence. I have what you need."

"The price…"

"… for this task…"

"… is nine."

"You have to be fucking kidding me!" Hood said, aghast.

The one in the center hissed, rage twisting her hideous features. She opened her mouth unnaturally wide, hundreds of tiny, sharp, backward facing teeth arching out.

"We…"

"…don't…"

"…joke."

Hood gathered himself. "I thought it was three. One each."

"Three *each*."

"That's the price."

"Or we take you two."

Hood rubbed his hands together, staring at them. "All right. I'd planned for three, but…"

"Do you really…"

"… have influence…"

"… or not?"

The three of them shifted as if in a breeze.

"Nine then," Hood said. His eyes were haunted, his voice thin.

The creatures laughed, guttural bubbling.

"Well, well."

"If you fail…"

"…you will regret it for eternity."

"I'll have to arrange it, but I can pay. Will you help?"

"Yes."

"We'll come…"

"…to you."

"Okay. I'll be at the Stag and Otter outside Achlyness. Can you get there?"

"We'll be there…"

"… at midnight…"

"…tonight."

Hood backed away, pushing Sparks back with him. "Tonight? Right. Midnight tonight it is. See you then."

"Have nine…"

"…or we take…"

"… you two."

"Yes, yes. No problem. We'll be ready for you."

"Leave…"

"…a window…"

"…open."

The strange, pale incandescence faded away and the Sisters disappeared in the shadows. Hood turned, walking quickly, following his torchbeam.

"What the hell just happened?" Sparks asked.

"I made a deal," he said quietly.

"Yes," she ventured. "Nine what?"

Hood shook himself. "But it's worth it. I must have whatever that boy has."

"I can understand your desire, Mr Hood. But we don't even know what it is the boy has."

Hood sped up, clearly desperate to be out of the caves. "There is enormous power in this world," he said. "Magic that normal people couldn't even comprehend is scattered all over the place. But it's not the ultimate, Ms Sparks."

"No." She had heard this diatribe before.

"Nothing is greater than fantastic wealth. Magic is power among the few, but enormous wealth is power over everyone. And nothing is more valuable than magic. Therein lies my trade."

"I get that. But what did you just agree to? Nine what?"

"Think about it, Sparks. Imagine how much that boy's items could be worth! I was interested in them before, but then he was able to defeat the Subcontractor."

"He has a Kin woman with him. The Kin are strong."

Hood barked a laugh. "The Subcontractor ate Kin for breakfast. Literally, I expect. There's no way one Kin bitch would have been able to beat him. And definitely not a human whelp. So the deciding factor must have been whatever it is that boy's carrying. That's worth any investment."

Sparks shrugged. "I suppose. You know best, after all."

"Yes, I do."

"You think those… things will succeed where the Subcontractor failed?"

"I bloody hope so. I'm a bit out of ideas if they don't."

"What are they?"

Hood turned slightly as he walked. "Not a clue, Ms Sparks. I just know they are unbelievably powerful and utterly ruthless."

They emerged into the howling day again, the wind and rain a blessed relief from the damp confines of the cave. Sparks looked back into the darkness that had seemed so inviting not long ago. "So what on earth would they want, Mr Hood? What kind of payment could they care about?"

Hood stomped on, pointing back down the valley. Curly and Higgs hopped up and led the way.

"Mr Hood, nine what?"

Hood looked back over his shoulder. "Souls, Ms Sparks. Nine innocent lives."

Sparks gaped at him. "Nine lives? Innocent lives? What does that mean?"

Hood clapped Curly on the shoulder as they walked. "We're going to need six more," he shouted over the wind.

Curly glanced back, surprise evident in his face. "Six more?"

"Yes. By midnight."

Curly stopped, turning to face him. "Midnight?"

Hood pushed him, forcing the stunned man back towards the car. "Yes, Curly. Six more. By midnight. Make it happen."

Alex arrived at Halifax airport tired and demoralised. What could he do now to discover this last piece of the Darak? And if he found it, what then? Would he really have the power to do anything about the book? Silhouette dragged him to a counter and enquired about a flight to Rome. It didn't take long for her to ask him for money again.

He pulled out his credit card. "This'll take me close to my limit," he told her as the clerk processed the payment.

"We'll be fine, Alex."

"My bank account is empty, my credit card is full. I have money in investments, but there's no way to get to that any time soon. We have very little finance, Sil. We won't be fine."

Silhouette took their tickets and led Alex towards the check-in desks. "We'll get money. We may have to steal it, or charm it from people, or whatever. But we'll get some. Money is the one mundane commodity even folk like us have to worry about sometimes, but don't be so... so human!"

"What do you mean?"

They stood in line to check in. "You ever see me get up early and go to work, Alex?"

"What?"

"I don't earn an honest buck, but I get money when I need it."

"How?"

She frowned. "You really haven't thought about this? You think I'm a monster as it is."

Alex flustered. "Well, I don't think you're a, you know, you're a..."

"You do. You think I'm a monster and I *am* a monster." She lowered her voice, whispering in his ear. "I eat people. Quite often, when I do that, I take their money. Sometimes I enchant them into loving me and giving me all kinds of gifts while I play with them. And *then* I eat them. And then take their money. I break into places and steal things that I sell on the black market. I'm like Catwoman." She leaned back, looking earnestly into his eyes.

Alex was unsure what to say. She was being completely honest with him and he had to admit he had been an idiot to think any differently. "I suppose I'd never thought about it."

"In this world, Alex, life feeds on life. It happens throughout the natural world. When people start to usurp that order, the hunt has to adapt."

The only person helping him was a monster and a thief. He was loath to admit it, even in the privacy of his own thoughts, but he felt as though he were falling in love, even while he struggled to trust her. Was it some kind of purgatory to love a monster? Would he become one too? What did it really mean anyway, to be a monster?

The queue shuffled forward. Silhouette's eyes were sad, watching him. "I want to be with you, Alex. I want to help you. But you *have* to accept what I am."

"I know. It's a lot to process."

"I'm closer to humanity than most of my kind. There aren't many like me these days, first generation Kin. I really do try to tread lightly. I try to feed off bad people whenever I can. I steal from the corrupt and the greedy. I'd be lying if I said I'd never taken innocent life, Alex, but I try."

He kissed her. "I want to understand. But you have to realize how hard this is for me."

"I know. Your whole life has changed. But I'm into you, Alex. I want to help you and I want to stick around with you. But you have to want me too."

"Oh, I want you more than you can possibly imagine."

"You're becoming something incredible. You know you're already something more than human, right?"

Alex raised an eyebrow. The energies of the stone vibrated through him, constant now as he tried to contain it outside himself while owning it on the inside. But why had she said that? "More than human?" he said quietly.

Silhouette gestured with her chin. "Are you the same as this lot any more?"

People milled and queued all around, their shades dull. Their lives seemed empty, boring, after the things he had seen and done. But he envied them. "These people are lucky. It would be awesome to be as ignorant as them."

"Maybe. But that's beside the point. You're not like them any more, Alex Caine. You're something more. And becoming greater all the time. You already have more power at your disposal than any Clan Leader I've ever met. You've defeated Kin in combat and then some. Whatever happens, you'll never be like *them* again. And, in their eyes, you'll be some kind of monster too."

Her words stung, but rang true. He had taken his first steps into a world none of them could imagine and there was no going back. At what point would that lead him to prey on them in ways similar to Silhouette? He wanted to rail against the possibility, deny that he could ever use people the way Silhouette suggested, but he was nothing if not a realist. She had a point. What degree of monster was she, and what kind of monster would he become?

"The Subcontractor thing had us beaten," he said miserably. "I'm still too human to have defeated that."

"Get over it, Alex. You survived, even if he beat you. And you learned, grew."

"I suppose."

"I'll show you what I can of how I live," she said, resting her head on his shoulder. "I'll help you in every way. But you must accept me and my ways."

He nodded, kissed the top of her head. "Everything's changing."

"It's already changed. You just have to keep up."

TWENTY-ONE

It took a long time to get back to something resembling civilisation and little was said on the way. There was tension in the Land Rover, Hood's nerves, Curly's trepidation. They eventually reached a bigger road and before long pulled off into the gravelled car park of an inn. A large sign on a black frame proclaimed *Stag & Otter, Bar and B&B*. The building stood stark against the desolate landscape, black tudor beams crossing dirty white walls, slate tiles across the roof, rough with age and weather. Two more Land Rovers stood by the front doors, dark oak wood under a porch like a lychgate. Warm orange light from the windows made a welcome sight against the miserable, gray day.

"We staying here?" Sparks asked hopefully.

Hood nodded. "We are. Tomorrow we should have everything organised and we can go home and wait."

Inside the pub was warm, low ceiling beams leading over a flagstone floor to a dark, shiny wooden bar. A huge fire roared in a central hearth. Sparks hurried up to it, casting her coat off onto the back of a chair as she went. She stood before it, knees pressed together, rubbing her hands as she tried to suck the heat in. She saw a number of other men, dressed like soldiers, lounging around the room.

Curly strode in. "Right, you lot, there's work to do. Cavey still upstairs on guard duty?"

One of the men sat up straighter. "Yes, sir."

"Good. Leave him there. The rest of you come with Higgs and me." The men stood and gathered coats, heading outside without question. Curly turned to Hood. "I hope we can find what you need," he said, the implied question regarding the cost of failure.

Hood's face was serious. "You better had. Nothing I've ever asked you to do has been more important."

Curly stared for several seconds. Eventually he said, "When I mentioned my conscience could be bought…"

Hood held up one hand. "I know. Three times the expected number, three times the pay?"

"Okay." He turned and left.

Sparks and Hood were alone in the bar. "No one else here?" Sparks asked.

"There's one lad upstairs, guarding the three we already have."

"That's all?"

"That's all. I own this place. I own many places. I had the guests turfed out and compensated. It's hardly busy at this time of year anyway."

Carpet-covered stairs led up from one corner. "Three what?"

"I think you probably know."

"I hope I'm wrong."

"I doubt it." Hood watched her with narrowed eyes, judging her reaction.

"What's innocent these days, Mr Hood?"

He stared.

"It's children, isn't it?"

Hood went behind the bar, took a whisky bottle and two glasses from a shelf. "Have a drink."

"I think I need one."

Hours passed. The day sank into darkness by late afternoon and Hood sank into a pensive mood. Sparks self-medicated with alcohol, trying to numb her thoughts without becoming thoroughly drunk. He had never gone this far before, at least not to her knowledge. He'd already secured three children. Now he'd sent for six more as casually as ordering takeaway. Certainly, Hood had killed before. She had too, on his orders. Life was cheap and those with power controlled their destinies. Was this really any different? Her own childhood, passed from one abusive bastard to another, had hardly been idyllic. Perhaps death before adulthood would have been preferable for her. A part of her baulked at the thought of using kids this way, but the larger part of her had long since lost any compassion for anyone else. People were fucked, they did horrible things to each other and you either took control or you got screwed over. Hood had taught her that. Children would only grow into bastards like the rest. She deferred to Hood and no one else and that's the life she planned to hang on to, whatever the cost. Her hands were shaking, though she'd long since warmed through. She drank deeply once more.

Soon after seven o'clock the sound of several tyres crunching on the gravel outside roused them. Hood sat up in his chair but didn't rise. Sparks, unable to help herself, looked out a leadlight window. The three Land Rovers, close to the front door. Hood's men got out, dragging others with them. Seven young boys in Cub Scout uniforms, eyes wide and stained with tears, were hustled inside. Last out of the vehicles was Curly, dragging a short, fat, middle-aged man. The man wore a Scout Leader's livery, his face twisted in abject terror.

Hood remained seated as the captives were presented to him. "We got lucky, after a fashion," Curly said. "A Cubs group down near Ullapool. Seven members. We weren't sure what to do about this bloke though." He shoved the short man forward. "Or the extra kid."

The Leader shook like he had a severe palsy. He clenched his hands together, beseeching Hood. "Please, whatever's going on here, please let the children go. Do anything you want to me, but let them go."

"Such a noble sentiment," Hood said. "But it's the children I need. You, not so much."

The boys sniffed and sobbed, watching their leader with a horrified lack of understanding. "Please," the man begged. "What do you want? Please let us go."

Hood addressed Curly over the distraught man. "Take him outside. Sparks, go with them."

Sparks jumped, not expecting to be addressed. "Go with them?"

"Remember Bashir, who tried to stiff me over that Djinn situation?"

Sparks immediately remembered the Arab on his knees, begging for his life, apologising for his foolishness, Hood stepping up behind him, placing the barrel of a semi-automatic pistol against the base of his skull. Pulling the trigger. "I remember."

"Do that to him. Curly will help you afterwards." Hood's

expression showed deep disinterest. He was testing her. Perhaps all her questions had shaken his faith in her.

"Right," she said. "No problem."

Curly dragged the blubbering man through the pub. Sparks followed. She heard Hood order Curly's men to take the children upstairs, put them with the others.

Outside in the dark, the wind whistled, icy cold and wet. Sparks winced against it, pointed to the far corner of the parking lot, deep in inky shadow. Curly pushed the man forward. "You gonna need this?" he asked, pulling a pistol from his pocket. It gleamed with a dark menace in the night.

Sparks took the weapon. The Scout Leader craned his neck, trying to see what they were doing behind him. Sparks indicated a clump of gorse bush, its dark green spikes and sparse yellow flowers black and white in the darkness. "Look at that," she said.

The man turned his head and Sparks raised the gun, pressed it to his skull and fired. He jerked, his legs flailing out from under him as his face exploded. Curly stumbled under the sudden weight, raising his free hand against the spray of blood and brains. "Fucking hell, woman!"

Sparks handed him the gun, turned back to the pub. "Get rid of him." She walked away.

"That was quick," Hood said.

"No point in fucking around." She went to the bar, poured more whisky. Her hands shook harder than ever. She tried to ignore the fine red spray drying on her wrist. "What about the seventh kid?"

"We can hardly let him go. I'll offer him to the Sisters, I suppose. Nothing else to do with him."

"What are they going to do with them?"

"I have no idea. I have to admit, I'm rather intrigued to find out."

Sparks swallowed, poured again. "So what now?"

"We wait till midnight."

She sculled the next drink. "Well, in the meantime, Mr Hood, how about you take me somewhere in this place of yours and fuck me."

"My dear woman, you're a mind-reader."

Over the Atlantic Ocean Alex fought against the desire to murder. Silhouette gripped his hand, whispering to him, trying to talk him down. The entity bound into the book cajoled and infuriated him, fired his nerves with an untouchable itch. His entire body sang with a tension that could only be released through blood and havoc. Visions of himself, powered by the Darak, ripping through the passengers on board swam in his mind. He imagined tearing flesh from bones, crushing skulls under his flying fists, biting chunks from screaming people, blood spraying in arterial beauty throughout the tight, clinical cabin. He panted, sweat poured down his face. He imagined kicking out a window, watching people sucked out the tiny hole, skinned and filleted on the way through.

"Use the stone to resist the book, Alex!" Silhouette tried to hold his eyes. Her concern was clear, deep in her pupils, her fear that he would slip away, run berserk.

He ground his teeth, clenched his fists. He pictured his foot smashing the cockpit door down, his knuckles mangling the flight crew, taking the controls and pointing the aircraft straight down at the churning waves. He could hear the whine of the engines along with the laughter of Uthentia, singing out from somewhere in his pocket and realms away simultaneously.

He turned to the tiny portal beside him as Silhouette tried to shield them with her body from the unfortunate man in the aisle seat. She hissed as he crushed her hand in his grip, his other hand rising. The book urged him on, its desire to feel him drive his fist through into the screaming cold air rushing past outside terrible to resist.

The man beside them leaned forward, a mixture of disgust and concern on his face. "Is he all right?"

Silhouette didn't look around. "He's fine."

"You sure? He looks like he's having a heart attack. I'm gonna call a steward."

"No need." She leaned close to Alex's ear. "Use the Darak," she whispered. "Resist this!"

He felt as though his muscles would burst, desperate as he was to start laying into every stupid face around them. Fucking sheep, stupid mortal, mundane losers, running on a wheel every day, good for nothing, achieving nothing, fucking useless bags of meat. He gasped, gripping Silhouette's hands almost hard enough to shatter them.

She let out a small cry and it twisted a knife in Alex's heart. He concentrated only on the sensation of magic from the Darak, drew it through every part of his body, threw it like a cold, wet blanket over the fire in his mind. Uthentia's cajoling became howls of rage as Alex used the stone to quell the urges burning through his veins.

"You're doing it!" Silhouette said.

He concentrated only on the Darak and his breathing techniques, years of practice lending assistance to the magic. His body pulsated with destructive urges, but he forced a command over them. It was like trying to hold onto a hurricane, but he refused to let go.

"I think I need a deeper...dialogue with this book," he said through clenched teeth.

"You think you can communicate with it?"

"I have no idea. It's something way beyond my understanding. I never really know what to make of it. I just get vague impressions of what it means. But maybe I can try. It's alive in there, I can feel its anger. It's like a living, sentient disease inside me."

Silhouette looked around. The man in the aisle seat studiously ignored them. Other passengers slept or stared at tiny screens. "I can't see anyone obviously magical around, but they'd be masking like us. You'll need to be careful."

"I can extend my own shields around the book. I can feel how to do that. I'm getting better control all the time." He grinned, even while shaking with the effort.

"Good. Use the stone for yourself, use it against the book. Don't let the book use it against you."

Alex collected himself together. He gathered the stone's power, his power, and built an impenetrable bubble around himself, locking down any emanations beyond the light bouncing off him. A thought occurred to him and he blocked the very concept of light as well.

"Alex!" Silhouette's voice hissed urgently. "Alex, what the fuck? You've vanished!"

He let the light back in. "Did that work?"

Her eyes were wide. "You just disappeared completely. All I could see was an empty seat."

He laughed. "Cool. Neat trick, eh?"

"How?"

"Dunno. I just sort of figured something out, a bit like the wards we use to cover our auras and colors. Sight is just another shade, I guess."

A half-smile tugged at her lips. "You scare me a little bit, Caine."

He kept the rest of the shields tight and slipped the book from his pocket. It writhed and shivered in 'sign, tendrils grasping at his hands and arms, crawling towards his face. He mentally wrapped them up and tucked them back around the grimoire, the energies of the Darak flowing with his will. He was learning to channel it more by the second and it felt good. He shivered with a pulse of fear and excitement, quick visions of sorcerers from stories flashing across his mind. The book's malevolence and anger throbbed in his hands. He cast his mind into it, deliberately trying to address the shred of whatever entity lay trapped within. *Let's have a chat, you and me.*

He opened the cover and the personality thrashed out like a heatwave, the pages flickering. They came to a sudden halt, script twisting and swirling. Alex let his eyes sink through it, let the meaning out. *Tiny, ragged, senseless thing a million million times insignificant. The universe alive with powers outside, the denial of all and the trappings of all.*

Alex slammed a thought through, trying not to read for a moment. *You can't finish me! I can resist you and I will destroy you.*

The script writhed again. *Insignificant. The power of stone and book and world, all combined, all through me.*

Alex smiled. It had never referred to itself before. *So there you are. You're just a trapped scrap of nothing. I will destroy you.*

It seemed to swell and burn in Alex's hands, pure, shining rage. Silhouette looked at him, worried. "Are you pissing it off?"

"Yeah, I think I am."

"I don't know how wise that is, Alex."

"I can't actually stop it right now, but I can tell it I'm going to be no victim."

He turned his attention back to it. *You hear that, fucker? I'm not going to be your victim. I'm forming ideas, Uthentia. I'm going to get stronger and I'm going to finish you.*

He let his eyes relax again, looking into the text, allowing Uthentia to speak. *Tiny, mortal mundane faeces. Nothing, you like others. Generational lives, destroyed in flames, in essence uncontained, so many more before and after now and then and always eternal.*

Alex could feel more, understand more. He got how it worked, building up in him until the fury became overwhelming, unignorable. The power was almost cyclic, suppressed every time Silhouette helped him to vent that rage in another direction, like a pressure cooker valve releasing boiling steam. Only this time he'd done it with the Darak. It still churned, not nearly as quelled as when Sil gave him release, but denied enough for now. It would be back sooner, stronger, but he'd bought himself some time. *I will survive you*, he thought at the book and slammed the covers closed.

Its wrath swelled through him as he slipped it away, out of sight. He locked his wards back down into the normal, familiar pattern he was used to, concealing his fast growing magic as easily as nudity concealed by a long coat. There was no question this trapped entity was awesome. No question it could destroy him, consume him. But with Silhouette's help, with his own growing ability, perhaps he could make good on his words. He would certainly need the entire Darak. With two thirds of it, he could barely hold off the inevitable. To beat it he needed more. If they came up empty in Rome, he had no idea what to do.

Silhouette reached over, squeezed his hand. "We'll find it," she whispered, reading his mind. Maybe just reading his face.

"I hope so. I really hope so."

TWENTY-TWO

Ten kids huddled in the corner of the small room, seven Cub Scouts, two little girls and one boy no older than four. They hugged their knees, rocking. Tears flowed from many, all faces pale, haunted. Hood and Sparks stood with their backs to the door as Curly and Higgs kept guard outside. An icy breeze pushed in through the open window, a square of blackness in the far wall. Sparks huddled closer to Hood, trying not to catch the eyes of any whimpering child.

"What time is it?" she whispered.

"Two minutes to midnight, by my watch."

Hood stared at the window, expression blank. Sparks knew there was a level of terror somewhere deep inside him and that scared her more than anything else. Regardless of all the crazy stuff Hood had done over the years, he'd always been in absolute control. Or at least he'd seemed to be. That was good enough for her. But talking to those horrible things in the caves she'd seen his fear. Pressed against him now, she could feel it. If Hood was scared perhaps he had gone too far.

A hissing cold sweep the room, sharper than the autumn air already blowing in. The children fell silent, their eyes, like hers, turning to the window. A dull bluish glow edged the wooden frame and dark tendrils of something scrabbled around the edges. Young voices cried out as the tendrils became fingers, then hands and arms, followed by lank, black hair and long, leering faces. The Sisters crawled through the aperture like four-legged spiders, one over the sill, one around the edge, one from above, slipping around the top of the frame as easily as a lizard scales a wall. They swarmed around the inside wall briefly, seeming to number more than three, before dropping to the ground in swaying, insectile crouches, hissing, licking the air. The children screamed, tears flooding from all eyes. Hood stiffened.

"So, you…"

"…have delivered…"

"…as we asked!"

Hood sucked a quick breath, clearly steeling himself. "I have, as I said I would. There's even a bonus child."

The Sisters stretched, craning thin, ragged necks, bobbing up and down as they counted. Long fingers marked out the offerings one by one and they turned to face each other in a tight circle and cackled. Fast, guttural words flashed between them. A wave of unease passed over Sparks, a sense of dread beyond the terror she already felt. Her loins trembled icily, her stomach fluttered.

"I trust all is as you require," Hood said, his voice betraying his own concerns.

"Oh, yes..."

"...this is..."

"... more than perfect."

"Good, good. What should I do now?"

The Sisters skittered across the room to duck and weave before the terrified children. The kids shrank back, wailing, hugging each other, trying to compress themselves away to nothing in the corner of the room.

"Nothing..."

"...until we take..."

"...your tribute."

Hood and Sparks stepped back, checking up hard against the door, as the Sisters fell upon the young like dogs on trapped rabbits. They each stood, grasping a child by the shoulders, pulling them up from the floor. They hung terrified like ragdolls, urine staining clothes, tears and sobs pouring from them. The Sisters stared hard at the eyes of the victim they held, long black tongues flickering. Their yellow eyes turned black and emanated a dark blue light slowly, like oil across the space between them. As the light hit, connecting their eyes, the small form arched in their grip, legs kicking feebly, their cries becoming weak, muffled.

Each child began to blacken and crease, their very substance disappearing as the darkening skin sucked tight against bones. Their faces shrank, stretching like leather across bared teeth, eye sockets and cheekbones rising like rocks from a draining lake. Their cries cut quiet as the screams of those remaining intensified. The

Sisters seemed less gray and drawn, less skeletal and lank.

The others broke and ran, scurrying around the room. Hood dove for the window, screaming at Sparks. "Cover the door, let none leave!"

He reached the window at the same time as two kids, caught one as he threw himself out. He dragged the thrashing child back into the room with a grunt of effort, pushing the second to the ground with a kick.

Sparks pressed herself against the door, covering the handle as children pulled and tore at her, pleading with her to release them.

A banging against her back, Curly's voice. "What's going on in there?"

"It's okay. Just make sure this door stays shut!"

She heard a bump as Curly clamped a grip on the doorhandle from the other side, presumably pulling against it to keep it closed. There were more screams, cut short, as those near her were plucked away. Her mind raged at her, *What the fuck have I done?*

Unable to bear it, yet unable to ignore it, she turned to look. Six tiny, black, desiccated corpses littered the floor. The Dark Sisters held three more aloft, rapidly draining. One last little girl sat frozen in the corner, eyes and mouth wide in horror, a thin, high scream piercing the air. The six blackened corpses had become nine and the Sisters had become young, beautiful, graceful, with flowing, lustrous hair, one blonde, one brunette, one redhead. They were glory incarnate, basking in the glow of their transformation. They turned to face the last child.

"Now what about you?" Blonde said, smiling like a favorite aunt.

Brunette laughed, a lovely, tinkling sound. "The extra one, unexpected."

"She can't be wasted," said Red.

Sparks shivered more violently than ever. For some reason, seeing them normal like this, hearing them talk in complete sentences, seemed more terrifying than anything she'd seen so far.

They advanced on the remaining child, crouched before her. She sat frozen, even her trembling stopped, the sound whistling from her throat faded to nothing. The Dark Sisters leaned forward, radiating blue light once more. Slowly, more slowly than the others, lasciviously drawn out, the young girl shrank in on herself, crumpling into a pile of bones, covered tight with thin blackened parchment that moments before had been freckled, strawberry skin.

The Sisters turned to Hood, still guarding the window. He swallowed hard, unable to prevent his eyes roaming up and down their naked perfection.

"You like?" Blonde asked.

"I think he much prefers us this way, judging by the swell at his crotch," Red said.

"I'm sorry," Hood stammered, trying to look away, failing. "I'm overwhelmed. Truly, you are more than I expected."

"Such a nice man," Brunette purred. "I think he's found a new respect for us, the man who delivered ten."

Hood's Adam's apple bobbed. Sparks's mind swept with revulsion and pity. On one hand she couldn't blame him for reacting as he did, these women so lovely and bare. But he knew as well as she did what they were, what they'd just done, what existed beneath the skin. Her nerves screamed with foreboding. This was wrong, everything about it utterly wrong.

"I have every respect for you," Hood said, regaining some of his trademark confidence. "I trust our deal is sealed."

"Sealed?" asked Blonde. "Oh yes, it's definitely sealed."

"So what would you have us do?" asked Red.

"I need you to track down and kill a human and a Kin and deliver to me whatever magical items they're carrying. Can you do that?"

"Of course," said Brunette. "You've bound us and tasked us, so we must do as you ask. Are you sure you really want these things?"

"Most definitely."

"Always get exactly what you want, don't you?" said Blonde, a smile pulling at her full lips. "Quite a powerful human, no?"

Hood drew a shuddering breath, trying to keep his eyes above the neck, failing. "Certainly, at whatever cost."

"And where are these two you would have us hunt?" Brunette

asked.

Hood raised one finger. "Let me check how far they've got." He scrabbled in the pocket of his jacket, pulled out a phone.

The Sisters, bored, turned to Sparks. An invisible hand thumped deep in her gut as their gaze fell on her. She watched them nervously, eyes flicking from one to the next.

"Love him, do you?" said Blonde, nodding towards Hood.

Sparks, tongue dry in her throat, managed a strangled affirmative.

"Follow him anywhere, would you?" asked Red.

Sparks nodded, dragging that tongue over her teeth. "He's been good to me," she managed.

The Sisters cast sidelong glances at each other, smiling enigmatically.

Hood's voice interrupted. "Jackson? Update, please." He listened, making occasional grunts. Without another word he hung up, turned back to the Sisters. "They're on a plane to Rome, apparently. I have a planesbird following. They're due to arrive in about seven hours. Can you get there? Find them?"

Blonde laughed, tipping her head back. "Oh, Mr Hood, we can get anywhere."

"Do anything," Red said.

"To anyone," Brunette said, staring hard at Sparks.

"And a human and Kin travelling together should be easy to spot," Blonde added.

Hood slipped his phone away. "Can I arrange anything for you? Clothes, travel, anything?"

Blonde shook her head.

"How will I stay in contact with you?"

She stepped close, gripped Hood's head between her palms. He arched back, a moan of ecstasy or agony, hard to tell which, slipped past his lips. When she let go he dropped to his knees, quickly staggered back to his feet.

"You feel me now?" Blonde asked.

"Yes, yes," he stammered.

"Yes. Lucky you."

"So you'll go to Rome? Let me know any news as soon as you have it?"

Blonde tipped her head to one side, looking at him almost lovingly. Almost predatory. She raised one hand, flicking a finger at him to move. As he sidled away from the window a cold burst of air pushed through the room and the Dark Sisters were gone. A sensation of incredible drag pulled Sparks's clothes briefly.

She slumped against the door, sliding down, dropping her face into her hands. Sobs racked her, chest heaving as shock pulsed through, finally released. Hood came over, slipped an arm around her trembling shoulders.

"That was more intense than I anticipated," he said quietly.

Sparks just sobbed, not trying to control herself. She had never felt such dread or seen such atrocity, even during her many years with Hood. She couldn't help feeling that things would never be the same again.

"Curly and his boys can clean up," Hood said, presumably referring to the shrunken corpses.

"Get me out of here, please," Sparks managed, voice muffled by tear-soaked palms.

Hood stood with her, keeping an arm across her shoulders. He banged on the door with his free hand. "Curly, open up. Let us out, please."

The door clicked, swung open. Curly stood framed by soft orange light from the corridor. His gaze slipped past Hood and Sparks, his eyes widening as he scanned the room behind them. "Fuckin' hell."

Hood stepped by him, leading Sparks. "I need you to sort this out," he said as they passed Curly. "Somewhere they'll never be found."

"Righto. I'll see to it."

Hood put a hand out, stopping Curly from entering the room. "I'm serious, Curly. Absolutely, under no circumstances, *ever* found."

"Yes, sir. Don't worry. These will be dust by morning."

"Good man. Thanks. You've really earned your money this

time."

Curly barked a humorless laugh. "Fucking right I have."

Alex and Sil stepped off a grimy train into the bustle of Rome's Termini station. Vast atrium ceilings, pale brick and glossy tiles reflected light from high windows and higher fluorescents. They trudged with the crowd, emerging onto a sun-soaked street busy with impatient traffic. Alex stretched, basking in the warmth. "Man, autumn in the Mediterranean is a vast improvement on everywhere else I've been recently," he said to the sky.

Sil smiled. "You're spoilt where you come from."

"Spoilt or burned to a crisp? It can get a bit extreme in Australia sometimes. Still, I'll take it over a northern European autumn or winter any time." He stopped, staring hard into the pastel blue. Something moved up there, glowing with magesign, making loops and whorls against the clear sky. "What's that?"

Silhouette followed his gaze. "What's what?"

He put one arm around her shoulders, drawing her close, pointing with the other hand. "Up there, really high. It's tiny, but definitely there, you can see the 'sign."

Sil squinted, eyes straining along the line of Alex's index finger. "Hmm. There's something there, but I can't focus on it. Can you see it clearly?"

"Not really. I think it's watching us."

"What makes you say that?"

"Dunno. I can feel it. Let's get somewhere quieter."

"In Rome?"

Alex headed away from the busy station. They walked a few blocks, always turning down the emptier looking street or alleyway, slipping between tall pale buildings, hanging with ivy or blackened by city grime. Something about the thing in the sky filled Alex with trepidation. He couldn't explain why, but he felt a strong connection to it now he'd spotted it and knew, intrinsically, that it meant him harm. It looped high above them. He stopped, scanning ochre buildings on either side of the thin street, wooden shutters open like wide eyes, drawing autumn sun into apartments. No one seemed to be looking out their window, the street empty. "Keep an eye out," he said.

Silhouette watched him anxiously. "What are you doing?"

"I'm going to bring this down."

"How?"

Alex ignored the question. He pictured the air around the thing high above without looking up. He could sense it, hovering over them. He gripped the stone through his shirt, drawing on it. He was learning all the time how to control and channel the incredible power. He ignored the anger and displeasure of Uthentia, concentrated on the Darak, the air, the flying presence. Magic surged from it.

Silhouette gasped. "I see it clearly now, some kind of creature. What are you doing?"

Alex locked his mind around the magic that encased the thing and took control of the air around it. He spun the air into a vortex, a tiny whirlwind spinning the surprised being like a top. "It's trying to escape!" he hissed.

"No shit. It's bending space, you can see reality tearing around it."

Alex gritted his teeth. The thing above tore at his brain. It was like trying to hold back an accelerating car with a rope. He powered up the whirlpool of air, spinning the thing into a blur, desperate to disorient it, break its power. With all the mental might he could muster he hauled on it, drawing it down towards them.

"It's coming!" Silhouette said.

"When it's close enough, you'll have to grab it! I can't hold on for long. As soon as you can, kill it, don't waste a second."

"Are you sure?"

Alex grimaced, trying to hang onto the thing as it thrashed and spun high above them. "I've never been surer! It's a danger to us."

"All right then." She bolted from his side and scaled the wall beside them, leaping from shutter to windowsill, heading for the roof with incredible agility and grace.

Good girl! He concentrated on nothing but countering the magic of the thing trying to leave this realm, dragging it down. Silhouette made the roofs and started running. He drew the creature down above the alley and Silhouette leapt from the edge, arcing out into the sky. She snatched the thing from the air and landed on the opposite side. Her shoulders flexed, her elbows flaring briefly as she struggled for a grip, then she twisted violently. The magic died, the presence of the creature, whatever it was, snuffed out.

Alex leaned against one wall, catching his breath. He was pleased to notice that his control had been clearer and his exhaustion less total. Already his mental stamina was returning to normal.

Silhouette landed lightly beside him. She held something out to him, her expression slightly disgusted. It hung slack and leathery.

Alex took it, held it up. It looked like a featherless bird with the wide, thin wings of a bat. Its black skin wrinkled at its joints and neck, pulled taut across its body. It had a sharp beak that gleamed like obsidian. "What the fuck is it?" Alex asked.

"I think it's a planesbird," Silhouette said. "I've never seen one before, but I've heard of them. Quite powerful. It was definitely following us."

"I guess this explains how that Subcontractor kept finding us."

Sil grimaced. "You think this has been on us all this time?"

"I don't know. But let's hope we finished it before it told anyone else where we are. That Subcontractor guy said something about Black Diamond and someone called Hood, remember? Maybe he sent this."

"That was a bit of a struggle just then," Silhouette said thoughtfully, "but it certainly wasn't worse than the thing we fought in Canada."

"Which means," Alex said, "this is probably a lookout. A scout."

"So something else is coming."

Alex looked up and down the alley, checking it was still empty. He threw the planesbird to the ground and agitated the air around it, visualised the consuming flames of a furnace. After a few seconds his magic surged and he immolated the weird bird, leaving nothing on the ground but a dark stain. "We'd better fuck off then," he said, turning to trot up the alley. "Let's put some distance between us and that thing."

Silhouette jogged alongside. "You're getting good at this stuff, eh?"

Her voice was jovial, amused as well as impressed, and that annoyed Alex. "I wish the circumstances were different."

"Of course. You don't want to be in this situation, but you love the power. Don't try to pretend otherwise."

He had to admit she was right. "I suppose so. Just a shame I had to find out this way."

"If it wasn't for the book you wouldn't have discovered the stone. Be rid of the book and keep the Darak and you're laughing."

"If that's even possible."

Silhouette put a hand on his shoulder, slowing them to a walk. "I truly believe it is, Alex. If anyone can do it, it's you. You're a prodigy. You have to figure out how."

He looked into her eyes, looking for signs of patronising, consoling. He saw none. She seemed to really believe what she said. "I hope you're right. But what if you're wrong?"

"Who knows."

Alex stopped, turned to face her. "I'm serious, Sil. If I fuck this up or lose control or whatever, I could cause serious damage. What if I try to fix this and release Uthentia again instead?"

"I don't think you will. I think you can beat this. Besides, I'm always on the lookout for excitement and nothing has been this exciting for a long time."

Alex sneered. "Is that why you're with me? For the excitement?"

"Yes. And no. I started out with you for the excitement. I've stayed because it's still exciting and because I want to hang out with you." She looked coy. "You still intrigue me."

He stared at her, wanting to ask questions he was afraid of hearing the answers to. He chose not to ask, shaking his head. "I hope you're right," he said again, walking on, trying to block visions of loosing some nightmare on the world. The presence of Uthentia in his pocket trembled with mirth, mocking. He flooded himself with energy from the Darak, silencing the book.

They enjoyed the sunshine and warmth. Rome hummed and buzzed around them, the dirt and soot from the overcrowded roads pervading everything, yet exotic nonetheless. "So where is this Den?" Alex asked eventually.

"We're nearly there. Look." Silhouette pointed as they emerged around a corner. The massive bulk of the Colosseum rose before them, ancient stonework on a scale hard to conceive.

Alex grinned. "Fuck me. I've seen pictures, but I had no idea it was so huge."

"Pretty cool, huh?"

The original arena of combat, the first cage, where warriors and heroes were made and died. He felt an immediate connection, imagined himself a gladiator, striding across the sands to face soldiers, lions, anything the Romans threw at him. It was a romantic image, he knew, but one he couldn't avoid. He'd read about the enacted battles, trapdoors to lift ferocious beasts directly into the arena, the flooding to recreate naval mêlée. Now it had scaffolds all around the lowest arches, hoards of tourists swarming over it. He could see thousands more inside, standing in the shadows of bloodthirsty Romans who had bayed for pain and slaughter. Crushed though it was under the weight of tourism, this thing still spoke to him. He blinked. "Wait a minute. You're saying the Rome Den, one of the oldest Dens, is the Colosseum?"

Silhouette laughed. "Kinda. It was, but times change. The Den is still there, just a lot lower down."

"Underneath?"

"We just have to convince them to let us in. And you may have to fight again. Just because you won your rights at my Den doesn't mean you've got any rights here."

Alex grinned. "Really? Freaking sweet!" The opportunity to fight on this hallowed ground? The thought moved his soul. The book rejoiced, wanting him to die here, bested by powerful, ancient Kin. He threw his mind into it, pushing his thoughts out to the piece of Uthentia trapped there. *You watch me, fucker. I'll win here as well and be one step closer to destroying you.*

The book's blistering rage burned his mind and he shut it out, following Silhouette towards Constantine's arch, standing magnificent beside the Colosseum. Tourists wandered all around, dozens of cameras clicking and flashing. Silhouette stood by the fence that surrounded the arch and cupped her hands around her mouth. She howled a quick, incomprehensible sound that rang across the palazzo. People jumped, turning sharply then looking away again. Several minutes passed before a hard-faced man with black hair and dark tanned skin strolled towards them. His face bore an expression of serious dislike. When he reached them Silhouette smiled disarmingly. "Hi there. We'd like to see Lorenzo."

Hood read reports, shuffled papers, checked online news, all the things he usually did, but his distraction was apparent. A tremor still ran through Sparks, the trauma of their trip to Scotland refusing to leave her. She couldn't shake the feeling that Hood had crossed some boundary. Not with her. The love she had for him encompassed everything and anything he did. Nothing he could do would sever her bond to him. But something had changed. Something shifted behind the facade now and it scared her. His obsession with this situation, the lengths he was prepared to go, were terrifying. More often than not he bought his way into the things he desired and somehow managed to turn a profit. Often he'd killed, or had someone do the killing for him. Now he found himself with a desire that appeared to be beyond his grasp and his obsession with it had become destructive. He didn't even know what it was he chased. It might be something so pointless that even he couldn't turn much of a profit on it. But he was driven to these lengths and Sparks couldn't shake the feeling that it would cost him dearly. A rapid, insistent knocking surprised them both.

Annoyance flashed across Hood's face. "Yes, what?" he said. The door swung open and Jackson stood framed by dark wood, wringing his hands. "What is it?" Hood barked.

Jackson gasped like a fish, trying to speak. He stopped, swallowed, tried again. "It's gone, sir."

"What is?"

"My bird, sir, the one following the man and the Kin."

Hood stared, the muscles around his jaw twitching. It was several seconds before he spoke. "Gone?"

Jackson nodded vigorously, staring at his writhing hands. "Just blinked out, sir. I felt a struggle, then nothing."

Hood leaned back in his chair, clasping his hands across his forehead, staring at the ceiling. "What does that mean exactly?"

"Mean, sir?"

Hood's eyes snapped back to Jackson, made the terrified man take an involuntary step backwards. "Gone," Hood said again. "What does that mean?"

"It means dead, sir. They killed it."

"How did they catch a planesbird?"

Jackson whimpered. "I don't know, sir, it's not possible. They just slip away, slip between realms. Harder to grasp than smoke, sir."

Hood leaned his elbows on his desk, his chin on his clasped hands. "I really, really want whatever it is those two are carrying."

Sparks sat quietly, wondering what they had. Every time anything happened it deepened Hood's desire. She had to admit it appeared to be powerful, but what if it wasn't the things they carried but the people themselves? Had he considered that?

"So we've lost them?" Hood asked.

Jackson nodded, staring at the floor, misery embodied.

"Then I suppose I'd better inform the Dark Sisters."

A cold wave swept through the office. "We know," said a voice like ice.

Jackson spun around, looking everywhere. Sparks stiffened, not daring to look, not wanting to see. Hood sat quite still. "Where are you?" he asked.

"Travelling, with your mind-print. What you hear, I hear."

Hood shot to his feet, scanning for the disembodied voice. "That was never part of the deal!"

Frosty laughter floated through the room. Sparks felt as if her bladder would betray her any second. "What deal, sweet man?" the voice of Blonde said. "We agreed to fulfil your task. The details are our business."

Hood sat, his face distraught. "You can read my every thought?"

"If I chose to. But I have other things to occupy me, little man."

Hood dropped his face into his hands. He rubbed his cheeks. "So what now?"

"We will speak to the planesbird keeper."

Jackson visibly trembled.

"He can hear you," Hood said.

More cold laughter. "Of course. But we need a rather more personal audience with him."

"Do you?"

"We'll be there soon. Do make sure your security people know. We wouldn't want any unfortunate encounters. Negotiating modern buildings is such a chore."

Hood's eyebrows shot up. "You're coming here?" The chill dissipated from the room, silence heavy in the suddenly warm air.

"They've gone," Sparks said, almost whispering.

"Not for long. Sparks, wait downstairs please. You're the only one who would recognise them."

Sparks shivered, terrified at the thought. "You'd recognise them too," she said, without thinking.

Hood rounded on her. "You'd have me stand around in the lobby? Waiting?"

Sparks jumped to her feet. "Of course not, no. I suppose we have no idea how long they'll be."

Hood smiled, completely without humor. "I suppose not."

Sparks marched through the building, taking some solace in the staff scurrying before her, terrified that she might approach them, task them with something. Her authority was second only to Hood's, and he was a rarely seen figurehead, more concept than person among the underlings. *She*, however, was very real, very present, very much in evidence. She barked orders as she went, invoking their fear to mask her own as she made her way down to the lobby.

She sat in the reception of the Black Diamond tower for several hours, sending anyone who looked her way on a pointless errand. When the Dark Sisters arrived a cold gust washed through the wide glass doors.

They strode into the lobby, well-dressed and confident. The handful of people around paused involuntarily, all turning to watch. The Sisters mesmerised every eye with their presence. Sparks dragged herself to her feet, trying to conceal her terrified shakes.

She forced a smile. "Hello, ladies."

"So nice of you to meet us," Blonde said with a condescending smile.

"You couldn't just crawl in the window like you did before?" Sparks asked, surprising herself.

Red laughed. "Oh, do we irritate you?"

Sparks bit her lip, said nothing.

Blonde swept an arm around. "All this glass and metal and technology, it's disorienting. We slip through the gaps in open places, travel faster than your modern vehicles, but only in the natural world."

Sparks nodded, chose not to ask any more questions. "This way please." She turned and led them away without giving them a chance to respond. As her high heels clicked across the marble floor a terrifying thought occurred to her, an image of the three Sisters pressed against her in the lift. Muffling a whimper of distress she pushed the button and waited. She could feel them standing behind her, refused to look around.

"Your fear is delicious!"

Blonde's icy breath across her ear made Sparks stiffen again. She clenched her teeth lest a scream escape.

"You know, you really have nothing to fear," Blonde whispered, still mere millimeters from her.

"Really?" Sparks cursed internally at the weakness of her voice.

"You follow that hideous man, but you're not to blame."

Sparks laughed despite her fear. "Oh, I've done plenty wrong."

"No, you haven't. You've survived, whatever the cost. The things you've endured, the things men have put you through, yet look at you now. Not only surviving, but thriving."

"How do you know what I've been through?"

Blonde's breath was like iced water across Sparks's neck. "I know everything Hood knows. I know everything you do for him."

"He saved me," Sparks said, her voice a strained whisper.

"I know. And you've made it that way. It's him who should be scared, not you."

Sparks frowned, half turning to see Blonde. "What do you mean?"

The lift arrived with a metallic ring. Blonde gestured to the doors as they opened. "Shall we?"

Sparks stepped in, the Dark Sisters following. "What do you mean, he should be scared?"

Blonde ran one fingertip under Sparks's chin, like the stroke of an icicle. "You'll be all right," she said with a smile.

Sparks looked away, unable to hold the gaze of those terrible eyes. She swiped her security pass, pressed the button for the top floor. They rode through the Black Diamond tower in silence.

Sparks led the Sisters from the lift to Hood's penthouse offices. Jackson sat opposite Hood. Sparks stood at the door, letting the Sisters through. She resisted the urge to turn and run away.

Hood rose, a forced smile splitting his face. "Welcome, welcome. Firstly, in future, please speak directly to me, rather than so publicly as you did before. I suppose you…"

"This is him?" Blonde said, ignoring anything Hood had to say. "The keeper?"

"Yes, this is Jackson."

The Dark Sisters walked casually over to the old man trembling in the chair. A dark stain spread rapidly across his groin as he sat transfixed by their eyes. The Sisters crouched before Jackson, leaning in towards him. "We need to know what you know," Blonde said. "What your bird knew."

"I'll tell you anything," Jackson said in a reedy, shaking voice.

"You can't tell us," Brunette said.

"But we can take the knowledge," said Red.

Sparks's fear surged again as tendrils of dark blue swam from the Sisters' blackening eyes. She relived the terror of the children as those malevolent wisps writhed across Jackson's face. Jackson cried out, his voice muffled, shifting like his seat was hot.

Jackson's hands flew up, grasping either side of his head. He howled as his skin blackened and grew taut across his skull. He shrivelled to a black skeleton, slid to the ground. The Sisters stood.

Hood looked over his desk at what used to be Jackson. "Did you have to kill him?"

"Of course not," Blonde said. "But we were hungry."

"He's been with me for years." Hood's face showed genuine regret.

Red shrugged. "He failed you, did he not?"

Hood looked at her, frowned. "Well, no, not really. It wasn't his fault they caught his bird."

"Oh well, too late now."

The Dark Sisters turned and headed for the door. Sparks pressed the button to call the lift.

"That's it?" Hood called out. "You've got what you needed?"

"We have a print of them now," Blonde said, without looking around. "We'll find them."

"And you'll contact me as soon as you know anything? Keep me informed? Privately?"

"Yes, yes."

"No need to see us out," Red said to Sparks.

They entered the elevator and the doors closed with a slight hiss. As the lift headed for the ground the chill in the air went with it.

Sparks let out a deep breath, thankful the hideous things had gone. Hood leaned on his desk, still looking at the blackened corpse of Jackson. "Fucking hell," he said, almost to himself. "I liked that man."

TWENTY-THREE

A lex could see the opening in the old stone wall, but his new understanding of his skills told him he shouldn't be able to. "Can you see the door?" he whispered to Silhouette.

"Only because it's Kin magic. You shouldn't. No one should that isn't Kin."

"I can."

"I'm not surprised."

Hundreds of people milled around them, gawping at the majesty of the Colosseum, of Constantine's arch, heading for the boulevards of the Roman Forum. The man who had reluctantly answered Silhouette's call, who had equally reluctantly introduced himself as Louie, reached the doorway and stopped. None of the hundreds of tourists and local hawkers paid him any attention. His face still showed nothing but disdain. "Your human..." he began.

"Can see your doorway clearly," Alex said, deciding to treat this man with respect equal to that which he was shown. "Take us to Lorenzo."

The dark man growled, lips peeling back in anger. "Who the fuck do you think you are?"

"Who I am is of no importance to you."

Louie took a step forward, fury twisting his features. Silhouette stepped between them, putting a hand to Louie's chest. "He's with me and you will not threaten him."

Louie sneered. "Who does he think he is to talk to me like this?"

"He's more powerful than you realize. And not really human. Take us to Lorenzo, please."

Louie ground his teeth, staring hard at Silhouette for several seconds. He turned and stalked through the hidden opening without a glance at Alex.

Silhouette leaned close to Alex, the wards dragging against them as they passed through. "What are you trying to do? You need to show some respect if you want help here."

"He pissed me off. I'm sick of being treated like the ignorant little human."

"A fine time you've picked to be all superhero. You're deep in Kin territory. Very old Kin territory. Please, be a little humble."

A haze seemed to shift from his mind. "Uthentia's making me act like a fuckwit," he whispered. "Trying to get a fight started."

"Please, Alex, second guess every time you're tempted to speak. The thing is wily. It can tell you're getting stronger, that you're closer to breaking its grip on you. You have to stay aware of it."

"I'll try. Did you mean what you said to him?"

"What?"

"Not really human."

Silhouette's eyes were pools of sympathy. She leaned forward, kissed him softly. "Yes. I did."

Alex walked on into the darkness of the passageway ahead of them. The entrance that looked like solid stone to everyone else led to a narrow passage that curved down and back on itself. Alex caught up to Louie. "Excuse me, I apologize. My business is dangerous, it makes me surly. I shouldn't have been so rude to you."

Louie looked over his shoulder as he walked, confusion distorting his brows. "A strange one, you are."

"You have no idea. Again, I apologize."

"Whatever. It makes no difference to me. Lorenzo will decide your situation."

The passageway continued down, lit by small glowing orbs of light that hovered near the arched ceiling, magesign twisting around them. Alex tried to get his bearings. "So you guys were here before the Colosseum," he asked.

"This Den has been here for millennia," Louie replied proudly. "We built the arena and fed on its human warriors for centuries. Now it's a fucking tourist attraction." He spat the last two words out like poison.

"The world changes," Silhouette said. "We have to change with it."

"Fuck that. We should take over. There are enough of us."

Silhouette rolled her eyes at Alex. "No, there aren't. The humans are tenacious and furious. Trying to take over would be suicide."

Louie cast her a disdainful look. "Says you."

Alex wondered how many other Kin thought like Louie. Kin, the nightmares, the bogeymen, the death in the darkness. They were real and they walked everywhere. And he was becoming more like them. But one thing he promised himself: he would never become like Louie. He would hold on to his self, defend his kind. He refused to descend into the depths of monstrosity that yawned before him. The power he did crave, but it would never cost him his humanity. Even as he thought it, he wondered how possible that was. Would he laugh at these thoughts at some future date? "How many of you are there?" he asked Louie.

"In this Den?"

"No, I mean globally. How many Kin are there?"

Louie shrugged. "Fuck knows. That's probably the biggest problem. Internecine wars and conflict, a complete lack of any kind of organisation. We just seem to lack the collective will."

"That's the real sticking point," Silhouette said. "No one really knows how many of us there are and no one will ever be able to stand up and rally our various Clans. We're as tribal as humans."

A slight relief washed through Alex. "That's good for us, I guess."

Louie growled a noise of disgust.

They reached a heavy wooden door, crossed with iron straps held down by massive nails. Louie pulled a heavy iron key from his pocket, the lock making a heavy *thunk* as he turned it, and led them into a huge open space, marbled columns marching away from them, supporting striated marble slabs high above. Kin walked the rooms, stood talking, sat and read or conversed. It was reminiscent of Silhouette's own Den in London, only bigger and smooth marble where Sil's had been domes of rust-colored brick. Orbs of arcane light hovered here and there throughout, up high near the ceiling, casting an almost daylight glow throughout. They were led through rooms and corridors to a quiet area, eventually to large double doors. Louie turned. "Wait here."

The rage of Uthentia was as evident as ever. Its desire for violence, death, blood. Alex suppressed the urge to turn back to the crowded main area and start brawling. The insistent desire to fight made his fingers twitch. He drew power from the Darak, to calm his muscles, soothe his mind. The more he used the stone, the more he was able to control it. The book vibrated in his jacket with fury. He could imagine the thing bursting out, pages thrashing like manic wings as it buzzed around, battering at him. He smiled. The almost-god was juvenile when it didn't get its way.

The door opened and Louie beckoned them inside. "Lorenzo will see you."

They followed Louie into an enormous chamber, brightly lit with dozens of untethered orbs, floating randomly around the high ceiling. All manner of sofas, divans, beds, chairs littered the floor, cushions and rugs scattered among them. Several people lounged around the space, many with vapid expressions, as if drugged. Alex probed for their shades. The inert ones were all human, mundane, enchanted somehow into insensitivity. Food for Lorenzo and his friends, presumably. The thought was too disturbing and Alex pushed it from his mind. He picked out a few Kin among them, alert, watching him from beneath hooded brows, suspicious.

At the back of the room a man lay back among a mountain of silk cushions. He was strongly muscled, wearing linen pants and nothing else. His skin looked like the marble of the walls around him, smooth and somehow hard, impenetrable. He had long dark hair and eyes that seemed solid black. He emanated an incredible sense of age and power. Alex saw shades around him unlike anything he'd experienced before. The man did nothing to conceal his true nature, exulting in his ancient strength. Alex had got used to seeing hundreds of years in people's colors. Welby, Joseph, Isiah. But this set a whole new level. He saw millennia in this one, more centuries of existence than he could conceive, colors and shifts he had never seen before. The man idly chewed what looked suspiciously like a human finger. Silhouette dropped to her knees before him, elbowing Alex on her way down. He knelt beside her.

"Lord Lorenzo," Louie said, reverence in his tone. He bowed and moved away, out of sight behind them.

Silhouette lowered her head, speaking very quietly. "It is an honor to meet you, Clan Lord. Joseph, of London, sends his deepest respects."

Lorenzo looked from Silhouette to Alex and back again. "Must we speak in English? Such a foul tongue."

"My apologies, Clan Lord, my Italian is not good."

Alex thought he should mention that his Italian was non-existent, but chose to keep his mouth shut. He concentrated on using the energy of the Darak, kept it flowing through his body to suppress the urgent, insistent drive of the book. Images of himself leaping onto Lorenzo, driving fists of iron through the ancient leader, flooded his mind. Even without the stone quieting Uthentia, he knew such an action would be suicide. Clenching his teeth, he endured.

"How is young Joseph?" Lorenzo asked lazily, doing nothing to conceal the fact that he wasn't vaguely interested in the answer.

"He is well, thank you."

"And why has he sent you here?"

Silhouette took a deep breath. "We actually come of our own volition."

"Oh?"

"We would request your assistance, Clan Lord."

Lorenzo flapped one hand at her. "Forget the formalities, child. Call me Lorenzo. And why have you brought your pet?"

Alex bit down the surge of rage that pulsed through him. It wasn't his, not his offense, but Uthentia trying to goad him into acting on an anger he didn't own.

"Not my pet, Lorenzo. My friend. This is Alex Caine. A human, yes, though only starting to come into his power. But he finds himself in quite a predicament and would ask for your help."

Lorenzo turned his full attention to Alex for the first time. The ancient Clan Lord's mind swept over him, probing deeply. Alex kept his wards tight, trying to stay private without seeming rude. Lorenzo smiled. "You do have something about you, don't you, pet."

Lorenzo's seeking changed pace, feeling around for the source of power. He touched on the stone and his eyes widened. He sat up sharply. There was no finesse now as he stripped away at Alex's wards, like a policeman patting down a suspect in a dark alley. His mind stopped at the book in Alex's jacket and sudden intense motion swamped Alex's senses. He lifted and flew back, hitting the stone ground with a breath-shattering impact, sliding several meters. Lorenzo stood among cushions, his eyes flashing fury. "How dare you bring that into my Den?" he roared.

Alex raised both hands, staying down, vulnerable as a flipped turtle. "Please, I'm so sorry, but I can't help it. I need your help to be rid of it." People moved, gathering around him, ready to pounce the moment Lorenzo gave the word.

"You don't get rid of it." Lorenzo's voice was dangerously low. "It's the price we paid a long time ago, before even my time, to be safe."

"Please," Alex begged. "I believe I can be rid of it, but I need your help to find the last piece of the Darak."

"The last piece?"

Alex pulled the stone on its cord from his shirt, held it up. "I have two pieces already."

Lorenzo bent close. Alex hadn't even seen him move. "Just what are you doing, human?"

"When it's whole I'll have enough power to break free from this book."

Lorenzo was mystified. "You really believe that?"

"I do."

"A book now, is it? I'd heard that, but it's been a long time since I bothered to follow the movements of that thing." He straightened, returned to his cushions. "You can't be rid of it, human. Who knows how much damage you'll cause before it kills you now you've bonded with that stone."

"I'm learning to use the stone. I can control it."

Lorenzo tipped his head back and laughed. "No you can't. No one can. *Nothing* can. I would annihilate you and take that stone for myself if I could, but that would only risk the book latching onto someone here, even me, perhaps. You're lucky. That's the only thing stopping me from destroying you right now."

Alex cautiously stood, returned to Silhouette's side. At least he wouldn't be killed outright here. He did see the twisted irony in the situation. "Will you help me? I need to know where to find the last shard."

"Those pieces were scattered far and wide for a reason. Why would I help you restore it?"

"I can be free."

"So what? What do I care whether you're free or not? The most powerful Kin mages of the age were unable to banish that thing. What makes you think you could do any better? Death is your only freedom.

"What selfish human weakness you show. You want to be free at whatever cost? Imagine, for a moment, that you could be. Then what? It moves on to someone else and the cycle is repeated, as it has done for centuries. It's going to happen. Why would I make it occur any faster? You hold incredible power already. With the Darak complete you could be a new destroyer of worlds. The risk is too great."

Alex clenched his fists in frustration, binding his mind down tight against thoughts that threatened to betray him. "I have a plan," he said, "but I need power. I need the Darak."

Lorenzo just laughed, shaking his head.

"You could benefit from this," Alex said.

"Really? What would you have to offer that I couldn't just take?"

Alex took a deep breath before speaking again. "Assuming I can't defeat this thing, and I die like you suggest."

"Which you will."

"Then I would be dead, and the Darak would be whole and there for the taking by whoever happened to be nearby. That could be you." Silhouette flinched beside him.

"You think I haven't thought of that?" Lorenzo tapped the side of his head. "This mind is very old, human. Very wise. Don't presume to out-think me. Your plan bears the same flaw I mentioned earlier. The same reason I won't kill you and take the stone now. The book would immediately latch onto someone else. That's something even I won't tangle with."

Lorenzo flicked one hand, dismissive. "Enough. You're talking in circles, human. You're a child in an adult's game and you have no idea what you're about. You're doomed. That's the way it is. That's the settlement the Kin mages came to all that time ago. It is inevitable."

Desperate, Alex tried to keep him talking. "Is it true the Kin who exiled Uthentia were from here?"

Lorenzo looked bored. "A history lesson now?"

"At least let me know the whole story if I have to die for it."

"This happened before my time. Before history," Lorenzo said. "But yes, it happened here. The battle was mighty and it cracked the stone and nearly destroyed everyone involved but the banishment was done. Mostly. That one sliver of Uthentia's consciousness managed to hold on. Wherever it is now, it has that one tenuous link to our realm and through that it plays games. Attaches itself to some physical item here, seeps into it and makes it indestructible and unshakeable, and plays. Seems it's landed a good one with you."

Alex pressed on while Lorenzo seemed talkative. "And the Kin who hid the pieces of the stone came from this Den?"

Lorenzo smiled. "You can stop fishing. Yes they did, but what does that tell you? The worst thing that could happen would be for you to find the third piece. Frankly, I'm stunned you've managed to come this far. You could be quite something if you weren't cursed."

Alex grunted. "I've heard that before. Why would it be so bad for me to find the third piece?"

"Oh, so many reasons. One, you would be incredibly powerful and that could be disastrous while you're under that thing's influence. Two, there are those who think the stone, if made whole again, could draw Uthentia back to this realm."

"That doesn't make sense, though," Alex said. "If that was true, surely Uthentia would be using his influence to make people like me find and remake the Darak."

"Perhaps. Uthentia is Fey and chaos. We can't begin to fathom its mind. Even the true Fey treat Uthentia as a god. No one should be able to survive long enough to reunite the pieces. Any that have been cursed by Uthentia in the past haven't lasted very long at all. You're something new."

Alex glanced to Silhouette. "We've found a way to temper the influence."

"Is that right? Well, good for you, you've lasted a lot longer than most."

Alex thought back to Peacock and Welby. It all seemed so long ago. "The human who had this book before me hung onto it for a long time. He didn't seem affected by it."

"A Keeper. That thing has been a book before. It's been a ring, a religious icon, many things. It slips from item to item and often lays dormant with someone of little or no ability, waiting for a worthy victim to come along. Uthentia is eternal. It has patience to match."

What if Uthentia had spent all this time waiting for someone capable of finding the pieces of the stone, re-forming it and releasing Uthentia from exile? Was he being played, coaxed into freeing an abomination that would destroy the world? If the greatest Kin mages had accepted this price, maybe he needed to accept it too. If so, he should die now, before his strength grew. Before he caused any more death and carnage.

"You begin to accept the hopelessness of your situation, human?" Lorenzo's eyes were mocking, but there was a hint of sorrow in his voice.

Alex refused to acknowledge that his life would end here. And what if he did give up? This book would move onto someone else, it would keep killing. Why should he allow that? Ghosts of a plan kept sweeping through his mind and he pushed them away. He didn't dare to think about them in detail, risk the presence of Uthentia seeing his ideas. Ridiculous though it might seem, such arrogance on his part to assume he could outplay this chaotic god of the Fey, he refused to give up. He was a fighter. That's what he did, it defined him. He would fight this all the way to the end. "I'm not quitting," he said, his voice strong.

Lorenzo clapped his hands sarcastically. "Bravo. I admire your courage. Don't give up. But this meeting is at an end. I will not allow you trial by combat for that book would be free in my Den. You've survived your visit, now you leave. You're not welcome here." He pointed at Silhouette. "You can return, without him, if you like. You are Kin, even if you do seem to choose your pets unwisely." He paused, eyes searching Silhouette's face for a moment. A slight smile tugged his lip for a second then vanished. "But for now, you both go," he said.

Several people moved in from all sides, their presence insistent. Silhouette stood, signalling to Alex with her eyes. He followed. They were led back to the heavy wooden door and out into the Colosseum plaza. The sunshine and city air was very different to the cool underground conditions of the Den.

Silhouette put her arms around Alex's neck. "I'm so sorry, Alex."

He shrugged her off. "It's not over yet. I'm going back in."

"What?"

"Lorenzo said the Kin who hid the shards of the stone were from his Den. You said all Dens keep good records. There must be something in there that'll give me a clue."

"But you're not welcome there. They won't let you in."

Alex winked. "They won't even know."

"What?"

"I'm going to need your help. Let's get somewhere quiet."

They sat in dappled sunlight in a small park. Silhouette had doubt in her eyes. "I don't know if you'll be able to pull this off."

"I did it on the plane, without even really thinking about it," Alex said. "You're Kin and you know me intimately. If I can hide from you, I can hide from them."

Silhouette was not convinced. "Not necessarily. Lorenzo is ancient. So many of the Kin there are far older than me. I might not be such a good litmus test."

"You'll have to do. What other choice do I have?" He saw her protestations seep away. "Okay, so I'm going to lock down. You have to tell me how complete it is."

Her mind swam over him, watching his physical and magical self in detail. He began constructing shields, starting with the standard tricks to conceal himself from casual magical eyes, drawing in his shades and colors.

"You look completely mundane again now," Silhouette said.

"Good. That's the easy part." He remembered sitting on the plane, blocking out light itself from touching him. He drew on the power of the Darak and closed himself off from everything. He let light pass right through him, made his shields permeable to everything.

Silhouette laughed, slight shake of the head. "You're gone."

"Completely? You can't see anything?"

"Not a thing."

"Try to crack the wards."

Her magic crawled over the space he occupied. He closed up tighter still, drawing himself away from anything she might be able to feel. She frowned. "Say something, Alex."

"Like what."

She burst into a smile. "You're really still right there?" She shot one hand out, slapping into his arm. "Shit, I thought you were mucking about and you'd snuck away. I honestly can't see or sense a thing."

"Even when you touched me then?"

"No. That's a good point. It's not like an illusion. You stayed invisible to my eyes and mind even when I could feel you with my hand."

Alex let the guards down, slipped back into view. "Well then, that'll have to be good enough. Let's go."

"Right away?"

"No time like the present. I don't want to risk something like that weird bird catching up with us. I feel the need to keep moving."

A short walk took them back to the Via del ForiImperiali, a few hundred meters from the Colosseum. Across from them a smaller road led up to a gelataria and coffee shop, looking directly across at the arena of combat. Alex pointed. "Wait for me in there. I'll be as quick as I can."

Silhouette held him hard, kissed him passionately. "You better make sure you come back to me, Iron Balls."

"I will. I promise."

"Don't get dragged into any mischief."

"I won't."

"And don't use any magic. It'll shatter your cover."

"I know. I'm learning, you know. It might take me some time to find anything. Be patient, okay?"

"I've been around a long time," Silhouette said. "I can wait for days if need be."

"Let's hope that's not necessary."

He stepped back and flicked up his wards. Silhouette's face fell as he vanished. "Come back to me!" she called out.

"I will."

He turned and trotted across the road, dodging between cars. As he walked past the Colosseum he calmed his mind. If ever he needed his training in physical and mental control, he needed it now. So many lessons with his Sifu, the hours of training, of meditation. He centerd his mind and his breath, drew the power of the Darak through his entire being and merged with it, locked down his wards and shields. Like a ghost, he slipped through the Kin's secret door.

Silhouette made her way up to the gelataria, her mind a maelstrom. She pulled her phone out and dialled Joseph as she walked.

"What news?" he said gruffly.

She bit down on her annoyance at his rudeness. He was her Lord, after all. He'd saved her, and her mother. "Not much, I'm afraid. I think we've hit a dead end."

"That's most unsatisfactory."

"I know, my Lord. I'm sorry."

"So perhaps I'll come now," Joseph said.

"Come here?" Silhouette asked, surprised. "What for?"

Joseph's voice became angry. "I will not allow a human to bear the Darak, Silhouette. The Eld made that stone. If twothirds of it is all he can manage to recover, so be it. Twothirds of it will be mine."

"But, my Lord, the book…"

"Let me worry about the book, little one. This foolish game ends now."

Silhouette took a grip on her panic, steeling herself. "Give it a little while longer, my Lord. Alex is investigating one last avenue and there's a slim possibility he might turn something up."

"Don't play with me, Silhouette!"

"No, I'm not. Let him exhaust this last lead, at least. I'll call you again as soon as I can and let you know what happens. It might be a while, but it seems a shame to let him get this far and step in before the end."

"Earn your true place among us, child," Joseph said. "I'll expect to hear from you soon." The line went dead.

Silhouette pocketed her phone, chewing her bottom lip. She went into the gelataria and ordered a strong coffee.

Alex's first problem presented itself almost immediately. The heavy wooden door at the end of the passage was impenetrable. He could probably knock it down, but that would hardly be the way to start this incursion. He crouched in the corridor to wait. After ten minutes, he began to wonder if it would be hours until someone showed up. As a sense of despair descended the door clicked heavily and swung open. A Kin woman stepped out, talking to someone over her shoulder. The gap between her and the frame was thin. Alex didn't take time to second guess. He dived forward, twisting in the air to slip through. His jacket brushed the woman's legs as he landed inside and rolled. Without a pause, he stood and moved several meters into the room, dropping down against the back of a large leather sofa. The Kin woman glanced down at her legs absently, not breaking her tirade about someone called Michael or Miguel. Another Kin stood inside, nodding her agreement. The moment passed, the women parted ways. Alex breathed a sigh of relief.

He concentrated on the magic of the Darak, kept his cloak total. He marvelled at his position, in the midst of a Kin Den, unseen. But however clever his newfound skills, they were useless if he couldn't find any information. He crossed carefully to the wall and kept to the edges, staying intensely aware of his surroundings. He stalked through, searching, building a mental map of the place. Many doors were closed, doors he didn't dare open. He logged all the dead ends for later investigation. Then luck turned his way. Not far from Lorenzo's chambers was a library unlike anything he'd ever seen.

Alex had always been a fan of books, a voracious reader. Great works of fiction enthralled him, books containing all kinds of knowledge fascinated him. He had dreamed of a library of his own and had converted one room of his house into the closest thing he could manage. This stood beyond his wildest imagination.

The room was vast, ribbed columns supporting silver- and gray-flecked marble slabs across the ceiling into the distance. Dark wooden shelves stood in ordered row upon row. A mezzanine level ran a ring around the entire massive space, more shelves, more books. Alex stood mesmerized, breathing in the heady smell, intoxicated by it. He could see 'sign swirling around several shelves, all manner of grimoires and volumes less than mundane in rough groups here and there. Some of the shelving held things that seeped age, clearly ancient tomes, priceless and fascinating. Alex scanned from the shelter of one corner. If these Kin kept records, surely they would be somewhere in here.

Several people wandered the library, browsing. Others sat at numerous desks or in leather armchairs, lost in their reading. Alex slipped quietly between shelves, exploring the layout. At the far end of the room a sectioned-off area looked enticing. Several rows of almost identical books, spines pressed with gold lettering. He crept in, looked closely. His heart skipped a beat and he cursed his stupidity. Every word was Latin, incomprehensible to him.

Why hadn't he considered such a simple point? Had he really thought he would be able to wander in and read the ancient records of this magical race in a foreign land? Lorenzo had been right, he was child lost among things he didn't understand. His disappointment, his internal rage, swam off him. The glee of Uthentia pulsated from his pocket, threatening to burst forth, smother his mind with fury, force him to smash into Lorenzo's apartments and demand the information he needed.

Don't get dragged into any mischief.

He sucked in a shuddering breath, dragging together the strands of his disguise. His eyes flicked furtively around. Thankfully no one stood near. The words of his Sifu floated in his memory. *Power is dangerous without control. At all times, maintain control, maintain focus. Any obstacle, however seemingly insurmountable, can be bested with controlled focus.*

Alex reminded himself that giving up was not an option. He smothered the book raging deep somewhere in his thoughts and turned back to the shelves. The grimoires he'd already read weren't in English either. He could understand and absorb those arcane scripts easily. What was a foreign language if not another form of arcane script? Language itself was a supernatural thing, the transmission of stories and histories perhaps mankind's greatest magic. He stared at the spines before him, let his vision open. Like watching for the move of an opponent before the opponent themselves knew what they were going to do, he looked for meaning behind the written words. Those meanings became clear.

Histories of The Den Of Rome, Vol. CCLVII

Volume two hundred and fifty-seven. Left and right were dozens of similar books. One of the oldest Dens obviously had one of the longest histories. He had found exactly what he'd been looking for, but it turned out to be a haystack. He had no idea when the events surrounding Uthentia's exile had happened, therefore no idea what the needle he sought looked like. As soon as he overcame one obstacle another dropped into his path. It would take years to look through all these.

He drew deep, even breaths, refusing to let despair sink him. He had come this far. Each volume had dates stamped below the title. He remembered Lorenzo's words earlier that day, *This happened before my time. Before history. But yes, it happened here.*

How old was Lorenzo? Old even by usual Kin standards, he knew that. How old was history? He cast his mind back, remembering how Lorenzo had felt, compared to others he knew were beyond mortal years. Welby, Silhouette, Joseph, Isiah. They all counted their age in centuries. How many more walked the Earth holding secrets like theirs? Silhouette had said that some Kin counted their age in millennia. Could Lorenzo really be over a thousand years old? Two? More than that? The thought twisted Alex's mind. What would it be like to have that kind of experience?

This sort of thinking would get him nowhere. He needed the volume that covered the exile.

He checked around again to be sure that no one could see into this corner of the library. Reassured he was alone, he let his mind out, as tightly controlled as he could manage, let it creep across the shelves of books. He filtered his thoughts through the Darak, asked the stone to seek itself in the hundreds of thousands of pages before him. He let his thoughts drift back through the histories of the Roman Kin, past volume after volume of events important to them, mentally fishing with magesign. As he neared the beginning of the shelves he thought his plan would prove fruitless, his methodology flawed. Then something caught. His eyes were drawn to a volume very near the beginning of recorded Kin history.

He slipped it from the shelf, turning pages like slivers of dead skin as carefully as he could. He read about the threat of Uthentia, the rise of the Eld, the mages who fashioned the Darak. He learned of the battle when they faced Uthentia and used the power of the stone to banish the Fey godling from this realm. It was all recorded here. He read of a council meeting, of their decision to let that last shred of Uthentia be. Their agreement that nothing could be done about it and periodic chaos, watered down in that form, was an acceptable price for the largely successful endavor they had embarked upon. The book described the three pieces, kept separate, the power denied recombination. The council agreed a stone this powerful must never be re-formed.

Alex's excitement grew as he read of the decision to task three

Kin to hide the shards and then kill themselves, so those shards might never be found.

There were no names, no places. No clues. Alex's mood deflated, the book dropping into his lap. The story was confirmed, but he was no closer to an answer than before. Despondent, he slipped the ancient volume back onto the shelf, staring at the faded gold leaf printed into the leather.

His eyes grew wide with sudden realization. He remembered Silhouette's words when Meera had suggested they investigate Rome. *Every Den keeps an account of its history, its members and genealogy.* Any genealogy would keep birth and death dates. How often would a seemingly immortal race like Kin lose their members? He knew when the Darak had split. The date three Kin members had been tasked with the ultimate sacrifice. Would their deaths be listed on that same date?

He turned, searching. The genealogy books were not far from the histories. Moving carefully, quietly, he selected the correct book by date from the dozens of volumes recording births and deaths. Three names were listed as dying the very day of the council's decision. Surely too much of a coincidence to ignore?

Alex spent hours cross-referencing the names, looking up their family trees in various volumes, looking for anything that might help.

He ended up in despair, with a huge list of names, descendants of the Kin who had borne that terrible task. At least, the three he suspected. Far too many names to investigate, follow up. Millennia of births and deaths since those days had created a many branched tree, hundreds of Kin descendants. Curdled excitement and despondency spun through his mind. All the events as described to him seemed true, yet his leads had disappeared in a morass of information, far too complicated to follow through.

Desolation rose into a red-tinged anger, melting quickly into fury. He would not be destroyed by this ridiculous situation. Uthentia poured rage through him, exhorting him to burst out of hiding, take on every Kin in this Den until a new answer presented itself. His heart beat a frantic cadence to match his mood as his temperature rose.

Grinding his teeth, hanging on to the rational part of his mind, he concentrated on the Darak to suppress the irrational thoughts bounding through his forebrain. Why would any Kin here know any more than he already knew? He held himself in check and crept away through the lines of shelves. With almost painful care he slipped through the rooms of the Den and out when a group of Kin left. He let them move ahead of him along the dim corridor then followed them out into the balmy autumn night.

Silhouette's face dropped as he walked into the gelataria. She was clearly pleased to see him, but could tell instantly he wasn't happy. She jumped up, slipped an arm around his shoulders and walked him straight back out the door. "Hold it together," she whispered as they emerged onto the street. She turned them right, heading down a cobbled alleyway between high shuttered apartments and scaffolding supporting renovations. "No luck, huh?"

Alex leaned into her, wordlessly thankful for her support. "I learned a lot," he said. "Mostly I learned there's no way to use any of their records to help. At first I had too little info, now I have too much. What I found only confirmed the truth of what we already know. Or it confirms the myths, at least. But there are hundreds of tenuous leads. Far too many, we'd never be able to follow everything up."

Silhouette squeezed him as they walked. "You're burning up here. How close are you to losing it?"

He barked a laugh. "Pretty close. But I'm actually managing to maintain some level of control."

"Really?"

"Sort of. I'm getting better at channelling the Darak. Where are we going?"

"Anywhere. Away from the Den, mainly. Tell me everything that happened in there, everything you learned."

They walked steadily, keeping to the quietest streets. Alex told her how he had snuck in, all he had discovered. As he reached the end of the story his anger welled up stronger than ever, the retelling fuelling his resentment, and three men stepped out of the shadows.

Silhouette froze, a soft growl sounding deep in her throat. Alex sucked in a deep breath, fingers gripping air reflexively. The men spread across the alley in front of them. Alex's heart pounded, his bloodlust rising like an orgasm. Uthentia exulted through his veins, throbbing with excitement. He read their shades and a wave of fear pushed through his anger. "Kin," he said sidelong to Silhouette. "Did Lorenzo know I was there?"

"Not Lorenzo's Kin," Silhouette replied. "I'm so sorry, Alex, I tried to prevent this." She slipped back, letting darkness fold her out of sight.

Alex didn't take his eyes off the three ranged in front of him. "You betrayed me," he said, resigned. *I knew you would.*

Alex's skin tingled, his blood rushed. He drew his center in tight, breathed control over the adrenaline as hundreds of fights had taught him to do. He watched the colors of the Kin, read their shades as easily as he would read a child's picture book.

"Don't blame her, Alex." Joseph's voice, somewhere out of sight. "She's been beholden to me for a lot longer than she's known you."

"Are you too scared to face me?" Alex growled, searching the shadows for the Clan Lord's shades. He was obviously very well warded.

"Not really. Just a healthy caution that's seen me survive this long. Giles, remember what I told you? Just the book."

Another Kin stepped from the shadows. "Just the book." His voice was slurred, like his tongue was too thick. "Search his pockets when he's dead and take just the book."

Alex studied his shades and saw colors of damage and retardation. This Kin had an injury of some kind that affected his thinking, his intellect. "You setting up a simple-minded puppet, Joseph?" he asked. "That's low, even for scum like you."

"Scum?" Joseph's anger washed out and Alex caught a flash of furious red, a diaphanous shade up and to the right. He knew where the Clan Lord hid.

"Joseph, please," Silhouette said from the shadows. "Not Giles. He doesn't understand."

"Of course he doesn't understand. But he's faithful and knows his duty. Isn't that right, Giles? You do the right thing by the Kin?"

Giles's face split in a vacant grin. "I do what my Lord says."

"Exactly." Joseph sounded pleased with himself.

Alex's fury bubbled over, his skin burned, his thoughts narrowed to a scarlet focus. The stone, *his* stone, scorched his chest as he drew its energy, thinking of nothing but showing Joseph his error. If the Clan Lord thought Alex had been powerful to beat Ataro, he would learn now how far Alex had come. It seemed an insult that only three Kin stood before him, even though they were clearly very old, very strong. The Kin crouched, tensed. Their shades flooded out, their intention nothing but violence and death.

Alex moved even as they burst forward and slammed low into the center Kin's abdomen, sending him flying backwards. Everything moved like treacle. Alex used the Darak, drew it into his every move, his every intent. Time stretched out. The Kin he'd struck went down and Alex's elbow crushed his head against the cobblestones like an overripe melon. Uthentia howled. Joseph roared somewhere miles away.

Alex kept moving, rolling over the dead Kin as the other two charged from either side. His mastery of the Darak was purer than ever. He swept a foot around in a long sweep, pivoting on one hand. The legs of the first Kin flipped up, his surprised face slamming into the cobbles with a dull crack and a spurt of blood. Alex caught the arm of the second man and twisted, standing as he did so. The man yelped as the bones of his forearms crossed well beyond their natural movement and snapped like dry twigs. He might be strong, but Alex was stronger. He held the Kin back by his broken arm and thrust a kick into his chest. The Kin flew back, his arm ripping from its socket with a wet suck. He screamed, slamming into the wall and staggering forward again. Alex dropped the arm and spun around, whipping one heel up and across. The kick landed true on the man's temple, knocking his head brutally fast to one side, sending him sprawling across the road.

"Finish him, you imbeciles," Joseph yelled.

The first Kin, who had gone facedown into the street, clambered to his feet, weaving unsteadily, trying to focus. Alex took one step towards him, drew back his elbow and hammered an iron fist into the man's face. His nose and cheekbones folded back into his head, blood bursting out around Alex's knuckles. He collapsed backwards, limp. Dead.

Alex turned back to the other Kin. He lay on the road, eyes wide open, seeing nothing, blood seeping from a skull cracked by Alex's heel. Alex tipped his head back and bellowed, bathing in the power of slaughter. Uthentia roared with him.

Shape and shades moved swiftly from both sides. "Don't just stand there!" Joseph shouted as he emerged from hiding, barrelling towards Alex.

Silhouette shot out of the shadows. As Alex raised his hands to defend himself he read her colors and sidestepped. She flew past him and crashed into Joseph's chest before the Clan Lord could close the gap. She cried out in pain and rolled aside.

Joseph fell back and leapt to his feet in an instant, his face twisted in fury. Silhouette crouched to one side, tense like a bowstring. Alex moved to her, her shades the most beautiful thing he'd ever seen. "You make a terrible choice this day," Joseph snarled.

"You yourself said I'm too much human and too much Fey," Silhouette said, her voice tinged with sadness. "Even if I helped you, the Kin would always hate me. I love you, Joseph, you've done more for me than anyone. You saved me. But I can't let you kill him."

Alex stood ready, convinced Joseph would attack them both. The Clan Lord's shades were all rage and violence. He might be powerful enough. The dead at their feet were strong, but had been no match for Alex and the Darak. Would Joseph be a different matter?

"A terrible choice," Joseph said again. Alex tensed as the Lord's aura surged, but he turned and vanished at a preternatural speed.

Giles stood to one side, his mouth agape, eyes haunted.

"Go with him," Silhouette told him. "Can you find him, follow him home?"

"I think so," Giles said thickly. He pointed to his slain friends. "They... they..."

Silhouette put one hand on his shoulder. "Ask Joseph to explain it to you. Quick, before you lose him."

Giles turned and ran.

Alex let the exultation and tension slip through him, drew deep breaths to breathe it away. Uthentia revelled in the murder, but Alex pushed the pleasure away too. He let the Darak smother Uthentia's joy, reminding himself that he had acted in self-defense, however much he may have enjoyed it. A shudder passed through him.

"I'm so sorry," Silhouette said.

"I wondered if you would sell me out."

"Alex, I didn't know what to do. When we went to Joseph for help he told me to get him the stone. He can't bear to see it in human hands."

"He'll hunt us again, won't he? Next time he'll bring an army."

Silhouette crouched, closing the eyes of the dead. "Maybe. I don't know. Joseph is a complex creature. If he knows that to get you he'll have to kill me too, that might give him pause."

Alex remembered the color of Joseph's shades. "I don't know," he said dubiously. "I think you may have severed any loyalty he has to you. Why did you do that?"

"I'm a pariah among my own kind. I always have been. Joseph told me that if I helped him get the stone from you it would prove to the Kin that I was one of them. But that's not true. They would never accept me, not really. But Joseph's words made me realize something else. For the first time, with you, I've found someone strong enough to actually be with me. With you, I don't need the Kin."

Alex wanted to believe her. He needed to believe her but couldn't help wondering if she was just keeping him and his power for herself. If she was such a pariah, did she intend to take his stone and use it to take over the Kin? He recognised Uthentia's influence in his thoughts, and cursed the book again. But he couldn't ignore it. "I hope you're right. How did Joseph find us?"

"As Clan Lord he can find any of his Kin, wherever they are."

"So he can track us easily, with far greater numbers?"

"Possibly," Silhouette agreed.

"He underestimated me," Alex said. "He won't do that again."

Silhouette gestured to the three dead Kin at their feet. "These were powerful men. Ataro was big and strong and deadly, but Joseph thought you a human then. These are older, more experienced. Between them they were a far greater threat than a beast like Ataro. But you went through them like butter."

"I'm owning the power of the Darak more all the time."

"Clearly."

"If Joseph comes again, with ten Kin, or twenty, or fifty, what then? However powerful I might be, there are odds I simply can't stand against."

"I think Joseph might lick his wounds for a while at least," Silhouette said. "We'll just have to wait and see. We have to go, before people come to investigate."

"Where?"

"Let's just find somewhere private while we decide what to do."

TWENTY-FOUR

T he Dark Sisters stood outside Termini station in Rome. They were dressed in modern skirts, blouses, and fashionable boots. They drew appreciative glances, exuding confidence, revelling in their soul-stolen beauty.

"This is a little loose about the middle," Red said, tugging at the soft silk.

"I told you she was heavier than you," Blonde replied absently. She looked across the busy street. "I feel them. Faint. This stench of humanity and their oily technology disgusts me, but I sense them. This way."

Red stepped up to her sister. "Yes. They are quite unmistakable. But the trail is getting old."

"We are restricted by the nature of human time," Blonde said. "All we can do is follow where it leads."

She walked across the road. A car screeched to a halt, skidding sideways, horn blaring. A stream of Italian invective burst forth, the driver hanging half out the window, gesticulating wildly. Blonde turned a smouldering look on him, not breaking her stride. The driver melted quietly back into his seat. Red and Brunette followed their sister.

They walked three abreast along cobbled alleys, faces tipped to the air, reading the weak presence of their quarry, to eventually emerge into the wide open space dominated by the Colosseum. Blonde turned a small circle, frowning.

"The trail is confused here," Red said.

"We must follow in the order it was laid down," Brunette said. "But there's a part missing."

Blonde sneered. "Mortal temporality. So limiting. What are we missing?"

Red drifted towards the wall at the back of the palazzo. "This way," she called. "It vanishes here."

"We should combine," said Brunette.

The Sisters faced each other, joined hands. They murmured, ignoring the curious looks from passers-by. Their eyes closed, heads down, the murmuring became faster as they used their collective will to feel the way their quarry had passed. All three snapped their heads up to stare at the door to the Kin Den, no longer hidden from them.

"Kin," Blonde said, almost a hiss.

"Naturally," said Red. "Of course they're allied with Kin. One of them is Kin."

"Almost as childish as humans," Brunette said disdainfully. "Trying to hide in plain view all the time."

"Is it so different from us, sister?" Blonde looked amused.

"We're hardly hiding."

They shared a smile and turned to the magically concealed doorway, striding purposefully down the passageway until they reached a heavy wooden entrance. Blonde reached out and stopped. All three turned to look back down the passage. A man stepped into view.

"What the fuck are you doing?" he said, his face derisive.

Blonde stepped forward. "It's no concern of yours, little man."

"Little man?" His face became furious. "I am Louie Vertigno, Warden of this Den and I demand to know just what you think you're doing!"

Red stepped up next to her sister. "Oh, Louie, you're cute." She reached out, index finger crooked to stroke under his chin.

Louie grabbed her hand, drawing his other arm back to strike. His face twisted in pain as he sucked in air, dropping Red's arm as if it was red hot. Brunette joined her sisters and they bore down on Louie. He fellto his knees, babbling incoherently. The energy of the Sisters drifted out, encompassing Louie's face. "What are you?" he managed in a weak voice before his skin tightened black across his skull.

The Dark Sisters straightened. "That was nice," Blonde said. "It's been a while since I tasted something so old."

"So much better than humans," Red agreed.

They turned to the door. Blonde put one palm against it and shoved. The door burst inwards in a shower of dark splinters. Several Kin turned and rushed as the three Sisters strolled nonchalantly through the wreckage of the door into the Den. Shouts and screams erupted as Kin were tossed aside like rag dolls, some merely broken, others partially consumed before being discarded. Panic broke out, weapons appearing as Kin swarmed the Sisters in a wave. A huge voice boomed out.

"CEASE!"

Kin dropped back at the command. Lorenzo stood across the large central room, his face hard. Several Kin groaned, writhing on the floor in pain. Others lay still.

"What is this?" Lorenzo demanded. "Who are you?"

The Sisters looked around, ignoring him. Some Kin rose to rejoin the battle. Lorenzo strode across to them, his hand staying their actions. "You do great insult to this Den," he said, stopping several feet from the Sisters. "What do you want?"

"We're seeking someone, that's all," Blonde informed him. "It's no concern of yours."

Lorenzo saw the blackened corpse of Louie in the passageway. "It most certainly is my concern when you break into my home and kill those I'm sworn to protect."

"Are they here?" Red asked.

"Who?"

Brunette stepped forward. "Come now, Kin-King. You've not had any strange visitors lately?"

Lorenzo's lip curled in distaste. "I should have known trouble would follow them. They're not here."

"What did they want?" Blonde asked.

"Information. They wanted help. I told them to leave."

Red tipped her head to one side. "You didn't help your own kind? One of them at least is Kin, no?"

"One of them is Kin and I told her she was welcome here any time without the human. An ancient evil clings to him and will destroy him."

"And you didn't help?" Brunette asked.

"I couldn't help if I tried. I don't know what they needed. So I sent them on their way. I don't want that curse infecting this Den." He gestured at the bodies of his fallen friends. "Even so, it seems that chaos still trails them. You're the Dark Sisters, right? I thought you myth. Who invoked you?"

Blonde gestured dismissively. "No one you'd know. We're tracking these two, that's all."

"If you tracked them here, surely you could tell they left again?"

"It doesn't work like that. We can only follow their intent, their learning. We're restricted to the course they took."

Red drifted off towards the back of the room. "Can you sense the overlap?" she called back over her shoulder.

Blonde and Brunette walked to join her, Lorenzo forgotten. He raised his voice. "Don't do anything to hinder these three. Let them go where they will and they'll leave when they're ready. Right, ladies?"

Blonde flicked a smile back over her shoulder. "Of course."

They headed deeper into the Den. Lorenzo followed them into the library. "They didn't come in here," he said tiredly.

"Yes, they did," Red said. "Well, the human did." She stopped, concentrated. "They left together," Red said.

"But the human came back," said Brunette, brow creased in concentration.

Blonde pointed to the back of the library. "He spent some time there, reading through your records."

Lorenzo frowned. "What? How? We would have known."

Red smiled. "Apparently not. He's using powerful magic, this human."

"This power, it is what the Hood wants," Blonde said.

"But the curse is strong too," Brunette added. "The Hood doesn't know this, perhaps?"

"How can he? He would never risk that," said Blonde. "This is becoming quite interesting."

The Sisters strolled back through the Den, ignoring all the Kin.

Lorenzo stood in the main room, staring up the passage after they passed along it. Eventually he shook his head, dropping his gaze to the carnage. "Get Louie's body in here and fix that door. We need to hold a ritual for the brothers and sisters we've lost today."

Kin moved about the Den, faces downcast in frustrated sorrow.

Silhouette slipped from the hotel bed, pulling her clothes back on. "That was awesome." She leaned over, teasing Alex with her breasts, planted a kiss on him.

He smiled, disappointed as she covered herself with bra, then T-shirt. "Makes a nice change to do that and not try to kill you too," he said.

"It certainly does. You really are getting a handle on controlling this stuff, huh."

"Those Kin in the alleyway took my rage for a while."

"I like it."

"I'm glad. I like it too, a lot. But we're procrastinating. We have to think of what to do. I can't keep slaughtering Kin."

"Don't pity them, Alex. They would have killed you. They tried to kill you. It's Joseph you should blame."

Alex climbed from the bed, began dressing. "I do." A tight knot deep in his gut twisted every time he remembered the fast, decisive slaughter. Perhaps it was a good thing that he held a level of guilt about what he'd done. How long before he didn't care any more? As a fighter, his Sifu had instilled in him a respect for every warrior. *Whenever someone steps up to test themselves against you, they deserve to be honored by you. It takes courage to walk this path.*

But that didn't apply to people out to kill you rather than test themselves. And next time there would be more. How many could he kill? He had made a life of fighting and never killed. He had beaten and broken opponents, and had enjoyed every minute of it, but he hadn't taken a life. His stomach jumped slightly when he realized that he had now and already he'd lost count of how many. It started with Peacock, then Ataro. The island was where he lost count, unnumbered lives swallowed by the cold ocean. He slammed a door shut on that train of thought and Uthentia's joy. With a frown he picked up his jacket, shrugged into it, trying to ignore the weight and presence of the book.

"I've had an idea," Silhouette said, breaking his reverie.

"Yeah?"

"I think you're trying too hard."

"Is that so?"

"I think the answer is hanging around your neck."

"What do you mean?"

Silhouette sat on the edge of the bed. "You said that in the Den you used the power of the stone to find reference to itself. You set it to seek itself among the pages of the books there."

"Yeah."

"So can't you do that to find the actual piece you're after?"

Could it be that simple? Why hadn't he thought of that himself? The Darak he already had could track down the last piece of itself. He would need to let the power out across the world, to seek itself on a global scale. Perhaps it would be worth a try. "I don't know. Maybe."

"The more you learn about this thing, the more you can do. You've learned something, so use it."

Alex sat cross-legged on the bed. He closed his eyes, emptied his mind. How long had it been since he'd had a chance to meditate like he used to? To train properly, to rest. He mentally shook himself, pushed away the thoughts, let his consciousness sink into the void. Something dragged at him, interrupting. He pulled his jacket off, the book in the pocket, threw it aside. His mind cleared slightly as he gained some space from it. If only it was that easy to be rid of it completely. He imagined himself walking naked through a forest somewhere, no pockets, no book. But he knew it wouldn't work. It would dog him everywhere, even if that meant it kept turning up nearby. Nothing this powerful would ever be that simple.

He remembered sitting in the Kin library, letting the Darak soak its presence through the shelves of books. He had put in mind what he wanted to find and used the magic of the stone to seek it. He let the process repeat, but directed the energy out. Without a focus in mind, like a bookshelf right in front of him, it felt like waving his hands in a dark room, stumbling around after a light switch. He panicked at the scale and his eyes popped open.

"You okay?" Silhouette asked, concerned.

"This is hard. I don't know where to go."

"Don't go anywhere. Tell it to go."

He pictured the stone whole, the pure Darak as it had once been, but had not been for thousands of years. He let the desire to re-form it become the only focus. Rather than try to travel with it, he simply let the energy go.

Vertigo swept through his body. He deliberately relaxed, refused to be knocked off center by it. Let it travel where it would and come back to him. And something cried out in the darkness. A sudden sense of oneness flooded his mind and body. As quickly as that, the stone had found itself. Consciously calming his breathing, not letting any excitement disrupt the process, he let the message in. *Where are you?* he called out across the aether. And the Darak cried back. He felt the enormous energy the combined stone would be, almost alive, its desire to be re-formed almost sentient. But it wasn't life that cried back across the aether. It was magic. Pure, unfettered, incredibly powerful magic, desperate to be recombined.

In his mind's eye Alex saw a burnt, arid landscape, gray rock, drifting smoke. A cave, isolated. A man in the cave, old as time. The man looked up as if he'd heard an unexpected sound. He gasped, his mouth forming an O of surprise.

And Alex knew where the last shard lay.

He opened his eyes. "I know where it is," he said, his voice quiet, incredulous. "I could feel its magic across the world."

Silhouette kissed him. "You can do this, Alex!"

"Maybe. I won't give up the fight."

"So, where is it?"

"You feeling charming?" Alex asked. "'Cause we need to fly again and I'm all out of cash. I hope Iceland's nice this time of year."

Hood strolled through a hermetically sealed warehouse in the basement of the Black Diamond tower. Sparks followed him, notebook PC balanced on one palm as she tapped away with the other. A tall, thin man with long, dark hair walked in front of them, eyes panning left and right. His sharp pinstripe suit rustled in the silence of the space, the only other sounds from Sparks's heels and fingertips. She checked their location on the inventory map. She'd only just managed to have the goods moved to the back of the warehouse before the client arrived. Hood insisted every buyer walk the length of at least one storage area on the way to see whatever they were interested in. The impulse buy was not to be underestimated.

Racks of shelving, glass cabinets, heavily sealed trunks, created walkways. A location popped up on Sparks's screen. Luckily the stuff had been moved before the three of them walked into the far wall. The staff knew better than to fail her directions. "This way, please."

She turned down an aisle then paused at Hood's subtle cough. The client crouched before a tall display unit. "What's this?" he asked, his Russian accent heavy.

Hood rubbed dry palms together. "Well, what an eye you have. One of my favorite pieces, actually." He crouched beside the man. In the cabinet stood a statuette, a foot tall, carved from obsidian. The figure had the head of a dog, two pairs of sweeping wings, a long scorpion tale. A serpentine penis twisted before the creature's chest as he pointed upwards to some unseen celestial relevance. "Pazuzu," Hood said quietly. "Demon King of the Winds."

The client looked at Hood with disdain. "I know *who* it is, Mr Hood. I asked *what* it is."

"Of course, Mr Doschenko. The icon there is quite powerful. It can be used to invoke plague, famine, storms. Should you wish to disrupt the plans of a landholder, for example. Of course, that's what it was created for. You don't need me to tell you that it can be used for so much more than that, especially by someone with your skills."

Doschenko stared hard at the statuette, his eyes darkening. Sparks took a step away from the pair. She had grown used to people using magic around her, but would never become comfortable with it. It might have made Hood his fortune, provided her with an escape, but she would never trust it.

"Open, please," Doschenko said. His voice sounded distant.

She hurried forward, finding the item on her inventory. It supplied a code number. She tapped the code into the small access pad on the cabinet and the glass front popped open. Doschenko reached in, lifted the statue reverently. He closed his eyes, running pale fingers across its night black surface.

"This is genuine. And quite powerful," the Russian said.

Hood inclined his head. "Of course. Very few items of Pazuzu are left, but *everything* here is genuine."

"Where did you get it?"

"Mr Doschenko, please."

Doschenko sneered. "I often wonder just what it is I finance when I buy from you."

"You finance my ability to find more of the things you desire."

"Of course." Doschenko's voice drawled with sarcasm. "So, how much for this one?"

"Two fifty." Hood knew the price of everything in his possession. His ability to remember exactly what everything was and how much he deemed it worth never ceased to impress Sparks.

"Quarter of a million dollars?" Doschenko's eyebrows rode high on his forehead.

"Pounds, Mr Doschenko. Pounds sterling."

"Ha! Even more expensive. Really, Mr Hood, you can't expect to charge these prices."

Hood straightened up, suddenly uninterested. "Well, if you don't want it. You can always get one somewhere else, I suppose."

Doschenko still cradled the statuette. "One of a kind items cannot be got somewhere else."

Hood opened his palms. "Which is why they command such unique prices."

Sparks studied the Russian, so like Hood in appearance apart from long dark hair where Hood was smoothly bald. This afternoon they had an appointment with a client the complete opposite, short, fat, constantly sweating. He coveted so many things in Hood's possession and seemed to have an endless source of funds to indulge himself. The next day they would be seeing the strange lesbian pair who Sparks secretly suspected were also sisters. One thing all these disparate souls shared was their inability to resist Hood when he saw their interest piqued.

Doschenko would buy this statuette. She tried to remember how Hood had gained possession of it but couldn't. Perhaps it had been on one of his secret personal missions, the occasional jaunts into an underworld he wouldn't expose her to for reasons he would never explain. Her mind often tumbled with suspicions as to why there were certain places she would never see when so much of his business he placed willingly before her. Now, as then, she stopped considering it. Anything Hood didn't want her to know about was probably something she would be glad not to know. In any case, Hood would never have paid close to a quarter million for this thing, if he paid anything at all. Doschenko would prevaricate some more, but he would buy.

"You are the most magical mundane I have ever known, Mr Hood," Doschenko was saying. "How do you recognise this stuff as genuine without abilities like mine?"

"I have my methods, Mr Doschenko. And many, many years of experience."

Sparks thought of the subcontracted agents Hood regularly employed. And wondered for the millionth time how mundane Hood really was. She suspected he was rather more magical than he ever let on.

"This item is genuine, but it is not worth a quarter of a million pounds." Doschenko's voice was strong, persuasive. Sparks recognised a kind of enchantment that many clients tried to use. Most, in fact. She and Hood both wore pendants that protected them from such charms.

Hood made a rueful face. "No, you're right." Doschenko smiled, clearly pleased with himself. "It's priceless," Hood continued. "You simply can't put a price on a unique, one of a kind item like that."

Doschenko's eyebrows and smile sank like stones through honey. He stared again at the shining black wind demon.

"But," Hood said, his voice jolly, "you want it. So I'm prepared to let it go for two hundred and fifty thousand pounds."

Doschenko put the statuette back in the cabinet. "I'll take it." His voice sounded tired, resigned.

Hood clapped his hands together, flicked a wink at Sparks. "Good man!"

Sparks keyed in the relevant information. Funds would be exchanged, secure delivery would be arranged. Hood had got his man. Again.

"So," Hood said, striding down the aisle, drawing Doschenko's attention away from the demonic icon while his desire still burned. "You were actually here to see the Scroll of Attenuatea. A powerful spell." He cast a serious glance at Sparks.

"This way, gentlemen, please."

Hood cried out, dropping to one knee. Sparks spun around, frowning at the pain evident in his face. "Mr Hood?"

Doschenko stepped back, eyes wide. "Where are they?" He looked frantically about the large space.

Hood pressed one hand to his temple, grimacing. "Not... here. They're just... communicating."

Doschenko took further steps back. "I should leave. Maybe return another day."

Hood drove himself to his feet, pure force of will. "No, please. Just give me... one moment." He grunted, pressing the other hand to the side of his head, like he was trying to crush his own face. "Yes," he hissed. "Yes, good. Okay." He paused, listening. "Are you sure that's where they're going?" Listening again. "Right. I've changed my mind. I want to be there, to see this. Yes. Keep me informed." He staggered back, as if a pressure against him had been unexpectedly removed. His eyes swam for a moment as he gasped, pulling himself together. He smiled, trembling slightly. "My apologies. Shall we?"

"What was that?" Doschenko asked. "Something grave was here."

"Just some... employees, doing a little work for me, that's all."

Doschenko followed them along the aisle once more. "Not your average employee," he said. "Something truly wicked. You take enormous risks, Mr Hood."

Sparks agreed with the Russian. The risks Hood took were not only enormous, but seemingly unnecessary. He would tell her it's how his empire was built, how he attained his fortune. And she couldn't argue with that. But when did the empire outgrow the man? When did the risks overtake him? When was the fortune big enough? He had long since gone beyond the pursuit of money; he already had more than he could spend. The sport of it drove him now. She wondered how far it would drive him this time.

The Dark Sisters stood in a tiny hotel lobby, a dark, desiccated skeleton at their feet. "So now the Hood wants to be there," Blonde said.

"He probably won't make it in time," said Red.

"I wonder why he wants to be there," Brunette said.

"You felt his mind." Blonde turned to the door, strolling out into the sunshine. "To see this creature he has tasked us to kill. He wants to be a part of the hunt. His obsession is delicious."

"So what if we catch up to them before Hood arrives?" Red asked.

"We'll see. We've been given a task by the man who gave us ten."

The Sisters laughed, a low, broken sound, and strolled through the autumn sunshine.

TWENTY-FIVE

Alex sat in a hard plastic departure lounge chair, watching flight numbers and times flicker across a giant screen. He had insisted on Silhouette doing the mind trick things to get them through passport control even though she maintained he would be able to do it himself. The thing that scared him wasn't that he might mess it up, but that he believed her. He had watched her sweet talk the customs official, read the shades of magic about her while she did, sensed the official's complete obliviousness to the manipulation. Alex had the power in him now. He could do exactly what she did. Even without the Darak he felt he would have the knowledge and ability still. The stone acted as an incredible amplifier, but the skill had become his own. That's what scared him about it. How much of his old self made room for this new Alex? This magical Alex.

He turned to Silhouette, slumped beside him. "We only just made it in time," he said, casual conversation to take his mind off things. "That taxi driver was a bit of a lunatic."

"I think the guy in the hotel gave him a bonus to make sure we made the flight."

"Funny, given it was the hotelier's own money that I'd just snatched from his till."

Silhouette grinned. "Your disappearing talents are proving all kinds of useful."

Alex smiled half-heartedly. He didn't like stealing. "Lucky that hotelier has such a good travel agent contact."

"They all work like that. Backhanders for referrals. The whole world turns on bribes and favours."

"Feeling a bit cynical?" Alex asked.

"No, not at all. Just being a realist. That hotelier will get a cut of the airfare that we paid to the travel agent. He'll get cheap taxi rides from the driver he called to bring us here. They give him the bonuses because he gives them the work and they get jobs that might have gone to other people. That's the nature of the human social animal."

The human animal. "As opposed to us?" Alex wondered.

Silhouette gave him a smile. "Starting to accept your ascension to more than human?" She kissed him as he winced. "Don't worry, Iron Balls. If it's any consolation, the same social system plays out in my world too. In every world, I expect. It's all about who you know."

Alex sighed. "I think that's one of the things I enjoyed most about fighting for a living. You train hard, you learn, you practise. When you step into the ring it's just you and him. No one to buy you out. It's all you."

"There's something beautiful about that."

"Of course there is," Alex said wistfully. "There's nothing more pure. It removes the social from the animal, but not the emotional. There's no hate in the ring, not usually. Two warriors who respect each other's ability, each other's efforts and sacrifices. You're just there to test yourself, body, heart and soul, against someone else. If you lose you congratulate the other person, you learn, you grow."

"I don't think you lost much, somehow."

Alex remembered broken bones, swollen eyes, jaws that couldn't manage anything but soup. "Oh, I did, early on. I got my arse handed to me on many occasions until I put the bravado aside and shut the fuck up long enough to listen and actually hear what I was being taught. Then I trained properly, trained hard, did everything the proper way, not the quick way."

"But your vision always gave you an edge, right?"

"Not at first. My vision grew with me, I had to learn to use it. The better a fighter I became, the more I relaxed into the flow of battle, the clearer I could see."

Silhouette stroked his cheek. "You were a master of your chosen field, weren't you?"

What made a master? Usually it was something someone else called you. He couldn't imagine ever calling himself that. His Sifu was a master. The man was beyond anyone Alex had ever met, not only in skill but in wisdom, awareness. Perhaps Alex had grown to become something like him. But he had always been a student, never a teacher. "Maybe," he said softly, reluctantly. "I don't know if I could ever really be called a master until I'd passed my knowledge on to someone else. I think that's the real definition."

"You could. Teach someone else, I mean."

"Not every great fighter is a great teacher. And I just loved to fight."

"You miss it, don't you?"

"Fuck yeah! My life was so simple. It was exactly what I wanted it to be. I fought and had everything I needed. It's not like I was striving for something from life. I was living it."

"But now you have so much more. You can see that, right? The life you were living, it was all you ever wanted only because you didn't know how much more you could have."

Maybe she had a point. If he stopped to imagine what he knew now without the burden of this book it made his previous life seem incredibly small. There existed more in the big wide world than he'd ever imagined and could he really picture himself not being a part of it now that he knew? "I suppose so."

"You stood up against things unlike any opponent you've ever had, Alex."

"That thing in Bonavista had me beat, though."

"And how long has it been since you were beaten?" she asked. "You went through three Kin like they were paper. You're improving all the time. More than you'd ever have improved otherwise. If testing yourself against other well-trained humans was the pinnacle of life before, you've just levelled up big time."

She made a certain kind of sense. His life now was a lot like his life in the ring. But the ring had changed. Instead of a fenced-in octagon, the entire planet had become his arena of combat. Instead of trained fighters, literally anything might step up. He hadn't lost a fight against a human for a long time. At least these recent encounters were seriously challenging him. He kissed Silhouette. "Levelled up," he said, with a shake of the head.

A happy voice sounded over the tannoy telling them it was time to board. Alex shouldered his backpack and held Silhouette's hand as they walked along the tunnel to the plane.

Sparks returned to Hood's office after seeing Doschenko safely from the building. A sense of trepidation hung heavy on her, following Hood's strange behavior in the warehouse. The longer this obsession with the human and Kin pair had gone on, the more it consumed him. And the less she liked it.

Hood was tidying his desk when she entered. "Well done, Sparks. A most profitable meeting, no?"

"Definitely. The impulse purchase was worth a lot more than what he came for."

Hood pointed one long index finger at her. "Showrooms lead to temptation, my dear!"

"You know your business, Mr Hood."

"That I do, Sparks. That I most certainly do. Now, let's pack our bags."

"Another trip?"

"Yes. To Iceland."

Sparks frowned. "Iceland? Why?"

"Because that's where the Sisters say our elusive pair is heading and that's where they'll catch up to them."

"So why do we have to be there?"

Hood stopped tidying. His gaze was hard, a sheen of anger making her stomach tight. "*We* don't have to. *I* have to. I'd rather like it if you came along but you've become quite garrulous lately, not to mention argumentative."

Sparks chewed her lower lip, thinking. "I don't mean to annoy you," she said eventually. "It's just that I've never seen you this…"

"This what?" His voice was dangerously low.

Sparks had a fear inside she couldn't shake off. She needed to give voice to her concerns, even if it cost her Hood's wrath. "This obsessed," she said, tensing at Hood's narrowing eyes. "Please, you've barely thought about anything else since you learned of this human and what he's carrying."

"And why should that bother you?"

"We don't even know what it is!"

"Are you serious?" He moved towards her, almost tenderly. "Sparks, this man bested the Subcontractor. No mere human could do that. Whatever he has, it's powerful beyond even my imagining. What price might I put on *that* piece of merchandise? Is that so hard to understand?"

Sparks looked at the expensive rug underfoot, a despair deep inside. "No, I can understand your desire for something so clearly powerful. But do we have to go to Iceland? Can't we rely on the Dark Sisters to get it for us, like you asked them to?"

"Well, I don't know," Hood said. "Maybe, maybe not. I've never used them before, and they seem... capricious. I want to be there. I want to see what this human and Kin are capable of."

"It might get you killed!"

"Ms Sparks, so sentimental. I'll be sure to keep the Sisters between myself and the prey. And when the human and his Kin bitch are dead, I'll get what I've paid for and sell it to the highest bidder. But I want to be there, Sparks. I want to see the battle."

"Why?"

He was suddenly angry again. "Because life is becoming increasingly fucking dull, that's why." Spit flew from Hood's lips. "Nothing has moved me like this in years."

Sparks still stared at the complicated weave, wondering why she felt so scared by Hood's condition. What made her fear for him so? She voiced a concern she'd held in check until now. "You haven't fucked me in a long time."

A slow smile spread across Hood's pasty face. "Is that what this is all about? Have I been neglecting you, flower?" Heavy sarcasm.

"You used to share your excitement with me," Sparks said, not able to bear his mocking eyes. "The more you've focused on this, the less time you've given me."

"Really?"

"You haven't touched me since Scotland."

"Sparks, that was only a day or two ago!" His voice seemed softer.

"It seems longer."

Hood walked around his desk, approached her with mischief pulling at his lips. "Let's go and pack, Ms Sparks. And while we're in our suite, with the bed right there, let's make you feel a little less left out."

She couldn't help a smile slipping onto her face. It really wasn't the point she'd been trying to make. What she really meant was, *You haven't loved me in a long time*, but that admission could not be allowed out.

Hood did business, he told people how it was going to be and that's how it was. When things got tough, he got people in to do the dirty work. Always in control. It hadn't been a long time since he'd touched her. It seemed a long time since he'd been truly in control. That's what scared her. But he was certainly taking command now. He reached her, took her in a strong, passionate kiss, squeezing her arse so hard she cried out, pleasure and pain.

"It's touching that you're scared for me," he said, squeezing again. "And it's quite funny that you feel neglected."

She pouted. "Don't mock me."

He turned her towards the lift. "I'm not going to mock you, Sparks. I'm going to fuck you. Then we're going to Iceland and we'll watch the Sisters do exactly what I want done. That's how the world works for me and you, is it not?"

Sparks pushed away the nagging doubt. "Yes, it is."

They entered the lift and she pulled open her blouse, pressed Hood's face into her cleavage.

lex and Sil joined the sea of people disembarking. As the crowd veered off for luggage they went directly to Reykjavik customs. Alex felt a sense of finality descending. Everything that had happened since Welby darkened his changing room door back in Sydney came to a head here. He knew, one way or another, things would end in this place. Maybe he would end here too. As they stood in a queue, a half a dozen people lined up before them, Alex said, "Sil, if I die, you need to stay away from me."

She frowned at him. "What?"

"If I die here, I don't want you saddled with this fucking book." He hefted one side of his jacket for emphasis.

"One, you're not dying. Two, I know better than to touch that."

"You're so sure I'm not going to die?"

"Someone has to be! Where's your fighting spirit gone?"

"I'm going to fight," Alex said. "I just don't know if I can win."

"You have a plan?"

"I'm not sure "plan" is the right word. Everyone seems so convinced it's impossible to be rid of this curse. Even with the power of the full Darak, the Eld were only able to exile most of Uthentia. If they considered the last part of him, lurking around like this, acceptable collateral, then how can I hope to change anything?"

"You're different to the Eld, Alex. This is a different time, a whole new situation. You have skills they didn't."

"Really? The greatest mages of their time and you think I have something they didn't?"

"The way you've learned to cope with this is already more than most people manage, by all accounts."

"With your help."

"I'm not planning on going anywhere."

He stroked her cheek with the back of one finger. That did genuinely make him feel better; he certainly wouldn't have got this far without her. But he couldn't rely on her always being around.

Life wasn't like that. What if something happened and she walked out on him and left him to his own devices? What if she did plan on taking the Darak for herself somehow? Or if Joseph came back with an army of Kin? "Even if I re-form the stone and I'm able to suppress the urges of this curse, I don't want a lifetime of violent sex and a constant compulsion to kill and maim. Right now I'm actively resisting the urge to start laying into the people ahead of us in this queue! At some point it'll get too much and I'll snap. I'm already becoming a monster. I don't want to tip over."

Silhouette raised an eyebrow. "A monster? Like me?"

Alex kept his face neutral. "Yes. Like you. You expect me to accept that I'm becoming more than human. Have you accepted what you are?"

She laughed, surprising him. "Fuck, yes. Of course. I'm not an idiot. I don't really like the term, but you're right. Call it what you like, what you're becoming is something more than you were. With the added power of the complete Darak do you think you could live with this?"

"No. And if I had the whole stone and I did finally crack and let loose, the damage I could cause is unimaginable. Everyone else has said so, and they're right."

"So you get the rest of this stone, you master it and you figure out a way to be free of Uthentia before his influence breaks you."

Alex hung his head. The ghost of a plan flitted through his mind again and he pushed it aside. "If only it were that simple."

"One step at a time, Iron Balls. Get the stone first. Then we'll see what happens." They'd reached the front of the line. Silhouette stepped back, pushed him forward to the desk. "Your turn," she said with a wink.

A wave of panic washed over him. *Bitch!* The customs officer sat taciturn in his little glass-walled booth. The man waited patiently for a moment before hitching an eyebrow. "You want to come in to Iceland or not?" A sardonic smile.

"Yes, sorry. Miles away." Alex stepped up to the little desk, drawing power from the Darak as he did so. He breathed deep into his stomach to flatten the butterflies looping around in there.

"Passport, please."

Alex let his magesign swell out, pushed his will over the man behind the glass. He constructed the perception of a passport in perfect order, the official's satisfaction that he'd seen exactly what he needed to see and handed it back. Silhouette stepped up beside him, her approval apparent.

The customs official smiled. "The purpose of your visit, sir?"

"Just a holiday," Alex said. His voice sounded tight, nervous to his ears. He kept pushing thoughts at the official. Stamping the passport, handing it back. He was clumsy, battering the poor man over the head with his awkward magic.

The man dragged a hand over his face. As another bubble of panic rose in Alex's gut the man said, "Thank you. Have a nice stay."

Alex's hands trembled like an alcoholic's. He strode away from the booth, not waiting for Silhouette. She caught up a few moments later in the corridor. He turned on her as she reached him. "What the fuck are you thinking?"

"Not the most delicate manipulation I've ever seen, but you did it."

"You could have got me fucking arrested or something!"

"I was right there, I'd have helped you out if it went wrong. But you did it."

"Barely."

She took his shoulder, pulling them to a stop. "You did it. You made a bit of a meal of it, but that was your first time. Do you know how long it takes people to learn things like that? You're a natural, Alex."

He frowned, still angry. "I feel like a clown."

They began walking again. "For years and years you've been honing your skills," Silhouette said. "You had no idea of the scope of the things available to you, but for years you've been reading people. You've been reading them and enhancing yourself even if you didn't know it. You've put in a lot more training than you realize. Now it's just a case of directing that training in new directions. Coupled with the stone, your power could be awesome.

If you let it."

"And coupled with this book, it could be devastating."

"So what? It could be what you need to destroy Uthentia."

"Destroy it?" Alex was incredulous. "Don't you remember Welby's house? We took out an entire street trying to destroy it. Who knows how many innocent people I've already killed."

He could feel the book, weighing heavy in his pocket. It flooded his mind with images of crushed people under the rubble of their homes. It pumped images of the Kin in the street in Rome, skulls crushed and bleeding. He saw Ataro, his head a bloody, pulpy mess mashed into the floor. He felt the exultation, Uthentia's approval, the rising bloodlust. Silhouette slapped him hard across one cheek.

He growled, his face stinging, and a red veil slipped over his eyes. One hand shot out, grabbed Silhouette by the throat. She caught his other hand as he drew it back to strike, visions of punching her head clean off her shoulders flashed through his mind.

"Alex, get it together!" Her voice was strained, crushed by his grasp.

He heard her as if she shouted from a distant room, muffled and irrelevant. All he cared about was blood and murder. He would finish her off and move on to whoever he saw next, killing his way through the airport, out into the street, wiping out everyone he saw for as long as he could. Fuck it all, why bother fighting this?

Silhouette pulsed with energy, driving him backwards with one hand. She coughed and gagged as she pushed. His back hit something that gave way and they stumbled backwards into a clinical, tiled room. He smelt disinfectant and soap, his senses preternaturally sharp. As they went down inside the door Silhouette shifted, her throat pressing out against his fingers. She snapped at him, feline teeth grazing his face as he twisted away from her.

She morphed again, crouching low. "Control it!" she growled, wearing her own face again.

He rushed at her, grabbing. She dodged to one side. "Look inside yourself, Alex! Where's the real you?"

Alex ground his teeth. His heart hammered, his breath was short and high in his chest, the desire to kill almost irresistible. Almost. He concentrated on nothing but the Darak and focused it against the only part of himself he could still feel, his desire not to give in. Like a fight, never refusing to admit you're beaten, battling on. With a yell of fury he turned and slammed one fist through a ceramic sink, shattering it.

"You can do this, Alex! Don't leave me!"

Her voice cut through his rage, cut through the howled cajoling of Uthentia. He dragged breath deep into his body, refused to be controlled. His fingers were clenched into a fist that he couldn't release and he smashed another sink even as he forced the anger aside. With nothing but will he made himself relax. His hands clutched at empty air, fingers grabbing for something unattainable.

Silhouette stepped up, took his face between her palms. "Let it go. You've got this."

His rage began to flutter away at the edges and he collapsed to the floor. His pulse still pounded against his ribs and temples, his breath still came in ragged gasps, but he soaked himself with the magic of the Darak. He thought of nothing but calm stillness even as Uthentia raged. He looked up, his eyes red, haunted. "I can't go on like this," he said, his voice desperate. "It'll finish me."

"We'll beat this, Alex. Don't give up on me."

He let her drag him to his feet and staggered after her out into the airport and through sliding glass doors into cold air.

Alex and Silhouette found a bar. They sat in a quiet corner, Alex sinking a shot of whisky that burned deliciously against the back of his throat. His trembling slowly eased. He could feel her tension.

"I'm okay," he said. "Well, for now."

"Close one, eh?"

"You could say that."

"You're getting stronger."

Her admission worried him. "How long till I'm too strong for you?"

"You already are. By a long way. But you're still you in there too."

"And one day I'll lose it and you won't be able to stop me?"

"Yes. Eventually."

"We need to fix this," he said. "Or I need to stop."

"I know what you mean by that and you can change that train of thought right now. Don't you dare give up on me!"

"What the fuck am I supposed to do?" he shouted. "I'll kill myself before I kill you!"

Several faces in the bar turned to look at his outburst. Silhouette chuckled. "Easy, Iron Balls. You're scaring the locals."

He couldn't help smiling too. Whatever else occurred, there was an absurdity to their situation he couldn't avoid. "It's true, though," he said, his smile fading. "I won't be responsible for your death."

"I'm a long way from dead."

"Maybe."

"So what now?" she asked. "Where next?"

Alex closed his eyes, let his thoughts settle. He slipped his jacket off, laying it on the floor beside his chair in an attempt to distance the interference of the book. He drew on the Darak, used its power to sense itself. "I can feel the direction," he said, his voice low. "I don't know where it is, but I can feel it."

"A long way?"

"Yeah. A few hundred kilometers maybe. It's very rough terrain. All gray rock and smoke and no signs of life. It's like the set of a *Star Trek* episode."

Silhouette pursed her lips. "Maybe we need to charter a helicopter. Would probably be the best way in."

"Probably. But we're skint. We robbed the hotel in Rome to get here! Unless you can work your magic tricks and charm us a helicopter flight we're screwed."

"No, we just need more money."

Alex sighed. "Is this where I become a little bit more monstrous?"

"Depends how you look at it." She looked around the bar, eyes hooded.

"You thinking of robbing *this* place?" Alex asked.

"Well, it's busy in here. Been open a while. They're serving food and drinks, so they must have a pretty good turnover. You reckon the tills would have enough to cover our expenses?"

"I have no idea! Strangely enough, I don't know what it costs to charter a helicopter, or the average takings of a busy Icelandic pub."

Silhouette stood. "Well, let's start here and see how we go. Here's the plan. You do your invisible thing, I'll make a distraction and you empty the tills."

"What? Wait a minute..." Alex glared as Silhouette walked purposefully from the table. She scanned the ceiling, then the walls. She turned back to him briefly, raised her palms in question. He returned the gesture. She scowled at him. With a sigh he drew his shields tight about himself again, enhancing the usual masking with everything else he'd practised and slipped from view.

She moved incredibly fast, slipped around a corner. A sudden shrill ringing burst out into the bar, people turning with shocked faces. As sprinklers rained down, Silhouette ran across the room. "Fire!" she shouted. "There's a fire, everybody out!"

A barely controlled panic broke out, people grabbing bags and coats and heading for the nearest doors. The bar staff tried to call order, organise people, yelling out words Alex couldn't understand. Silhouette flicked a wink back in his direction as she left with them. In seconds he sat in an empty bar, the fire alarm drilling into his ears, sprinklers soaking through his clothes.

He realized he probably had a very short time before the fire department arrived. Grabbing his jacket, pulling it on, he ran behind the bar, studied the tills. There were three, lined along under racks of spirits. One in the middle still had a key in it, above the keypad. The others had their keys removed, the staff having the forethought to protect their employer's livelihood.

Alex frowned. He didn't have time to work this out. He thought his fingers hard as steel bolts, pressed his fingertips into the small gap between the tray and the till and pushed. The metal buckled. He got a grip of the edge and pulled the tray open, notes and coins bouncing in the drawer as it sprang open. He grabbed handfuls of cash and moved on to the next till. Twice more he repeated his violent theft and hurried from the bar, hunched against the indoor rain, notes stuffed into his invisible pockets. He had no idea how much it was but it felt like a lot.

As he ran past the people milling about outside he had a wave of panic, imagining his fingerprints everywhere. Too late now to worry about that. Maybe the sprinklers would help.

He saw Silhouette across the road, walking slowly away from the pub. He chased after her. Checking that no one looked in their direction he slipped back into view, making her jump.

"You're wet," she said with a laugh.

"No shit! Nice plan." He pulled a face to make sure she got his sarcasm.

"Was a great plan if it worked. Did you get it?"

"Yeah, we're rich. Maybe."

"Good lad. Don't feel bad, Alex. They'll be insured."

"I guess so. It's still wrong, though."

She laid a hand on his shoulder. "Right and wrong is a malleable thing. It's not like you're just stealing for the thrill of it. There's a lot at stake here. Come on, let's keep moving."

Hood and Sparks sat on the Black Diamond jet, sipping champagne. A pretty young hostess with a tiny skirt and apprehensive eyes served them smoked salmon hors d'oeuvres. Classical music piped through the small plane. "Do you feel a bit more looked after?" Hood asked.

The warmth in Sparks's stomach wasn't only from the booze. Hood had certainly done his bit to reassure her, but she knew she had given in too easily, ignored her deep sense of unease. But she didn't care. This is how it worked in her world. Why she loved him. "You know how to treat a lady."

"You do mean everything to me, you know that?"

She wondered if he mocked her again. Always she had been

unable to tell when he took her seriously and when he had fun at her expense. But in this instance his eyes seemed sincere. "Really?" Her voice sounded nervous to her own ears.

"Really."

"I'm never sure why you put up with me," she said. She knew how much her insecurity irritated him, but this seemed like an opportunity too good to pass up. He never spoke this intimately.

"I wonder myself sometimes." He leaned over, stroked the frown from her brow. "But you know the answer I give myself?"

Did she really want to know? She twitched her shoulders slightly.

"You give me everything I want."

"Do I?"

"Well, you're damned efficient as a PA. I might have the business mind, but you keep the whole thing running like clockwork."

Sparks smiled, though with little humor. He was right; she knew how bloody good she was at her job. But she rather hoped she was more than that.

"But that's just the start of it," he said, sitting back. He crooked one finger at the hostess. She brought the tray back over and Hood snicked a crispbread piled with salmon and avocado, took it whole into his mouth with a snap of his teeth. "You also give me everything else my extensive appetites require," he said around the delicacy. He chewed slowly.

That was more like it. The business be damned, it was the other services she supplied that mattered. She'd learned very young that taking control meant giving a lot more than a person might otherwise consider reasonable. It soon became apparent to her that the more she gave, the better she maintained the safety and security she desired. And she enjoyed it too. Her own appetites were beyond those of most people, it seemed. She flicked her eyes up to the young hostess, back to Hood. The hostess licked her lips nervously.

Hood slid one hand up the back of the hostess's leg. She stiffened, but didn't move away. "Would you like a pay rise, sweetheart?" he asked her.

"What do I have to do?"

"Nothing so bad," Sparks purred. "You just have to play with us. The three of us, another hour or so flying, nothing else to do ..." She raised an eyebrow, lazily undid the top few buttons of her blouse.

The hostess laughed nervously. "Well, I could certainly use the money. Seems like a pretty nice way to get some."

Hood pulled the girl down onto his lap. "That's the spirit!"

Sparks saw the reluctance in the girl's eyes, her fear. She knew the internal struggle, the girl fearing for her job if she refused, regardless of the raise she'd been promised. *Let me teach you a little something about survival*, Sparks thought as she moved around to join them.

TWENTY-SEVEN

"I feel them," Blonde said.

Sour-faced people swept water across the floor of a bar, brushing it out onto the pavement.

"Strong, for a human," Red said.

"Very recent," said Brunette, licking her lips. She looked into the bar. "Havoc they caused in there, I think."

"Yes," said Blonde. "We're very close now."

"The Hood will never make it," Red said with a quiet laugh.

"Will he be very disappointed?" Brunette asked.

"Certainly," Red answered. "Oh, it's been a while since I've had this much fun."

Blonde turned away from the bar. "The mortal realm is a truly engaging place."

They moved away along the busy street. People's eyes were drawn to them, eliciting occasionally shivers as the Sisters passed.

Alex and Silhouette sat in a charter office while the man at the desk checked rosters. A wooden triangular sign in front of him said, *Hi, I'm Frigeir.* He sucked on his teeth as he flicked through printed pages. "Urgent, you say?" he asked, his accent barely noticeable.

"Yes," Alex said. "We really need to leave right away."

"What's the hurry?"

Silhouette leaned forward, all cleavage and smiles. "We're just anxious to catch up with some friends. We're running late and don't want to get into trouble."

"Late for what?" Frigeir asked.

"That's classified, I'm afraid."

Alex flicked her a sidelong glance. What was she playing at now? *Classified?* his raised eyebrow asked.

Frigeir checked his printouts again. Alex felt her will swell out, watched the magesign twist through her shades like cigarette smoke in a sunbeam. "We could really use your help," she said, her voice low.

Frigeir seemed suddenly drunk. "Mm-hmm. I'm sure I can sort

something out. Classified, you say?"

"We're part of an international task force," Silhouette said. "You'd be doing the right thing by several important agencies if you can get us out there quickly."

Alex frowned. He watched the interplay of her magesign with Frigeir but doubted the man could possibly fall for her ridiculous claims. Yet he seemed to buy it. Alex wondered how much of it was subtle Kin magic and how much pure animal attraction. He'd never seen anyone use their femininity and sex appeal as confidently and expertly as Silhouette. She could seduce anyone into doing anything she wanted without the magic, he was sure. Her self-assurance and power impressed the hell out of him, made him fall for her more every time he saw it. A nervous flutter in his stomach made him catch his breath. He was in a world of trouble and saw death looming real before him, but right now all he felt was love. He had fallen totally for Silhouette. Did she feel the same? She acted like she did, but was she just having fun, enjoying the adventure, after his stone? Or did she really feel about him like he felt for her?

Frigeir put his papers aside. "Well, the thing is no pilots are available until tomorrow at the earliest and then, of course, we have to check the weather first."

Silhouette pouted. "What about you? You're a pilot, aren't you?"

"Well, yes, but someone has to man the office."

"What about if we pay you really well?" She nudged Alex.

He jumped, pulled wads of notes from his pocket. He held the bills up for Frigeir to see. Their haul from the bar had been quite substantial. Drinking seemed to be something people always found money for. "How much will it take," he asked. "We have to get out there today."

Frigeir eyed the money. Alex saw the temptation rising in him. Silhouette still coerced the man with her will. Alex let his own magic out, drew against the Darak and tried to slip gentle images in the man's mind of the three of them in a helicopter, flying out over gray, rocky wilderness, wads of money stuffed in the pilot's pockets. He tried to be as subtle as Silhouette, tried to emulate her style. He peeled off the majority of the notes he had stolen, completely clueless to their actual worth, slapped them on the desk. "This enough?" he asked. "Sorry they're a bit damp, I got caught in a shower."

Frigeir sat back in his chair with a sigh, doing a fair job of covering up his astonishment at the amount Alex had just laid out in front of him. Alex wondered how much he'd given away. "Well, I guess no one will worry about the office being closed for the afternoon. But I'll have to be back before dark."

Alex couldn't be sure how much of that success had been his work, how much down to Silhouette's magic and feminine charms, and how much the lure of cold, hard cash, but the result was exactly what they wanted. "If you can fly us out there, wait for a while and fly us back, that would be great. I don't think we'll be there long." Frigeir frowned. "We just need to catch up with our friends briefly," he added quickly, trying to hold their ruse together. "We shouldn't need to be there more than an hour or two."

"And where exactly is it you need to go?" Frigeir asked.

"Well," Alex said, drawing a nervous breath, "I'll have to direct you as we go."

Frigeir locked his hands behind his head. "Really? More classified information?"

"I'm sorry this seems so strange," Silhouette said, jumping in while Alex gaped, trying to find an answer. "But we're paying you well." She nodded at the money on the desk. Alex added a couple more bills.

Frigeir raised his hands, stood decisively. "Let's go then." He took the pile from the desk, pushed the notes deep into his pocket.

He led them out to a smaller airfield beside the main Reykjavik airport and across dark gray tarmac. Lines of various colors criss-crossed under their feet as they walked past small planes. Tiny wheeled vehicles buzzed around them with fuel and luggage. They hopped into Frigeir's helicopter, *Icelandic Sky Tours* emblazoned on the side, and put on the headsets he handed them. The helicopter was shiny, new looking, and smelled strongly of pine air freshener.

Frigeir talked to the control tower in rapid Icelandic and fired up the engines.

Alex pulled the mic down, covering it with his hand. "I've never been in a helicopter before," he shouted over the rotors starting up. He leaned forward, catching her chin, and planted a kiss on her lips. She was surprised for a moment, before kissing back enthusiastically. "Thank you," Alex said as they parted.

She gave him a quizzical look, slight shake of the head. She kissed him again.

Frigeir looked at them over his shoulder, one eyebrow high on his forehead. "Ready to go?" he asked, unable to keep the smirk off his face.

"Ready!" Silhouette said.

Alex buckled himself in. Maybe she did care for him, after all. He needed to believe she did. That this was more than just a bit of excitement in her long life. He felt the warmth of her still on his lips and chose to believe this meant more to her.

Frigeir powered up the helicopter and took off with a stomach lurching drive. He guided the chopper out of airport airspace and turned, a question in his eyes. Alex let the Darak swell out from him, felt for the missing piece. A sensation of gentle drag tugged at one side of him. He pointed past Frigeir. "That way," he said.

Frigeir nodded. "Okay then."

Sally Beaton suppressed her tears as she watched Mr Hood and Ms Sparks from the safety of the galley. They would be landing in about twenty minutes and she would be free of them. So many people had warned her about working too closely for Black Diamond but she hadn't listened. *How bad can it really be?* she'd wondered. Pretty bad, it turned out. She trembled, desperate to get to a hotel, to a steaming hot shower, to wash the last hour off herself. She felt as though the stain of it would stay with her for life.

She had known that refusal would have been trouble. No court of law would understand, but something about them told her without a shadow of a doubt that if she'd said no to their advances she may never have returned to London. And for a promised pay rise? Was that all she was to them, some whore? She'd thought the opportunities in Black Diamond had meant more, that her hard work would pay off in a solid career. Had she been moved closer to Hood just for her looks?

She swallowed hard against tears rising, her throat tight with shame. What would she tell Peter? Could she tell him? *I had to agree, or they'd have killed me!* How could she expect anyone to believe that, even while she knew it, deep in her soul. She didn't doubt for a second it was true. Hood's eyes had been saying something his voice and smile had never articulated. She squeezed her eyes shut, trying to block out the memory of a look that held black depths of despair and said, *Do what we want or suffer the consequences.*

She felt violated in every way possible. The pay rise, their sweet words after the things they'd made her do, her job, none of it mattered one bit. She wouldn't make the return journey with them. They would almost certainly expect the same from her. She'd barely held it together this time. No way could she do it again. When they landed she would act exactly as they expected her to, all smiles and saucy looks. Then she would run to a hotel, certainly not the one they'd booked. She would scrub and scrub until she felt clean even if that meant taking off her own skin. Then she would book a flight home and disappear from Black Diamond forever. No job was worth this.

The pilot's voice buzzed over the intercom, making her jump. "Prep for landing, Sal."

She pressed the button. "No problem."

Hold it together, she told herself. *Just a little while longer.*

She leaned through the curtain. "Buckle up, please, we'll be landing in a moment."

Hood licked his lips lasciviously. "I don't think I'll be landing for quite a while yet!"

Sparks laughed, that horrible, bubbly laugh. Sally forced a smile, swallowing more sobs, and slipped back behind the curtain. She started stowing trays and locking cupboards, covering her mouth with one hand, unable to stem the tears any longer.

The Sisters stood beside benches outside Reykjavik airport, smiling at the appreciative glances of passers-by.

"Irritating," Blonde said, looking into the distance. A tiny speck flew towards bright white clouds.

"Easy enough to follow," Red said.

Brunette made a noise of annoyance. "Perhaps the Hood will make it after all."

"It's been a while since I got excited about anything," Blonde said. "I intend to enjoy this final play. I'll talk to the Hood again." She tipped her head back, eyes half closed. "Do I hurt you, little man?" she said quietly, laughter under her breath. "Ah, so close you are. You travel fast for a human." She listened. "Really? Very well."

"Well?" Red asked.

"The Hood arrives any moment. He wants to travel with us. Apparently he has a helicopter arranged."

"A human flying machine? How... interesting. So, he will see the end after all."

"The end?" Blonde said thoughtfully. "Yes. The end indeed."

Brunette smouldered at a passing businessman, trapping his eyes with her look. "It should be most entertaining," she said under her breath. The businessman tripped, blushing as he hurried away. Brunette slipped from the group, gliding after him.

"Don't be long, sister," Blonde called out. "The Hood will be here very soon."

TWENTY-EIGHT

F rigeir swung the chopper around for a second pass, twisting to look at the ground below. "No way, sorry. Nowhere safe to put down."

Alex and Silhouette saw nothing but ridges of gray-black rock and shale. Smoke twisted across the desolate landscape like gossamer snakes. "How close can you get us?" Alex shouted.

Frigeir lifted higher, scanning the ground. "I can put down over there." His voice was tinny over the headset. "It won't take you long to walk. But are you sure this is right? I can't see anyone else."

"This is right," Alex said. "Put us down as close as you can."

"Okay then."

Frigeir sounded dubious and Alex couldn't blame him. The Darak burned, throbbing with anticipation. He was in no doubt whatsoever that they were virtually on top of the last piece. Yet Frigeir was right. No one and no thing but cold rock. He remembered the vision he'd had when he set the stone to find itself. A cave, a surprised face. It must be somewhere they couldn't see from the air.

Frigeir put the helicopter down on dark shale. "I can wait here," he said, killing the engine. The blades *whup-whup-whupped* through the chill air, slowing down. "But you've only got an hour at most before it starts to get dark. I'm not flying in the dark. If you're not back here, I'll go without you."

"Fair enough. We'll be back." He hoped Frigeir and Sil couldn't hear the uncertainty in his voice.

He hopped out of the chopper, Silhouette close behind. "This way," he said, taking her hand. He was close. So close he could feel it, could imagine the completed Darak and the power it could yield. Dark thoughts ghosted across his mind, loose ideas that flitted past his consciousness like bats in the night. He hated himself for the things he considered. He looked back at Frigeir sitting in his helicopter, imagined the man's wife, children, parents. He might not have a family, his parents might be long cold in the grave, but

Alex didn't know. Couldn't know. Could he really go through with the things he considered, the only other option he could conceive? He had no right. If anything would make him a true monster, it was that. Better he do terrible things to himself.

He ached at the thought. Silhouette walked purposefully beside him, beautiful, powerful. She had supported and protected him all this way, but if it was a choice between true monster or sacrifice, only one option really existed. He hoped she would understand. He hoped he would be able to do it.

Uthentia in his jacket bucked and thrashed, the distant, massive voice of it hurling rage through every part of him.

"What's happening?" Silhouette asked.

"It's getting angry because we're getting close," Alex lied.

"Read it, maybe?" Sil suggested. "See what it has to say?"

"No way. It can get fucked. I haven't given it a chance to voice itself for a while and I'm not going to now."

"Fair enough. Keep it together, Alex. We're nearly there, right?"

His stomach fluttered with his love for her. Or was it fear that she'd betray him yet? "You know, there's an old yarn my Sifu told me," he said. "It's a kind of warning tale."

"Oh yeah?"

He plunged on. "It talks about a little boy who stalked a tiger. The tiger had been terrorising his village, killing the people, and the little boy decided to be a hero and hunt it down. When he finally got near the tiger he snuck close through the undergrowth and grabbed it by the tail. The tiger got furious, started spinning around, snapping and clawing at the boy. The boy hung on for dear life, running left and right, staying safe only by staying behind the tiger. The boy panicked. He thought he'd caught the tiger, but really, the tiger had him. There was nothing he could do to defeat it and the moment he let go of the tail it would get him."

Silhouette reached for Alex, put a palm against his cheek. "Why are you telling me this?"

He ignored the question. "The point of the story, I think, is to warn people against starting something they can't finish. Going in blind or without a plan."

After what seemed like a very long pause she said, "So what did the little boy do?"

"Well, he couldn't let go and he knew he would tire long before the tiger. All he could do was drag the tiger around. They were near a waterfall and the boy kept ducking and diving, avoiding the teeth and claws, moving nearer and nearer to the edge. Knowing the tiger had to die for his village to be safe, when they got near the precipice, the boy jumped."

"Alex, no."

"He hung on to the tiger and took it down with him, saving the village."

Silhouette stopped walking. "Fuck that, Alex! There has to be another way."

Alex winced, looking at the ground. "At what cost?" he asked, his voice strained.

"At whatever cost! Don't you dare leave me, Alex. Not after all this!"

"Really? I mean that much to you?"

"Fuck!" She spun around, walked away a few paces, turned back. "Fucking yes! All right? It started out for me as a bit of an adventure. Something interesting at last. For a time there I even thought about doing what Joseph asked of me. Then I thought about maybe trying to take the stone for myself. But the Kin would still hate me either way. I would still be alone. I told you before, you with the Darak means I don't have to be alone any more. I can live with being an outsider if I'm not alone."

He trembled all over. "I love you, Silhouette." The words felt like cotton wool balls, dragged reluctantly from his throat.

She stepped up, kissed him hard. "I love you too, Iron Balls, you fucking stupid little human."

He laughed, despite his anguish. "You are so romantic."

She had tears in her eyes. "The last person I said that to was my mother, Alex. Don't you dare leave me too."

He kissed her, held her tightly, her body pressed against his. Could he really give in to the monster, to keep a monster? He didn't want to be alone either. Keeping to himself was one thing, but being really alone, lost in all this power, was terrifying.

"Don't give up on me," she said into his neck, her breath sending shivers through his spine. "Find another way."

"I'll try, Sil." And he meant it. He hated himself, but he meant it.

They walked past a shoulder of dark rock, Alex's mind churning with formless emotion. The voice of his Sifu drifted through. *Never be distracted while you are engaged in battle. If the fight is not yet won, nothing else matters. Nothing!*

This fight was far from won. The Darak pounded against his chest like a second heart. The last part lay somewhere nearby. For thousands of years the stone had existed apart from itself, broken, incomplete. It had an almost sentient desire to be whole again, channelled through him. And Uthentia, trapped in a book, washed white hot fury through him, filling him with images of murdering Silhouette in hideous ways, getting Frigeir to fly him back to Reykjavik, sending the chopper to crash in a fiery spectacle in the most crowded street he could find. He forced himself to focus only on the Darak. Ignoring Uthentia was like ignoring a red hot branding iron pressed against his mind. He breathed, focused, brought all his training to the fore. *Just a little bit longer.*

As they cleared the rugged boulders, a narrow channel appeared through the rock. Someone stood in the shadow of the passage. A Kin, ancient and powerful, his presence unchecked in this uninhabited wasteland, miles from anyone. "I've been expecting you," he said in a deep voice.

Alex recognised the man's face from his vision. "So you know why I'm here."

"How did you do it?" the man asked. "Find me?"

"I wasn't looking for you."

"No, of course not. How did you find the shard?"

"The two pieces I already have were able to trace their lost brother," Alex said.

The man nodded, his expression resigned. "Of course. Then it is true."

"What's your name?" Alex asked. He sounded tired. He knew a fight was coming.

"Ovidius. You?"

Alex recognised the name from his research in Lorenzo's Den, though his mind had trouble grasping the concept. "My name is Alex Caine. I'm afraid I'm going to take the stone."

"Yes. I suppose you are."

Alex was stunned. Surely this guardian of ages would stand against him. "Really?" he asked suspiciously.

Ovidius dropped to his knees and pulled his shirt off over his head. Bare-chested, trembling in the cold, he laid a heavy dagger on the shale before himself. "Over a thousand years ago I first had the vision. Already I'd spent so many lifetimes protecting the piece of the Darak that had been entrusted to me. That first premonition of you nearly destroyed me."

Alex crouched to maintain eye level with Ovidius, but kept a safe distance between them. "Premonition?"

"They began after I'd already guarded the stone for several hundred years. I was supposed to be dead, but I knew others would find it. I defended it time and again. The visions would warn me, help me prepare. Then I saw you. Not very clearly, I don't recognise you now, but the same assailant appeared to me again and again. That first time, when the vision showed me broken, bleeding, dying, I despaired. For a thousand years I've been seeing variations of that same prophecy. I've thought of hunting you down, forcing the confrontation, but I couldn't even know if you'd been born yet. I've ventured forth occasionally, when I've needed to feed. I've watched the world, studied history passing. Waited for you."

"I really don't want to hurt you," Alex said. "I'd rather not hurt anyone else." He ignored the insistent cajoling of the book, drumming thoughts of murder into his brain.

Ovidius flashed a grin that disappeared as fast as it had appeared. "Isn't that just it, though?"

"Is it?"

"How much do you want to kill me? Not when you think

about it, but when you let your true feelings rise?"

"I want to rip you limb from limb," Alex admitted. "But those aren't my true feelings. That's the book at work. Uthentia's desires."

Ovidius' face twisted with discomfort. "Interesting," he said. "You still differentiate."

"Haven't you seen all this?" Silhouette asked. "Don't you know what's going to happen?"

Ovidius laughed, a high, shrill sound, sudden and short. "The visions are always different. I knew you were coming. For a thousand years I've known you were coming, but every time it's slightly different. Sometimes we fight, sometimes I die."

"Do I ever die?" Alex asked quietly.

Ovidius lifted his face, his eyes haunted. "No."

They were silent for several moments. Alex wanted to get the shard and move on, but this strange old Kin deserved some time, some chance. Would he really let Alex pass? The dagger sat on the stones between them like a gate.

Ovidius's shades were every color of despair and disappointment, sadness and melancholy. He showed no intention of fighting, of trying to stop Alex. He moved so quickly that Alex was on his feet, crouched and ready, almost before he realized he'd moved. Ovidius held the dagger out in front of himself. He pointed the hilt at Alex. "Use it," he said.

Alex kept his distance, still tense. "What?"

"Kill me."

"I don't want to."

"I should have died aeons ago, Alex Caine. What difference does it make now?"

Alex relaxed his ready position, tried to stand more casually. "You were supposed to kill yourself," he said. Uthentia howled his rage through Alex's brain, the Fey creature's wrath almost deafening in its intensity. Alex gritted his teeth, tried to shut it out. "It's not my desire to kill you."

"You don't want to give in to that urge?" Ovidius said, his eyes wild. "I can see it in you, I can see the 'sign pouring off you. Your bloodlust is enormous. Imagine the thrill you'd get plunging this blade into my heart! Think of it, finishing one as ancient as I!"

Uthentia thrashed at Alex's mind, forcing Alex to stagger forward against his will. He concentrated only on the stone at his chest, tried to ignore the hurricane of desperation pulsing from the presence of Uthentia. "I will not kill you!" he yelled, his throat raw with the effort. "Uthentia does not rule me!"

Ovidius smiled, his hand reaching out to wrap around the other already holding the dagger. The point trembled as it pointed in towards his chest. "Perhaps there is some hope then," he said and slammed the blade into his body. He bucked, his mouth dropping open with a cough of surprise and pain. He twisted, grimacing in agony as his blood flooded over his hands to spatter on the dark gray rock under his knees. He stared into Alex's eyes and Alex watched a life unimaginable blink out.

Ovidius fell forward and was still.

Alex pressed his palms against his face, shaking with the force of Uthentia's furious dissatisfaction. He sucked in air and kept his mind focused on the Darak, let its magic soak through his body, infuse every vein and fiber. "I deny you!" he growled and the rage subsided to the dull roar he had come to accept as normal.

Silhouette crouched beside Ovidius, closed his eyes. "Poor bastard. I seem to be seeing a lot of old Kin die lately."

"Even when I refuse to kill, this whole situation ends in death," Alex said. "Hard to believe he's been here all this time, protecting the stone, and it ended for him like this. So quickly."

"He should have died a long time ago. Shouldn't have still been here."

"He was testing me." Alex felt Uthentia's muffled joy at the death of such a being even while it raged that Alex hadn't done the murder. He did his best to ignore it.

"You passed," Silhouette said, putting one hand on his shoulder. "You resisted."

"To what end?" The sound of a helicopter made them both spin around. "Frigeir...?" Alex started to say.

"No," Silhouette said sharply. "Alex, this is someone else

arriving. You better find the shard!"

Alex stared at the approaching chopper. For some reason it struck him as very strange that whatever had been tracking them all this time would arrive by helicopter, just as they had. Maybe there *was* another way.

Silhouette dragged at his sleeve. "Alex, come on!"

They turned and ran into the dark cleft between tall, cold rocks.

TWENTY-NINE

Sparks pressed herself as tightly into the corner of the cramped cabin as she could. Hood sat stiff beside her, buzzing with excitement. How could he bear the proximity of the Sisters, sat opposite them, smiling? They lounged in the seat, sexuality pouring off them, letting Hood drink them in. Sparks could barely contain her disgust, yet Hood seemed mesmerized. Perhaps their magic only worked on men.

Since meeting them at the airport and transferring quickly to the waiting chopper, they had been in a bubble of ice and terror. Sparks's skin crawled in the presence of these creatures. Their exquisite exteriors did nothing to quell the memory of what they really were. What they had done. And the fear that had knotted her stomach ever since Scotland bound ever tighter.

"Looks like we've found them," Hood said, pointing.

Another helicopter sat inert on the dark ground below. Smoke from fissures in the barren landscape twisted up and away in their downdraft as the pilot brought them down next to it. As they landed a man with close-cropped blond hair and a friendly smile approached.

Blonde leaned forward. "Ooh, he looks nice." Her sisters giggled and Sparks's stomach tightened another notch.

The five of them clambered out, their pilot staying in his seat. He had been uncomfortable from the moment they met and clearly had reservations about his passengers. Sparks noticed he kept the engines running, the rotors whipping the cold air as they slowed to an idle.

Hood approached the other man, a broad smile across his face. "Hello there," he called out.

"Hi." He shook Hood's hand. "I'm Frigeir. You're colleagues of the other two? I think they expected you to be here already."

"Really?" Hood kept his smile in place. "Where are they?"

Frigeir pointed. "They went that way, only a few hundred meters. The man thought he knew where to find you."

Hood nodded a thank you. "That's okay, we'll find them."

Blonde stepped up, offering a hand to Frigeir. "Lovely to meet you," she said, her voice like warm, silky chocolate.

Frigeir shook the offered hand, a frown forming at her touch. Sparks saw the sudden concern in his eyes.

"Not now, please," Hood said. He jerked his head, gesturing to their own pilot. "We don't want to scare anyone off."

Blonde pouted. "How boring."

Hood strode off in the direction Frigeir had indicated. "Come on, then! Let's find them."

The Sisters followed Hood, chattering to each other and giggling. Sparks lingered, incredibly uneasy. A deep sense of foreboding dragged at her.

Frigeir caught her eye. "You okay?"

"Fine, thanks." She turned to follow her lover.

"You're a strange bunch, if you don't mind me saying so," Frigeir said with a nervous smile. "What is it exactly, your business here?"

"You wouldn't understand. Sorry." She hurried away, swallowing an urge to tell the kind-looking man to get in his helicopter and fly away, pretend he'd never seen any of them.

Hood looked back. "Come on, Sparks!"

"I'm coming."

Hood paused, gesturing for the Sisters to take the lead. When Sparks caught up he slapped her hard on the butt, fell into pace a few meters behind the Sisters. "Here we are then. At last!"

Sparks smiled at him, but felt her lips trembling. "Yes. Here we are."

Uthentia's fury threatened to tear Alex apart. The Darak pulsated with urgent longing. He turned through a narrow channel between high, dark rock and found the cave he'd seen in his vision. A simple bed in the corner, with blankets piled high. A small fire burned in the center of the space, providing a wan dancing light but little warmth. A few belongings were scattered about, mostly books. Ovidius had lived like a monk, doing the one thing he had been tasked with at the exclusion of all else. He had shown a devotion to his cause unlike anything Alex could imagine. And he had died selflessly for it. Alex bit back his shame.

Silhouette stopped in the entrance, glancing nervously back over her shoulder. "Hurry, Alex!" she hissed.

The Darak burned against him, trying to drag him into the shadows in the cave's depths. He pulled the stone on its cord from his shirt and it burst into blinding light, filling the cavern like a thousand flashbulbs firing at once. An answering burst of light lit a deep alcove at the back. Alex stumbled forward, barely of his own free will.

The third shard sat before him, tiny, almost insignificant. For so long it had waited, hidden in these folds of rock, silently guarded. How many people had passed close by and had no idea? How many times had Ovidius had to defend his secret? Alex wondered if there were legends in any nearby towns about these wastes. There should be.

He reached for the tiny shard, his hand trembling. As his fingers touched it an electric bolt of raw magic thumped through him. Uthentia howled. Alex arched back, gasping in ecstatic agony. Pure, raw power stretched the seams of his being as blinding light wiped everything else away. He distantly heard Silhouette calling his name.

The third and the first two pulled towards each other like magnets. He took hold of the stone he wore in one hand, the shard in the other, and slammed them together. A pulse of magic burst out, lifting him high, throwing him back through the cave. Silhouette cried out. He hit the ground, sliding across hard rock that felt icy against his burning skin. He bucked and twisted, trying to squirm away from the blaze that racked his body. A slow howl of pain, starting low, rose from his throat until it became a piercing wail of anguish. He couldn't hold it, he was surely incapable of containing this energy.

Silhouette screamed at him from a million miles away. "Alex, take control, please!"

He dragged air into his lungs, still writhing in pain. When he tried to speak he screamed again.

"Alex!" Silhouette shouted from another planet. "Please, you have to control it before it destroys us!"

He heard her pain, her desperation. Why didn't she run away, leave him here to burn? He wanted to cry out to her, tell her to save herself from this nuclear explosion of magic he had no hope of managing. He ground his teeth, tried to shout but only screamed again.

"Please, Alex!" There were tears in her pain now, sobbing as she pleaded with him.

He had to save her, had to be with her. If she wasn't going to save herself he had no choice but to best this energy. He remembered how it felt to channel the power of the stone when he fought, taking the energy through his body, making it a part of him. Through the screaming pain, through the raging red mist of agony in his mind, he remembered how he had owned it before, when he had only two parts of the whole. The three combined were exponentially more powerful, incalculably more potent. He ground his teeth again, biting down the pain. He forced it to comply with his boundaries. His body stretched, his molecules threatening to burst apart and wash away in a wave of uncontrollable magic. He braced every muscle, held himself together by force of will.

He held his hands up before him, the stone between his fingertips. It was terrible and beautiful, larger than the three pieces should be combined, like a flawless black diamond the size of a hen's egg. It shimmered and rippled with the flood of magic it produced. *Own it. Make it a part of you.* He remembered the corpulent horror on the island off Canada, the shard buried deep in its body. *Make it a part of you.*

He couldn't tell if he heard something from his memory, something from the Darak itself or Uthentia's mad cajoling, but it was the only thing that made sense. He couldn't control this level of power from the outside. It had taken a group of powerful Kin mages, the Eld, to wield this thing. How could he hope to handle it alone? He had to be one with it, not apart from it. Uthentia roared in sudden anticipation, sensing the power to be free again.

With a yell of repentant rage Alex slammed the stone against his chest, opening himself to bond with it, willing it to become a part of him. He arched off the floor as a thousand bolts of lightning tore through him. He clenched down on it, forced his mind to focus, channel the power like he had before. Not from outside, but within, guiding the magic through every cell. Guiding power that wasn't coming from something he held but from something he was. Something he had become.

The energy found pathways through him. The chaotic explosion of pure force now contained started to race in his body, following the ancient meridians of his body's own energetic lines, engorging them, empowering him. The Darak had become Alex Caine and Alex Caine the Darak, inseparable. The magic pulsed through him in wave upon wave of agonising fire, threatened to burn him to a crisp from the inside out. He willed it to conform, drew against his training to control the energy flow through his body, balance his essence and his spirit with the power. The pulses grew less violent, less painful. His heart beat hard and fast yet slow compared to the vast ripples of magic scouring through him. He tried to calm it to match his heart, then command his heart to slow down, back under his control.

The burning ebbed from the cave as he lay on the cold floor, gasping massive, desperate breaths as his body buzzed and trembled with barely contained power. As he mastered his breathing he finally began to settle.

Silhouette scrambled across the cave floor to hold him, her cheeks tear-streaked, her eyes wide, red. "Are you okay? Alex, please tell me you're okay!"

He tore open his shirt, staring at the stone embedded in the flesh of his chest. His body merged seamlessly with the large black gem of the Darak. He ran his fingers over it, still gasping, hardly able to believe it was done. "I think so," he managed between gasps. "But what have I done?"

Silhouette rained kisses all over him. "I don't know, Iron Balls, but you're blazing like a supernova."

"You don't have to tell me!" His breath slowly settled and the Darak pulsed with his heart, matching his heartbeat, but inside now, not separate. As blood flowed through his veins, the power of the Darak flowed through him too. It felt incredible, unfettered energy filling every atom of him. He laughed, more a cough than real mirth. "I feel awesome!"

Silhouette smiled through her apprehension, kissed him again.

A man's voice shouted from outside. "Anyone there? Come on out and play!"

Alex grimaced. "Fuck me, here we go again."

He leaned on Silhouette for support. As he took a step something bolted through him, made him stagger. He felt Uthentia, thrashing in the no-space between realms, battering against his bonds. He felt the pressure of a galaxy against him, the consciousness of something unfeasible roaring through his mind, trying to use him as a conduit.

Silhouette pulled him upright. "Alex? What is it?"

He began to shake in panic. "It's Uthentia. He's trying to come back and I don't know if I can stop it."

Silhouette looked him hard in the eye. "He was exiled once before, Alex. With that." She pressed one finger against his chest. "Now you and it are one. You have the power."

"Come on out or we're coming in!" The voice outside was loud, confident, amused.

Alex pulled free of Silhouette's grasp. "All right, then. Fuck this. All at once, let's finish this thing."

He strode through the cave, back between the high, cold rocks. Silhouette hurried after. He emerged from the shadows to see three stunning women, dressed for a summer in the city, standing in a row some fifty feet away. A safe distance behind them were a tall, thin, bald man with pasty white skin and a lithe woman with long blonde hair and a stark, angular beauty.

The three women in front, one blonde, one redhead, one brunette, leaned forward as one when they saw him, their eyes going wide. "Look at you!" Blonde said. "I've never seen such a thing."

Alex's body racked with tremors from the magic coursing through him. After everything that had happened, a welcoming party of two suits and a trio of supermodels struck him as hilariously absurd. "What kind of fucking circus is this?" he said through laughter. The sensation from the women drifted over him, cutting through the miasma of his magic like a draught through a warm room. They exuded a malevolent, destructive essence far from anything human. "Really," Alex said, more serious. "What are you?"

"They are your death," the bald man called out. "You've eluded me for long enough."

Alex looked past the three women. "And who the fuck are you?" he called back. "You're the one been sending things after me? You're Hood?"

Mr Hood smiled broadly. "You know my name? Marvellous. Yes, I'm Hood." He indicated the woman beside him. "And this is Sparks. And I will take what you have now."

Alex could feel realms bending and shifting around him, through him. He sensed other worlds, space and time itself, a malleable, interchangeable thing. Through it all Uthentia pounded against the nothing that held him trapped, clawing at the last shred of himself trapped in the cursed book in Alex's pocket, desperate to pull himself back through to reality by the re-formed stone that had exiled him. Uthentia remembered the magic that had trapped him and strove to use it again. And the magic remembered him.

Alex existed across time, saw *through* time, felt the near panic of the Eld as they battled to control the Darak they had created. He saw them struggling to direct its power against Uthentia. Kin fought tooth and nail with Fey while the Eld fought a creature more god than animal. And he understood their compromise.

The sliver of Uthentia trapped in the book was a memory of the godling that nearly destroyed the world. It couldn't be cast out any more than a person could forget to breathe. However much people might like to forget the horrors that befall them, the memories are always there. It was the memory of Uthentia that was trapped and that was his power, what he clung onto from beyond. The part which could never be exiled. It was necessary.

Alex pulled the grimoire from his pocket, held it up. "You

want this?" he asked. Magesign swirled around it, thick as smoke from burning rubber. The three women straightened as one, took a few paces back.

"What are you doing?" Hood yelled at them.

Alex pulled off the ragged remains of his jacket and shirt, his bare torso still slick with the sweat of his struggle to control the Darak. The stone gleamed darkly, dead center of his chest. "You want this?" he shouted, pointing at it.

Hood's voice sounded strained, panicky. "Sisters, you are bound to me! Do as I say. Kill him and take those things!"

Blonde turned to Hood. "You have no idea what he has. That magic is a blight beyond anything you could imagine."

"I don't care!" Hood screamed. "*Do as I say!*"

Blonde shook her head. "We can't give you that power."

"It would bind with us the moment we killed him," Red said, backing away further.

Hood's eyes were wide, his face flushed red in fury. "You are bound to do as I command!" Tendons stood out in his neck like shipping ropes.

Blonde laughed. "No, Hood."

"We asked for nine," Red said, still backing up.

"You gave us ten," said Brunette. She and Blonde stepped back as well, the three of them moving aside.

Alex faced Hood across an open expanse of cold, hard stone and shale. Volcanic smoke drifted across the ground, curling about their legs like curious snakes. Sparks stood beside Hood, looking stricken, torn between staying beside him and running for her life.

Hood shook in anger, his hands clenching before his chest. "You cheated me!" he screamed.

Blonde bubbled with laughter. "You cheated yourself, little man. You can't play with us. Who do you think you are, really?"

Alex began vibrating with the power coursing through him. Uthentia strained at his bonds, desperate to break through, and Alex planned to let him. He gestured towards Hood with the book. "You want what I have?" he said, his voice quiet yet travelling preternaturally across the distance. "Catch!" He spun the grimoire like a Frisbee through the air.

Hood gasped, shoving Sparks aside. He stepped forward to catch it, confusion twisting his features. As it landed in his hands Alex let Uthentia out.

The air ripped with the sound of realms tearing and the earth shook. A massive inconceivable entity pounded into the world, laughter booming through the sky. Everything darkened in his shadow, everything froze in his passing. Frost instantly rimed every rock, crackled crystalline on every bit of skin. The book burst into confetti in Hood's hands, the memory rejoining the actual. The Dark Sisters and Sparks scrambled away as Hood dropped to his knees in the face of absolute chaos. Alex thrummed with power. Silhouette cried out behind him. "Alex, what have you done?"

"I'm fixing a mistake," he said, gritting his teeth as he held onto the force that threatened to tear him apart.

Uthentia, whole again and fifty feet tall, arched up into the clouds, screaming his joy at the firmament. His memory had been removed from its attachment to Alex's soul, the book destroyed. Alex called out to the reminiscence of the Eld, begging their help wherever they might be.

Uthentia sensed the Darak. He spun around to face Alex, enormous, black and twisted. Alex's mind struggled to understand what he saw, tried to conceive more dimensions than he knew existed. Uthentia stood tall, a monstrous, heavily muscled creature, wrapping and warping through multiple forms. His skin shone dark and thick, rippled with scales and scars, then smooth as ice. His limbs seemed human, then animal, first four, then six, then eight, taloned and reaching. His features swam through one hideous form after another. He roared from a lionesque mouth before his lips writhed into reaching tentacles. His eyes burned with fire, gleamed blackly in the daylight, shifted from two to four to eight to two.

Alex gathered every bit of power he had and channelled it through the stone embedded in him. Uthentia remembered the Darak and the Darak remembered him.

The incomprehensible godling bellowed, striding across the

distance in two mighty steps, raising arms that twisted and turned through dimensional impossibilities to crush Alex into the rock. And the Darak worked its magic again. Energy poured out of Alex in luminescent waves and pulses, engulfing Uthentia. Alex dug in as the magic he wielded drove him back. His feet gouged furrows through rock as he stood against a god. The Darak had the power, the Eld had created it, he had to channel it. Only he had bonded with it in a way the Eld never had. He controlled it with himself, the same way he controlled himself every time he fought. Uthentia screamed in rage as realms bucked and folded, wrapping the Fey godling up again. His deafening voice cracked across the sky, like a thousand demons shouting at once. "Memory is eternal!"

Alex understood that. He had learned from the Eld. They had to let a shred of Uthentia stay and so did he. But they had been surprised. He was prepared. As Uthentia split and churned between the walls of realities he cast forth that shred of his consciousness again, looking for a hook in reality. Alex directed the power of the Darak and caught that memory, wrapped it in the magic the Eld had imbued in the stone, and guided it. This is what had cracked the Darak before and would do so again, but not before he made sure it was contained this time.

He fixed his eyes on Hood, still on his knees across the broken ground, shaking and piss-stained. Using every bit of power the Darak could muster he sent that piece of Uthentia's consciousness directly at the bald man. "You want what I had?" he yelled. "You can have it!"

Hood arched backwards, lifted from his knees and flew back across the loose ground. As the Darak forced Uthentia once again into the exile of nothing between realms, screaming, Alex released the full potential of the stone and the part of Uthentia that had been the book became Hood. Alex shrieked in agony, his chest exploding as the Darak cracked again.

Hood shrieked, slamming his palms either side of his head. He thrashed and writhed on the floor, pulling at his face. Sparks wailed, running to his side. She dropped to her knees, sobbing, trying to hold him as he writhed on the ground. She looked at Alex with pure, uncomprehending hatred.

"Oh, that's beautiful!" Blonde shouted at Alex. "You trap Uthentia in a man! But it won't last long. It will destroy his mind in minutes and move on."

Alex grimaced with concentration, eyes watering with the pain of his ruined chest, desperate to stay conscious. "It needs another person if it plans to move on," he said through gritted teeth. "That's how it works, moving from one thing to the next, living on in one item or another, making that thing indestructible." He drew against his own magic, his own authority. He remembered the pages of Welby's grimoire of elemental magic, water, air, fire and earth. He sent his mind down into the earth beneath them, drove his will between the rocks and into the liquid red magma below. The shattered Darak burned like shards of red hot iron, embedded in his flesh. It still held power and he used it. He forced his mind through fissures in the rock directly below Hood, cracked the earth itself wide open. Hood cried out, scrabbling at the shattering rock as it opened up around him. Heat shimmer and smoke belched up from the glowing red pit beneath. Sparks scrambled back on hands and heels as Hood slipped down into the furnace lake, his fingers clawing desperately at the edges.

Sparks screamed, clapping her hands to her mouth as Hood slid inexorably, fast running out of anything to slow him as his newly indestructible fingertips shredded the rock. She stood frozen to the spot, her hands stretched out across the gap between them. "ROBERT!" she cried.

Hood's eyes were wide, terrified, as his grip finally failed and he slipped from sight into the burning fissure. "CATRIONAAAAA!" his voice howled as he fell into churning depths of molten rock. The name became screams of unimaginable agony as his body burned. But the screams didn't stop, echoing on and on. Hood burned but couldn't die, indestructible with the shred of Uthentia's consciousness trapped inside him.

With the last of his power, as darkness closed in all around, Alex slammed the broken earth shut, trapping Hood and Uthentia in an eternal prison of fiery liquid torture. He heard the Sisters' laughter and Sparks's screams as he gave in to the pain. Silhouette rushed forward, grabbed hold of him, and blackness closed tight as he collapsed.

THIRTY

S trange noises swam around Alex's mind. Blackness surrounded him and the weight of a planet pressed down on his chest. He hitched a painful breath. Given the discomfort he decided he probably hadn't died. The sounds resolved into voices, an odd lilting language he didn't recognise. Perhaps it was Icelandic. He tried to open his eyes.

A shadow moved over him and as his eyelids peeled apart he saw Silhouette. Her smile lit up, relief and love in her eyes. She pressed her lips against his, murmuring through the kiss. He sucked in a breath as she moved away. "Don't suffocate me!" he said, his voice weak. "Not after all that."

She laughed, moved around, kissed his cheek, his forehead, his chin. "You son of a bitch," she said. "I thought you were dead."

His eyes focused on soft, low light hovering around a room of rough-hewn gray stone. Other faces floated by, looking on with interest. "Where am I?" he asked.

"Safe," Silhouette said. "This is a Den in Selfoss." She smiled at his confusion. "We're still in Iceland."

"Frigeir actually waited for us?"

"No way. He fled. So did the pilot who brought the others in. You remember the Sisters?"

Alex winced, recalling the hideous evil they exuded. "Yeah. They helped us?" He found that hard to believe.

"Kinda. They were so entertained by what you did to Hood they passed word on to this Den to come and get us. I looked after you in Ovidius's cave until help arrived."

"Wonders will never cease. Funny ally to find in all this. What about that Sparks woman?"

Silhouette grimaced. "They took her with them. She was gibbering mad anyway, I think."

Alex wasn't surprised. He felt a twinge of guilt at what he'd done to Hood. For all his efforts at trying to avoid turning into a monster he had condemned that man to an eternal torment, a literal hell. But he'd had little choice and Hood was hardly an innocent.

Alex found it hard to believe anyone could really be bad enough to deserve what he'd done, but the man had tried to have Silhouette and him killed. Why should he care? For aeons Uthentia had found pockets of torment in one form or another, trapping and killing people throughout history. While Alex may have damned Hood to something unimaginable, no one would ever suffer like that again. He would carry the guilt of what he'd done forever, but at least he could try to console himself with the thought of all the lives he might have saved. Including his own. Or was he just rationalising his selfishness?

Silhouette stroked his cheek. "You did what you had to," she said quietly. "I can see you struggling with it, Iron Balls. Don't. You did what you had to."

"Really?"

"No one has ever managed what you did. You've stopped the final influence Uthentia has in this realm."

Alex frowned. He couldn't get the image of Hood burning for eternity out of his mind. "At what cost?" he asked, his voice breaking.

"What you did to Hood was no less than he deserved," Silhouette said.

"No one deserves that."

Silhouette shook her head. "Really? You know what those creepy Sisters told me? Hood had tried to secure their services with the lives of children. Only he'd given them ten children when they'd asked for nine, so his binding didn't take. They thought it was funny." Her face twisted in horror. "He sacrificed ten kids trying to get to you and they'd been toying with him all along."

Alex couldn't understand. "Sacrificed?"

"Hood kidnapped children and fed them to those evil bitches, Alex. He deserves to burn forever."

Alex closed his eyes. "Fuck me," he said. "Maybe he does, after all." His hand crept up to his chest, feeling gingerly across the tender flesh. It was hot and swollen.

"Don't touch it," Silhouette said. "It needs to heal."

He shifted up onto one elbow, pulled the cover aside. His chest was a ragged network of puffy red scars, throbbing with pain. There were three dark shards like glass merged with the flesh around his solar plexus. He touched one gently, felt it pulsing with power in time with his heartbeat. "The Darak," he whispered.

Silhouette nodded. "Andrea said it's a part of you now. It's broken, but it can't be removed because you and it are one and the same thing. She said you have amazing strength to have survived that. And those pieces are still very powerful, even I can feel that."

She was right, the strength of the Darak, even cracked, coursed through him, pulsed with his lifeforce. "Andrea?" he asked.

"She runs this Den, the Clan Lord here."

Alex stared at his chest. The pressure, the constant, insistent rage that had been part of him, had vanished. He felt lighter, clearer, stronger than ever. Even though the stone had broken, its magic engorged him, unfettered by Uthentia's desire. "Part of me." It already felt like the Darak had always been there.

"Yes." Silhouette ran one fingertip gently over a piece of the ancient stone. "You've bonded with it, become part of it. You always will be. It would kill you to remove it and effectively kill the Darak too. So there's really no point in anyone hounding you for it any more."

"Joseph," Alex said. "I wonder if he'll ever forgive you."

Silhouette made a rueful face, but there was mischief in her eyes. "Ever is a long time. Besides, Joseph has a soft spot for me."

"So do I," Alex said. He ran one finger over the shards again, a deep ticklish sensation thrumming in his heart. "For a moment there, while it was whole, it was incredible."

Silhouette smiled. "I remember. But it's still whole. You and it together. It just bears scars, like you do."

The power of the stone travelled through him like his blood and his breath. "More than human, eh?"

Silhouette kissed him. "A lot more."

The End

About the Author

Alan Baxter is an award-winning British-Australian author who writes dark fantasy, horror and sci-fi, rides a motorcycle and loves his dog. He also teaches Kung Fu. He lives among dairy paddocks on the beautiful south coast of NSW, Australia, with his wife, son, dog and cat. Read extracts from his novels, a novella and short stories at his website – www.warriorscribe.com or you can find him on Twitter at @AlanBaxter and feel free to tell him what you think. About anything.

www.ingramcontent.com/pod-product-compliance
Lightning Source LLC
Chambersburg PA
CBHW031658170626
46808CB00005B/1503